I0763849

THE BRIDGE
OF
EVON
To Walk Where
Mountains Sleep

Also by Marshall Cunningham

**The Bridge of Evon Quartet**
*The Taste of Riverwater*

# To Walk Where Mountains Sleep

Written by
Marshall Cunningham

Published by Noble Theme Publishing

Book Cover by Alexandra Allden

Map Illustration by Jenna Warren

First Edition 2026

*To my parents*

*Scott and Sherry*

*Who always made sure I had love in my heart*

*and a story in my hand*

# ACKNOWLEDGEMENTS

What a *ride* it has been! Just a few short months ago Evon and all its secrets were still mine to hoard—but now, with *The Taste of Riverwater* out and Book II in your hands, travelers from across the globe have begun their adventure with Foxtamas, Foxlaris, Acirema, and Bunns.

In that time I've been able to meet so many of you lovely, incredible people that have taken a chance on my work. If I met you at the launch signing in January, behind the counter at Bean's Books, online or at events, *thank you!!* Every time I get to sign your copy or explain how it took me fifteen years to complete this story my heart overflows with true, genuine, and honest joy.

With the release of *To Walk Where Mountains Sleep*, The Bridge of Evon Quartet is halfway complete! I've been asked which book of the four is my favorite and, well...all of them, duh, but by that I mean this one. It's the adventure story, the travails of *The Fellowship of the Ring*, the Lantern Waste to Aslan's How, the trail you take out of the lilac wood and to King Haggard's Castle. I spent the majority of my time writing trying to perfect very section. It's a quick concept to grasp, journeying out from one place to reach the next, but in it lies an infinitesimal gap with which to fit worldbuilding, new characters, new places, challenges, victories, revelations, etc., etc. *That's* why I adore it such. So much can happen, *will* happen. It's a field vast as it is deep, and these pages are your chance to frolic within it.

Better yet, no one's the same after a journey, neither your nor the characters. You feel yourself covering the ground beneath your feet. When you return to these words after you've made it to the back cover, you'll know what I mean. The adventure physically unfurls through the widened world and fresh faces, the dangers deterred and merriment made. You too will walk to where mountains sleep when all is said and done.

The feeling this book gives me is what led me to write *The Bridge of Evon* to begin with. I crave that exploration. It's never a linear thing (for the better) and means the finale is still far off (for the best), but what you get in return makes time you spent time worthwhile. And what's better than that?

As before, I want to extend my never-ending thanks and love to all of those who helped this book and the entire Quartet come to be. Some are the same, some are different, but without any there would be no journey to undertake.

God, first and foremost. My Savior, my Life, the only reason I breathe here and now. Let my words continue to be Yours. I thank You so dearly for everyone below.

My parents, Scott and Sherry, for reading through book one *so* fast I thought they were lying to me when they said they finished it.

My brother, Bo, who I was blessed to share a childhood with, one filled with the Lego playing, forest exploring, and video making that created the foundation of this book. Love you, Passa.

MoMo Kessie for her endless, ceaseless love, and for giving me the notebook that I wrote the first inkling of this book within. *I love you!!*

MoMo Mary and PawPaw George, in whose home I typed the official first chapter, and who supported my writing wholeheartedly both on earth and in Heaven now.

Abbey and Emma, my cousins, and the very first eyes to ever read this story.

Bean, my reading and writing buddy, my schnauzer girl who never left my side and made the many, many hours of writing all the less lonely.

My girlfriend, Caitlyn King, for her dear love in the final days of finishing this project, and for being the only person actually happy I put my dog above her.

Garrett Bullock, my longest friend, Employee of the Year, and Evon's biggest fan. How hollow this story would be without you always by my side.

Matthew Gilleran, for his unceasing dedication on the audiobook side of things and for not leaking the voice note of me singing the songs in these books (Of *course,* Marshall, I could never, would never! How touching of a statement, I'm honored beyond measure!) ;)

Mrs. Jenna Warren for her *astounding* work on creating The Map of Evon, and for letting me beat her in *Lord of the Rings* Trivia Pursuit.

Ava Bramlett who finished beta reading this book (and the others) on Christmas Eve.

Mrs. Rhonda Robinson, Mrs. Mary Nabholz, Mrs. Shandi Summers, and Mrs. Laura Shelton, my high school English teachers, for allowing me to express my creativity in poems, projects, and plays. I wouldn't be here with the chances y'all gave me and the literature y'all opened my eyes to.

Drew (Coach) Miller, my eighth grade Bible teacher who I promised to name a character after. He's finally in this book. And he's still awesome.

Dr. Hawkins for being my mentor during my Capstone project and enriching my life by introducing me to Christian writers I can now call my new favorites.

My college friends of Braydon and Caroline Bivins, Kristína Coggin, and Chloe Emmerling for their unlimited uplifting and support for anything I write. Few people have purer hearts.

John and Clive. My heroes. I hope I do y'all proud.

And, finally, to everyone who supported *The Bridge of Evon* Kickstarter! We raised over $7,000 to fund the publishing of these four books in July of 2025. Just thinking about it now, many months after the fact, brings me to tears. Thank you, thank you, thank you. All y'all made this boy's dream come true. ***Thank you!***

Joe and Stacye Austin, Scott Austin, The Barron Family, Heath Besowshek, Loren Biggs, Carol Bradford, Ava Bramlett, Kelly Brogdon, Garrett Bullock, Katherine Burns, Jaxon Charlton, The Cole Family, Bo Cunningham, George Cunningham Jr., Greg Cunningham, Malcolm Cunningham, Sherry and Scott Cunningham, Jackson D. McDonald, Essie Decuir, Jon Dor, Ron Duggins, Tierney Earnest, Josh and Brooke Evans, Madison Evans, Nick Flesher, Florentina, Ftost-Frame, Lauren Grasso, Olivia Henry, TJ Johnston, Jared Jowers, Kylei Keever, Samantha Keil, Andrea & Ben King, Jace Kramer, Claire Lee, Topanga Leslie, Kristy Linville, Kevin and Donna Lyon, Drew Miller, Katherine Malloy, Matthias720, Durgan Maxey, Megan Mercer, Mary Nabholz, Rebecca O'Neill, Grace Olivia Martin, Linda Petit, Ringmaster, Rhonda Robinson, Anna Samons, Karen Samuhel, Melissa Seme, Tara Shuster, Christine Sterling, Drew Strickland, Giselle T., Michael

Taylor, Tonia, David Trotter, Corrina Van Brunt, Georgann Whitley, Thomas Williams, Marti Wilson, Ben Wrobbel, and Julie Wynegar.

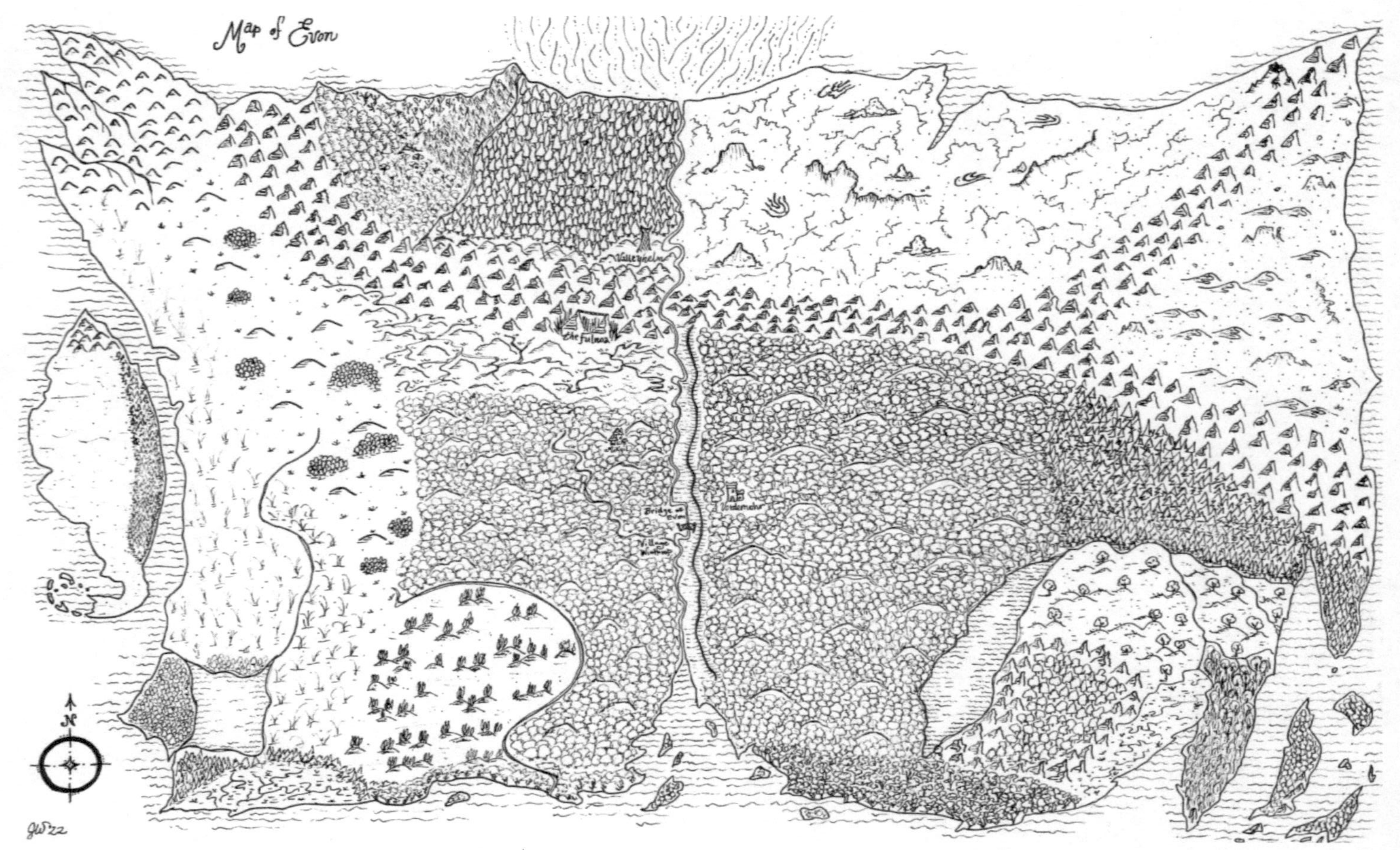
Map of Evon
Valleyhelm
Bridge at Evon
N

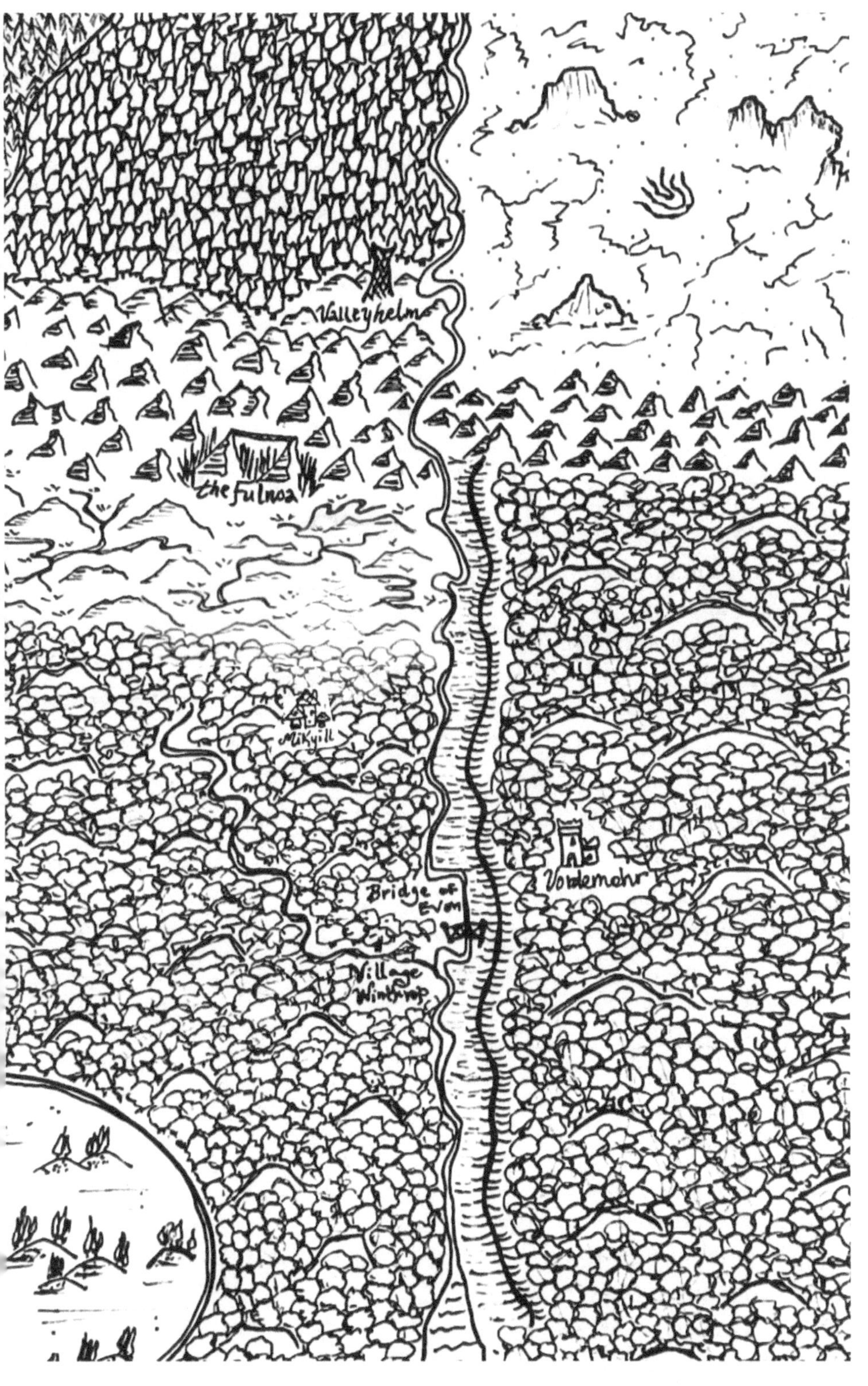

Valleyhelm
the Fulnoa
Mikyill
Bridge of Evon
Village Winthrop
Vordemohr

# PRONUNCIATION GUIDE

**Acirema:** *uh-SEER-uh-muh*
**Adalgiso:** *uh-dahl-GEE-soh*
**Aisar:** *AYE-sar*
**Cammont:** *cuh-MONT*
**Dubyr:** *DOOB-yer*
**Enaled:** *eh-NAHL-ed*
**Evon:** *ee-VOHN*
**Feiht:** *fee-HET*
**Foehn:** *fane*
**Foxlaris:** *FOX-ler-iz*
**Foxtamas:** *FOX-tuh-mus*
**Fulnoa:** *full-NO-uh*
**Garona:** *GUH-ron-uh*
**Getophry:** *get-OFF-ree*
**Ghroat:** *gr-OTE*
**Gniw:** *new*
**Gregabbit:** *GREH-guh-bit*
**Hucksubtle:** *HUCK-sut-ul*
**Iota:** *eye-OH-tuh*
**Lordell:** *LORD-ul*
**Losrym:** *LOZ-rem*
**Mechmilne:** *MEH-chuh-milne*
**Mikyill:** *MEEK-yill*
**Nohsis:** *NO-sis*
**Omaya:** *oh-MY-uh*

**Ratatoskr:** *ruh-TAT-oh-sker*
**Reinden:** *RAIN-den*
**Roihelm:** *ROY-helm*
**Rokanoe:** *ROW-ken-oh*
**Ruel:** *ROO-ul*
**Tarasque:** *TAYR-usk*
**Tauronon:** *TAR-oh-non*
**Tirsol:** *TEER-sul*
**Tywyll:** *TIE-why-el*
**Velvedier:** *vel-vuh-DEER*
**Vordemohr:** *VORD-more*

# Book II

## To Walk Where Mountains Sleep

# I

# "CAST ACROSS THE MOUNTAINS BOLD,"

Dead.

The entire first patrol.

Reports flooded in from those who arrived after the initial invasion. They found poor Rapol and the others slain, shot dead across the sands. Few had seen the attackers, and those that had flew back to Vordemohr to inform their Vorde.

"What did they look like? Were they waiting? Did they know about the patrol!?" Velrick sputtered out. He turned a frantic red eye to the reporting bugbear general, Breyhuf. The beast tried to keep up as the wolf and Getophry flew down the long, stone hall.

"I, um, I don't know, my Vorde. A scout said one looked like the orange boy you brought in, a-a-and the other was horned, another striped—"

"And were they *WAITING!?"*

"I-I-I'm not sure, my Vorde, but the patrol didn't see them coming. So, um, perhaps—"

"Enough, Breyhuf!" The wolf stopped right before the hall's end, setting a parcel down outside of an ornamented door. "Clarify all you know, get a scribe to spell it out if you must. I want more squads sent over with you and Reyhuf leading. Find these murderers and scout the West, learn quick their roads, towns, people, *all of it."* His claws sprang out, gripping the bugbear's maroon tunic to the point of tearing holes. "You're my eyes," he whispered. "You've heard the rumors. Skirmishes like these can be life or *death* for us, for our land. I know you understand. Am I wrong about that?" Breyhuf's body quaked as he flung his head left and right. "Then leave at once. And please take whoever you need."

"Yes, m-m-my Vorde." The bugbear, though beastly and dressed his part as a soldier, bumbled off down the hallway, a child scolded by his parent.

Velrick shook his head and knocked on the door before him, muttering to Getophry as he did.

"Make sure he follows through. I'll be busy today." The cockatrice nodded and started off. No questions asked.

Velrick cleared his throat before knocking again. "Hello, Foxlaris? It's Velrick."

"Come in," came a stifled response. The door eased open, revealing the injured castaway. His outline was bathed in the dance of a few dim, flittering candles instead of the light leaking past the curtains. The fox worked his way around the room. His steps, while small, slowly adjusted to walking with both a peg leg and eye patch. Balance had been the first hurdle, but the morning practice started to settle in. Now his concern lay in making a straight line.

"Why, one step ahead of me today!" The peppy voice of Velrick took a minute for Foxlaris to register; the barrage of new sensations had forced him to extend his focus towards his senses.

"What was all that yelling about?" he asked between steps. His scarred face turned to Velrick, who lowered his gleeful countenance.

"Ah yes…*that.* Well, my boy, I was hoping to hide this from you, but…no, you deserve to know. It's about the West." The wolf gently grabbed Foxlaris' arm and shoulder as he walked. It provided him the safety to try larger steps without falling.

"What about it?"

"Rumors. Word has been spreading since the bridge incident. People are scrambling to find a reason or cause for it all. Their attention has, to our dismay, turned Eastward. We're being assigned the blame."

The fox's single eye shot to his helper, growing in disbelief

"How? You've done nothing wrong!"

"I know, Foxlaris, I know."

"I was there, we...we all were!"

"But they need that release," sighed Velrick. "Smoke forced up by the chimney. Worse, I fear, is reports about our patrols." His head fell lower. "Dead, killed by soldiers waiting to ambush them. Oh, it's all a horrible, twisted business."

Foxlaris stopped his walking and fully turned to the wolf. The golden tunic adorning his body sagged, the blackened robe guarding it hardly holding on. Such news wore on the leader.

"Well...what can be done now?" Foxlaris asked softly, trying not to stir any resounding emotions.

"I've ordered who I can to negotiate where they can. All tedious work, the kind I'm *far* from cut out for. But that's not why I'm here." With that, he gathered the strength for a soft smile and eased the fox over to his bed. "How've you been this morning? Any aches, pains, coughs? I'm amazed you've already begun to walk!"

"So am I. But yeah...the scars and splinters, they're still hurting a good deal. And my eye. The healers came by again to change my bandages and give me some real awful draught. I managed to dress, though, and light the candles."

"I noticed," said Velrick. Foxlaris had indeed changed from the surgical wrapping of the days prior to something a tad fancier. He kept with the apparent Vordemohr style, dawning a patterned maroon habit and gilded trousers. All the clothing tucked away in his room had the same elegance to it. It felt important. It felt royal. "And I am deeply proud of you. I suspect few else could have moved about as such." Without warning, the wolf sprang up and back towards the door. He dipped behind it, pulling in his parcel. "But, like I said, you skipped a step in my plans for today."

"What's this?" asked the fox as Velrick presented him with the package.

"Oh, just a small gift to help you through our day today. Here, let me help you." The pair both worked at cutting away the string (a perfect use for Foxlaris' hook) and tearing back the paper. Beneath the wrapping lay a cane, formed from a mixture of burgundy wood and obsidian, with the sculpt of a silver wolf head welded to the top for a handle. Foxlaris let himself beam. "I want to show you Vordemohr today. You deserve to see your home for the time being, and, despite all your hurt and struggle, you deserve to see it with *ease*. What do you say, my boy?"

"I think…" Carefully, the fox raised himself up with the rod, stretching back into a walking stance. The pommel fit well to not distress the gashes still healing in his hand. Walking with it gave him good support, enough to move somewhat freely. It would take time, of course, but the cane was the next step in regaining who he was. "It's great. Thank you, Velrick."

"For certain, my boy, for certain. Now, if you'll follow me, we'll start this tour. If we're lucky, we'll even get to see a few surprises along the way."

They exited the room at the hallway's end, albeit a tad slow for the sake of the fox. Small lanterns clung to the black stone walls. Their glow did a fine job illuminating the hall, revealing the fine craftsmanship that had gone into smoothing the brick into a mirror-like surface. As they traversed farther down, the light grew brighter, and the stone faded into a dark, marooned wood. Before he knew it, Foxlaris found himself in a massive keep. The ceilings above vaulted high, revealing at least four more stories rising above. Glass windows took up the entire length of most walls. Outside of them waved trees coated in an ugly, dark green so muted it could have been black. Their gnarled limbs and roots looked to have attacked the palace over years of a stagnant war.

Inside the chamber, multiple hallways just like the one they had entered from began and ended. Some were well lit and tall, leading to important rooms or courtyards, while others sneaked away in the shadows, hoping to keep their secrets close. A similar scheme adorned the staircases. The central spire rose from the middle, gracing each level as it reached up to meet a meticulous stained-glass window topping off the room.

For the small village boy, the keep was from a story, nay, a *dream.* The velvet under foot; the light glistening past the fortified foliage walls; the miraculous array of creatures passing by—the *creatures!* Why, he'd barely noticed them! An entire array of busied folk rushed around, each dawning either a habit like himself or some gilded cloak. A few he could make out as alps or bugbears; others were new, with massive wings or hulking tails. They had to be the same beings talked about in Western stories, meant to keep children up at night or inspire the brave warrior to finally make that journey out of Mikyill. But now they were real. And in front of him. And off to do some business he had no mind to even imagine.

"This palace you stand in now, Blue Rose," Velrick began, breaking the dream surrounding the fox, "is Crimsdon Hall. It's but one of four the buildings that compose Vordemohr. The others we will get to surely, but for now, I assume you want to marvel a bit, yes?"

"More than you know," Foxlaris uttered. Smiling, Velrick watched the lad struggle with his steps forward, spinning around to take in the sight. "All this wood. It's…red. We don't have anything like it in the West."

"Oh, I'm *well* aware." The wolf chuckled. He patted him on the shoulder and started their walk again. "It's an, um, 'gift' of sorts from…"

Foxlaris felt the hand upon him quiver. Turn clammy. The wolf tongued his teeth and swallowed hard, squinting until his eyes burned.

"Oh, from…gah, the bird, the…the blue one—"

"Roihelm?"

"Yes, yes, him." A stab of shock puckered his face, like an arrow plunged into his back. "After the War that Split the World, he cursed our land in many a way. One was that, for certain trees, when they are cut, they 'bleed' and stain their wood. It's a reminder of what he claims we did. Dirt in the eye as far as I'm concerned. The truth is, it's *spite,* Foxlaris, petty spite. Well, we were not ones to let such punishment rule us. Thus, we took those trees and used them, made them our home. Their name came to be known as Crimsdon; thus, Crimsdon Hall."

So much raced through the fox's head. Velrick talked about Roihelm like he knew him, like he wasn't some story or ghost too high above to know. His parents worshipped him, and he too believed the Phoenix to be real, but here, he seemed…tangible. Like a person. What legends were real over here? And how could they take such magic so plainly, so normally? And this…War!?

"The War's not a myth? I thought it was just some tale to explain away Nohsis."

"A myth? Oh Foxlaris, it's the full truth! There's more to it than you or I may ever know. But don't worry yourself with it now, we have more than enough priorities here."

"But—"

"Trust me."

The fox grimaced. No matter the bruises or bandages, his old angst still shone through at a moment's notice. But…Velrick was right. He was a guest, nay, inhabitant of Vordemohr now; it would do him good to be acquainted with it.

The next stop took them up the stairs, passing by robed toads and vultures as they did. Each time someone passed, they performed a quick bow for their Vorde. The fox found it odd at first; by the time they reached the fifth level, it felt customary.

Velrick led on through the twists and turns of darkened halls that lured Foxlaris in. What history lay within some random room? How many secrets were formed and told, lives touched and lost, history created and changed? It ate at him. But he forced himself out of it, focusing on the passing comments of Velrick instead.

The issue was, he'd known that pull before. With Foxtamas. Taking over his soul and imparting upon it some wish for adventure. A call to explore.

Those thoughts…they were pointless. Had to be.

The journeying slowed at a narrow hall that opened into a wide circular courtyard. A tall obsidian wall arose around the open field of grass. Inside, a squad trained in spear exercises. Some high-ranking troll officer sprayed out drills, and the small army followed them without a single misstep. But Foxlaris only gave mind to a single thing: the breeze.

He'd yet to breathe anything other than the muggy air of brick and Crimsdon. Now, his ruined lungs took in the outside freedom, seeing the blissful blue sky above as they did. The last time he'd seen such had been Grammo Day, before mounting the Bridge. When he'd been with his friends. When he'd lived a different life that—

*WHOOP!!*

The minute tickle in his throat ricocheted into a brutal coughing fit. The cane did little to help as Foxlaris fell to his knees. His mouth gasped for air. All that came was the struggle for breath amidst crazed, howling coughs.

Velrick rushed down beside him, smacking his back as if to burp his own child.

"Slow, Foxlaris, slow. You'll be alright, one breath at a time." The shuffling metal noises behind them had stopped. The wolf glanced back at the trainers and commander glancing their way. "Continue on, Crollow. He'll be fine." The troll nodded, and the grunts of the spearmen resumed.

Foxlaris soon caught his breath, but not without a dizzying headache shaking the sight of his single eye. The pair took their leave in pleasant seating against the wall. They sat in silence, letting the noontime sun linger past and the dedicated soldiers drip in the sweat of determination.

"You know," Velrick started, "the surgeons prepared me for such an event. We thought it would be lesser, but, well…"

"I'm fine. I just…need to adjust."

"Certainly. We all do, my boy. Times like these are unprecedented for us all." The wolf helped himself up and extended an arm for the fox. Taking it, the two dusted off from the grass and took one final look around. "I brought you here in the case you'd want to train, spar, or whatever it is you find to fancy. It's all yours, as is everything in Vordemohr. But with your condition, I'm not alone in the belief of your avoiding it."

The fox hardly recognized they were once again on the move. Velrick led him again along the stairs, this time back down to the main chamber and through a vast, open hall ending in a pair of Crimsdon doors so tall they scraped the ceiling. Four guards stood before them. Each bore the Vordemohrian colors of red, black, and gold, with dark plated armor rising to the top of their necks. Long, burgundy V's climbed in the same fashion up their chests. At the simple nod of the Vorde, the crew turned and shoved apart the portal.

The sight brought Foxlaris back to his senses. The way forward was not another stairwell or hall, oh no. Crimsdon Hall parted into an expansive wooden platform, extending out past the ridge on which the palace sat. Three small towers were raised upon it, one for each side. From these extruded two sets of long, wound metal wire that sloped downward somewhere beyond the tree line.

Gasping, the fox shuffled out further to understand what it was he'd been led to. Two of the lines—those to his left and right—trailed north and south, respectively. These reached further along the ridge whereas the one directly at his front appeared to bend down along its slope. As he studied the line, however, it began to sway, jostling and twinging until, riding up it and towards the platform, there came a *carriage.*

Hard, heavy grunts welcomed it home like the trumps of a parade. Four hulking beasts worked at the platform's edge to twist a wooden wheel wrapped in wire and chain. Their shells at first made them out as turtles (despite the spikes and dreary color of green and black); but as the creatures pushed on, Foxlaris saw their lizard-like tails, six bear feet, and ugly, snorting lion-like heads with disheveled manes and snarling teeth.

"Don't be afraid of them, Foxlaris," Velrick reassured him, pushing him further out upon the platform, "they are only doing their duty. Tarasque are brutal beasts, but beautiful in the same breath. Yet look beyond them! You now stand in the true heart of Vordemohr, the key which controls our operations: the Styelines."

The longer the fox looked around, the more it made sense. By now the carriage had reached the top and unloaded its variety of passengers. Their departure allowed room for a small squabble of alps to hop aboard. The structure itself was fairly open, with a small gate and railing to enclose the riders and, hopefully, ensure their safety. Even when halted by the tarasque, the Styeline still wobbled in the busy wind.

"Originally, Vordemohr *was* Crimsdon Hall. Our armies, leaders, visitors and the such stayed in the stories I showed you. Let me tell you, my boy, how cramped we all were! A horrible oversight. So, at the bottom of the Vordemohr's ridge, a village was constructed, meant to ease our stifled suffering and grow the cause. Then when *that* grew, we built the North and South Patrol Towers." The pair crept closer to the wooden transport as Velrick labored on. With each step the excitement within the fox flared. He caught a glimpse of the village Velrick spoke of below, like a semicircle of wood and rock connected to Crimsdon Hall by a silver string. "To bind it all together, we enlisted the East's finest, drawing from the minds down in Thistis and the metal workers of the An-Zeen. Does the West have anything close to this?"

"I-I don't think so," Foxlaris stuttered out, "not even in stories."

A quiet, prideful smile slipped out of the wolf.

"I figured as such. From what little I know of that side they are too slow, you know, too disconnected to work for something better. Marvels such as these are dreams to them. Now, come along, the Village is our next stop."

With that, the wolf and the fox boarded, but not before the tarasque (and fellow riders) bowed to Velrick. Once more, the grunts picked back up, and the palace and platform began to slowly ease away. The carriage's shake forced Foxlaris into one of the seats lest his balance give way.

He took the break to watch the darkened forest surrounding them. It felt similar to Mechmilne, with the rising ridges bursting out across the land; however, they did not ease back down towards the forest floor, instead dropping off with sheered cliffs. The very one on which Crimsdon Hall sat did much of the same. Perhaps that is why the Village sat so far away.

"Does this Village have a name? Or is it just 'The Village'?" asked Foxlaris while taking in the sights.

"Oh, surely. It's officially titled The Village of the Vayne."

"Vayne?"

"Yes, Vayne. It's the one who guards and maintains order down there, tracking all routes of business. Being so far Westward, we rely on other regions for supplies, such as rations and metals for the smithy. If you peer out now, you can see that very trade happening."

Looking over the moving rails, Foxlaris did spot the Village's opening gate, guarded by walls that rose around the entire town. A long line of vendors, carts, and baggage trailed off into the thicket. Whoever stood dealing with them was in for a long day.

"If the Vayne is not too busy, I'll introduce you to her, though I'd hate to interrupt."

"But aren't you above her? And all of them? Or is a Vorde not…" He cut off before his assumptions could embarrass himself. To his surprise, the wolf nodded and answered with a perk in his voice.

"No no, you're quite right. My Vordeship is a unique power. Think of it as…a kingship, only I oversee a mission, not land alone."

"So that would put you above a king."

"Some believe so."

"Are you one of them?"

"If only it were that simple. Overstepping in my role unbalances the flow we aim to maintain. The more reserved I am, the better work we do. It's all about observing, my boy, and taking action after the fact."

Velrick presented him with a kindred smile and soft pat on his back. The Styeline carriage continued, rattling down as it went.

The Village of the Vayne bustled with the daily activities of the Vordemohrian Army, traders, trainers, and Easterners visiting the renowned battle station. Thousands scuttled through the maze of stout stone buildings. The alleyways between were turned a pulpy slush of gray, the earth beneath rubbed away like a rash. It smelled no different. A thickness coated the incessant energy every moving part produced. The grime between the bricks, the unceasing chatter and clanging and banging and batter, it built up like grease squeezed from over-twisted wood, the rusty drip off wagon wheels far beyond their change. The Village didn't look as it did for lack of care, but rather because it cared *too much.* Worked *too hard.*

The Styelines landed at the town's back, being met with a similar platform and tarasque array as found above. Velrick and Foxlaris wasted no time departing and joining the noontime fray.

By now, the fox had grown far too curious for his own good about the new species and races passing by him. As they walked towards the barracks, Velrick worked as his guide. Tarmin, Foxlaris learned, were the oversized toads he saw croaking about, often oozing an oily slick. Some moved with ease; others rolled about. Past them were korrigan, impish delights that looked the part of slim, sickly gnomes. Following them he met both orcs and trolls (exactly as ugly as the stories made them out to be), as well as a couple mossokin, soft, subtle creatures covered in the overflows of moss and mushrooms. These and many more he discovered whilst surfing the Village streets. It all registered that the East was not some wild jungle as he and many other Westerners believed it to be—it was a new world entirely.

Their walk eventually led them to a large, squared-off stone building that stood out amongst the smaller structures. Its roof and doors shared an accent of Crimsdon wood, although the multiple stories between them appeared ready to topple over one another.

"Here lay the barracks. Our current soldiers and draftees house here. Generals, officers, and others of high rank may stay in the Hall, however. If you look down the street—" He pointed a ways down towards a similar building, only far flatter and with smoke billowing from its many darkened chimneys. "There are the kitchens. We of course have rations in Crimsdon, but if you want a *real* treat, make your way down. That's not the only exciting thing down here…" Velrick took off once again. He led his guest through the flanks of soldiers leaving the barracks and heading down for lunch. They steered through narrow paths before reaching a lane of smithies. Roughly seven shops—each roaring with multiple wicked flames and steaming welds—lined the row, covering both the low-framed roofs and cobbled road with soot. Despite the smog, Velrick pushed through to the main station, denoted by its second story and velvet finish. Wafts of smoke met their noses.

"Hold, stay back for a moment. I don't want Smitemaster Ulisil's ashes choking you to death." The wolf passed him a quick wink and stepped inside.

Foxlaris tried to follow what little conversation leaked from within, but before he knew it, Velrick emerged, and with him a rugged metal box.

"What's that?" Foxlaris asked.

"In all truthfulness, nothing you probably need. The surgeons, well, they got to talking with the old bat in there after they fastened to you the many metal parts he crafted. It's an experiment more than anything. Still, you have the right to test them for yourself." Carefully, he tilted up the lid, revealing a pile of metal so polished it glistened like crystal.

"What are these?" The fox took one in his hand. It had the dimensions of a dagger, only with a thickened screw bolted to the end of it.

"Replacements for your hook. Here, let me show you." He proceeded to tug the fox's faux-paw and twist it. With a *POP!*, the hook detached, leaving a perfect hole in which to fit the attachment.

"No…*way*." By his tone, Velrick couldn't determine whether he took a liking to the gift—that was, until he slammed in the dagger, twisting it tight. Foxlaris aimed the blade to the sun and watched the metalwork glimmer. The light bathed him. In doing so, it relit some cursed, broken part of his soul. His lost hand has become a *gain*.

The fox couldn't stop himself. He dug through the others like a child on a riverbank, taking notice of axe heads, forks, spoons, maces, and even a metal fist. His singular brown eye glimmered as he looked back up to Velrick. "I get to keep them, right?"

"I don't see why not! I'm rather surprised you have such an interest in them. Here, re-attach the hook. I'll have a servant bring these up to your room while we meet the Vayne."

"I didn't think we'd actually get to meet her."

Velrick chuckled while Foxlaris worked the hook back on his arm.

"We will whether she likes it or not. Figured I'd see myself as a bit of a king after all," he replied, a touch snarky. The fox shared in his grin.

As they approached the main gate, the noise of busied merchants and deliverers echoed to the point of nausea. Some were allowed in and hauled their grain carts through the crowd; others began shouting matches with the Vayneguard (denoted by their ivory armor and halberds). One voice, however, carried itself high and clear above the senseless chatter.

"You are required to turn away *now!* Vordemohrian law strictly *forbids* the selling of Jontlian tea and olswinges. I will not be asking you again. Good *DAY!"* shrieked a furious female voice. Foxlaris squinted in the hopes of seeing the speaker. Once they neared the towering obsidian gate, he found her.

She was the Vayne alright. Her hair, white as the clouds above, rolled down her back, highlighting the grayness of her skin. She tossed a quick glimpse their direction, revealing two soulless gray eyes. Not a shimmer. Not a spark. Both her ears and teeth came to a razor point. They paired well with the sharpened gold plates of her armor.

"Stay put. Our Vorde approaches," delivered her stinging, raspy voice. A single look altered a guardsman to fill her role and continue the struggle with the mossokin merchant.

"Seems I didn't have to say a word," Velrick chuckled, pushing himself and Foxlaris closer to the Vayne. "Iota! Busy day I see?"

The tall woman dropped to a single knee before him. Her cape, striking as her hair, dirtied itself in the commotion without a second thought.

"Yes, my Vorde. Your call for more supplies was heard clear across the regions. Yet some filth still tries to sneak through." Cold came her words. The fox noticed the warnings of older age upon her. The gray skin was pulled taught to her sleek muscle and bones. For a moment, he could hardly tell if she was breathing. Who was this corpse standing before him?

"Ah, well, I should have suspected as such. A good thing I put *you* in charge! But I came to introduce our newest guest. Foxlaris, meet Vayne Iota Nightsong."

"Nice to meet you." The fox extended his good hand. Iota gazed down with a smirk, meeting it. As they touched, Foxlaris could have sworn she'd buried him in the deepest of a Pradifore's snow. A frost pumped through his nerves. It didn't chill or sting as most colds, but numbed, melting his fur and the skin beneath to a dead, unrecognizable weight.

"A pleasure," she replied. Her matte eyes watched him recoil and hide the paw within his habit sleeve.

"He's the same soul I rescued from the West, the ones our healers worked with day and night. The boy's better than we could have ever hoped."

"Oh..." the bitter tone of her voice cut off. "A Westerner?"

Foxlaris felt the flick of her eyes scan over him. They reached deep, slices of her pupils detaching the broken fox from the Eastern metal holding him together.

What could he do? The very fabric of his being was undressed before him. What did she seek?

"My thoughts exactly. More than a rarity around here—an utter *legend!*"

Iota nodded, then turned back to her master.

"I see. But I have more news, my Vorde, past the suppliers. Scouts claim to have spotted cultists approach, others having talked with them and refusing their demands. An attack could be imminent. I was heading up to the South Tower—"

"And so are we!" cut in Velrick. "To the North, actually, but our route up to the Hall remains the same. We'll journey together, and I'll alert the Northern Patrollers. A plan?"

"Surely, my Vorde." The Vayne responded with a bow. As she went back to inform the Vayneguard of her departure, Foxlaris glanced at Velrick in confusion.

"Cultists? What's going on?"

"The Cult of the Bird. Pests we can't seem to rid ourselves of. I'll explain more at the tower. Just know that the West isn't the only force we're defending against…"

The Styelines rattled as the carriage flowed upwards. Due to the special news they carried, only the trio of Velrick, Foxlaris, and Iota were aboard. As much as he tried, Foxlaris could hardly take his eye from the woman. Something intrigued him, like an itch aching to be scratched.

"Are you an elf?" he suddenly blurted. The thought had barely entered his brain before being tossed to the wind. Both leaders exchanged glances.

"No. I'm a healt," she shot back, words strict and laced with bile. "Are you one?"

"No, I'm a fox. Can't you see that?" fired Foxlaris with equal gusto.

"I can. But we have no foxes on this side of Evon. Just as *your* side has no healts."

Velrick nodded her direction, red eye beaming. She knew the sign to yield. The Vayne softened her approach and took a seat beside Foxlaris.

"Elves were the Bird's Chosen, created with the sole function of serving him. When the War came, a sect decided to think for themselves and sided with the Eastern forces. Their choice locked them away here. The only place suitable for their survival was the forest south of the Sea of Pont, guarded by mountains tall enough to hide them from the Bird's eye. They thought themselves safe. Until Roihelm cursed it."

There Iota paused. Her eyes squeezed tight, breathing drawing slow at first, then quickening in pace.

"He stripped both them and their land of all life. All color. We were no longer elves; the change to our land reshaped our lineage, forming a new creation. Elves of dead skin, sharpened features, stale eyes. Healts." The Vayne let silence fill in the rest. She parsed past the fox's scars and bandages as he studied her, comparing the breathing being before him to the sketches planted in his brother's books. There was no stopping his intrigue from bubbling out. "I hail from there, our Silvestwood. Vorde Velrick traveled our way many a year ago looking for warriors. I joined him and well…became Vayne."

"I see…" A grave reply from Foxlaris. Before him legends were both born and killed. Elves were…real. But so too the strings that bound them, forced them away just as the stories told. Their refusal of the fabled fate sat next him. A colorless symbol of freedom.

"I guess life there's not easy," Foxlaris finally added. To his surprise, the slightest of snorts sputtered from the Vayne's frozen chest.

"Do you know what it's like to live in a world where your entire existence is a shade of gray? Where your eyes burn in their yearning to fulfill their true purpose?"

"I've been out at night."

"And you think that's the same?"

Foxlaris shrugged. "Sure."

He could tell that, without Velrick's protection to still her hand, she'd have run him through and dropped his body into Forguile below.

Instead, she laughed. Far from how a *normal* creature would. Stifled, a stern puff of wind. But a laugh nonetheless.

"Westerners are as the stories claim," she said, a tad breathless.

"And how's that?" Foxlaris asked.

"Behind."

The tarasque grunting soon met their ears, and the Styeline basket softened down to a halt. Together they made their exit and thanked the monstrous hybrids as they did.

"I must be off, my Vorde," said Iota. She tightened her sword belt and realigned her silk-like hair to fall an inch above it. "The information will be relayed, and the soldiers shall be alerted."

"Thank you, my Vayne. We'll relay it to the North and await any news. Farewell."

"Farewell, and to you. Fox."

"Oh, uh, yeah, farewell." Foxlaris had not expected the address. A soft, cold smile melted its way upon her countenance. With a turn, Iota the healt disappeared amongst the crowding platform.

Before long, the pair were traveling up a second Styeline, this one bound for the North Tower. Going up was a far different sensation than going down. The rolling mounds of green below lost their detail, clouding into strokes of a painting rather than tangled scraps of wire.

The ridge upon which the tower sat lay fairly close. They arrived in less than half the time it took to reach the Village. Their carriage eased not towards the base, but directly to the top, a few stories shy of the open roof. Like the Hall, it too was formed from a mix of Crimsdon and obsidian. Within spiraled a winding staircase that touched an assortment of rooms. These served as extra barracks and armories for patrollers set to keep watch. Most residents served only the Tower Patrol, not blending into the army; although, in times of need, some unlucky Village soldier would be forced upon the teetering walls early on a treacherous morn.

Velrick wasted no time hauling the fox up the flights. Yes, the stairs still proved rather unruly, but the practice with both peg and cane was well needed. He appreciated the push upwards once they reached the top and the hidden spectacle revealed itself: an aerial view of East Evon.

Foxlaris felt the chilled sting of the obsidian through his sandal as he stared out over the tall, guarded battlements. The air tasted bitter, a prickly dryness shriveling the tongue. Heavy gray clouds had begun to roll in. The pale light of the sun peered through, brushing past—but never parting—the dark and dense forests below.

This new vantage point revealed a daunting truth he hadn't fully understood when in Crimsdon Hall—these woods offered no life like Mechmilne. The sweeping trees beneath mimicked a rising storm, drenched in the thrashing sounds of impending danger. Sickly were the greens and broken were the browns. They stalked and howled in the ill wind as if haunted by wayward souls, the kind doomed to walk the endless forest paths, goalless, ghouled. For miles the gloom spread, up and over small knolls and hills, crossing sparse dead valleys, toppling over the occasional ridge. But to the West, in a hue of dormant mauve, a high line of ridges stood, blocking whatever stood behind it. Was it Nohsis? Could it be that, after all these years, he finally found what lay beyond the Eastern blockades?

"It's so different from the West, but…so much the same," came Foxlaris' quiet comment. He and Velrick stood still, letting the wind wash over them. Even the patrollers at their backs took care to keep their steps quiet.

"So is such because it used to *be* the same. The Splitting of Evon changed your forest to Mechmilne and ours the Darkwood of Forguile. Rather nasty, isn't it? Too murky and sinister, even when no one's around. But more happened during that time…" Velrick lifted a claw, pointing Westward at the mighty purple wall Foxlaris observed. "He put that up the same day. Like a wall to keep us in, to avoid gazing over at his precious West. Practically mountains compared to the rest of the ridges. But he did even more." Next the claw pointed up to the sun, slowly drowning in the sea of raiding rain clouds. "The sun's pattern changed. Instead of rising from the East, it now sets here."

"Why?" asked the fox.

"To make it look as if we slaughter it every night, like we steal the light from this land. It's vile, Foxlaris. That and all else he did to us."

Foxlaris nodded deeply. A thinking nod.

Who even *was* Roihelm? The storied Author of his youth? The good blue Phoenix who gave life to all?

No.

That couldn't be true.

There was nothing good about the Eastern state. Curses had been imparted, from the Crimsdon blood to lifeless Silvestwood. Betraying the elves, his *hand-picked* people? Hiding all Easterners with the ridges, reversing the sun? Look at Forguile. How it swelled and blistered like a boil ripe with pain. Is this any condition for one's Creation to live? Especially when, miles off, paradise roamed in the valleys and hills of Mechmilne?

Worst of all, everything had existed as such for thousands of years. *Thousands*. Generations, nay, entire *family trees* came and went while choking on the tainted air and surviving amidst the volley of plagues. Whatever transpired within the War that Split the World, it led to this.

Led to an Author dispersing malice and injustice. Led to half a world burdened by their mere existence. Led to one poor, broken soul left to hold it altogether.

And it was to that soul he turned. Velrick's red eyes marbled with tears. What about, he could not tell. Perhaps the very fight he now understood. Keeping oneself alive was enough; running a small kingdom, meanwhile, would kill any beast. *Should* kill them. But in that moment, Foxlaris saw that his tears weren't ones of hatred or fear. They were silent cries for help. Invisible screams from a soul destroyed by his very Maker.

It clicked.

Everything, from the moment he awoke half-conscious on that metal table, started to come into view. Why Velrick saved him. Why he was welcomed in Vordemohr. Why he brought him gift after gift and made him an Easterner despite the blood inside that deemed him a fox, an outsider, a Westerner.

He shared their pain.

The curses from Roihelm were the wounds of the Bridge. The taunts of his friends. The lies of love and care by his own family, his own brother. They had ruined him. Stolen his very autonomy and flesh. Left him to rot out of fear of what they'd done.

Foxlaris Scottsworth bore the scars of brokenness and betrayal.

Vorde Velrick bore the scars of brokenness and betrayal.

East Evon bore the scars of brokenness and betrayal.

The world ebbed back into view. All the troubling thoughts racked his brain and, along with the altitude and splinters still stinging the length of his body, sent waves of a headache blistering across his skull. His impaired vision cleared enough to see Velrick leaning over the wall's side.

"Foxlaris, look!" cried the wolf. "The cultists move down the ridge!"

The fox stumbled closer and peered down. Sure enough, bright blue dots scurried beneath through the Forguile floor. Some had already reached the end and had begun barreling down the sheer-faced cliff via hooks and rope. "Patrollers!" Velrick shouted, spinning to face those on the upper floor. "Cultists invade from the North ridge, heading down for the Village. I want fire relays sent to those below, and airborne soldiers taking the first strike. The rest start a full rush down to meet them, now!"

Not one dared disobey. Within the minute, a blue flame erupted upon a pyre near the tower's base. An identical one appeared within the Village moments later, the notice of a signal received.

Foxlaris gawked at the precision of the shuffle. Dozens of soldiers scrambled downward in organized pairs. Those blessed with flight hurled off the edge and took to the forest, targeting the blue spurs and diving beneath the leaves. All the while, Velrick kept the pair stationed tight on the upper platform.

"Don't worry, my boy. They'll have the attack finished before we can even make it down. Hardly an issue for them these days."

"But who even are the cultists?" the fox asked. "You said you'd explain."

"Ah, right, just about slipped my mind. We call them, as I said, the Cult of the Bird. Others say Helmists, or Blue Caps. Personally, they go by the Old Evonian name of Meki Totodora, meaning 'Your Servants.' The 'Your', of course, referring to…"

"I know."

"Good. This cult is the last remnant of power that bird holds here. We've faced them for *years* now. They claim their crusade against us comes from these 'visions' he bestows upon them. Since they started, it has become their singular duty to besiege our fortress. Why? I'm none the wiser." Velrick shook his head and chuckled. "This ends soon. The battles, they're more frequent, more violent than usual, *especially* since your incident. I don't know what he feeds them, but it is about to lead to their deaths. I can feel our final war coming, Foxlaris. 'Tis near."

The wolf started back towards the stairs as distant shouts reverberated from the ridge and Village. Yet those final words lingered with the fox. These cultists…they're all Roihelm had left. A strike against them would be a guaranteed protection, nay, service to the very folk who'd taken him in, shown him care and honest love. The Easterners deserved that service; *Velrick* deserved that service.

The hook twisted into his arm suddenly felt out of place. He craved the dagger.

Watching the wolf walk away only convinced him of this mission. He'd face the Cult of the Bird. How? He didn't know. He could barely make it up a single step without a wheeze, but he'd power through it, grow strong, worthy, then outgrow even that. He'd prove that, without a doubt, Foxlaris was not some bandaged boy to drag around, oh no. He was an Easterner. A force against Roihelm and all the damage he unjustly wrought.

It was time to earn his keep.

"Hurry along, my boy!" cut in Velrick's silky voice. Foxlaris shook his head to look beyond, seeing him awaiting him at the stairs.

"Are we going down there?" questioned the fox.

"No, far from it. No reason to have you near this battle, as short as it may be. It's not your place." "We'll take the tunnels back to Crimsdon. I've the one last surprise to show you."

Obvious by the muggy air and lichen-stricken walls, the tunnels of which Velrick spoke saw little to no use. Some poor soul had been forced to light a few torches to illuminate most of the way. It did little in helping the pair avoid askew puddles of muck and dangling moss hiding the dim turns like a pair of curtains.

The passageway ended in a decrepit dungeon hall. It led either to a flickering light on the left or an eternal abyss of darkness to the right. Velrick grabbed a torch. Foxlaris felt the obsidian walls recoil as the orange flares brightened the right-side corridor.

Down, down, down they traveled. Hall after hall. Room after room. Finally, with a change of structure from sloppy to patterned, Velrick halted. The pitter-patter of their steps echoed out—the walls around them were thin, the passage finally above ground. The wolf's hand swiped past the wall. It rested on an ashy, protruding brick which once held a sconce. He gripped it tight and pulled.

*CrEaK!!!*

The door beside them flung open.

All looked black to the fox; not so for the wolf. He slipped into the passage and trotted down another set of stairs. As confused as he was, Foxlaris was given no choice but to follow.

The flight concluded in a chilled, barren room. Large, the ceiling vaulted with flicks of chipped tiled patterns along the top. Something further down within, however, stirred in the small lapses of firelight. At first, it looked to be just two small stacks of smoke. Candles, even torches, left to simmer, once again prepared ahead of time.

Then the flames revealed the bones filling the floor.

Taking the torch, Velrick tapped it to a small line of oil lathered below the tiles in a thick, deliberate scratch marred into the soot-soaked wall. The entire chamber roared to life in a flash. And in it sat the beast.

Foxlaris choked. His eye followed the full, heavy body for what felt like lifetimes. Scales large as shields, as *doors,* covered it like chainmail, their color that of rust and darkened metal. His heart skipped a beat as the talons, glistening like an axe head, shifted just enough to signal life.

Lanky spines rose from the beast's head. They traveled a great ways down its back, starting white but ending the same rich hue of the scales. Spikes of similar size and ferocity anchored themselves upon its hulking wings and hind quarters. Behind them hid its snaking tail. Long as Nohsis and thick as a Pradifore giant.

But what terrified the fox beyond measure, sending chills up his back and beads down his head, were the colossal, blood-colored eyes.

The pupils matched his height. Even though the creature lay asleep, the hideous eyes sat open, those hideous, hideous eyes. They were two wide portals forced awake, the dark, creamy crimson calling forward its victim. A strike of fear pierces you the second you wander too close. Its gaze engulfs you like fires and molten chains, clenching around your body. You're unable to move. Unable to breathe. Heavy grows the burden as it sucks you into a pit of no end, only cascades of darkness, a blistering fall that twists and turns you and gorges you on helpings of helplessness. Emotions—known not by name, but by feeling—smother you with the presses of blades stinging like a million deaths. Then, when all being has finally whisked away from you, and you're only the pain beating from a bleeding, bleating heart, you open your eyes. And the beast is before you once again. Hideous eyes still open, but glaring at you now from within another world.

The world he had let you peer into.

A world he cannot escape.

"D-D-D-Dra-a-g—" Foxlaris' breath left him. Luckily, Velrick was quick enough to steady him and ease the air back towards his lungs.

"Easy, Foxlaris. It's a dragon indeed. Beasts like these are but myths in the West, and here so too. But come with me. Admire him. See not the fear he extrudes, but the beauty brimming beneath."

His hand shook as he placed it within the wolf's. One snap of those sword-like fangs was all it would take to end the life barely clinging to his body.

"There, nothing to fear. He's dormant as can be." Velrick brought him away from the eyes and further along, letting him soak in the layering of the scales and heat radiating deep within. "He's called, in an old dragon tongue, Dearg-Fu'Ath. The Red Ash."

"H-H-How did you even get him? And here, here in room this small!?" Foxlaris asked, fear leaking from his mouth like spittle.

"That story could take *days* to tell in full. In short, I found him myself, lost far in dragon country across the Lostlands of Vollow. Beasts such as Dearg come not from the wild, but of their own culture, own kingdoms. My stay there was long, and the tongues I learned years in the mastering. He was younger then. We both were. We'd begun to bond and connect on a level of the spirit when he pulled him away from me. The *bird*. His call upon my dragon was far stronger than any I'd felt or witnessed. We battled for his very *soul*, Foxlaris. Such a terrible sight. One I see even now when I sleep."

As the Vorde continued, the fox glared deeper at the living legend. Rashes and scars like those of a rope burn rounded his neck. They ground into the scales and reached to a sinewy layer of skin below. Thick patches of elongated spikes appeared to be missing. Cuts, clean and focused, lay in their place. Strewn across the underside of its belly were a series of gashes. They'd scarred over with a pale redness. From them flowed small puddles of pearly slick. Was this…blood? Infection? The fox couldn't tell. The wounds, however old they were, had yet to fully heal.

"Why have him?" questioned Foxlaris. For some reason, the words he asked stirred a new emotion in Velrick. His breezing around topics and issues and worries dropped with a single glare. "Why not use him instead of locking him up down here, and—"

"Because he's our key, boy," the wolf cut back. His eyes softened, jaw unslaked, but words pointed as the end of a spear. "I've...not made it very clear, have I?" Velrick closed the distance between them. Both claws held Foxlaris by his hand and hook. "Everything in Vordemohr has but one goal: to fight, and win, the war against the West.

"Wait, what war?" asked the fox, gulping.

"The one of inevitability," sighed Velrick. His grip tightened. "Both sides have grown apart for thousands of years, and now once more they try to converge. It was bound to happen. We, this world, is a cycle. One we can't break, only anticipate.

"But you, Foxlaris, you're the *first* to see the secrets each hold from the other. A seer omniscient as the bird himself. We've both weapons, both armies, both people to fight for and protect. The East and the West slumber with sword in hand, battle-ready. And it's there, in that readiness, we find what we fear the most.

"We *must* defend ourselves at all costs. Had Vordemohr not taken the correct steps, the gnawing of such fright would have us as dented bones, not the muscled warrior we stand as today. Every measure has been taken to ensure we lose not an inch more than we already have. Yet, as much as I deny it, and deny I do...that fear is being realized. Has been for years. Despite our efforts."

His hands departed. The wolf faced away, hiding his expression. "Do you realize," he uttered, rhythm cold, meter still, "what the Bridge of Evon truly was?"

One eye faced back. Tears shielded it.

"The first step in conquering our lands. All of history, Foxlaris, *all* of it led to those timbers spanning the phoenix-wrought waters that shield us from one another. It's an act of *war!* Of *violence* to our kind!"

In a swirl of his cloak, Velrick spun back towards him, gripping him by the shoulders.

"Our fears were *right!* We've known the West too long to have turned a blind eye. What they did once in the War that Split the World they can do again, with ease had we not been prepared. Listen to the rumors now. The Bridge failed—but a catastrophe took its place. Even better for them, boy, even *better!* The blame falls to us! We're no longer exotic, oh no, we're dangerous, we're hungry for their children and wives, their quiet, precious ways of life! Watch it, just watch it! War will be at our doorstep. They will think us weak in comparison to their dwarves and bears, ghoulish beasts deserving the abolishment we ourselves brought to *their* shores."

His snout graced Foxlaris' one good ear.

"That, my dearest Blue Rose, is why we have him. Why we have *everything.*"

The truth was almost too much to bear. Foxlaris pulled away, shaking his head, trying not to induce another migraine from the menacing words and flickering lights. Still, he understood the Vorde. He'd worked at Bridgeburrow, heard the motives behind the Bridge. The East was to be sapped dry. Incorporated. *Invaded.*

All lined up.

"I see, Velrick. I'm...sorry for misunderstanding."

"Do not apologize to me, nor anyone. It's a fault my own for not telling you sooner. With this knowledge, however, you must promise me..."

"Whatever you ask," Foxlaris replied. The weight of the moment prodded him to add a small bow.

"Try bonding with Dearg-Fu'Ath."

Silence, apart from the flames licking the wall, filled the room.

"I...I-I don't understand...bonding?" asked the fox, low and timid.

"Exactly that. There's a...magic within him. You witnessed it, I'm sure, when meeting his eyes. But let it daunt you not. The longer you work with the bond, the quicker you'll heal. His might will become your own until you've risen to a fuller stature, one meant to strengthen what you have, replacing what you lost. Quicker too will you feel at home. I've already notice you're adjusting." Smiling, Velrick once more touched the fox's hand. This time, he raised it near the dragon's nostrils. "He won't hurt you. Neither will I. All that pain is behind you, Foxlaris. Let us heal and prepare to fight back that pain. Together."

Velrick pulled back his paw. The hand of Foxlaris, still cramped by the aches of splinters, hung within the air. It would be his move to touch Dearg, to take the first step in becoming the servant East Evon needed.

One long breath escaped him.

The cooling touch of the maroon scale tingled his hand.

Velrick grinned.

# 2

# "LIKE SILVER POURED FROM CRAGGED MOLD,"

"So, that's why I think we should go there. I know it's crazy and far and the exact *opposite* direction of where we need to go, but…gah, what other choice do we have? They have the knowledge and soldiers we need to get over there. We just gotta, well…hope they share it with us."

Foxtamas' voice wobbled as he spoke. The trio had plopped themselves upon Bunn's master bed in anticipation of the news. The blistering light of dawn illuminated his friends, bathing them in the young colors of rising reds and opening oranges. Bunns, still groggy from his late-night adventures, bobbed his head and squinted his eyes to avoid the morning. Acirema sat beside him—less tired, but less impressed. Foxtamas recognized the look. It mimicked his own fear, only twisted with rationality and reason. It wasn't worry. It was anxiety, and the gaping chasm which separated the two.

"Are you guys alright with this? We can think it through and find some other way, or—"

"No, Foxtamas, it's great," Acirema replied. She met the fox's gaze. "Just…if we go through like this and *actually* leave for the Fulnoa, all of this becomes…real." The princess knew her words weren't making sense. Deep in her stress, she reached beside her for a pillow, burying it in a hug. "Think about it. We're not too far from home. We could easily go back like nothing happened. And, well, I *know* that's not true, trust me. Foxlaris is still lost and we're right alongside him in that. It's just we've never done something this…*grand*…before."

"Queenie," cut in Bunns, rubbing his eyes, "wha' do yer mean? Our adventure has barely even started!"

"Bunns, hush," Foxtamas shooed, shooting his friend a stern look. The jackalope shriveled his nose in protest. "I get what you mean. If we need to turn back and let you stay—"

"No. You won't believe me, but…Bunns is right."

Acirema took them both off guard. The boys glared at her for a moment (as Bunns, of course, let a cheeky smile slip through). A light giggle escaped her. "I just never thought our quest would lead us, you know, to the *Fulnoa*. Are you *certain* this isn't just to fulfill some childhood fantasy?" Her sarcasm proceeded her, and it was Foxtamas' turn to protest, this time with both hands raised.

"Promise. It seems we just got lucky," he replied, winking at Bunns who, in turn, rubbed his paws together in a mix of anticipation and excitement.

"More than tha' laddie. Think it—weh're gonna walk the halls, see their weapons, peryton, all of et! All them stories weh made are about tae come *true*."Foxtamas smiled wide. He'd barely had time to imagine the reality of their destination between the fright of his friends abandoning him to return home.

A hand suddenly grabbed his own. He looked up and saw the quiet countenance of Acirema beaming his way.

"I know it's crazy, and far, and the last place I figured we'd end up, but it's okay. We'll follow you anywhere, Foxtamas. For him."

A second, calloused hand joined them.

"Aye. Anything tae bring ol' Rizzeh back. Ah reckon he'll bae mighty jealous when he hears 'bout where weh've been!"

Hucksubtle Tavern sat empty. All the lanterns had been blown out, taking the nightly buzz and crowd with them, and replacing the commotion with sunshine and an elderly porcupine nestled in a corner, sipping on a warm tea and slowly picking on a pair of blueberry scones.

Teardic, however, kept wiping down the counter as if nothing had changed. His ears turned him towards the three as they creaked down the steep stairs. As usual, along with his dress of a pleasant green apron and tunic, his custom smile welcomed them to the new day.

"Mornin' boys, m'lady! Sleep tight I reckon?" asked the chipper coyote.

"Never better!" Bunns replied. He hopped up on the barstool before the others, clear pep in his step.

"To be real honest with ya', Mister Bunns, I wasn't think' you'd be too, well, y'know—"

"Nae, Yotesy, takes more than a lil' drink tae take meh down! Et's the Elk in meh, swear et on mah mum's antlers."

"Hah! Should've guessed. Always the tough type, them Flapdragon champs." Foxtamas and Acirema joined their horned friend at the bar. The quiet, cozy nature of the morning could have lulled them to sleep had Teardic not stoked the conversation. "So, y'all Eastbound today, huh? To find your brother an' all?"

"Well, about that…" Foxtamas gave Teardic a nervous smile before spilling the news. As he did, the coyote whisked up from under the bar three cups of tea, dispersing them as he went along. His face twisted into shock. A trip to the Fulnoa wasn't *quite* in the right direction.

"Well looky there! Wasn't what I was 'spectin', but I ain't the 'venturers here. Seems like y'all'll be needin' a few things, won'tcha?" he winked, speeding off through the small door behind him. Acirema raised her arm in protest, on the verge of speaking out against the charity. Thankfully Foxtamas and Bunns were there to hold her back. If he was offering something, they would take it. End of story…and humility.

Odd *clinks* and *clanks* sounded from behind the bar, but Teardic still emerged peppy, barely able to hold the multiple sacks of provisions, flasks of ale, and withered maps fumbling from his paws. He plopped them down with a resounding *CRASH!*, somehow keeping everything from breaking

"We'll worry 'bout them vittles and such later. First up is gettin' y'all a way up to them Mountains. From what Mister Foxtamas was tellin' me last night, y'all ain't the most-well versed in Mechmilne country, right?"

"I mean, I've gone to a fair few villages, but nothing as north as the Fulnoa," said Acirema.

"Exactly what I figured. Now, I gotta make runs up to these parts every now and again, so I know some roads. Here's the choice ones."

He unfurled the map across the bar and stretched it for the trio to see. It detailed the entire region of Mechmilne Wood, stretching from Winthrop at the bottom to the Stone Twins at the top. Nohsis took up the Eastern side; nothing stretched beyond it, like an ocean at world's end. Everything, from the ridges and valleys, moors and lakes, had been charted on the crumpled brown paper. Foxtamas quickly noted where Hucksubtle (and Hucklebee) were located. Their trek had taken them farther than he thought, a good way northwest. Still, in relation to where they needed to go, Acirema was right. Home would be long behind them.

"I call it the Riverside Ride." Teardic traced up the map's right edge, sliding past dots of ink and their respective titles. Names like Fornrose, Rorison, Soardon, Vawdege, and Dink all appeared either right along Nohsis or scarcely shy of it. The road connecting them looked to be a straight shot north. If the party took it, their only turn would be West upon reaching the Dwarfmoors (the open, plain, moorish country north of Mechmilne). "It's all easy walkin'. Had my cellar cart 'long there no problem. Thing is…"

His green eyes turned upwards, securing their attention. "I've had some Fornrosers come my way. Ain't good up there. Grammo Day done wrecked their foundations, tore through the 'tire town like a storm. Hit the same way up to Soardon, and on this here road, it'll be y'all's last stop."

"Yer thinkin' thieves will want tae take their own stops tha' way?" questioned the jackalope.

"Certain, Mister Bunns. Not sure it's the route for y'all three."

"I'm thinking the same thing. What are the other ways?" Foxtamas asked, studying the map.

"Well, they need y'all to answer a big question: are y'all wantin' to head through Mikyill?"

Together, Foxtamas, Bunns, and Acirema stared at each other, a little stricken by such a question. The Fulnoa were one thing...but Mikyill? The *Grand City* of Mikyill?

"We've...never been there before..." replied the fox.

"Aye, an' yer would think tha' Queenie would have been—"

"And I may not be able to go now." Acirema's words returned the room to silence. "Before we left, I heard from some of the Watchers that Gniw cut all ties with Winthrop. I'm not sure if he blames us for the tragedy, or losses, or something, but the blood between our village and the City is...bad, to put it lightly."

"You ain't need to worry, m'lady," spoke the coyote, tapping the Mikyillian marker with a smile spreading his cheeks, "the place is brimming with raccoons just like yourself. Trust me, I've seen 'em with these here green peepers. You'll fit right in. Wouldn't hurt to keep a low cover, though. Hood up, no eye contact, rules like that."

"Are you sure? The last thing I want is to have us holed up in a jail or some dungeon—"

"M'lady," Teardic leaned in closer, tilting his head to slow her rambling words, "I ain't about to send royalty to that big ol' hedge maze without a warm home and friendly face. Selida, my baby sister whose room I stole last night? She'll be *more* than happy to take y'all in. She's got her own Inn up there. You tell her this rascal sent ya' and you'll be takin' *her* room for a change!" The bartender giggled to himself, yet infected Acirema all the same. The stripes over her face slackened in relief. "But really, I reckon y'all take to Mikyill. You walk straight through and find a million an' one roads leadin' up to the Fulnoa. Say what you will 'bout that Bridge, but it got these big places connected better than any politikin' I've seen."

"So, if we keep north and turn a little to the west, we'll make it there, right? It looks like the road leads through a few stops," said Foxtamas. It was his turn to trace out a path, taking the route of least resistance through the towns of Ernwell, Daisy Creek, B'bonrey, Tresbotton, and Kinsdale.

"Ya' beat me to it, Mister Foxtamas! You very well could. Makes the most sense, don't it? Plenty of places to stop an' rest, warm beds, good food, all that. But you see that road? Look at all them zigs, them *zags*. Y'all followin' it would practically *double* the trip to Mikyill. Beats the broken villages, but costs ya'. *Deep.*"

"Nae nae nae, enough of tha'. There no other way? Not sure these lassies can handle tha' long of a trip." Both friends fired at Bunns with loaded side-eyed glares. Amongst the shots, Teardic sizzled his hands together to the point of popping out a spark.

"Oh, there's a way, alrighty. We call 'em…the Oldtrails."

Again he took the map, only this time with a lead piece in hand. The trio watched as he etched a clear line Westward out from Hucksubtle. It curved away from just about every known village and road, instead trekking across ridges and rivers until concluding at Mikyill's left edge. To their surprise, when drawn out, it came up considerably shorter than the other two routes.

"Old towns and hamlets may've gone off an' gotten lost to time, but not the trails that connected 'em all together. A good slew start just a few hours north of here. Y'all take 'em, even through the woods and valleys an' all that, and you'll be to Mikyill faster than a Ratsy. It's the way I take to Selida when I visit. I reckon you'll be seein' my cart tracks 'fore long." As he spoke, he began to roll up the map. "Even better for you, m'lady, is there won't be a soul on there to recognize that royal mug of yours. Safe, secure, speedy. Only kinda quality we offer here."

*WHACK!*

Teardic slapped the condensed paper against the bar, grin bright on his face. "Sound like a plan?"

Foxtamas looked over to his friends. Both nodded. Not just ready, but *enthused.*

This was it. This was the plan to save Foxlaris.

"Oldtrails it is," the fox heartily replied, matching Teardic with a smile of his own.

"Perfect! I knew y'all folk were the smart kind. Had my doubts last night, but we're on past that. Now, let me tell y'all 'bout the supplies..."

In short, the coyote filled each of the travelers a sack containing just enough drink and vittles to make it to Mikyill. The flasks contained fresh water, their orders from the night prior, and an extra sip of Hucksubtle Mug (*not* the Bunns kind). As for food, scones, tarts, apples, and a few stray loaves of bread were tucked away. It beat out whatever Winthropian scraps the boys had snatched before leaving.

"How long do you think this trip will take?" Foxtamas piped up while settling the supplies in his pack.

"Varies. Quickest could be two weeks, but most who take it average 'round a month or so," replied Teardic.

The fox's heart sank. Was it really *that* long? The bartender's words charged against his walls, hacking before slashing, striking the stone hot until a gap expanded just wide enough for fear to slip in. Its army took the chance. It charged headlong, at the exact time another voice rang out.

"Hah! Watch et laddie, weh'll bae there in ah week flat. Mark mah words!"

"Marked 'em, Mister Bunns!"

Foxtamas did too. The builders soon arrived, and his castle's holes were mended not by stone, but by steel, pliable from forging in the warm fires of friendship. There his trust could always lie.

Once packed, Foxtamas, Acirema, and Bunns stood ready to go. The fox tightened his crossbawns and cleaned off his cape; the raccoon adjusted both her quiver and bow before dawning her purple hood; the jackalope double-checked his star pouch and stretched wide to loosen the bruise. A finer party was never seen.

"I'm not sure I can thank you enough for your generosity, Teardic," started Acirema, clasping his hands. Tears began to ring at the bottom of her eyes. "When this mess we're in gets resolved, I'll bring all of Village Winthrop here and have them spend every last Top they can spare. Promise."

"Oh, no, no, m'lady! The pleasure's all mine. Think it, ol' Yotesy gettin' to help on a royal, Evon-spannin' quest? Never thought I'd see the day!"

"I'll be sure to tell you all about it when we find Foxlaris," Foxtamas added.

"Aye! Thank yer laddie!" With that, the company moved towards the door, taking their first steps back into Mechmilne. This time, however, they were prepared, well-rested, and journeying with a goal.

Foxtamas turned to give one last wave to Teardic. His blue eyes met his green, and the toothy grin he produced just about blinded him.

But…something came over the fox.

A feeling he knew was more than a thought, more than a dream. A prophecy. Promise. One which assured him that, the next time he saw such a smile, he'd be different.

An entirely different fox indeed.

Outside the tavern lay a waking dream. The mid-morning sun blistered through the foliage overhead, sparkling upon the leafy floor like light from a green stained-glass window. The wind twiddled in the air with a whistle. Hands on an invisible flute. The mood it set was that of a dance fluttering far, fluttering wide, down even to the plump drops of dew, their coats diamond bright.

Gentle whispers of beauty brushed against the trio. They lingered to listen and feel the words fill their weary souls with wants for wandering, hope for hospitality among the far-out fields and forests. All Evon stretched out before them, beckoning with this very call. Had not the pebbled road at their feet led Northward, all three would have easily succumbed. Gone in the glory. Lost on the eternal trail...

"Look there, past the trees up ahead," Acirema suddenly broke in, taking the first steps away from Hucksubtle. "I think that might be Hucklebee." Indeed, the small outlines of houses and smokestacks peeped past the trunks safeguarding the gravel path. It created a stark divide before the tavern, one that cut a line through the trees and formed ditches on either side. A road-side stop all its own.

"It's gotta be. You'd think after so long they'd at least try to make amends," Foxtamas added.

"I know. I can't imagine an entire *village* holding such a grudge."

"Yer know wha'? Ah say good on ol' Teardic. Lad's makin' ah fair ol' livin' for himself. Last thing he needs is all tha'."

"But it has to get lonely, right? To provide for so many yet still be shunned?" asked Acirema.

"Maybe after ah while yer become numb tae et. Like et dinnae matter one way or another wha' those laddies think."

"I hope that's how he feels."

"With a smile like that?" the fox chimed in, already ahead of the pair on the road, "I'm sure of it." It was obvious by his walk that just being in the wide, open air changed him. Like Bunns in a battle, or Acirema with a poem.

"Well, aren't you excited?" asked the princess, smirking.

"And you aren't? Like, I know the urgency and danger around us but...just look at, Acirema. It's enchanting. And we're going to the *Fulnoa*. I'm not sure I could *get* any happier!"

"That's the spirit, Scottoh!" Bunns hopped on ahead from his lagging spot with the princess, joining his friend in admiration of the forested road ahead. "Just don't bae gettin' all scared on us, got meh?"

"Whaaaat, me? Not sure we're talking about the same person here, Bunns."

Acirema giggled and caught up to the boys. A smile found her somewhere between the crunch of the pebbles and slinking shadows waving across them.

"So, since you two are the resident dwarf-lovers, what are we expecting to find when we get there? What will it be like?"

Oh, how that sent their minds racing. While Foxtamas fumbled with the map, Bunns turned to her with mouth agape.

"Callin' *us* dwarf-lovers, eh? Yer the one who *met* the Lordies at Grammo Day!"

"*Hardly*. Father had me smothered in that tent with Gniw the whole day. I know you saw when you peeked in. The only dwarf I caught a glimpse of was the one on stage. Are they always that, um…down? And I figured there were supposed to be two of them."

"They're usually jolly as can be. As for there being two…" Foxtamas held up the map for the raccoon, pointing to the Brother Mountains at the top. "The left one, that's the Blue Mountain, and the other is the Brown. I believe the one we saw on stage was Enaled Wolverton of the, well, Wolverton clan. They've been Wolvertons for the past however many centuries, so you can always kinda assume the current ruler is from that family. Anyway, he matched the descriptions I've heard and bore the Blue Crest. Foehn, his cousin, rules the Brown while he rules the Blue." The fox rattled off the facts. He constantly looked over at Acirema to make sure she was keeping up. Inwardly, however, she kept hidden the fact she knew everything he spoke of. Politics gave her such a breadth of knowledge about the who's and what's of Evon; it was depth, however, she was always waded away from.

"Of course, should've remembered that. But don't they also have some…forest…right? I remember it coming up in some game we played, where Foxlaris was a tree—"

"Aye Queenie, the Cranarbor!" Bunns replied with gusto. He shot his paws over to snatch the map, only for it to resist.

"What do you need the map for?" asked Foxtamas, pulling it away.

"Tae show Queenie the ol' brutes an' make sure weh're still headin' the right way."

"Oh, so *you're* the leader now?" he snarked back.

"Ah figured so!"

"Nope, not after last night. You might only remember your win, but the chaos you caused—"

"Didn't hurt ah soul! Yer gotta give meh ah second chance here."

"I will. If you earn it." Foxtamas beamed him a look of victory and held the map closer. Both Bunns' ears tucked back behind his antlers. He knew the fox was right. But he'd show him. He always did, didn't he?

"As you were saying, Bunns?" said Acirema, stifling a laugh.

"Oh, right." He motioned for Foxtamas to spread out the map again, making sure this time not to grab it. "Look, right around the Fulnoa. See tha' big ol' ring of brown? Tha's the Cranarbor Forest. Big bunch o' trees, Ah mean *huge*. Legends say they can come tae life if the Lordies need 'em tae."

"So let's hope we don't make them angry," added Foxtamas.

"I doubt I'll be included in that 'we'," Acirema replied. "But it does sound intriguing. Are you sure the stories will be able to live up to the real thing?"

"Oh, I bet. We'll just have to wait and see."

The Fulnoa-founded conversation continued, and the path wound forward along its open, clear-cut way. A small side ditch with long graceful patches of grass ran beside it, accompanied by light, bountiful bunches of local Centryfold (A hairy, almost mossy flower with a blue tint), Ramsons, Midnight Orchids, Sea Rose, and many a dinky lilac. Bushes covered the other side, all the frost berry variety, and brought along a few early fallen leaves of autumn. Summer's green would soon fade, and the ripples of red and yellow would flood across Mechmilne and Evon. Foxtamas made certain to drink in the scenery. He caught the grasshoppers poking their sleepy heads above the grasses, the bees and wasps swirling around hives hidden in rotten stumps.

Traveling, it seemed, lived up to his dreams.

As the day progressed, the wood changed around them, the sites shifting from those beyond what surrounded Winthrop. Parts of the forest opened to plains rising up the nearby ridges. Wind-whipped grass stole the place of trees, splashes of yellow daisies pocking here and there. Many an old fence lay right off the road's edge. These were not forged with metal and stone like some sunken battlements guarding a homestead of families past; no, these were wooden, and these were quiet. Their trail tumbled in and out of messy green tufts winding up their chipping spines. The purpose of their holding was gone now. A farm, maybe. A yard, the guarding line where children weren't supposed to run past. It outlived it. It outlived them. And now it traveled a ways with the passersby, learning new accents, catching glimmers of old tales refreshened and retold, before petering out as sprouts of spruce and pine returned, the end of another journey, yet only a part of someone else's.

The sunset grew along the outlining ridges without the trio even noticing. Golden cast the light, making the farms by which they walked flare with gilded grain. Beyond them, deeper in Mechmilne, sat an old cabin, perhaps passed down from one generation to the next. An old frog farmer waved at them as they passed. Oh, how tasty did his apple trees look, blueberry bushes smell. The hominess was hard to resist. It stayed with them until dusk grew darker, and a new issue rose to their attention.

"So, guys," Foxtamas began as they turned the bend. The larger forest giants returned, clinging over them with bended boughs. "Teardic's line says the start of the Oldtrails should be there, past the trees on our left. But I don't see anything…"

"What do you mean?" Acirema tiptoed to glance over past his shoulder. Sure enough, the lead mark suddenly shot westward, departing from the line distinguishing the road.

"Wha're weh waitin' for? Let's head on in," proclaimed Bunns. The jackalope started towards the wall of green but stopped when his friends stayed hunched over the paper mid-path. "Hello?"

"Bunns, just wait, okay." A hint of worry stuck to the fox's words.

"So yer ain't trustin' Teardic now? After all he did—"

"No, i-it's not a trust thing. I just need to make sure," he replied, squinting deeper at the lines of black and gray. The faltering daylight didn't help. "There's just no marker, and I swear we should see *something.* Say he placed it a little too far back, or a little up ahead. We get lost in there, o-o-or on some other road, we're lost, *just* like we were before. It's not worth trusting it if we don't know for sure."

"Nae Scottoh, the lad knows these trails. Wha's et gonna hurt tae start lookin' anyway?"

"Oh, I dunno Bunns, *everything!?"*

"Guys, quiet down, we can ask this family up ahead," Acirema said. She pointed down the road where a small rabbit family strolled towards them. The father rolled a stout, wooden cart behind him as his young girl and wife walked beside. Their simple clothes of tunics and sandals exposed them not as Mikyillites, but hailing instead from one of the smaller villages strewn across the map. Once closer, the princess raised her hand in a wave.

"Excuse me! Might we ask you all a quick question? No need to be a bother."

"Yes ma'am," replied father rabbit with a hoarse voice. Once beside the travelers, he quitted his carriage and stretched his back, the cackling cracks aged and audible. "What's seemin' to be the matter?"

Foxtamas scurried beside him with the map and pointed out where they sat on the path.

"We're taking the Oldtrails to Mikyill. Our guide, he drew the start of them here, but we aren't seeing anything saying we're at the right spot or not. Do you happen to know if he's right?"

"Hmmm," came the gruff reply. The husband gazed closer to where Foxtamas indicated. The browns of his eyes reflected Teardic's hasty marks. A shift. A scrunch of the eyebrows. "Son, sorry to tell ya', but I ain't quite so sure one way or 'nother."

"But you shouldn't take them."

The group turned to the new voice, the one cold, belonging to the mother rabbit now holding shut her daughter's tall, floppy ears.

"Wha' do yer mean?" Bunns asked in confusion.

"The Oldtrail way takes y'all right through Hermit's Glum."

Foxtamas exchanged confused look with his friends. The name hadn't rung a bell.

"Hermit's...Glum?"

"Bless you, dearies, y'all must not be from these parts." She tried to chuckle, but only a cough came out. "It's an ol' spot on the Oldtrails where exiles from Mikyill and the other towns go off an' die. All stories of the place say that, even in death, their ghosts ain't got a place to go, so they haunt the whole country thataway." By her deadpan, glazed-over look, truth lay in her words. Or, at least, truth to her.

"I'd listen to her, kids. It's done served me well. Keep on this road here and you'll make it up to Ernwell. Town's got plenty good places to sleep." Acirema nodded, coaxing a smile as she did. Though, behind her, she could feel the heat leaving Foxtamas. Fear in the form of potential Hermit's Glum ghosts were already haunting his mind.

"Why yes, we shall. Thank you so much, both of you," she replied with her political politeness. Father rabbit nodded. His worn, calloused paws fitted themselves around the wagon's handles once again. As the wheels turned, so did their feet, rolling and trotting past the trio. Until his raspy words called back.

"Y'all ain't from Winthrop, are ya'?" His brown eyes turned around, squinted. They found their target in the princess. Acirema could tell he suspected something. Something dangerous.

"Oh, um, no, we're from Mikyill. Just...taking a different way back," she responded with shaken voice.

"Why are yer askin'?" Bunns stepped up a bit in front of his friend. Though none could tell, his hand was angled at the ready. Any foul movement from the man and a star would fire fast and true.

"Heard the place is tied to raccy's like yourself, miss. I saw the lot of 'em up there on Grammo Day."

"Then we must be cousins or something!" she giggled, hoping to relieve the tension. "Well, thank you again—"

"And I blame them Winthrop bastards and all 'em on that stage."

Breath gone.

Words lost.

Eyes frozen.

Acirema tried to produce something, a nod, a smile, a shake, *anything.*

Foxtamas, meanwhile, found himself stuck in the exact same place. Oh, to run away from it all! Where could he go, what could he do! His thoughts diverged, some racing towards the perfect path to flee, and the others scrambling for reassurance in his friends. Bunns would protect them. Fight them off. Already Foxtamas gleaned the star pouch easing open. And Acirema, her words could fight just as well, maybe call off the entire impending catastrophe ready to explode before them all and kill them and slay them and ruin everything and leave Foxlaris to die—

There, in the back of the cart.

His blue eyes collapsed shut, but he knew what he saw. Nothing looked out of the ordinary at first. Bags, provisions, a stray doll. But behind it all sat what every Evoneer, parent or not, never dared to fear.

A small coffin. No larger than the size of a child.

"For tha' Bridge?" asked Bunns yet again.

"For my son."

The others found what Foxtamas had. Behind it, the rabbit family held back tears lest they betray their stout, stoic emotions.

"We're takin' him to the sea," spoke the wife. "He always wanted to go. He still tells me…still, even now. Even now…" She was beyond solitude. The woman, it seemed, was haunted.

"Our condolences," Acirema responded, bowing her head.

"Thank you, miss. Y'all journey safe now."

"Same to you."

Once the rabbits made the turn, the friends released gasps of worry, confusion, and relief.

"You weren't about to hurt them, were you?" Acirema asked to Bunns, wiping sweat from her forehead.

"Nae, just tryna scare them if they tried tae get ah bit close—"

"I thought we were gone, I thought we were gone," repeated Foxtamas between breaths.

"Scottoh, weh fought ah buncha Eastern beasties, an' *tha'* had yer scared?"

"You heard what he said about Winthrop! You saw the casket! A-A-And his wife, saying she could still hear him. Oh, I'm scared sick, Bunns, *sick!"*

"Easy, Foxtamas," Acirema patted the fox's cloaked shoulder, rubbing in her gentle words. "Just be glad he didn't find out."

"And what if he *did?* Didn't that get you upset?" he looked up at the princess, meeting her eyes, watery to the point of tears.

"No, it…it did." Each word came out quieter than the last. That father…he couldn't be right. She did nothing to kill that boy. Neither did her own father, as wicked as he could be.

But…

Winthrop *had* played a part. One so inscrutable, inalienable, that had they not given a quarter of a Top to Gniw, that little rabbit boy would be splashing through the waves of the sea, not buried beneath its sands.

A shiver, chilled and sharpened, shattered through the princess.

Foxtamas wrung out his hands before rubbing them against his head.

"Oh, what are we gonna do now? I'm not even sure we should take this way."

"We have to," Acirema finally whispered in response. Her low tone took both boys off guard. "It's either try our luck here or meet someone else further down the road. You saw how close one family was to figuring us out. We can't risk that again."

"And what about the Hermit's Glum place?" the fox retorted. "We're just supposed to not mind strolling into some *haunted wood?"*

"All ah load o' junk. Yer saw tha' lass, mad as ah manticore. Ah reckon et's ah couple old huts, nothin' more," chided Bunns.

Foxtamas realized his chances of winning the war were dwindling. Both were right, of course. Acirema couldn't risk being found out, and the dangers of delay would hurt worse than any ghost, ghoul, or goblin waiting up ahead—

*SNATCH!*

Without warning, Bunns whisked away the map from Foxtamas, bounding away from him and into the darkening forest.

"Wha—Bunns! Give that back!"

"Can't do, Scottoh!" he shouted, poking his head out from behind a tree. "Weh need ah leader who can point us the right way, *so,* Ah'm thinkin' et's mah turn for ah second chance!" The jackalope crunched and trunched through the thicket, and as he did, Acirema gave the fox a light, sideways glance.

"You *did* promise him…" she said, defeated. But not for her sake.

"Yup, that's it," grunted Foxtamas. He hiked his pack upon his shoulders and smacked his lips. "I'm not saying a *word* more the *rest* of this trip."

With that, the pair trudged after Bunns. The twilight behind them unfolded over the East, twisted pinks laced with gold and matte clouds sinking beneath the horizon.

# 3

# "OUR HOME AROSE IN QUAKE OF MORN,"

Lunch never tasted so good. It was partially due to the tarts still crisp from Hucksubtle, their flaky edges leaking a homey twist of honey and apple butter; it was also because of the dusty, leaf-covered Oldtrail running alongside them.

The dense canopy overhead stalled any hope in searching for the route the night prior. So, at the behest of Foxtamas, camp was made. Acirema experimented with roasting slices of apple and pairing it with her cider while Bunns scoffed down a scone and called it a night.

Almost.

He tossed and turned. Then turned and tossed. Something, he complained, kept rubbing too close to both his back and bruise. Sure enough, when the easing light of morning sifted down through the leaves, the jackalope found his makeshift pack-bed rolled out directly upon the rocky, dirt-cut Oldtrail. They denoted it by the cart tracks rolling deeper into the forest. The great ruts had done little in helping a certain Bunnclar Cammont catch a wink of sleep. Still, Teardic was right: a trail of his *was* upon the route.

Another morning began as the trio followed the road before them. No longer did they have the gentle slopes and wide, grazing fields to enjoy; they were back, yet again, in the wilds of Mechmilne. It didn't matter to Foxtamas. A journey was still a journey, after all.

He kept his head high and watched the dazzles among the leaves, the peaks of blue, sunny sky like stars spread against a green night. So too did he dwell among the trees. Some, like the ashes or oaks, paraded as wise, as creatures in their own right, unconfined by bark and branch. Something about that grandeur drove his steps deeper into the ruts of the trail. A vigor of defiance warmed his chest. He was one of them now. A part of this world, shifting forward beyond the simple reaches of home.

Others brought out differing flares of feeling. Those that drooped and sagged with leaves of sun-beaten green ignited memories of exhaustion and the tendrils of dusk. They were paced out by the smells, sights, and staggering height of the pines. Through their presence, Foxtamas found breath. Felt the wind rustling past him. The refreshment reminded him that no limbs or lungs of his own ached. This day was still young, and with it both himself and the unfolding adventure ahead. Such truth rustled through him until a singular dead tree crept into view. Its scarring snaked across the grayed trunk, slicing away many a limb and carving inward until only a rotten husk remained. Lightning could have been the cause. Or the lone strike of a fire. Either way, it brought to life a fear the fox had forgotten since yesterday's encounter: Hermit's Glum. Now, as he smacked on his tart, the thought only rooted deeper into his mind.

"So…think we're in Hermit's Glum yet?" he asked, low and hushed. The trio had stopped in a quiet meadow. Two twin oaks loomed on the outskirt, with roots large enough to sit between conjoining at the middle. While Foxtamas and Acirema each took a tree, nestling between the earthen legs, Bunns hopped and skipped through the grass. He chewed on a pear while passing through the small wildflower brush of red and purple. Beneath them slept large, square-cut stones sunken deep into the ground. They dotted the whole field. The more he paced, the more he realized their lunch had led them to the remains of a village.

"Gah, Scottoh, yer still on tha'?" the jackalope spat back.

"And you're not?"

Bunns stopped his investigation and turned back towards Foxtamas.

"Not ah lick. Look, everything's been the same all day an' not scary like yer thinkin' et'll bae. Just…think o' somethin' else. Like Ah said, tha' lady was—"

"Mad as a manticore, you told me. What else should I focus on then? Hm?"

"What do you hope to see on the adventure?" Acirema asked. With the touch of a mother calming two toddlers, the princess gazed out from her oak, taking in the gentle sway of flowers tickling her legs. Foxtamas looked across at her. She knew exactly how to shut him up—or, in this case, start him going, just on something new.

"Umm…I don't really know. Something classical, y'know, like in the stories."

"Such as…?"

"Like a Wizard's Tower, or a magical something-or-nother."

"You think we're going to see *magic*?"

"Anything's possible, I guess. I always thought legends had to have some sort of truth behind them." For the briefest of moments, the thought of Roihelm flickered through his mind. Was it the mention of magic? His own worries of facing a reality he'd rather run from?

No answer came to him.

"What about you?" the fox asked back, a tad sarcastic. "What do *you* wanna see?"

"Nothing for a while. I think just sitting here is nice enough. No kings, no presidents, no travelers wishing death on me." Both boys, even Bunns off hopping from stone to stone, chuckled. "But in the terms of what *you two* like, I would say…a manor of sorts, with a nice humble witch hidden inside."

"A witch? You just doubted that I'd see magic!"

"I said a *humble* witch. Do you see any magic in that?" protested the princess.

"Yeah, in the word *witch*."

"Well maybe she only has curses for healing or giving extra vigor to her garden."

"That wouldn't be a curse, it'd just be a spell."

"A gardening spell it is then." Acirema failed to hide her smile. How could she help it? Foxtamas' cheeks hastened towards a rashy red. Was it anger? Embarrassment? Or just frustration at her lacking so much of the knowledge of which he knew too much?

"Of course yer tae would want witches an' wizards," Bunns finally commented, crossing past them to fish something from his pack.

"What's that supposed to mean?" questioned the fox.

"Aint like yer tae want tae take on ah dragon or sneak past guards for some treasure. Yer just keep it simple, yer know?"

"Well look at where fighting a *minotaur* got you," Foxtamas shot back. Bunns' heated stare returned.

"Low blow, Scottoh."

"Ok, besides dragons and treasure, what else are you wanting to see? Thieves? Pirates?" Acirema added.

"Nope. Ah already got what ah want, nae thanks tae yer two. An' you'll bae happy tae hear et, Queenie."

She knew that grin.

That "brown eyes so tight the next move may cause pure terror" look. Sure enough, the jackalope pulled from his pack the Banjalope, its strings already tuned.

"Always gotta find yer ah good travelin' song for an adventure, right?"

"Well of *course* Bunns! Take it away!" The fox tossed a quick wink to Acirema as Bunns cleared his angelic voice. That seemed to clear up his cheeks.

The princess sighed. Long and defeated. Father was right—she should never have befriended the lowest of village boys.

Oh my darlin', oh my sweet love,
I lookit your lone window 'bove
And see that sight where it came to an end;
Many nights I sat below
And sang a song I know you know
Both to you and your House at Yellawood Bend.

The second these eyes saw you pass
In Ol' Miss Tubbard's schoolroom class
All I wanted was to be your friend.
You soon obliged and let me stay
Until your Pops done heard us play
And locked you in your House at Yellawood Bend.

All the folks they said you moved
But my heart knew it wasn't true,
So every day an' night I'd out there spend.
You heard me, yes, I know you did,
As I grew up to man from kid
And sang to your ol' House at Yellawood Bend.

I did all this 'till I was hoarse,
A weary soul with voice a ghost,
Had to sit for a while lest I meet my end.
It was on that cold afternoon,
My eyes grew wide, big as the moon,
When you came to your House at Yellawood Bend.

All old and gray, just like me,
But with someone else, new company,
Your…husband. Kids. And grandchildren.
You passed it by without a care,
Said, "Well lookit that, I lived there,"
Then up an' left your House at Yellawood Bend.

You didn't even see my face,
The one you loved when we were eight,
Like I had gone and just blended on in.
I know my skin's gone deathly white
And no one passes, says goodnight,

But darlin' I'm not leavin'
I'll be non-stop a-singin',
Until we're both fine livin'
In your House at Yellawood Bend.

As usual, Bunns gave a quick bow after strumming the final cord. Foxtamas clapped wildly; Acirema, begrudgingly, followed.

"Why such a sad song?" she asked.

"Yer wanted tae see ah manor an' Scottoh's been hankerin' for some ghosts, so Ah figured yer tae would bae all in." Smirking, he slung the instrument back down to the meadow and started putting both it and his emptied flask away, replacing them with the map. His paw traced along Teardic's line. They were on the Oldtrails alright. Just not that far along them.

"Alrighty laddies, weh best get ah move on. Weh got plenty o' ground tae—"

Without even the warning of a bristle on his back, a surprise gust of wind slammed against Bunns, smacking him down and ripping the parchment from his hands.

"Bunns, the map!" Foxtamas cried, leaping up from his spot. It circled further and further upward, the fox's height being no use in nabbing it.

"Stay back Scottoh, Ah got et!"

Bunns started into a sprint. The breeze tossed it up from their camp and along the meadow. Within moments, it would sail to the forest lining and ride over its waving crests.

Had not a star sprung into the jackalope's hand.

Right as the map met the tree line, a buzzing whirl sped through the air.

*THUNK!*

Perfectly pinned upon a pine.

Relief melted over them. Bunns (pride beaming from his dimples like dawn through drapes) turned back to reassure his friends.

"See? Nothin' tae worry about." Still grinning, he looked up to where the star had caught the map. But his brown eyes didn't linger on his stunning work of marksmanship.

They looked towards the darkening sky encroaching above him. And the rolls of thunder crackling no more than half an hour away.

The twin oaks and meadow lay long behind them when the first drops of rain began. The crisp noontime day had vanished; in its place clumped clouds like paint smushed on a canvas, their colors blues and blacks, spread across as bruises upon the sky's bright skin.

The Oldtrails had taken a sharp turn Westward. Wide were the forests with grassy plains between them, completely opposite of the thicket and overhanging branches they'd braced earlier. As the wind and rain picked up, however, the swaths of field beneath the trees held the water close. Both the dirt at their feet and the ruts on their path would slush into mud after too long.

Time was not on their side.

"There has to be some place we can take cover!" Acirema hollered, hood pulled tight around her head. The sprinkling had just about drenched her. "Some town, a cave, anything!"

"Not from wha' Ah can tell," Bunns offered back. The star-torn paper showed nothing but ridges and forests surrounding them. Further up, Teardic's marking grew thicker, just as they had at the entrance to the Oldtrails. "Weh just need tae keep pushin' forward! The forest gets thicker oup ahead!"

As hard as they tried to hurry, the darkness didn't wait to fully encompass the land. Night arrived early. No different than the storm that overtook Grammo Day. Although they could still make out the flailing trees, only the blaring stroke of lightning fully illuminated the path ahead.

The company braced against the torrents of rain. They wrapped themselves tight in their cloaks and kept their heads low to stay somewhat dry. If cover wasn't found soon, both supplies and map alike would fall to ruin.

It was then that the roars of the river overtook the groaning of the wind.

"Why'd you lead us to a river?" Foxtamas shouted over the noise.

"Ah didn't! The map said this was just ah lil' creek!"

Around the corner, cascading flows of muddy brown and filthy foam rushed westward at an unceasing pace. The waters rose high, chipping away at the land right before their feet. It left them on a rocky outcrop that used to be some twelve feet behind the shore. Now, one wrong move and the mud slathering it would give way.

"Should there be a bridge!?" Acirema cried.

"Aye!" The jackalope hopped from the path and scurried up the river's edge. Nothing resembling a bridge came into view. "Ah think," he yelled, "tha' it leads tae Nohsis! Tha' laddie got big, and so did this one!"

Acirema hunkered close to Foxtamas as Bunns staggered back. It was all they could do to avoid the battering gushes of water and wind.

"What do you think?" Her voice sailed above the chaos.

"We gotta turn back! I know it's open, but we'll find something!" the fox shouted.

"Nae!" Bunns shook his head as he rejoined them. "Weh'll lose Teardic's trail! An' tha' side's plenty thick!"

The opposite bank did provide the best cover. Aged oaks with roots that traveled deep into both the soil and raging waters alike built a wooden wall against the edge.

Foxtamas considered the option. But he stared too long.

The rattles of the wood swayed to a rhythm certain, not across the chords of random sound but to a song that signaled violence, malice from the heights of the lightning to the heart of the ground. The wind became both conductor and warring general in the course—a symphonic sinner, devilish dancer. He'd known that ferocity before, heard the cries of the sightless commander.

It led his mind back to a world it should never have returned to.

Murky rapids.

Broken bridges.

Brother sides…

The flashbacks started without remorse. He was back there…

No, *he* wasn't. But another fox was.

There! In the water, his brother! Foxlaris! Guys, hurry, jump in! He's close, we can get him, don't let him go down, hurry, go, go, please, *PLEASE!* Just reach his hand! It's so close, so close I can almost—

*K*
*A*
*Z*
*Z*
*A*
*K*
*C*
*K*
*!*

Lightning ignited behind them. It marred the sky and silenced sight and sound. The sizzling afterimage sprayed through the rain like a statue—first a sun-lit gold, then static bronze, then a crumbling of sparks that exploded forward, blasting the trio deep into the muddy trail.

Foxtamas felt numb.

Nothing moved to either his eyes or ears. Had the rain…stopped? Their journey, the river…was it all a…a dream? It could've been—and would've—had he not felt the poke of a hand attack his back, followed by the ringing of a faint cry, almost too faint to comprehend.

"*Foxtamas*...FOXTAMAS!"

"Uuunnggg," he moaned. Above him loomed the face of Acirema, again calling his name. She wiped the muck from his fur before tugging at his arm and helping him to his feet. The fox shook his head (and a good helping of unrelenting rainwater). He awoke back into the reality of the thunderstorm and their perilous way forward.

"Scottoh! Hurry, over here!" called Bunns. Foxtamas, still a bit dazed, found the jackalope pushing against a tree near the bubbling riverside. The bottom had taken the brunt of the lightning strike, blasting most of the wood and leaving the sides both black and sizzling. "Get yer axe!"

"What...what're you doing!?" The fox fired back. Bunns jumped and pounded the tree with his shoulder. The giant swayed.

"This tree's long enough tae bae ah bridge over for us. Yer chop et right about here, an' meh an' Queenie'll get et set tae cross, got et?"

"What the—Bunns, no, that's crazy!""Weh're crossin', Scottoh!""No, that's stupid! We'll drown!"

"Yer wanna get struck by lightning? Or lose the map an' get lost out here?"

"Just listen, we can—"

Bunns' eyes narrowed. He gripped the fox's arm, squeezing as he spoke his next words with a firmness Foxtamas had only seen him use on those he wished to strike with a star.

"Weh. Can. *Make et.*" He let his words ring, then snatched the axe from Foxtamas' side and pushed it against his chest.

"Chop."

Bunns turned away. Cold.

For a moment, the fox didn't know how to react. He felt the heat of pride radiate from his friend, practically steaming the rain pelting him. The situation was dire, yes, but this, that level of ferocity? Both wanted out of this mess. But Bunns... he wanted something more.

Regardless, Foxtamas obeyed. Swinging the blade felt odd at first, even considering the conditions. It handled differently from the axes used in Bridgeburrow. Each swipe took long to wrap around his body yet hit with double the punch. The clarity came when he realized it was meant to chop something much more threatening than wood: other Evoneers.

"It's almost there!" he shouted, cutting further into the core. Bunns and Acirema backed up behind him. By now the rain's firing was almost unbearable. Hoods and cloaks did little to slow the process, and everything except the very center of their packs fell waterlogged. With tightly drawn tunics and boots teeming with rain, the trio bunched together right as Foxtamas landed the final swing.

The pine groaned. Its thin wooden sinews snapped one after the other, tumbling downwards with a whistle. It crashing upon the other side with a *CrAcK!* echoing over the river's cholic.

"Yes!" Bunns cried. He motioned for Acirema to follow to the giant's ravaged end. With a hefty push, the tree snuggled itself closer on the other side. Strong. Secured. Ready to cross.

"Queenie, yer up first while Ah get Scottoh. Hunker down an' hug the side an' yer'll bae fine."

"Are you sure?" Her question reeked of fear. Bunns could tell by her furrowed brow that the chopping waves and pelting strings of rain frightened her. But he didn't care. He *needed* them on the other side. It was that, or…or…

He shook his head and shot her back a stern glance, softening it with a nod.

"Aye. Head on over, weh won't bae far behind."

While Acirema readied herself upon the log, Bunns guided Foxtamas over, despite his protests.

"Bunns, I-I-I can't, i-it's—"

"Yes yer can! Stop baein' scared for once an' *move!* Weh gotta go before weh get blasted like tha' tree!" screamed the jackalope. He hopped up on the makeshift bridge, dragging Foxtamas behind him. "Ah'm gonna walk, but crawl if yer have tae. Don't' take long!"

Oh, he had to.

Actually being atop the log flashed blazes of fear through his body, no different than shocks of lightning. He hugged that bark as if it were his own mother. The fox tried to scoot closer. His paws slipped against the soaked bark as he tried the simple task of adjusting his grip. Everything halted in that moment. Not even the rain or pounds of thunder convinced him to move.

Was this what Foxlaris had felt like? Seeing the rising rapids below him, ready to fall into their open, sinister arms? Feeling the storm hold his head down like a foot on the back of his neck? Had he felt the hopelessness? The realization that the only escape was down?

"SCOTTOH!"

"I-I know, I'm-m-m moving." His blue eyes glanced up as he began to inch forward. Acirema made it about halfway using the same method of crawling. He could do it too.

The more he carried on, however, the more he found himself tested. Little pine pegs and needles poked through his trousers and marked up his legs. Below, the water sprayed higher, dousing the tree and loosening his grip to the point of slipping off entirely. Over all of it billowed the wind and water.

He lay practically blind. His eyes seared when opened, and could only make out the rough outlines of Bunns and the log. Stabs of fear flicked his heart every time he stretched his soaked hands out into the whistling, whipping, ceaseless void of darkened, hazy gray. He couldn't make it. There was no *way* he could.

Yet when he stopped to swipe away the water from his eyes, he realized he'd already made it roughly halfway. The others were not too far ahead. Perhaps, after all the fuss, Bunns was—

*K*

*A*

*Z*

*Z*

*A*

*K*
*C*
*K*
!

Another strike. This one further upstream, past the bend that blocked their view. The trio halted to embrace the aftershock. It rumbled. But didn't stop.

*"Bunns! What's that!?"* Foxtamas couldn't bear to look around. Something had been upturned by the flash, and the grumbling earth below carried the dreadful news.

*"Just hurry!!"* came his cry, pained with a genuine choke of fear. The fox peaked one eye open.

He regretted it.

From around the corner barreled a wave of earth, mud, and water spanning the width of the river. They had but moments to complete the crossing.

"BUNNS!" Foxtamas fumbled getting up. He was only stabled by the jackalope stepping back and snagging his arm. Both scrambled forward. The grip of their boots slipped, but they didn't care. Together they raced ahead, senses overloaded, fear pumping their hearts into action.

The bridge's end raced into view. Only a few more steps. Only a few more lunges to reach safety.

But it wouldn't matter. Their fate was sealed the moment Foxtamas hacked into the tree.

*We never brace for moments*
*we see before our eyes.*
*We wait in fear and think beyond*
*to dreams just in our minds.*

*If time moves like a river,*
*we're bridged with bated breath.*
*Yet the moment our lips meet the waves*
*we drink of water's depth.*

# 4

# "A SHADOW BRIGHT IN EVON BORN."

Murky. Silty. A taste of earth long undisturbed. The concoction laps against his mouth. The only feeling he knows.

*HELP! HELP! I CAN'T BREATHE! I'M DROWNING, HELP!*

Weightless. Empty. Like...summer days on Nohsis. Floating along. Like the clouds, like the bees.

*THE WOOD IS PUSHING ME UNDER! I CAN'T SEE! IT'S HITTING ME, IT'S HITTING ME!!*

Coarse. Irritating. Rubbing somewhere in the distance behind him. It creeps beyond, snaking around.

*F-F-FOXLARIS! I SEE YOU! HELP ME PLEASE, PLEASE! I DON'T WANNA DIE, I DON'T WANNA DIE!!*

Plump. Light. The drops fall at random. No intention to disturb. But their dives echo to all the silents and dreamers drifting down the way.

It is those that wake him.

"*GHUUHH!*"

Foxtamas gasped as the spell of unconsciousness broke. His limbs flailed in the waters, now quiet, a wanton spray of grabs and reaches. Through the splashes he rose above the river. Both boots unplugged from muck of the shallows, but he felt them tangled in the one thing holding him from flowing further downstream: a net—or, at least, what remained of one. By the look of it, the web used to span the entire way across. The gorging of the stream had decimated it. Just like everything else.

He waded through the shallows and towards the shore, eventually sliding up the sand and onto a stump at the tree line. He'd no clue how long his slumber had lasted. Overhead, the blackened sky had crept to an almost equally dark night. Frigid air tore through his tunic and cape, chilling the soaked garments. His body shivered without control.

He tried to control his staggered breathing when the flashes of memory suddenly struck. The swirl of muddy waters. His head banging upon the grime of the river's floor. Choking on loam and dirt. So much spinning. So much gasping.

But within it all…Foxlaris was there.

Only for a moment brief. Foxtamas swam alongside him, both crushed under the billows and blindness. He reached out to steady him. Inches from his fur.

Then he was gone.

In the moment it felt so *real,* but now, awake and clinging to life in the dredges of the rain, he saw it as the illusion it was. A memory made from the horrors of Grammo Day. It had to be. Had to be.

The memory unfurled the longer he dwelled on it, pulling backwards to before the wave and the breaking of the log bridge. Back to the reason behind it. A sour taste overtook his tongue.

And it wasn't from the water.

"B-B-Bunns," the fox uttered. *He* forced him across. Made him crawl along the log despite the rain, despite the danger. Made him chop down the tree. Refused to find cover on that side, wouldn't listen to the sound, *right* judgement Foxtamas outlined before him. All for what? To incarnate their fears? Drown the company? *Kill them all!?*

No.

He knew the reason. He'd seen it time and time again in every game, every story, every job. Bunns wanted to prove that he could make it. It's all just a performance in his world, a chance to rub in prowess and leadership. Must he *risk his life* just to prove that he can, in fact, cross a creek? Well, look where it left them.

He failed. *Finally.*

Foxtamas shook his head and looked around. Where...was Bunns? Or Acirema? Had they not been dazed alongside him? He whipped around, hearing nothing but the howl of wind and putter of rain.

"Bunns? A...Acirema?" he yelled. The words didn't carry far, disappearing into the fog when hitting the misty shroud of Mechmilne.

It was then the malice slipped through his hands. What stupid reason did he have for hating his friend when he might be lost? Or in danger? Or...or *dead!*

He stumbled up on knocking knees. Before moving into the forest, he slung his pack around from his back. The scrappy leather had hardly held, keeping only a single flask of ale. All other snacks were either washed away or mingled into a mush at the bottom with the glass of the remaining containers.

The loss turned his stomach. He'd be hungry soon—if the shivering ever stopped. Then what would he do? His friends still had to have food, right? But if he never found them, he'd only have the ale, and between that and the cold he'd barely make it through the night, and even if he did *that,* where could he possibly go or run to or find with the map gone, the trail gone, everything everyone just just just just just *GONE*—

"BUNNS! ACIREMA!"

A hoarse, mangled cry. One that echoed this time, letting Foxtamas hear his own voice, shrilled. "Come on, come on," he said to himself as he finally stirred. "They c-c-can't be far. Just move, Foxtamas. Come on, *move!"*

His boots squelched in the thicket of the wood, as dreary and shadowed as himself. The overhanging branches gave cover from the rain, though what droplets made it through made him shudder, shake. Pinpricks of danger. *"BUNNS! WHERE ARE YOU! ACIREMA!!"*

Nothing replied.

He lost himself in the repetition. Each step felt like the last. Every call for his friends disappeared without reply. Even the trees, his companions and fellow travelers, became husks hidden in the night. Fatigue from both the river and the search began to set in. His shoulders sagged with aches, and lungs rose high, only to be met with stinging pain. No food. Little drink. What was he to do—

"*FOXTAMAS!*"

Soft. Distant. But his name nonetheless.

"ACIREMA!?!" shouted Foxtamas. He swung every which way, begging again to hear that sweet, sweet voice. "ACIREMA! *WHERE ARE YOU!*"

"FOXTAMAS!" Louder. Closer.

With his keen ears flared open, the fox pushed on to his right, using his last burst of speed to skip over tangled thorns and mossy outcrops. Something scurried amongst the tight gaps of trees. The quicker he ran, the easier he made out the muddied, exhausted form of Acirema Feiht fumbling towards him.

"ACIREMA!" he called again, right as her puffy eyes spotted him. Like a dandelion expelling her seeds, the princess soared, embracing her childhood friend with a hug pulsing of joy and relief.

"I-I-I thought y-you were dead, *dead!*" Acirema garbled out between her sobs. "I-I couldn't reach you two a-a-and you were gone a-a—"

"Shhh, it's okay, it's okay." Foxtamas patted her on her back, closing his eyes as his own salty sadness swelled. The fear rising within his exhausted body retreated. Comfort claimed them both.

Eventually, as her emotions steadied, Acirema looked up at the fox while wiping down her eyes.

"Have you found Bunns?" "No," he replied, gazing over her to the thicket surrounding them. "I was hoping you would've."

"I…tried. I couldn't catch you two after the wave hit. I checked downstream and up, in the rapids, under…under the debris…"

"Then that means he's still out there," Foxtamas said with the slightest glimmer of hope. It did good to see it reflect in the form of a smile on the princess. "If I got swept away and made it, then I know Bunns is *more* than fine. Come on, let's check back down where I ended up. We can hurry and get there before it's any darker."

A glance passed between them. Both knew the other couldn't make it more than an hour before collapsing. Nightfall would welcome them into its dreamy arms.

"Yeah…yeah, okay, let's go. I'll follow you."

The pair headed back to where Foxtamas had awoken. Amongst their calls for Bunns, they assessed the damage taken to their supplies. One apple. One flask. Nothing more between them. What little resolve remained journeyed off without a goodbye; dread took the place as their third companion.

However, right as the last hue of light faded, leaving them in total desolation apart from the occasional sprig of lightning bursting through the forest, a noise trickled in from an oak grove hidden just out of sight.

Foxtamas and Acirema felt it before it tingled their ears. Like a fish flopping on sullen shore, the choking midday sun sapping it of life; like ruins, lost in some wood unknown to generation after generation, tumbling down without anyone near to hear the sound; like the dripping of the year's final snow, melting away an entire season, an entire movement of the winds and the rains, in the pitter-patter of a lone, single *drip…drip…drip…*

Yet it was none of those things. Only the rare, runny sniffles of one Bunnclar Cammont.

He sat curled beneath the roots of a monstrous oak, knees close to his soggy, dirt-stained chest. Cuts and gashes sliced across his white fur; streams of tears paved yellow riverbeds down his cheeks. The cold throttled him. He couldn't breathe without a shiver. Despite it, the jackalope didn't hold close his pack or ring out his cape—he gripped the map instead. The bottom right corner. The only corner that remained.

No one dared speak. Bunns long heard them trampling towards him. He didn't move, didn't change. The duo eased closer to him, each taking a side beneath the tree. Foxtamas draped an arm over his friend, his adoptive brother. Acirema did the same, her warming touch opposing the frigid bitterness within.

The fox sensed it. It radiated the same worry that battled within his own mind. But the army in Bunns, it acted…differently. The feeling wasn't conniving, tactical, or cunning in its approach. No, this one…*raged.* Destroyed. Burned a bloody thirst.

Fear was not upon him. Anger was.

"Ah failed." A whisper so quiet only the jackalope knew it. The muttering made tears blur his vision, hand tighten around the soaked parchment. "Ah failed…"

The one thing he could never do. The one goal he could *never* mess up, *never* ruin. Failure lowered the shield that so long guarded him. The voices at the attack they…flooded in. Conquered his mind and focused every sense upon their words.

*Ah'm going away, son.*

*Yer don't get et, lil' brother, Ah don't have ah choice tae stay.*

*Don't leave meh too, mah baby. Please.*

*They're yer new brothers. Love 'em as yer own.*

*You're small, bunny-brain.*

*You'll get crushed after one smack.*

*Really? Stars?*

*You can't save a* thing!

How could he stop them!? Ghosts of his past, pulling away the mask he'd spent a lifetime crafting. They can't! Stop, *no!*

No one can know. They can't know his burden, can't know what he hides behind the smile, behind the jokes, behind the stars. Failing lets them in. Any second they could tear through and see the real him.

No. No, he'd stop them. He'd yell, he'd fight back. Anger would shield him. No one gets in.

*NO ONE!*

Yet…

Yet he had heads upon his shoulders. His friends were with him. *Beside* him. They saw the map. They'd been washed away upon his bridge. They trusted him enough to go along with his stupid, stupid plan. Even after all of that, they still sought him out. No scorning, no fighting. Just comfort.

A comfort his soul had hardly ever known.

All disappeared in the dark. Rain still trickled, and winds still blew. The trio remained huddled together in and out of a rest birthed from their exhaustion. No one had the will to face what would come next on their quest.

Bunns saw the glimmer first. It moved not as a leaf or far off strike of lightning, but with purpose. It dashed from tree to tree without disturbing a soul. Peaks of moonlight spotlighted its rags dragging over the branches. A living shadow sweeping closer towards them.

Bunns held his breath. His eyes shifted to every corner. The forest around him lay still apart from the pop of his opening star pouch.

*"TRAVELERS!"* boomed a grand, spacious voice, bold with the overcome trials of time and howling with the fervor of a tamed insanity. *"State thy business in this Glum!"*

The speaker entered from the darkness. See-through tatters clung to his bones; ghastly did the chains twist around his long, drooping body. The puckish eyes sunken within his skull glowed an alien gold. Above them twisted horns, gnarled like a crown upon his rag-covered face. The ghoul floated with arms extended, hovering above the trio and their oaken defense. He was not of the realm of the living. Nor the dead.

*"Speak I say!"*

*THUNK! THUNK!*

With but a flutter, the ghostly figure dodged both stars, letting them sink into the wooden giant behind him. His bright, golden gaze whipped towards Bunns who, with more stars in hand, stood before the fox and raccoon.

"Back off yer haunted *bastard!"* shouted the warrior. He looked no different from an angry child in his soaked, battered clothing.

"Yield, young one! My wrath is not easily faced," taunted the floating beast.

"FIGHT MEH!"

The ghost vanished in a blink. Gone. The trio, gagged by fear, twisted around, searching.

Bunns never saw it raise its weapon above his horned head.

# 5

# "TRACE WAY THE FOLDS OF KINSMAN TRAIL,"

*SLASH!*

The blade launched forward, cracking against its target with a resounding thunder. Once more it rose, and once more it swung. Beating until his arm grew heavy from the abuse.

Foxlaris tumbled back upon the grassy field of the training ground. His good hand carried a circular wooden shield while the other bore the sword attachment instead of the hook. Kyrell opposed him, the alp servant assigned to him by Vorde Velrick. The gangly creature held a shield of his own in preparation for the fox's next move. It wouldn't be one he needed to brace for. By now the fox moved at half his original speed, and they'd sparred for hardly half an hour. None of his attacks varied. Often the poor alp needed to move closer just for Foxlaris to mimic a hit. He'd been witness to hundreds upon hundreds of trainees over the years; none grew so weak or tired so quickly.

"Zihr, we cin shtop," Kyrell gurgled, doing his best to talk in the Western tongue as opposed to his native Eastern.

"No!" Foxlaris shouted, gripping the shield with a shaky hand. Sweat slicked down his fur from tip to stub of his tail; the rattle of his heartbeat shook his one-eyed vision.

Days prior, Velrick agreed to allow the fox to "fight" in the impending final battle with the Cultists. His health was fair enough to begin training, especially after his frequent visits to Dearg. Though, within, the wolf knew the steady pace his protégée needed. Kyrell was skilled enough in the basics to ease Foxlaris in, starting off with beginner blocks, swings, and the occasional kick (terribly difficult with just a peg).

Yet never had such a broken fighter wanted so *much*. Coughing fits flared immediately their first morning. Mixed with the aches of his scars and splinters, the fox barely could barely form proper stances and grips. Progress inched along. Despite it, the fundamental drive for glory and revenge upon all who wronged him strengthened each of his attacks, even when he couldn't find a breath, even when the most he could offer was a tap of his sword against a shield. Kyrell knew he'd never be the best—yet never did he doubt the persistence he showed.

"Weapon up this time! I want to meet the blade," Foxlaris called back out. Deep gasps interrupted his words. Too far and he'd collapse on the grass. The alp obeyed, however, and uplifted his sword, moving it away from the shield.

"Ready," replied Kyrell.

Foxlaris approached with a small trot. He kept his wooden barrier low but arm-blade high, swinging once near his servant. Bright *CLINGS!* and *CLANGS!* erupted with every hit. The entirety of his effort poured into the sword. And all the alp had to do was stand there. No different than a hay-filled dummy.

How was this *fair!?* He gave it all and Kyrell could still best him with a half-hearted swing. This...oh, this had to change. Neither he nor the East could fair another round of injustice. Someone had to take the stand against it, and as long as he felt air in his battered lungs, it would be *him*.

Foxlaris knew what others saw, though. What his outside looked like. No one wanted to give the cripple the blade. No one thought to turn to the Westerner in their time of need. No one ever guessed the sickly little fox would have the potential to *make something of himself*.

More sparks flung from the clashing swords.

What was this then? This training, this sweat lapping against his mouth like the tide. Was *this* tired? Was this too weak to go on?

They turned gold, then a sizzling white.

A vivid anger burned across his scarred face. It twisted him. Made his jaw sag, brow twist and scrunch over his empty socket.

The full weight of his body leaned into his arm.

How *dare* they look down upon him! How dare they think him lower, lesser, worse than all others—

The pressure of the blade became too much for Kyrell to hold back.

"Zihr! Zihr!"

He let loose his sword, only for Foxlaris to follow through with the attack, slicing directly through his thin, tattered wrist. The hand plopped down next to the weapon it once held.

"*RAH! GRAH! AH!*" the helpless cry was no different than that from a dropped babe. It broke the fox from his haze and opened his eye towards what he'd done.

Kyrell folded into a bloodied mess upon the grass. Consciousness faded from him as the pain shocked his body into an uncontrollable sleep, bordering on seizing. Foxlaris tried to move, tried to act, tried to do *anything*. He just stood still. Unable to speak.

"Men! Hurry him to the infirmary here. No need for the one in the Village," a silky voice ordered from behind. The fox turned to see Iota marching in from the darkened hall. Her faded eyes and pale skin tricked his eye, as if there was no way for her lack of color to exist on such a bright, cloudless day. The white-coated Vayneguard followed at her flank. With a nod, one solider slumped Kyrell over his shoulder while another carried away both blade and hand.

"I-I-I didn't mean to do it…I was hitting, and…"

"No use fretting." The Vayne stood beside him as the guardsmen exited.

"But I just sliced off his *hand!* Kyrell doesn't deserve that, he's been doing everything right!" fired Foxlaris, finding himself on the verge of tears. The healt remained expressionless over the crime. A harrowing opposite.

"You'll be seeing more and doing worse in days to come. Watching it now may ease the shock."

"But he's not some *enemy.*"

"Most in service work, especially to fighters, expect worse. Alps know their place. Everyone here does." Her rebuttal ended the talk. With long, certain strides, Iota drifted past the red-stained grass and towards the wall of arms near the yard's entrance. Glistening swords, readied axes, and sharpened spears hung with the likes of shields, maces, and bows. She began the conversation once more while deep in her admiration of the weapons. "The rumors are true then—you're joining us in the fight?" Still stunned from her bluntness, Foxlaris nodded and straightened up, trying to hide the swelling of pain within.

"Yes, it's my duty now. I'm no more a Westerner than you," he replied stoutly. It was *technically* true. The fox had no intention of returning to the West. He and Velrick both agreed they not only thought him dead but wanted it that way as well.

"Hm. At least you're training." Her long, lifeless fingers ran across the array of swords. All dazzled in the midday heat, cool and sharp to the touch. "What is the West like?" she asked. "You're the only one here who knows. Rather tasteful knowledge."

Was the question honest? Or just some remark to belittle him?

"Um, well…it's much lighter there. Or feels lighter, I mean. The trees are a brighter shade, the air's not as thick, and the people, they're…more like me, I guess. Nothing odd like an alp or bugbear."

"I see."

"But no one is as connected as y'all are. Mikyill's the biggest city and all, and I know so many different kinds of people live there, but that's it. The rest are spread out and isolated. They tried fixing that with the Bridge, but—"

"That ended in death and pain," said the Vayne.

"Yeah. Exactly." A silence hung between them. Foxlaris felt forced to stare at his superior as if waiting for an order. When no response came, he squeezed out a question of his own.

"What about your home? The Silvestwood?"

That caught her attention. Iota glanced back with a soft grin, stopping her search and focusing on the fox.

"We are like your West, cut off from most of the East. Few are able to pass through the surrounding mountains without trouble. We were the last to open to Vorde Velrick for a reason. My people, they're no different. Cold, brooding. The kind your type is best off avoiding."

"What's that supposed to mean?"

She eyed his broken body up and down in response.

"Don't you *dare* say a word—" Foxlaris threatened, only to be cut off by the wave of her hand.

"I've no freedom to form insults."

"Then say what you mean."

"I *mean*, fiery souls as yours cannot be tolerated. The kind of wanton passion you so flagrantly wield. Killers are *born* in the Silvestwood, not made. Every babe seeks its father's blood, not mother's milk. You break bread between the thief and the assassin, if already they're not your kin. Our…nature is violence. It is the urge that pumps the life through our hearts."

This time, the fox gave her a glare.

"The Village has tamed me. More than I like to admit. I've felt the crassness of my edges soften over the years as I help build towards a larger goal. A funneling of my desire for competition." Each word she spoke fell between exactness and embarrassment, like a truth she felt forced to admit.

"So…is that a part of y'all's curse? To want to kill?"

"What's left of a painting when you remove the color?" A rhetorical question, and one Foxlaris turned an eyebrow at. Iota let a silence hang as she took short, careful steps around the ring of field.

"I don't have a clue."

"Brushstrokes. Smudges of paint. A frame with nothing to hold."

"A real looker, then…"

"That is what the Bird left us as. Not a completed work of art, wherein all the elements mold together as one—no, we are the bones of something once beautiful. Strip away the wonder, the grace, the complexity, the morality, and that gray portrait is but the base, the *foundation* of all Evoneers. It's debauchery. The kind all of us bear, only instead of being covered by color, it's all we have left to cling to."

How was Foxlaris meant to respond to *that?* The Vayne still stalked around the courtyard like those she described, lurching with hands behind her back. He felt little sympathy for such a brutalist. And yet…the tale of her abandonment made his cheeks burn red. His core remembered the same feeling within himself.

"I see. I'm…sorry to bring it up. I had no idea—"

"It's no fault of your own. The question of our bloody nature being within ourselves or without as part of the curse is one no side has yet to settle in debate. Don't think us a raving band of savages, though. Our sophistication is our pride.

"We channel our energy into our arts, our knowledge, our history. The many cities in the Silvestwood resemble nothing close to the Village. We dwell in the academies and the libraries, the music halls and the citadels of those far wiser than we shall ever be. I've yet to find any region here as special as those homes. Crimsdon Hall, for its glory our Vorde holds to standard, hardly compares."

Hearing her words turn honey-laced made Foxlaris question all he'd known about Winthrop and the West. What was it like to value something he always saw as so…frivolous? To retrace your history not as a myth, but as a true, graspable reality? His thoughts traveled back to their encounter upon the Styelines. She recalled healtish history in detail to the point of memorization. If asked, he'd be incapable of doing the same beyond his own father and mother. What about every fox that *ever lived?*

"Then do y'all not fight? I don't know how you can have all that and still be…"

"Killers?"

"Yeah."

A light chuckle found her.

"Conflict takes many forms. We avoid the extremes where possible, but arguments on family lines, historical accuracy, land ownership, opinions—it's all there, just without the bloodshed. Imagine a bunch of bickering scholars who could slice your throat in a mere flash."

Foxlaris nodded, clearly put off by the thought.

"And if they *do* start slicing throats?"

Iota responded by thrusting a sword into his good hand. They'd rounded the entire field, ending up back at the patch marred by Kyrell's incident.

"You kill them before they kill you, and hope there's a healt left to tell the tale. But enough talking. We've a battle approaching, and I will not have a fighter be ill-trained. Switch your hand out for the axe then meet me in the middle."

"What about a shield?" Foxlaris asked while Iota began walking off. She turned with a smile firm to her face.

"You want to know about us healts? Then it's time you learn to fight like one."

With axe upon his arm and sword tight within his paw, Foxlaris approached the Vayne who had dawned weapons of her own. At first, they appeared to be gloves of sort, made from a thin metal that outlined the bones poking out from beneath her skin. The sharp lines traced up her hand and extended past her fingers, creating bladed claws at her fingernails like that of a beast. Such a weapon halted him from moving closer.

"What're you wearing?" asked the fox.

"They're called silvclaws. You use them for scratching," Iota replied, starting to adjust them. She lifted up her fingers and the pointed ends and metal lines from her fingertips, clenched her fist, and let the tips of the claws *launch* forward, leaving five deadly prongs protruding from her knuckles. "And stabbing."

Foxlaris gulped. But he declined to show fear. Instead, he planted his foot and peg opposite of her, readying for the lesson.

"I made you leave the shield because you can do as much—if not more—with two weapons by your side," said the Vayne as she found her spot. "That hand gives you an advantage you've yet to realize. Use the axe head to block my shots. The sword you'll use to attack, and even if you lose it in the flurry, you'll still be equipped with your other hand."

The fox nodded, keeping track of the new strategy she employed.

He heaved up his axe before his body. Without a sign to start, Iota dove towards him, scratching towards his face. Foxlaris swung up for protection. The bottom of the axe caught the silvclaws mere inches from his eye.

"Like that?" he spat, straining to keep her back.

"Yes, but you must be quicker. Again."

The pair repeated the routine. The healt slashed from all sides, nipping him at some, but teaching how a block could and should feel. She eventually let him add his sword and showed how to use both as means to cover extra extremities. It flowed into the next step Iota had planned.

"Use both arms in your swings. When the sword falls your axe should raise; keep moving, Foxlaris. Never leave them time to breathe or think. That is how they learn you, see you, and kill you."

The second her snappy words finished, the silvclaws flashed into action. Foxlaris met them with his double block, pushing her back before breaking the stance and aiming the sword her direction.

He heeded her quick lesson. A massive swing sent the blade forward, followed by the sudden rush of the axe. Though quick to avoid it, the healt nodded at the hasty retention. He learned well.

Foxlaris refused to let up. His approach was to block then get an early jump with the dual-wielding hit. Iota nearly wound up sliced as the fox kept the flurry of blades hot and heavy. The dance unfolded for longer than either expected the weakened Foxlaris to last. Once his breathing deepened and swipes faltered, the Vayne knew it was time for the finale.

One move tossed him upon the ground. She met the sword mid-air with the back of the claws, halting the blade and wrapping it in the metal strands. As Foxlaris went to lift the axe, she flipped around with a kick, knocking him down flat. The breath evaporated from his lungs. Deep gasps slowly recovered it, and as the world stopped spinning around him, the fox looked above to see the blank matte eyes meeting his.

They looked…familiar. A certain lift of the eyebrow. A fiery glow heating the iris. Yes, he could feel the superiority. Glaring down at him like some fool, some child her Vorde had taken in. Nothing more than a pet. An outsider. A *Westerner*.

The dominance she held over him for being less than hurt worse than the kick. It recalled feelings from the deep past that, like her healtish blood, kept his heart pumping. Foxtamas looked down upon him the same way when he lay sick and aching in bed; Bunns gave him the same stare the moment he proved himself unskilled or untrained; Acirema paraded around the same glare of supremacy, acting like a heroine to befriend such a lowly peasant.

Their malice pinned him in that courtyard years ago. Did Iota now dare make the same mistake? Did she not cheer the fact he'd never be like her, an Easterner, destined to the same damned fate as the rest of them?

No. This healt was *NOT* better than him. *NOT* worth more. *NOT* stronger. *NOT* superior.

He'd show her. He'd make her regret ever looking in his singular brown eye, touching his torn, ragged fur. He wasn't about to be an Easterner by circumstance alone, oh no.

He was to be one by blood and ash.

Without a word, Foxlaris struggled up, ignoring Iota's offer to help. He shot her a hard glare and tossed the sword to her feet. She returned him a modest grin.

"I'll have the Vayneguard alert you when the battle approaches. Be warned, you will face little combat. Read yourself to gain the experience of feeling battle. Not waging it."

No response.

The Vayne watched him dispatch the axe head from his arm, replace it with the hook, and hobble down the long, dark hallway exit.

Once the fox was gone, she followed suit. Her pace slowed as the torchless walls gave way to a small alcove sliced into the left side which, up until moments prior, had not been there.

"Report back that he's going down," the pale woman whispered, stepping into the small entrance. There, standing tall with shadowed cloak and readied halberd, was Getophry.

"Will do, my Vayne," he uttered. Every word he spoke came out more stilted than the last. He appeared lifeless even when compared to the healt.

"Any word on the Blue Caps?"

"Yes. Our spies have confirmed their final march will be at the Village's gates. All sects depart soon. Only days remain."

"He's placed Dol with us then?"

"Would you want any other?

"No. I hardly trust the other generals as is. Thank you, Getophry. My best regards to our Vorde."

"He shall receive the word."

The cockatrice melted into the darkness with a single move. In a few moments, their hiding spot would blend back in, and all traces of the conversation lost to time. Before the hidden door could activate, however, Iota imparted a long, confused glance into the void. A small hint of emotion twinkled in her eye. One thought extinct for most of her kind.

Regret.

*FWOOOSH!!*

Foxlaris followed the steps of his Vorde and lit Dearg-Fu'Ath's lair just as he'd witnessed. Fire trailed around the ashen prison, revealing the hulking, sleeping monster still lost within a world of its own. Already the memories of staring into his eyes attacked him. The terror. The waking nightmare buried in the soul of the beast. Such forces almost made him quit the endeavor then and there.

The reward was too great for that though. Every move and breath begat pain for the fox; what could anymore do?

Gently, Foxlaris kneeled beside Dearg. The scales still bore the long, thick ridges of red. Somehow the soul that harbored them would grant him healing, peace, and all else Velrick promised. How? The fox was unsure. Bonding of some sorts. Whatever the way, he had to try. No fear interrupted him.

"I trust you, Vorde," Foxlaris muttered to himself as his hand, forcefully steady, touched the heated body of Dearg-Fu'Ath.

He felt the air within his broken body swell. Like downing too much water or stuffing your face at a feast, a weight inside him doubled.

A weight of rage.

*This land is red, and this land is barren. This is the land of my home.*
*You are here now, Western Son.*
*And you are whole.*
*Your hand has returned to you. Your foot has returned to you. Your eye has returned to you. Your ear has returned to you. Your tail has returned to you.*
*Your spirit and fullness and life have returned to you.*
*I see you as you imagine yourself.*
*Yes. This you give me freely. This image upon my bloody stone.*
*I see them too. Those in the distance.*
*The Three you fear.*
*They carry weapons and you cannot run.*
*Or fight back.*
*The Crown steals back your hand.*
*The Horns hack off your leg.*
*And your Shadow plunges a sword in your eye.*
*I hear their jeers, and they echo louder than your pain.*

*You will never rise against them, Western Son.*
*Not in this state.*
*Not with this broken body.*
*Not alone.*
*Feed me this pain, the one that bleeds upon my dust.*
*Give me the anguish pouring from your limbs,*
*Beating with every pump of your heart,*
*And let me return you tenfold what was taken.*
*My own strength and wisdom.*
*My own spirit and fullness and life.*
*My hand shall be your hand.*
*My leg shall be your leg.*
*My eye shall be your eye,*
*And with it all I alone can see.*
*Release yourself from this.*
*Feed me what you cannot bear to taste.*

Foxlaris awoke, gasping, panting in a puddle of his own sweat. Flashes of the vision fluttered with every blink. The red desert. The feeling of wiggling his fingers. The crunch of dust in his mouth. The…dragon claw forming at his wrist…

Beneath that same hand the behemoth stirred. The heat of Foxlaris' rage burned within Dearg now; the memories of an abandoned young fox became his own. He felt it, not only in the dragon, but in the lessening of the weight upon his chest. Where it doubled before, now it shrank. In its place his limbs…relaxed. No, beyond that, became *nimble.* If he wanted, he could tumble and swing, dart to and fro quicker than in his Pradiforian prime. A vivid energy *pulsed* through him.

So too did it wash over his mind. The hook no longer felt like a replacement. He suddenly envisioned a plan to slay a creature both in battle and in bed, how to use it like an axe or sword. The buzzing current of skill and throttle flowed backwards to the battle he'd performed not even an hour prior. Every move between him and Iota soared across his vision, replayed in the finest detail and analyzed, studied. Foxlaris knew where he'd fallen short on the swings and blocks. It was as if he played a timid game of chess in real time instead of the thrusting back and forth of battle.

As he watched, a new insight developed about Iota, just from a glance. The intensity of her focus left her open to surprise. Take her attention, take her life. These analyzations and more poured into the mind, soul, and muscles of Foxlaris. New resolve controlled his body—he became a flower, finally above the soil and on the verge of bloom.

Thus, in the flickering fire of the dungeon, both creatures exchanged parts of themselves the other desired. One a spirit of fury to stoke the rage he wished to descend upon the world; the other the prowess to prove the truth that no longer wished to live inside.

Foxlaris knew not how long he kneeled. Time was not an element in their shared world. When he eventually awoke, he let a smile creep on his lips.

And a flash of red swipe across his eye.

# 6

# "FROM ICY PEAK TO INWARD GALE,

Bunns thought he was dead.

He braced when the ghoul dashed towards him, no stars or hammer quick enough to shield him. A resounding *THUNK!* crashed against his ears. Was it his horns snapping? Skull shattering?

Slowly, he peeped open his eyes. He was still in Evon alright, just pinned to a tree by black, gnarled talons and stared down by beaming golden lights.

"I'm not here to hurt you!" the rugged voice proclaimed. "Lay aside your weapons and you'll be offered my aid. *Conditionally.*"

Bunns nodded despite it paining his throat. He tossed aside the star clamped within his hand. The second it hit the ground, the beast retracted its grip. And clothing.

With a lift of the rags, the monster unclasped a hidden bracket beneath its neck, causing the foul horned head to fall back like a hood. In its place was no demon, no ghost; only an aged snowy owl. Scars of all length and depth drew themselves across his face. One chipped deep into his black beak, forming a skeletal window into his dry mouth, while others carved around his illuminated eyes. Wrinkles made his spotted feathers sag like ripples on a storm-wrought river. Time had left its abusive mark upon him.

"You may call me Rillem," he said, voice now stiff and low. "Come, it's time you three depart this storm."

It took a moment for the trio to gather themselves. He was just…an owl? Not some hellish creature ready to feast upon their hearts? Foxtamas held that quiet joy of relief close. Crossing the river must have led them *directly* into Hermit's Glum, the *one* place he hoped to avoid.

It wasn't hard to follow the bright white head topping the twisted body of dirty scraps and chains. By now the sky had begun to blotch, and the tosses of moonlight guided them into a thorny part of the Glum. After wading through the thicket, they came upon the ruins of an old hamlet tucked beneath tall, overhanging trees. Moss and lichen dripped down in the fashion of a lost swamp. A few houses remained by foundation alone, where others had fallen into unrecognizable messes of thorns, weeds, and vines burying any memories left behind. The bones of a single house still stood. Within it sat a hut, rounded like a dome and covered with dried mud to create a rough, white exterior. A small chimney on top puffed strong a graying smoke; flickers of light escaped from beneath the entrance.

Rillem led the party in without a word. Bathing the rugged round walls was a small fire in the center. It flickered within a circle of stones, roasting a pot hanging on a spit straddling either side. The meal cast rich, rising shadows against the interior, soaking the few benches placed around it as well as a wicker hammock nailed into place along the side. Below it was a small cellar door. The hinges appeared well-used with its bronze handle nearly faded. Besides that…nothing of note stood out. Simplicity reigned in the owl's hut.

The bird slid off his ragged costume and placed it on a small wooden peg dug into the wall. He wore a plain outfit of slacks and a torn tunic beneath. The guise felt a tad more fashionable.

"Take a seat. I'll pour out a bowl for all of us. It's nothing wild tonight, just shrimp stew." Once again, the friends were quick to listen. Bunns took one of the three benches for himself, and the fox and raccoon found comfort upon the other. Eeriness wrapped them like a blanket, more so than the warmth of the fire finally drying their garments. Something about the lap of flames, barren home, and choppy voice put them on edge. Like dancing on the precipice of a mountain.

Rillem poured the stew into four wooden bowls next to the pot. Instead of passing them out, however, he sat them on the empty seat beside him.

"I can tell you're not a company of thieves or evildoers," he began. A certain silence hung in the air between thoughts. Just long enough for one of the guests to shift their eyes. Sniffle. "I've been following you since your lunch at Persimmon Ruins. You're set to follow the Oldtrails, yes? That path doesn't come near this hut, but it seems the…accident…at the river forced you deeper into my Glum. It's not normal I do this, you know. But I wasn't about to let three kids starve and die out in that rain." His words halted at a long pause, one that let him scan each one of them individually. "This food and roof are yours if you tell me who you are and where you're headed. You must leave at dawn's first light. I'll lead you back to your trail down a way where you can never find this hut again. Take this deal and warm your stomachs, or I'll bid you three a good night. Choice is yours." They expected a grin to follow his words. Only the golden stare remained.

"W-Well," began Foxtamas, obviously shaken by the intensity of the owl's demands. What if he somehow messed up? Got caught in a lie he never intended to tell? Told him too much and got the entire trio killed!?

No. He couldn't think that way, not with his friends beside him. This old "ghost" wouldn't slow them down. "My name is Foxtamas. The jackalope, he's Bunns, and she's—"

"Anlana."

The word felt wrong from her lips. Like a forbidden verse, an old cry lost on deaf ears. She picked up the glances from her friends but refused to acknowledge them. They knew the name. It wasn't hers, yes, but someone almost as close.

Her mother's.

She kept her eyes on the owl with a stare of confidence turned calmness. It was a small step in taking control of her title, her prestige, and her destiny. She would say when the royalty of a Winthropian Princess preceded her; her right to hide it had finally been executed.

"I see. And your goal? You must be aware these Oldtrails are hardly used," replied Rillem.

"Yes," nodded the fox. "We were told they were the quickest way to Mikyill. B-But that's not our only goal, y'see, we're actually going, or, um, *doing* something a lot bigger..."

And thus, just as he had with Teardic days prior, Foxtamas retold the tragedy of Foxlaris, the resolve of Bunns and Acirema, and the journey the trio had embarked upon. This weaving was more resolute, though. Both his brother and their destination were no longer unreachable. Such a thought boosted the fox's trembling confidence enough to finish the tale and leave the owl with a slow, steady nod.

"Mm. Interesting. Interesting indeed. Few take on such...lofty...quests. The Bridge then, did you work on it?"

"Oh no, that was left to either the dwarves or people in Mikyill, I can't really remember. Me, Bunns, and Foxlaris worked on Bridgeburrow though, the village right there next to it," said Foxtamas.

"Carpenters, then?"

"Only recently."

"So, a couple of woodworkers take on these, what, gangly Eastern beasts without a problem? *And* a rampaging Minotaur?" The doubt on Rillem's voice sent shivers through the fox.

"W-W-Well it was m-mostly Bunns. He's trained an' all, much more than us. Wasn't too hard for him, r-right, Bunns?" The attention turned to the jackalope. It was obvious neither food nor the conversation interested him. His head hung low, his eyes a silky smooth.

"Yeah. Ah breeze." The response carried as much weight as the wind.

Rillem didn't care, it seemed, turning his full attention towards Acirema.

"And why did you join, Miss? Work in carpentry as well?" The question caught her off guard, not only in its absurdity, but icy delivery.

"I answered the call of a friend. Foxtamas needed all the help he could get."

"So you were that quick to abandon your husband then?"

Her face contorted. What in *Evon* did he mean?

"My...husband?" Acirema asked, bewildered.

"Yes. King Aisar."

The room froze.

Every breath escaped.

None dared to blink, none dared to think.

The bubbling stew rattled around with a noisy *clink,* chiming as fast as their hearts beat. The trio exchanged glances; Rillem, however, kept a deathly mark on the princess.

The next words had to be chosen carefully. They couldn't test their luck again, not after meeting those rabbits on the road.

"I...don't know what you mean, Mr. Rillem. I—"

"Don't play coy with me." His voice dropped an octave. From crisp to vile, a new, curdling roar ripped from his throat, like an actual ghoul infected his words. "I know your *scheme.*" "Sir, I-I-I think you have it wrong," Foxtamas tried to intervene, but it was too late. Rillem flung up from his seat, the fire doubling his size by covering the wall behind him in shadow.

"You *LIE* to me! With the name of a *dead woman* who *FREED US!* Is THIS YOUR *SICK GAME!?*" A dagger appeared in the grip of his wing. His talons scratched forward across the dirt ground as the bags under his eyes deepened. "You...you've not come for some brother, *none of you!* None travel this far, none use such *lies!*"

"Mr. Rillem, please!" the raccoon pleaded, but was shut down as his daggered wing pointed towards her.

"YOU'LL BE QUIET, WRETCH!" his voice boomed, echoing off the walls. "I won't hear a word from your lips, traitorous lips, *HIS* lips.

"Mikyill...fighting...carpentry...terrible liars he's gotten, but here they are, HERE. THEY. *ARE!*" His weapon waved between the three of them. Bunns, awake from his slump, once again brought a star to his paw. "Spies, little spies, spies meant to find my favor...*WHAT'S YOUR PLAN!?* Will you slit my throat *now* or before his *throne?* Dangle me before him for some *reward!* I've seen such rewards, rewards, rewards,

rewards worth nothing! *NOTHING!* IT IS LOSS! *LOSS YOU'LL FACE, ALL OF YOU!"*

He pushed past the fire and took a step too close. The trio bounded from their benches, raising what weapons they could grasp. Bunns jumped in front and made the gleam of his star evident to the crazed owl.

"HE WON'T HAVE ME! NO ONE WILL! KILL ME BEFORE I KILL *YOU,* COWARDS! HE WON'T HAVE ME! HE WON'T HAVE *ANY OF US! NEVER! AGAIN!"*

The blinding eyes of Rillem suddenly began to dance uncontrollably, shaking as if caught in a seizure. His body twitched in foreign, alien jabs, like a puppet pulled every which way. Wings fumbled to a confused salute, talons jolted to crush an invisible child between them. A storm flurried in his mind. A storm of utter madness.

In his rage, the dagger lurched above his head, his eyes growing wide casting a gaze of murder over the trio. Bunns reached back with a star. Acirema knocked an arrow. Foxtamas gripped his crossbawn.

A blink and it would be over.

*K*<br>*A*<br>*Z*<br>*Z*<br>*A*<br>*K*<br>*C*<br>*K*<br>*!*

"GUH!"

*THUMP!*

Nothing needed to fire. Instead, a blazing flash of lightning, followed almost simultaneously by a cacophony of thunder, rattled the hut, tasing Rillem in the middle of his attack. The shock forced some cry from him before his legs lost their strength. He collapsed to the floor.

The trio watched as his limp body began to seize in front of them. Out from his mouth spewed splashes of foam, the golden eyes still twitching between rapid blinks.

"What do we do!?" Foxtamas cried, stepping forward to get a better look.

"Head for tha' door! If he wakes he'll bae after us again!" rebutted Bunns, aiming a star for the aged, white head.

"No!" Acirema yelled. She snatched his arm before he could fire. "We can't leave him like this!"

"He just tried tae kill us! Remember tha'?"

"I don't know what's wrong with him, but he offered us help! I'm not going to *kill him* for that!"

Her words were final. Foxtamas, agreeing with the princess, followed her lead and knelt beside the owl. The pair grabbed the shaking Rillem the best they could and leaned him over. Foam drained from the hole in his beak. Bunns, begrudgingly, pulled a damp cloth from his pack to wipe away the spit and bile.

"What now?" asked the trembling fox.

"I'm, um, I'm not sure." Acirema's head swiveled for something, *anything* that could slow the jolts and jagged breaths. Nothing appeared. "Rillem, Mr. Rillem, can you hear me? Mr. Rillem, please wake up, please!"

Behind her, Bunns and Foxtamas waited with bated breath. The jackalope knew he was right to slay the monster then and there. But seeing such a ferocious villain diminished to a bubbling puddle of feathers...something about it softened his taught heart.

After more coaxing and begging, the rising of his chest slowed. Both eyes grew weary of their shakes, and, for a brief moment, Rillem appeared to be asleep in the arms of the princess.

"Ghrmmm," he muttered. One eye peeked open. Fell. Then rose again.

While it slowly began to recognize the young faces, they stared at it in return, startled. The bright, gilded color had faded; a muted, warm yellow now took its place, one that transformed his face entirely, pulling back the age and unfurrowing his brow. The monster had transformed into a kindly old owl.

"No…no…oh no, no…" Rillem slurred, his head shaking. "What've…what've I…done!?"

With the little energy keeping his body alive, the owl raised himself up, tears streaming down his face. "No, no!" He tried again to speak but dribbled into nonsense. Sobs overtook him. Torrents of regret melted down his cheeks.

Acirema couldn't take it. She scooted closer beside him and held him up. The boys behind her draping their arms over him. Still, his old, wailing cries continued. Nothing stings quite as hard as someone so far in life crumbling by pressures they long ago overcame.

"Shhh, calm down, it's alright," the raccoon eased.

"I-I-I-I'm s-so, so sorry," Rillem gasped between the tears. He didn't even try to wipe them. He felt them deserved. "I-I-I haven't, haven't had a fit in so long, s-so l-l-long-g-g."

"It's okay, sir, really." Foxtamas patted his back, but to no avail.

"N-No it's not. It's *not.* Y-Y-You're good kids. You're not bad, not spies. You…" He lifted his face from his wings and looked behind at those surrounding him. For the first time since their meeting in the woods, the old bird looked at ease. Alive. Awoke from a sleep consumed by countless nightmares. "Saved me."

Rillem lifted himself up to the bench. "I can't keep living like this. It's been too long. Look where it's gotten me." The trio couldn't tell if the words were for them or himself. That changed when his softened gaze found them. "I am…hurting…young ones. Long have I worn this mask, this…falseness upon me. It let me run and hide from what I wished to escape, but, in the end, consumed me, twisted me into that…beast. Killing kids…am I no better now? After all this time?" he asked with a cold chuckle. History gushed from his words, plaguing the mind of Foxtamas with mystery and intrigue. Who *was* this hermit?

"I don't ever think I can fully apologize for my actions, nor thank you for rescuing me from that attack." His mellowed eyes once again flooded with tears. "But…if you will, I would like to explain it all, show who this scarred old owl actually is. You're owed that and more, and I…must share it. If I hide any longer, I'm scared of what I might become."

The four sat in silence. Foxtamas, Acirema, and Bunns all felt the pull to know more about the man. His change was obvious; the one speaking now resented the Rillem who tracked them earlier in the day. Trust, relief, and honesty could be shared between them. If his sullen silhouette draped in firelight was anything to go off, sharing this story was worth more than any food, water, or shelter.

"We'll listen, Mr. Rillem," Foxtamas replied with a nod and quiet smile. "I don't think any one of us wants to see you hurting like that, and if it helps, well…" Like water bursting through a dammed stream, a timid grin flowed across the owl's face. So tight was it that his cheeks rose to cover his puffy eyes.

"Thank you, Foxtamas. And before I forget, please, take your stew, all of you. You've more than earned it and will need it for this tale. It's not one that ends happily—or, rather, after so long, maybe…maybe it finally has…"

# 7

# "IN STARLIT VERN OF KITH AND STOVE"

The owl's voice had no home, nor felt at one anywhere. A laugh would be welcome, but always fell overtaken by a cold breeze in the heart, a shudder of wonder with every word. You could tell the trouble and uneasy life he had led simply by a sentence. That voice had met many people and many lands, always knowing that in a short moment that fellow, the one soul close enough to call "friend", would be gone, and only exist, to him at least, in a memory long faded, forming a begging in his heart never to be fulfilled. A many lonesome song that voice did sing, about meadows, flowery fields, bright forests and breezes, the kind that appear once in a lifetime. Had he seen those things? Or were they thoughts from a childhood, deep dreams of the past? None knew, but the voice alluded. The voice knew the road and lost the way, could trace a trail but never follow its path. Such connections to the future could never last. Whatever it did hold—did feel, did know—would end. But the road…the road never ended. Perhaps that's why, in its solitude, a grizzled grayness had enveloped the homeless voice. Because without anyone to speak to, what good was the journey at all?

"I'll begin with my name." Having removed the empty pot, the biting firelight now filled the room, illuminating the low, rugged face of Rillem as he spoke. "It's not Rillem. Or, not fully. My official title is Sir Cowl Hangrich Rillem. When I first came out here, I tried to strip it from me and start fresh. But in that…I felt myself abandoning my family, the little semblance of who I was before…before everything.

None even remembered my surname. Or my full name. It worked well, then. For whoever had the unfortunate pleasure of meeting me.

"When I was Cowl, I lived in Mikyill, born and raised. Me, my sister, and our parents lived in a small room in the Rikenwehl. You mentioned never having been to Mikyill; well, it's what they call the western half of the city, past the first ridge that divides it. There our life was simple. Happy. Father worked as part of the Myriad but denied his place in the barracks to stay with us and Mother. She was…sick, all the time I knew her. But Father, that ol' oak, never let such stress get to him. He'd be chipper, we'd be chipper, and Mother would be too. Even after she passed, and we were still kids…it never got to him. I guess I tried to embody that."

The owl paused for a sip of the soup. At points when his words wandered, his body looked around as if it was listening to the tale for the first time. Buried were these memories. Older than the trees, it seemed, and older than the earth.

"Kids, I cannot tell you how I yearn to return to that era. The Cowl then had no concept of time, or fear, or anger; all of it passed without a thought. Can you imagine a life with no thinking? Just…living? Magical, simply, simply magical.

"But time gave me thoughts and grew me up, and it wasn't long until I followed Father's steps by joining the Myriad the second I could. We worked side-by-side for some time until his death, only a few years later. By then both my sister and I were more than capable of taking care of ourselves. I offered her Tops to keep our family's room, but she declined and moved Westward, working in some small kingdom out there. We wrote on occasion, even as the letters slowed and our lives grew further and further apart. In all honesty, I can't remember the last time I saw her face or read her hand. I…have trouble picturing her now, really…so pure that look, so…porcelain…pearl.

"Regardless. I was all that remained of the Rillem family in Mikyill. My, how determined I was back then! Nothing could get me down. I had my duty and my past to move on from—a goal and a force to propel me. So, like any good solider, I trained. Trained far more than I should ever have. I found daggers and throwing knives suited me best. Paired with my station as an aerial trooper, I pushed myself to be both accurate and precise and better than all in my field. And I did. I never stopped. It...consumed me, in a way. What else did I even have in that time? My mind is cursed with a wonderful memory. But those days of flying until I faltered or throwing until my wing almost broke...they're gone. Feelings come back occasionally. Never the sights, never the sounds. I became nothing but a dagger. And that's where he got me."

At that sentence he slowed and sipped on a spoonful of stew. It didn't seem to warm the chill rising through his spirit.

"Gniw had been elected shortly after I joined the Myriad. Although president, his influence affected us little besides the stout increases to our pay here and there. I didn't have time to keep focus on it. A few years into his term, however, a higher up called me out from one of our drills. He was some general of sorts that claimed a couple of my friends had put in a good word about me. I should've called his bluff—my friends then were slim to none.

"I was brought deep into Seasongold Palace where, in a room no larger than a cellar, a practice was held. I thought nothing of it at first; had to be tryouts for a promotion or mission of some sorts. Either way, I was more than prepared. They let me fly, throw, and run the course a few times until I wore thin. Afterwards, they led me back to my barracks. Simple as that. No word came back for months, and it fell through the cracks of my mind. Figured I'd been passed up or so. That was, until, one night, I heard a knock rasp my door.

"Council members I'd scarce seen around the Seasongold awoke me and forced me to pack away what little belongings I had. They tried explaining the details of an oath and forced selection as we scurried out, but my brain was too drowsy to comprehend. I only fully awoke once in Gniw's private quarters. That bird *bastard* sat before me, and at my side stood five others, equally drowsy and confused as to the situation.

"We were promptly told that, based on our aptitude for fighting and withstanding of a predetermined set of pressures, we had been selected for Evon's premier league of exemplary warriors: the Velvediers.

Forcefully, really. Anyone unwilling to join would be exiled from the city and forced Northward, somewhere in Pradifore.

"You see, children, no one was *ever* meant to know about this force. For as long as Mikyill has elected presidents, each president has too elected a group of their own, a hidden squad of secret servants. The man before Gniw, Topwrell Olk, formed the Topredirers. Each group is kept small, composed of just six members. Most of Evon is scoured for the perfect fit. After enough presidents came and went, though, the Myriad became a training ground of sorts, a pond, ripe for fishing.

"You would not *believe* how eager we were to join! This, this was *proof* of our hard work and achievements. I realized those endless days of dueling and sparring and racing and soaring until I wore out my wings, they'd been worth something. In that moment my life found...purpose, I suppose. I was chipper, I was useful, I was serving a man I thought righteous in every way.

"But kids...kids, I was a damned fool.

"Our tasks were simple. Or...started that way. We served Gniw in the shadows, doing whatever work he required. Sometimes we went ahead of him when he visited foreign regions or towns, disguising ourselves as locals so as to watch from a distance. Other missions sent us on trips within the city. We delivered packages, brought in secret shipments; we were never privy to the parcels, just where they were meant to go. You see, it was nothing severe, just an invisible wing for Gniw to use when privacy was better practice than public knowledge."

"What other tasks were there?" Foxtamas suddenly prodded in. The question took Rillem from his reminiscing and back to the growling fire and worn friends before him.

"I, um...there were many, Foxtamas, a good many. One time we staked out in the sewers for a week when we caught word of rebellion. Nothing came of it. Another had us solving the mystery of a dwarf who died whilst visiting Gniw and the Seasongold and...and now I can scarce remember the culprit. "Regardless, the fact remains that our job took us to places any regular Myriad would cower before. We were given unprecedented range and access to the entirety of Mikyill. Of course, the six of us had to be smart about who knew of our whereabouts and activities. But that...mattered little, I suppose. Because we had each other.

"The longer we worked together, the closer we grew as a family. It was me, Beeze, June, Geric, Eisley, and Meek..." Saying those names brought pain upon his jaw, aching as it formed words long forgotten to his tongue. A hint of regret followed each Velvedier. "Nicknames, except for mine. Cowl was always short enough. Each of us was chosen for something different. Beez, or Beasle Metaltalon, struck hard and fast in a flash. His surname was his specialty. My, what a friend. Greatest I had in the troupe, on my heart. Meek was quicker than any I'd seen, Eisely a natural born leader and master of disguise, and June and Geric, my, no truer of heart. I'm certain I had hundreds of assignments with each of them individually and even more together. They weren't just comrades or coworkers—these were my brothers...my sisters. We shared the same goal and poured in every drop of sweat we could to succeed. That changes you. Teamwork like that, confidence in completion and doing so with loved ones by your side. They...were my family. More so than my own blood. No doubt about it.

"I didn't just end up in this hut at random, though. Things had been stable for around five years until election season came upon us. Gniw told us in private his own plans to run, and whispers spread of a few other prominent officials eyeing the presidency. During these early stages we were tasked to deliver tonics and other odd medicines to certain districts. Nothing out of the ordinary, just a quick stroll in the dead of night. Yet only a few days later, a sickness spread to the *exact* locations we visited. We figured the cures simply hadn't worked in time. Afterall, we'd done similar missions before, and not everything can be a success. But you see, the ones who succumbed weren't random—they were those who, weeks prior, had started talks of an election bid."

"No," Acirema whispered to herself. "No, that...that can't be—"

"The news broke, and Gniw immediately held a city-wide wake for the fallen leaders," Rillem continued while eyeing her. "Those close to them were sanctioned to stay in their districts until proper cures were available lest a true disease break out. That owl just about had a catastrophe on his hands...from the outside. Everyone praised his stellar leadership and quick planning, securing him another five-year term. For months nothing but good word passed through the Seasongold. But us Velvediers...we had our doubts.

"Perhaps it was a test run to see where our loyalties lied, or maybe he truly thought he we wouldn't notice. I can't say, even all these years now. What I *can* is that we all knew, deep down, this 'sickness' came from our hands. Yet that was but the preface. Once re-elected, things changed. Forever. We didn't have to question Gniw's motives or actions...we knew. We knew what he'd selected us for all along.

"Beez, June, and I were sent to Fotherton one night, briefed little on the context. We arrived and met with an informant. She told us the mission: one of the Myriad had broken rank and deserted, threatening to expose a secret about Gniw once far enough from the city, probably related to the election. He'd spoken too loudly and to the wrong people a few towns prior—even the Ratatoskr couldn't spread word that fast. But our job wasn't to bring him back or test his loyalty...it was to kill him."

"This just can't be true!" The princess practically jumped from her seat. "I met this man, and he was *nothing* but kind! Treated me far better than he had any right to."

"That was always his trick," sighed the owl. "Play the babbling, bobbling bird *so* well that you practically succumb to the character."

"No, you *must* be lying."

"I wish I was." Rillem clutched his bowl. By now his stew had turned cold; the last sip a lost tang on his tongue. A shudder rattled through him. "I wish my whole life was a lie." His mellowed eyes found the fire and pulled away from Acirema, and the story continued in the lapse of flame. "You feel the same shock I did, Miss. That of confusion, of trickery, of being played the fool for so, so long. That I let myself be swindled into the role of a murderer by a man I thought as innocent as a babe.

"And yet...we did it. I like to imagine I stuttered before following the order. But I know I didn't. I *know* I didn't. Folks, I know how foul it sounds, how vile and evil and...and pathetic as a damned coward it was to kill a man more innocent than any on our team, but, in my mind, I *was* being loyal, was I not? Gniw knew. He handpicked me, picked all of us. Were we not sworn to be his? If killing was the only answer, so be it. My shepherd, his sheep."

The trio gulped. This...this was where his madness had been born.

"My dagger struck the man before June's arrow could. Beez tossed him in a hay cart without a second thought. We made it back to Mikyill that morning. When the dawn hit us, we weren't the same trio who'd gone into that night. We'd been born anew, as assassins by moonlight.

"We found out the other trio of Eisley, Meek, and Geric had followed similar orders in Daisy Creek. No one flinched. Together we left behind any doubts about the medicine, sickness, or plans of our leader. We worked as one yet again...just with blood-soaked blades and souls.

"From that point on we were solely assassins. Gniw briefed us on the changes, saying that the secrecy of ourselves and our missions could not, under any circumstance, leak into public knowledge, now more than ever. We weren't supposed to not exist—we were to never have *existed.*

"Thus, us six had to...fake our deaths. Forsake all attachments. For some it was easy. Others..." His warbling voice flickered again. The flames in his eyes rose. "But we obeyed—didn't we always? Cowl Hangrich Rillem died upon the bird's orders. I hate to say it, but...I'm not sure if my sister was ever given word. To her and the rest of Mikyill, we no longer existed in Evon. Only in its shadows.

"Once settled, we began the killings and espionage for our president. Most of the time we knew little about why a certain couple had to be executed or elderly gentlemen slaughtered. Over time the pieces would fall into place. Some were political opponents to Gniw whose knowledge could disrupt the image he displayed. Others were causing trouble for local kings and lords pledged to bird. Calling in a favor from the president was having some lowlife killed by 'falling' down the town well.

"You must understand just how, how *brutal* we were. Taking a life meant nothing. Absolutely *nothing*. I never felt a single pang or nudge of their grief o-or their agony. It was as routine as waking up and working on that Bridge Town you three mentioned. I kept it clean if I wanted. Other times…it just depended. Those who did die weren't just old, propped up dukes or whoever you may think. They were families. Children. Those…unborn." He could hardly catch the words as they left him, smoke wafting from the fire of self-loathing within. The tears dripping down from his eyes shook. Some dribbled down his beak. Others made indentions upon the brown, dusty floor.

"I…I can always recall their faces. Shock overtook most. Fear…twisted those who died slower. They were so *afraid* of what I'd done. What it meant. That they'd face death so soon…so soon. Some, blessed, never felt a thing. So many worry about their last words but never about who they'll be looking upon. How many spent their final seconds looking at my face? My hooded, haunted face?"

Rillem was breaking yet again. The same cadence as before mutated his words, and his eyes darted, left to right, up and down, into the fire and out to the ghastly figures clouding his vision like cataracts.

However, the soft hand of Bunns rubbed against his shoulder. Every pass eased the muscles twitching along his back.

"Easy there, lad. Just keep breathin'. Talkin'."

Something, perhaps the warmth of forgiveness, brought his mind away from the horrors. He nodded to the jackalope and took in a steep breath.

"B-B-But anyway, Gniw. His scheme through the assassinations was to ensure no one would ever run against him. He replaced his opponents with goons of his own choosing, all eager to do his bidding. We were none the better, I know. But the entire city accepted his façade.

"Have you ever wondered why he's the longest reigning president Mikyill's ever seen? Why no candidate has ever *wanted* to see him out of office? He corrupted his secret guard and trained them to be murderers. No Topredier would *dare* be asked to kill. It's hard to rationalize, but I truly believe Gniw started out righteous. He wasn't one to want power for the sake of it. No, gaining power gave him *leverage*, the means to enforce what he believed best for Mikyill, as false of a morality as it was. He fed our people *his* truth. The kind which, over time, corrupted into greed and death. And through it I was no better than a fork upon his plate.

"Our killings lasted ten years, two more election cycles. We were in the midst of preparing for another term and the troubles it might entail when Geric broke the news—he wanted out. We all figured him crazy, of course. The thing was, none of us even considered what would happen if we *did* want to leave. Was our original offer, that of being exiled to another town, still viable? Or…or was it 'till death did us part?

"We didn't know, and we weren't willing to find out. Geric though, that ruffian convinced us. His wife still knew he lived. And worse, she was expecting. The news shifted his worldview. He'd seen the pregnant mothers we'd beaten and the kids bleeding out on our blades. Who could guarantee that his child would be any different? Was it only a matter of time before they ended up on Gniw's list?

"The way he explained it…broke us. For the first time in over a decade our eyes opened to the misery we reaped upon Evon in the name of a man we thought incorruptible. Our missions were nothing more than senseless killings. It's all we were good for. Robbing so many of so much. Life was worth *more* than whatever Gniw wanted, whatever plans he baked behind our backs. We spent that night crying over one another in the darkness of our quarters. The consequences of our actions weighed heavier than…than…

"Every laddie in all the world," whispered Bunns.

"Yes…yes, that exactly. We mourned for those we'd murdered. We mourned for the lives we never got to live. We mourned for the realization that we'd never get the forgiveness we yearned for. And yet…we too realized an equally valid truth. That as long as we still breathed, we could start, for the first time, doing something genuine, something *good.*

"We would set Geric free from this life.

"The plan was to fake his death. Our expertise. The next outing was to kill a princess in Tresbotton. Geric made sure his wife traveled and waited there before we could arrive. We met with her the night of their escape. Geric he...he handed me his cloak, the fine fabric that hid his face from the victims he felled. After all those years, I think I finally saw the man who was hiding beneath it. One untouched by Gniw. One ready to be a father and correct the course of his life. I bid him adieu with one long, lasting hug. None of us knew where they ended up. I like to believe he went furthest west possible, somewhere in the Isle of Asda Fraye.

"It doesn't change the fact I never saw him again. Our family broke that night. But another was born in its place—born under the moonlight where too long we lived.

"We bloodied the garment and presented it to Gniw upon our return, lying about an ambush of royal guards and how Geric bravely stepping forward to save the us as we fled. He bought it. My whipped mind thought the news *actually* saddened him. He shed tears! His beak trembled in ways I'd never *seen!* But when I thought like Geric, I saw it wasn't melancholy for a fallen soldier, no, no, but an *irritation* at a plan heading south.

"So many of these moments plagued me as we went on. It plagued all of us, sickening us more so than the first time Gniw forced us to shed blood. We'd ruined lives without knowing why! How many generations rot in the ground because of some dumb word by a damned owl! What power does he have!? Oh, it riled me then and it riles me now, friends! Every person touched by him had their lives stolen, innocent or guilty. We were tired of being an extension of his malice. We, after so long, were ending it.

"Beez was next, my closest friend. Saying goodbye, it...made me want to run right then, right there. I believe he flew north, hopefully to the mountains. Those were his favorite missions. Soon after his escape,

Gniw voiced his suspicions, wondering if after fifteen years of service we were finally starting to grow weak. Whispers emerged then. Of new recruits already being looked at. Of the trainings and tests starting up once again.

"We found ourselves at a crossroad. The four of us remaining could easily oust the entire operation. Gniw would crumble and all Evon would be freed from his clutches of death. But what could four measly souls do? How many people would rather die than admit a fault with the bird? Mikyill was, and still is, consumed by his control. He'd somehow switch the blame on us. To the world we'd become nothing but liars murdering in his name. Worse, new Velvediers would just take our place. They'd be better selected, keener to perform the tasks than we'd been when the killings first began. The cycle would continue.

We felt…powerless. Even the most skilled assassins in Evon could not bring down the might of Gniw. Killing him was out of the question. Thanks to our clearing the way, Gniw replaced every seat around him with one of his own. They would surely fight for his position if he was dethroned, and the chaos unbridled would be worse than any work of a Velvedier. So, we did what we could to save the only ones we could: ourselves.

"The plan was rushed. We should have prepared far more than we did, but with Gniw's ire and suspicion over us, we weren't under the best of circumstances. None of us could stay. If we achieved that, then the rest didn't matter.

"We pulled it off about a month after Beez left. Gniw sent us back to Fotherton. For what? I have no clue. We never intended to make it to the town.

"Instead, the four of us sought shelter somewhere smaller and less regarded by Mikyill. It would be our jumping off point of sorts, the last stop before our lives changed forever.

"Village Winthrop."

They froze. He tried, but Rillem failed to hold back the soft smile at their shock. It felt strangely…welcome.

"No way! B-B-But that's—"

"Yes, yes, your home, I figured."

"Then how come we ain't ever seen yer before, eh?" asked Bunns, still at his side.

"This was, oh, more than two decades ago now. We came in at night under the guise of lost travelers seeking aid from the king. An older woman, Miss Tilly, let us board for the night. Did you three ever know her?"

"Oh yes," Foxtamas replied, memories crashing upon him. "She was a grandmother of sorts to us younger kids. Always had stories, treats, and flowers every time we went and saw her. She, um…passed not too long ago." Rillem bowed his head, giving the groundhog her moment of silence.

"I see. Few will ever share a heart like hers. For us, she arranged an audience with King Aisar. Our initial plan was to gain amnesty for a short reprieve and map out the new lives we were to take. Yet in our haste, we revealed our identities and plan to the king. We thought him, leader of one of the lowest hamlets in Mechmilne, with people of good, kind nature, sympathetic to our plights. But no."

"Guess he's always been that way," Foxtamas muttered beneath his breath.

"Immediately, he rejected everything we put forward. He claimed it heresy to Mikyill and Gniw, a betrayal of honor. We weren't dumb—we trained to see through lies such as these. Winthrop wasn't as far away from Mikyill as we first envisioned. Aisar, he didn't care about our betrayal. He was looking for power, ways to grow the poor village. Getting in good with Gniw seemed a quick and dirty path. Helping his secret ring of assassins betray him? Entirely out of the question.

"I won't lie, we feared for our lives that night. Word could be sent to Mikyill the moment we left his throne room and we'd be on the run, with no goal or supplies, forever chased by our replacements. But when we arrived back at Tilly's, someone greeted us…the queen. Anlana Feiht."

The owl's tired gaze finally returned to the fiery one of Acirema. This time, the name did not arouse questions or violence. Tears bubbled in the princess's wide, brown eyes instead. "She…she promised us safety further west. She was from those parts and knew routes we could take to keep low profiles until we made it to Dolioh country. We were also given her oath that our secret would never leave Aisar's mouth. For all his brutishness and grabs at power, she kept him in line.

"We thought we were being tricked. Kindness like this was unheard of, not only so far in our experience but in the line of work we were leaving. While Tilly housed us those few days, Anlana would come down nightly with word of safehouses and families willing to take us in. One time, she came with a tiny infant raccoon held tight to her chest, and her handmaiden, a jittery pregnant jackalope. Acirema was her name, and his was to be Bunnclar…"

Speechless. All three. Apart from Foxtamas, who snorted at the disbelief on the faces of his friends.

How…what…

This hermit, this *assassin* had known…their *mothers.* Not only their mothers, but *them!*

Acirema dropped her head into her hands, exasperated at the fact.

"I can't say I remember you, Rillem, but…I can't even believe…"

"Oh, I figured as such. You were a timid little thing. Every time June or Meek tried to wave and make you laugh, you tucked your head away from us."

"Yeah…sounds about right."

The owl chuckled. "Still, even with your mother's help, the threat of being found together was too prevalent. Each of us decided to head a different direction. June headed towards Efeters, her homeland, while Eisley ventured South and I further west. Meek was set to Roistlind, but…one of us had to stay behind. All four leaving without a trace would certainly stick Gniw's new guard upon us. He'd want his loose ends cut to size.

"I begged for it to be me. I-I-I couldn't bear having my family still suffer, and for *me* no less, a monster. I'd do anything for them. If Gniw found out I should be the one to be beaten, hanged, killed, whatever he saw fit, I'd go to my death without question. But Meek, he…the fool argued me out of it. He was younger and the closest to Gniw. If there was a chance of the bird believing anyone, it was him. Everyone agreed. I didn't have a choice, and I hated myself for it.

"On the night we planned to leave, he assured us he'd find a way out. I can't say if he did. Like Geric had to me, I handed in my cloak, bloodied and bruised from a faux attacker. Anlana gave us the trails and supplies. Our new lives were one step away.

"I remember our final hug only by the warmth. My mind couldn't take it. Thinking about the truth of that might've made my heart explode. I know I cried. I didn't stop for days. They were tears for my sister who I'd unjustly abandoned; for the brothers and sisters who were tricked into a life of unspeakable cruelty; for the innocent victims who left this world without a word. Worse…they were tears for the all the lives forever changed by my hand."

Finally, Rillem's tale concluded. Not even the crackle of the fire dared sound. All sat still, taking in the warped, twisted world the owl had somehow survived.

Was he innocent? Was he guilty? The answer didn't seem to matter. His story, one so long buried in a broken, twisted heart, had finally come to light. Relief filled him. Consequences of whatever kind were free to ravage him, but they could never take the freedom he finally allowed himself.

*That* mattered.

"So…how did you end up so close to Mikyill?" asked Foxtamas, low as to not disturb the peace. The story had been too astounding to end just yet. Rillem lifted his eyes, giving the question time to simmer.

"It was, um…to guard the others," he stuttered out. "If I couldn't be the one to go back, I'd do the next best thing. Any word of them hunting us and I'd seek them out before any Myriad or Velvedier could."

"And did they ever get close?"

"No, thankfully, but not for lack of trying, I'm sure. Hermit's Glum was a kid's story in Mikyill, meant to deter anyone from going down the Oldtrails and getting lost. For me, well, it was ripe for the taking.

No ghosts or ghouls of Mikyillites past ever haunted the place—except for me.

"I built this hut in the ruins of Fleetly, an old town, and made it my home. The folk tales usually keep travelers far enough away. When they do venture too close, however, I bring out my disguise to shoo them off. Only adds to the myth.

"But my fears of being found are…rampant. Paranoia controlled my every thought before you three showed up and pried this story out of me. You saw my fits…you saw what I've dwindled down to. I never thought derangement would come upon *me.* For so long every action I took felt sane. I-I-I was *strong,* I was quick, *capable.* But now, I'm lost, children. So, so lost. The poison's moved through my mind. Now…it's in my heart.

"I just can't see any good in the world anymore. You three, your mothers, you're all light, certainly. But one small spark. Look at Gniw. He still reigns. Same with Winthrop and your father, Acirema. Look at the Bridge, look at the monsters crossing our shores. Good's an exception to the rule. Hope is just a lie to keep you going from one day to the next. If the world wasn't so cruel, then maybe my family would still be together, and we'd be doing *good* for once.

"But it's not.

"There's no worth in doing anything but stalking my Glum."

The roar of the fire picked back up as Rillem tossed in a spare log. It cast upon the rounded walls four shadows, all lost in thought, taking in what the owl had said.

He…wasn't wrong. The three of them had lived their entire lives under the burden of oppression, be it of cold or king. They knew the taste of hopelessness—bitter, dry, the scratched throat of an impending illness. And now, for all the spices Rillem put in the stew, they still felt that sting in their mouths.

Acirema lingered in her mind. An image, one she squeezed her eyes shut to better focus upon, came into view. It was a mirror. The same one that hung on her vanity. In it shifted a fuzzy, blurred raccoon that, in the right lighting, could almost be a reflection of herself. The only difference was the Feiht Royal Crown sitting on the opposing lady's head, tall and golden. Denoting the woman as queen.

"What was my mother like?" her voice carried low, not wanting to disturb the silence despite so desperately needing to.

"Well," Rillem began, clearing the nihilism from his throat. "Very much like *you*, except for the eyes. Hers were this kindly green that always scrunched up when she smiled. And she smiled plenty. Your mother was lovely in all senses of the word.

"The Ratatoskr do stop by here on occasion, and Ruel passes on the major news, especially of Mikyill. But with word of the Bridge, Winthrop joined the conversation. I've since heard what goes on there. I can tell it in the clothes you three wear, the story Foxtamas told. It's…devastating, I'm sure." His words suddenly slowed. Something in his demeanor, between his relaxed features and lowered beak, made him appear not as some lost hermit, but a gentleman merely fallen a little off an already beaten road.

He breathed, regaining his composure. With smile softened, he reached his wing around the fire and into the hand of Acirema. "But, princess, I am more certain than ever that had your mother never left us, Winthrop would have changed trajectory entirely. She was honest, and caring, and stepped into the shoes of any who approached her. Only a child of hers could have saved me as you did. You have my thanks. I tell you now, you'll make a fine queen indeed."

Acirema forced her hand away to wipe the tears trickling down the stripes of her face. Yet she brought it back just as fast, snatching the lowly white feathers with a grip tight enough to crumple them.

"Thank you, Sir Cowl—"

"Just Rillem, please. I don't wish to taint the life of that man any more than I already have."

"Yes, of course. Rillem, I know so, so very little about my mother. She's just flashes in random memories to me. So to hear that she was as…as wonderful as I knew she had to be…my heart's warm. So, so warm."

Acirema rose and pulled the bird into a hug. Each let tears fall. One part in mourning for the former queen, another in celebration for the woman she'd been. "I only wish I could say the same for Gniw," she said as they separated. "I really did think the world of him when we met at Grammo Day. He dealt with my father for so long, didn't disregard him for his antics—I figured a man *had* to be good natured to suffer that and keep sane."

"I suppose he adapted to it after so long," chuckled Rillem. "It's all in what we choose to show the world. Some may carry good hearts in vile bodies; others the opposite. Or worse."

"Ah take et weh're not going tae Mikyill then?" Bunns shot in. His voice ran hoarse, eyes weighed down by bags of midnight blue.

Rillem laughed *again* to their surprise. "Of course not! You travel with the daughter of a former Mikyillite ally, who *knows* what chaos may ensue if she's discovered."

"You mean they'll kill her!?" blurted the fox.

"This new guard is a mystery to me still, but she's the type they may want swept under the rug, depending on what your father shared.

"Thankfully nothing," Acirema said with relief. "We've talked so little these past few years."

"Even still, your best way forward to the Fulnoa lies in New Lothlock. I'll explain more in the morning—the hour grows far too late for plans such as these. You'll be surprised to find, though, that this trip may not take as long as you first envisioned." With a wink to the jackalope, Rillem rose, stretching. He circled around the friends and collected their bowls. "Sleep as long as you care to. I'll be out patrolling the night and preparing your route for tomorrow. Figured I might as well pass on the same kindness your mothers gave me. Except for you, Foxtamas. I never met yours, so it's out in the rain for you."

A...joke? From...from Rillem!? Of all that had caught the trio off guard that day, that was by far the most unexpected. Change *had* fully enveloped him. Or, rather, perhaps the mask so long-set was finally falling off.

"Ah, well, wouldn't be the first time," he joked back. "Me and Foxlaris weren't in the picture 'till a little later."

"And I bet she was just as much a fighter," he replied with a smile. The owl bent down and lifted open the small cellar door, revealing a ladder leading into a darkened abyss. "I'm off. I'll stop back by here soon to check on you and the fire," Rillem said as descended, only to halt for a moment. He looked back to them. The potency of his yellow eyes was washed away with tears. "And…thank you. For saving me. Not only with your hands, but your ears."

"No, thank you for helping *us*," responded the princess.

"Oh, I did little—"

"It's worth more than you know," Foxtamas added. Stoic, Rillem bowed his head in honor.

"I suppose we all helped each other then. You kids rest up now. I'll see you in the morning. Goodnight." He winked, and the door plopped door behind him.

Each member of the trio cozied up with their blankets upon the hut's floor. The fire finished its drying as dreams started washing against their minds. Acirema stood somewhere in the Palace, speaking with her mother. Gray had begun to take the queen, but her dazzling smile and emerald eyes destroyed any notion of a slowing mind. Foxtamas ran alongside Rillem and the other Velvediers, fleeing from the gangs of bandits, thieves, and members of the Myriad chasing them westward. And Bunns…couldn't sleep a wink.

Too much still troubled him. He stared ahead at the door. There beside it hung the ghoulish mask Rillem had used. Something about it captured him. The twist of the horns; the chains tying it down; the wax along the cheeks that, from a distance, made the creature look like it was melting.

He…

He understood. Why Rillem put it on. Why now he'd taken it off. And he asked the same about himself.

*Why?*

*Why did* he *put on a mask?*

He squeezed his paws. Felt the callouses. Felt the sensation of the soggy, ruined paper staining them like blood.

In that, he found his answer.

# 8

# "WE'RE ALL ONE LINE OF VEINS BELOW."

Morning rays fluttered down through the small chimney of the hut. The fire had long passed away and made room for a new crown of light. With it whistled the lovely first hymns of the woodland wind, carrying the smell of a fresh day scented by yesterday's rain.

Just the rustle of the branches was enough to stir Foxtamas. His tired head rose, bringing with it aches and a soreness from the previous day's ride down the river. Sitting up felt like a chore. With all the days of walking ahead...had the Fulnoa even been a good idea at all?

The question faded when the smell of heated fruits and bubbling oats hit him. Foxtamas rubbed his eyes. The hut was empty apart from his sleeping friends and Rillem's simmering pot. Although not present, his presence was noted. The fox gently raised himself (minding the *Pops!* and *Cracks!* plaguing his young body) and hobbled to the cauldron. Berry-laden oatmeal steamed inside with three bowls sat beside it. The breakfast, it seemed, was his for the taking.

As he began to pour the porridge out for both himself and the others, flashes of the day prior started to relive themselves. The Oldtrails. The Storm. The Surge. The Ghost. Rillem...

Yes, Rillem. Was he certain that wasn't a dream? Some odd fantasy come to life, playing games of assassin and intrigue in his sleep?

"Ah'm brokeeeeeen."

Foxtamas turned from his chore to find Bunns rolling beneath his blanket. Groans gargled from his aching mouth, his short, stout limbs stiff as the antlers upon his head.

"Et's all locked oup, Scottoh. Everythin'. Yer gotta leave meh here tae die."

Smiling, the fox bent down and whipped the blanket off him, tossing it to the side with his packs.

"I'm feeling it too, Antler-Ears. Rillem already made us breakfast, so get on up."

"Uuuuunnnggggg," was all Bunns could comment back. The pain of his stomach *did* outweigh that of his body, however. He lifted himself up, reached out a hand, and presented his friend with the cheesiest smile he could muster. Foxtamas obliged. Begrudgingly.

"Go ahead and burn your mouth on it. Might stop all the moaning."

"Yer'd say tha' tae ah wounded soldier?"

"If you count as one, then yes."

The pair gobbled the hot morning meal. Small bits of blueberries and strawberries swirled in a creamy mixture of full, gritty oats that tasted earthen like a crisp autumn day. It was more than any village boy deserved.

As they ate, Acirema slowly arose, though skipped over the customary complaining.

"Goodness…what time is it?" She asked, groggy. "I swear I slept for a few years or so."

"Morning, thankfully. Maybe mid-morning. Rillem made us oatmeal, though. Here," Foxtamas replied, passing her a bowl. He'd taken a seat back beneath his blanket, forming a small circle with his friends.

"And you two trust it?"

Her concern stopped their shoveling. The fox and jackalope exchanged glances. Timid ones, at that.

Of course they hadn't thought that through. Had the owl so easily won them over? Odd things *do* happen when a sore body is involved.

"Tasted good, so Ah reckon so," Bunns finally said, setting aside his empty bowl.

"Just thought the skeptics would've been more careful," she said, taking her steaming porridge. "It's almost too much to take in, about

Rillem. Like…the stories, especially about our mothers, they took me off guard. Had me questioning what was real."

"Right?" Foxtamas added between bites. "Just thinking about what a day we had yesterday makes me wanna sleep again."

"Ah wouldn't mind…"

"But how much of it do y'all think was true?"

"Did you even *see* him?" Acirema asked with snark thick on her voice. "You can't fake the kind of passion he spoke with. He was just, you know, a little lost and had to find his way back."

"More than a little," said Bunns, rolling his eyes. A bite of bitterness still stung him. "The bigger issue is where weh go now. Trustin' his food is one thing; wha' 'bout trusting him tae get us tae tha' New Lothlock place?" Foxtamas shrugged. He set aside his bowl and began bunching up the thin quilt.

"Do we have much of a choice? We lost our map." Though his words weren't meant to maim, Bunns eyes fell ever so slightly. They *had* a choice. If it wasn't for himself, wasn't for his failure—

*SLAM!!*

The cellar door beside the trio flung open and just about cracked on the dirt floor. From its darkness peeked a white, feathery, rejuvenated head.

"Ah, morning, friends! Good to see you three up so early—I expected to see you at noon," announced Rillem, giddy. He hopped up and sat on the floor's edge, letting his talons dangle in the dark of the cellar. "I've been making preparations all night for your journey northward. Finish your meals and get packed, I'll be waiting down here to reveal the." He ended his news with a wink, and as quickly as he first emerged, the owl disappeared, this time shutting the cellar door with a gentle touch.

Acirema scooped up the last of her breakfast while the boys readied the packs. The river had left them with little. Nothing but the necessities of rolled-up blankets, half-filled flasks, and each of their individual weapons.

"Ready?" Acirema asked once finished, her bow and quiver fixed in place.

"Tae bae buried alive down there bae Rillem? Absolutely!" Bunns was forced to scurry down the stone ladder lest he meet the beating glare of Foxtamas. Who, in his silent reply, stifled a smile.

The steps down ended not in some dank, roomy cellar, but a long stone tunnel, lined with small alcoves for whatever the bird needed. Rillem himself was fiddling with something near one of the shelves. The torch he carried illuminated the trinkets, exposing staffs, costumes, bottles, and books, showing just how far the underground hallway went. He stuffed something in the pocket of his smock-like tunic right as the company arrived.

"Perfect! Now, follow me, and don't mind the clutter. This here's my escape tunnel that doubles as a pantry, a closet, and library. Parting is not one of my hobbies." The owl motioned for them to follow, taking the lead down the stuffy gray hall. "As I mentioned last night, going to Mikyill is not the best of options, even if it does lead quite nicely to the Fulnoa. There are only a few towns before the Dwarfmoors that have comparable roads. Luckily for you three, I've a vessel that leads right to one."

Perplexed, the trio looked around at each other. He could feel the stares behind his back.

"Ah…vessel?" Bunns asked.

"Indeed. You won't be going by foot—you're going by *boat*, one headed straight to New Lothlock. It's not much of a stop from what I remember, but the getting there is quick, and the inns and traders are of good stock. The road out, the one going northwest, leads to the Guardmonts and Fulnoa. You'll see the signs, no worries."

"And what about Old Lothlock? What happened to it?" Foxtamas asked.

"Same thing that happened to Fleetly and Persimmon. They grew up both before and after the Great War, then died off when people headed further West, away from the memories of carnage that plagued them for generations. New Lothlock simply took its place after a while."

The fox nodded, and together the company broke through the light bathing the tunnel's end. It opened into a wide valley, sprinkled with flowers of blues and reds and grasses tall, lazily swaying in the fresh morning wind. Down its gentle slope creeped a lake. Not terribly large, it rippled along the stern tree line at its opposite bank only to push past it, leading a small watery trail deeper into the woods. Closer to the travelers, however, and taking their attention from the morning, was a dock.

A scrappy dock. Not very steady, shabby in the right parts and neat in the wrong, it seemed to have been built by someone more experienced killing with wood than building with it. The same could not be said for the boat moored at its edge.

The main hull was crafted in the shape of a simple raft: a group of sanded logs tied together with globs of pitch spread between them. Atop the base sat a tiny little room, no larger than a pantry. It housed extra supplies, a narrow desk, and a surplus of quilts, patterned in ways bright and sharp and not native to Mechmilne Country. Two masts rose up from the hull, one in the middle with two paddles attached to the sides and the other, shorter, in front. Off the former pole clung two identical sails while a smaller one, much more navigable by the tug of a hook on the end of its stringing, lay upon the latter. All three had been tightened and appeared in fine condition despite a few small patches here and there. Topping off the ship (quite literally) was the crow's nest. It was about the size of an apple bushel, but had a plank nailed into the middle for a seat. On the vessel's side the words *The Losmo* had been scribbled on in a worn white ink. The penmanship was of a scratchy pattern—if owls were known for one thing, it was never their handwriting.

Everything about the boat, bobbling along the glittering waves, soaking in the soft presence of the sun, left the trio speechless.

Bunns forgot how to blink. And breathe. His mind drank on the mixture of relief and excitement until he fell drunk with peace. Rillem had been…right. They'd been given a route, a ship, a taste of hope! The map…the map *wasn't the end!*

"This, children, is *The Losmo*, called 'Wanderer' in Old Evonian. Felt appropriate considering my current station," he said while walking towards the dock. "I built her after getting settled here in my Glum. She was mainly an escape plan if Gniw ever found me, but I sailed her around these bends a fair time or two. An excellent girl, none better around. And perfect, I think, for the three of you."

"Mind if weh, um, explore the lass ah bit?" Bunns asked. He licked his lips in anticipation.

"Oh yes, go right ahead. Spent the night fixing her up, so there shouldn't be—"

The jackalope didn't hear him finish. He bounded off the dock and jumped upon the stern logging of *The Losmo*. Foxtamas joined, right on his heels. The pair began their quest, invading the room's smallest nooks, climbing the central pole's ladder, and feeling the thick cloth crafted for the sails. This ship was…oh for all the goodness in Evon, it was *real!*

What more could any adventurer ask for!

Their gawking made an excellent show for Rillem and Acirema. They watched the escapades from the dock, not caring to hide their goofy grins.

"You know," the owl started, "you can tell they're village boys stuffed in the bodies of young men."

"Oh, trust me, you don't know the half of it!" Acirema watched him break beside her. His laugh was one of deep refreshment both for his soul and hers, with squinted eyes and a ruffle of feathers. Through it, the line separating Cowl and Rillem blurred.

The exploration couldn't last forever. Both boys hopped back to the creaking dock at Rillem's behest, doing what little they could to hide their joy. Once settled, the owl pulled a small, patched sack from over his shoulder and plopped it on the ragged timbers.

"Now, before you all go sailing off like a band of good-for-nothing raft rats, I've, um...some words to say." His tone stiffened. He couldn't look any of them in their eyes—*The Losmo* held his attention. "I think I was given far too much time by myself last night. It was for the better, don't worry. You two probably saw, but there are two buckets aboard in the hut. One of fruits, the other small shrimps and fish. Use them as you may, I just...hope it refills the supplies the storm stole. I know it's not muffins and ale—"

"No, that's more than generous," the princess interrupted. Rillem flickered his focus to her for a single second, smiling as he did.

"Yes, well, use them wisely. But I've brought you more. A few gifts, I suppose you could call them. Don't get me wrong, I'm still stout in my belief of this world being too far gone for its own sake. But...I'd like to see how far I can help this little exception get." With a teary wink, he dug into the bag. First out came a bundle of journals, loose papers, and ink-stained notes grouped together by a gaggle of stray strings. "S.C.H.R." was scrawled upon the covers. Rillem handed the mess over to the fox, minding his confusion.

"I've much more to hide than what I told in last night's story. These...these are the journals and thoughts I kept during the years between my leaving and arriving in this place. I figured, in keeping with this new rush of life I've been given, that I need them out. Passed on. To someone much more eager to read these tales than I."

"But I thought you went straight to the Glum?" asked Foxtamas. The aged pages felt coarse in his hands, but also warm. Warm with the beating of a heart turned to ink.

"What can I say, secrets have always been my specialty. Do take them though, learn what I can't share with my voice. These memories...they've outstayed their welcome."

Foxtamas nodded. And gripped the gift tighter.

"Thank you, Rillem. I'll make sure to read them and keep them safe."

Nodding, the owl moved towards Bunns, fiddling again with his bag.

"For you, little warrior, I found something more suited to your line of work than a few old stories…"

Rillem turned over his wing and revealed a knife. It was shaped for throwing, with a sleek ebony handle and sharp, narrow blade. A sapphire rested on the pommel. Within it an "M" had been carved, but the middle "V" inside the letter was bolded with a refined, glittery silver.

"Laddie, et's ah beaut!" Bunns exclaimed. He flipped it over his fingers and found it weighed no more than a star.

"It's a throwing knife given to me when I first joined the Velvediers. I've plenty in my collection and thought I could part with one. Who knows, it may fling farther than a star."

Bunns grinned and squinched up his nose.

"Aye, weh'll bae seein' 'bout tha'!"

Finally, Rillem moved down to Acirema, who waited with bated breath.

"And, for the princess, something a fellow enemy of Gniw may need." His wing didn't dive for the bag. No, as if out of thin air, a pendant materialized in his wing. It was formed from a long, silver chain with the slimmest links the princess had ever seen. Draped at the bottom hung a carefully crafted pin. Its symbol matched that of Bunns' dagger—the metal "M" and "V" forming the logo of the Velvediers. Though, this time the "V" was etched from sapphire. Its brilliance could not be understated.

"Why…it's so beautiful, Rillem!" she gasped upon taking it in her paws. "I already adore it!"

"Oh, I'm glad. The pin at the end was once my hidden badge. We used them at certain places around Mikyill and villages to announce our arrival to other informants waiting for us. Like a key to lockless doors. It's mainly for beauty, but who knows."

"Well thank you, I'll wear it with pride. And use it to ward off Gniw if he gets too close." They both chuckled as the princess clasped the gift around her neck. The shimmering blue of the "V" contrasted with the lavender of her tunic. "You do know you don't have to do any of this, right? Your ship alone is more than enough—"

"Think nothing of it. Just clearing out some junk this old bird doesn't need." Before she could air her rebuttal, Rillem pushed his way onto *The Losmo*. He gave one final inspection as the trio boarded, packs and gifts in hand. "If you look out," he said upon the stern, "this pond drains into the Runnel. It's a river that heads northward from here. Both it and the tributary you three washed away in make the Glum's eastern border. Unlike that one, though, it should *not* be overflooded.

"The journey to New Lothlock will take roughly two days if I remember right. It peters out at an old mill. Once there, tie up the ol' girl; I doubt anyone will want to mess with her. And don't worry, I'll find a way up to sail her back down. I've done far more difficult things in my time."

He turned back around once done. Foxtamas, Bunns, and Acirema stood gazing at him, taking in the orders he laid out.

Rillem tried all he could. Oh, how he tried.

But nothing helped.

The friends morphed into the images of his own, becoming Beez, June, and Meek, young as if they'd never been recruited, as if time had finally come to a halt and the simplicity of that life wrapped them all in a beautiful, luscious love.

His soft yellow eyes swelled with tears at the sight.

And the truth.

He couldn't have them back. No matter how hard he tried, how well he hid, how *fervently* he prayed. These youngsters would take their place in the world. In doing so, they would become what the people in their life needed them to be.

And what the Velvediers could not.

"Well then. About time I bid you three farewell," he choked out. His wings flapped, and the bird soared into the air, hovering above them before taking to one of the nearby trees.

"Thank you so much, Rillem!" Foxtamas shouted up. "We won't forget you!"

"Hah! You'd be the first!"

Suddenly, without a sound, a knife fired from beneath his white wing. The rope holding the boat to the deck snapped in two. It forced the trio to grab a mast as *The Losmo* began to drift away from the shore. "Use the paddles and head for the Runnel!" Rillem called again. His voice carried across the lake, like that of a horn, played not for the arrival of a king, but for the joy of the sound. "Go find your brother! Go change this world for the better! Happy trails, happy trails!"

With a final salute, the snowy owl took back to the air. Shouts of goodbye trailed behind him. He was soon lost to the trio in the river of clouds above, gone and invisible like a gust of wind.

It was a narrow way out of the pond. Bunns and Foxtamas eagerly elected themselves to work the paddles while Acirema guided from the back. Their ship moved with ease along the smooth waters. However, once the boys got the hang of steering and rowing, the banks exiting the lake tightened. Overgrown grass tangled with clumps of eroded mud, thickening the sides and keeping long-drowned foliage blocked beneath the already shallow small waterway. Bunns, fueled by his excitement, simply started smashing away the blockade. It *actually* proved useful. He flung away large enough sections until *The Losmo* slid through, fully exiting the lake and entering beneath a darkened canopy of overhanging branches.

"You can tell Rillem wasn't keen on going down here," Foxtamas commented, trying to avoid thick trails of moss. They fell like ropes, long enough to slide against the logs of the hull.

"*Nae*, yer think so?" jeered Bunns. His paddle had no luck avoiding the brambles scratching up near the vessel's side. "For ah first sailin', yer think et would bae ah bit easier!"

"Yeah, not the way I was dreaming of our first voyage."

"Should bae out in the sea, Ah reckon. Nae moss tae tangle yer oup there."

"There's seaweed, supposedly."

"But can't yer eat tha'?"

"I think so."

"Then Ah'd bae out of there on ah full belly!"

Acirema just rolled her eyes and held on to the main mast. The hanging trees blocked out most of the sun. It would be a miracle if the boys didn't get the ship stuck in the first leg of their voyage.

Thankfully, light began to break through as the roaring of north-bound waves splashed at their ears. The Runnel was close! With a few more pushes along the narrow way, the canopy opened, and *The Losmo* swept into the fresh, open waves.

The Runnel flowed with a generous run, sticking well to the name. Its width was double that of the ship and give it plenty of room to navigate the peppy, choppy waves. Walls of trees flanked either bank, though the leftmost one was clearly the edge of Hermit's Glum, what with the thickened oaks and tight spaces. As Foxtamas and Bunns realigned the paddles and began their work in steadying the course, bends shifted the waterway, taking their focus and channeling it into navigating the way forward.

After what felt like ages, they'd returned.

This was their road.

This was their next step in reaching Foxlaris.

"Say," the fox called over once settled with his oar, "shouldn't we be going a bit faster? It seems, I dunno, kinda slow."

"Aye! Weh should bae flyin' down—" He saw it before he could finish the complaint. In their giddiness to launch the boat, they'd forgotten to untie the sails!

Bunns nearly tossed his paddle overboard and ran to the central mast. With one of the tallest hops of his career, he reached for the rope. The tip of his paw snatched the end. Held tight. And yanked it down.

*FWOOOOOSH!!!*

The forgotten sail slammed open, kicking *The Losmo* upwards and shooting it down the watery road. Spray blew into the air and misted back until the entire deck lay wet.

In the same motion, it flung Bunns to the ground. The pain hardly registered compared to what the journey had already put him through. Giggling, he cried out, "Haha lassies! Now weh're goin'!"

Foxtamas whooped out a holler. The sudden burst made his paddling obsolete. Instead, he set it aside and let the icy breeze spill through his fur. His blue eyes watched the brilliant colors of Mechmilne fling by. Every leaf became a blur, every trunk a streaking dash, but oh how he *felt* the history of it all pouring over him, ink upon a page. Its nature, its *essence*, that he saw in the splashes of green and umber, splashes of paint upon a canvas. He heard its voice—he saw its soul.

"I wish your childhood selves could see you now!" Acirema called out over the breeze. She took up a laugh at the thrill of skimming down the river.

"Which ones?" asked Foxtamas. "The pirates, explorers, spelunkers—"

"Or the hunters, spies, thieves," Bunns added from the floor.

In that moment, the raccoon found herself missing those fantasy outings. When she'd go along with their ambitions, where Foxtamas read aloud the tales they'd explore, and Bunns led the way through the forest, crafting with Foxlaris an arc for the day. Even after all the years they spent together, and how in that time they grew and matured, they kept safe that spark of life and love. Perhaps that is why she always joined them—not because of Mrs. Cammont's promise to watch over the young princess, but because they showed her, in all their stupid, goofy ways, what it meant to live with nothing but sticks and stones.

"The pirates. I remember Father taking me to visit the Gardens of Poppy Ridge, and when I returned you three bragged about sneaking out to the pond without me."

"Yes! We stole the fruit baskets from the garden and used them for boats." Foxtamas' face lit up as the memory danced across his mind.

"Yer and Rizzeh were lucky. Ah had tae take the fall for tha' an' got mah behind *whooped!"*

"And I'd do it again. Man, what a game to miss, Acirema. We paddled around, had wars, tried to loot each other—"

"Oh, I'm aware," she cut in, grinning. "I was reminded every time you three sang that awful, awful shanty."

Bunns scrambled to his feet.

His eyes met the shocked face of Foxtamas.

Their shared thoughts connected in the billowing wind.

Without a cue, the fox picked back up his paddle and began thumping it against the boat's ragged side.

"You mean this one?" he asked, grin pinching his cheeks. Bunns added to the beat with a slam of his foot before hopping up the main mast's ladder.

"W-Wait, guys, no, I didn't mean for you to—"

We ain't hail from isle or sea,
Locked in this pond mer-ci-less-ly,
Forced to sail amongst the green
Until we come to town and scream:

Hi, Hi, Hi-dey Ho!
Hi, Hi, Hi-dey Day!
Weeeee're the Winthrop Piiiiirates
And we've brought some good ol' hell t'raise!

Lock the doors to flower stores
When we sneak right up to your shores.
While them Watchers dream and snore
We'll be taking Tops galore!

Hi, Hi, Hi-dey Ho!
Hi, Hi, Hi-dey Day!
Weeeee're the Winthrop Piiiiirates

And we've brought some good ol' hell t'raise!

At the pond we will find rest
And count the coins that we've been blessed.
If your king comes to arrest
We'll grab the ships and flee out West!

Hi, Hi, Hi-dey Ho!
Hi, Hi, Hi-dey Day!
Weeeee're the Winthrop Piiiiirates
And we've brought some good ol' hell t'raise!
(One more time!)

Hi, Hi, Hi-dey Ho! (Hi-dey Ho!)
Hi, Hi, Hi-dey Day! (Hi-dey Day!)
Weeeee're the Winthrop Piiiiirates
And we've brought some good ol' hell t'raise!

HEY!

To their utter disbelief, the performers finished their song to *applause*. Acirema didn't even try to contain her laughter. Neither of them had skipped a beat or word, perfectly in sync to their childhood tune.

"Just as good as the eightieth time I heard it," she giggled.

"Oh, so et finally rubbed off on yer after ah decade, eh?" asked Bunns. He picked back up his oar and rested it against the waters. The ship's speed had finally adjusted, and the river now dragged the paddle by with a bold ease.

"What can I say, it just sounds better when you're actually *on* a ship."

"No, I don't think that's it," said Foxtamas. "Bunns, I think our most infamous critic *enjoyed it* as a *song!*"

The princess scoffed and turned her nose up to the wind.

"Nonsense. I guess a girl can't enjoy her friends acting the fool every once and a while then, huh?"

"Guess not, but she *can* enjoy a village ditty."

"Ah bet et makes her jealous of them fruit baskets weh had!"

Again, Acirema scoffed, this time turning towards the cabin.

"It appears the festivities have concluded," she said, prim and controlled, "and I am no longer needed except as a target for unbridled and unrequested ridicule. If you two have no prior complaints, I will take up the task of sorting the supplies graciously gifted to us by our previous host. Good day."

With that, she trotted off. To the rolling eyes of her friends.

"Ach, Ah'd rather lose mah ears than hear tha' princess talk."

"*Queen* talk," Acirema corrected from the door.

"How 'bout *annoyin',* eh?"

Bunns heard no reply.

Rowing on the Runnel didn't prove a challenge. All three sails puffed out their chests with honor. Every now and again the pair would shift the ship one way to avoid a sharp bend or the grip of an overreaching branch. In the simplest of terms, it was bliss.

"Feels good, don't et? Tae bae back on our feet?" the jackalope tossed to the fox.

"Oh yeah," nodded Foxtamas. "I thought it was something when we got on the trails outta Hucksubtle. But this, Bunns, I bet we're gonna cut Teardic's estimate in *half.* Heck, *fourths* if we're lucky."

Bunns noted the tone of excitement on his tongue. It came out often after he recited a story he'd read or one he himself wanted to create. Passion clothed him now, and the fox looked dashing in it. "Heck, it's making me wanna take up boating when all this is over."

"Boating!?" Bunns asked in confusion.

"Why not?"

"Weh ain't even at the Fulnoa yet, Scottoh. Might wanna hold back on the big ol' life choices 'till weh bring Rizzeh back in one piece."

"Hey, I can be an optimist at times. I mean, there's not really a Bridgeburrow to work on when we get back. You really just wanna repair roofs the rest of your life?"

"Meh, not tae sure. Guess Ah never think ahead tha' far." He knew that would get Foxtamas stirred up. Would've done worse to Acirema.

"I'm *well* aware."

"Weh could end up in Mikyill like Reinden an' Asterlyn. Ah'd find ah job slingin' stars an yer could bae some ol' storyteller like that one laddie at Grammo Day."

"Oooohhh, I see the vision. You either wanna get drafted into the Velvediers or killed by them, that right?" Foxtamas turned away from paddling to watch the sour scowl grip his friend's face.

"Ah could take the bonnies, easy."

"Like you did with Rillem?"

"Blame the river. Had mah whole head buzzin' around, wasn't on mah game."

"Mhmm. Whatever you say. Maybe boating isn't the best for you after all."

Silence hung between them for a moment. The whisps of the summer wind whipped by, and the occasional *splash!* sprayed the pair with its refreshing dew. Words, however, did peep out from Bunns.

"Well…Ah think Ah'd like tae have ah family, yer know. Ah wife, few kids."

"Really?" Foxtamas couldn't tell if he was serious. He searched past his response, looking to his off-set look, the gaze focused not on the river, or the forest, but the future.

Perhaps he was.

"Yeah. Et might bae nice. Imagine et: ah manor all mah own, built like ah castle with all the lil' Bunnses runnin' around—"

"Causing chaos? Not sure that's a dream, Bunns. Sounds more like a nightmare!"

Both friends chuckled at the thought.

"Nae, don't worry. They'd get whipped in tae shape bae the lil' Scottohs."

"I'd make sure of it alright."

"Aster would too."

The fox paused his rowing entirely to stare the jackalope down. But he couldn't keep it up. Bunns was already too busy giggling at his own joke.

"Real funny."

"Ah know, tha's why Ah said et!"

Foxtamas resigned himself to silence after that—Bunns kept up his grin, whistling the chorus of a song. *The Losmo*'s serenity gave the fox ample time to gaze up at the branches interlocked above them. Their shadows spotted him like an illness. Each passing leaf shielded the blazing sun but for a moment. A moment of reprieve, rest. Reflection.

Staring at the nature of Evon never bored him. Something always caught his eye and turned it from thought to tale. Was that not happening now? It was as if the fear that so often battled against his brain held no land here. Its sting wasn't felt—Foxtamas the Adventurer was free. Lost in the world. Drowning in the beauty, the possibility, that magic that drifted beyond the sky, the waves, the sea…

"SCOTTOH!"

Bunns' cry shattered the daydreaming.

Right as the fox recognized the urgency in his voice, the vessel rocked up and down, tall walls of water leaping on board. Foxtamas scrambled up from his spot and looked ahead.

Rapids.

White water cracked over itself like rolling mounds of breaking glass. The once quiet lane roared with a thunder, bending every which way in a quick, chaotic mess. Worse, the shore had changed. The Runnel now ran through the broken end of a ridge. It's sheer, rising rockface had crumbled down to a beach of pebbles both smooth and sharp. Crashing would rip not only the boat, but those trying desperately to navigate it.

Foxtamas gulped, then panicked. He raced for his paddle. The second he sheathed it into the spraying rapids, it hit him.

Literally.

*THUNK!!*

"GAH!"

The blistering speeds slammed it into his shoulder. Somehow he kept his grip, but not without a splintering pain running down his arm.

"Scottoh!" shouted Bunns again. He checked ahead for the upcoming turns in the waves before hopping over to Foxtamas. "Can yer row!?"

"Uh, um, I-I can try," he groaned.

"Good, just keep us away from the right shore!" The buzzing jackalope bounded back to the left side while Foxtamas stood up, gripping the oar until his knuckles paled.

"What's going on!?" Acirema peeked from the shack and almost fell overboard as the rocky waves beneath tilted *The Losmo* backwards.

"Just hold on!" Bunns yelled to her. He deterred his focus far from the biting breeze or constant bumps throttling the ship. No, he settled on the frontmost mast holding the taut, smaller sail. Rillem had built it on a connection that, once untied, could swivel, helping to lead the small vessel wherever the captain wished.

Good thing Captain Bunnclar Cammont was reporting for duty.

He unclasped the fastening in a flash. The sudden unraveling threw the sail left, causing the entire ship to careen towards the leafy shoreline.

"BUNNS!" Foxtamas bellowed as his side swung into the air, almost sending the fox into the white-crested waves below.

"Ah said HOLD ON!" A quick push of the sail corrected the course. Bunns hugged it for dear life. He used the hook at the end to drive the boat past the sharpened shoreline and wild, unseen bends.

Yet as he did, *The Losmo* increased in speed. The trio felt the steeper decline developing under their ship. Its front skipped across the waters. Each hit exploded into a misting spray that clouded Bunns' vision. Eventually, as the boat flung like an arrow down the Runnel, it blinded him. Trying to steer became useless. He was forced to let the waves roll them as they wished, like spinning in a gambler's hand.

The jackalope rushed back to the others to try and look ahead without drowning his eyes. Glimpses came through, thankfully. Glimpses of the foamy flow creeping to an end. Glimpses of the foliage pulling back to cradle the shores. Glimpses of...

Of...

"Yer blasted river..."

A drop.

"GRAB SOMETHING!" Bunns shouted, frantically pulling his friends closer and towards the room.

"W-W-What!?" stuttered Foxtamas.

"Just BRACE!"

*S*<br>*P*<br>*L*<br>*A*<br>*A*<br>*A*<br>*A*<br>*A*<br>*SSSHHH!!!*

All became weightless. All disappeared in a frenzy of white. And then all stilled.

No water bursting from over sides, no spray weaponized by the wind. All was calm.

Mostly.

In the cabin, the trio lay tangled amongst their packs, barrels, and supplies Acirema had meticulously sorted through.

"Everyone alright?" Bunns asked between breaths. His bruised chest rattled up and down, up and down, quicker than his heart, fear glowing on his face.

"I'm broken…" moaned the fox, trying his best to sit up from the wooden ground.

"I heard the paddle slap you," Acirema said. Luckily, she'd only been thrown against the wall and not soaked like the other two. "Are you okay?"

"Mostly…maybe."

Bunns helped them up, careful not to overextend himself. The pains of the minotaur and previous waters started to flare, both from the drop and his own worry.

"Tha's et," he sighed. "Ah'm *done* with rivers. Ah get how Rizzeh probably feels now."

"You can bond with him when he gets…gets back—"

Foxtamas shuttered and grabbed his arm. The spikes of pain rolled through it, like a dagger slicing at the veins beneath his skin.

Acirema caught him and led him to the chair by the desk.

"You stay in here and read the books Rillem gave you. I can take the shift."

"No, I'm fine, just—"

Acirema stared him down with a look that rivaled that of his own mother *and* Mrs. Cammont.

"Fine." He gave in and tossed up his good hand. "Just be careful."

"I will be." She winked before following Bunns out to the deck. Already the Runnel had calmed, rocking back to its original, simple gait.

A messy concoction of guilt, relief, pain, and intrigue brewed in the fox's stomach. The shoulder wasn't *that* bad, but using it anymore wouldn't help anything. Was it an excuse to leave the work to his friends? The very people risking their *lives* to get back *his* brother? And what was he going to do? *Read?*

It was too much. He went to rise from his seat, only to put too much weight upon his right arm. The fires singed him.

Acirema was right. A break wouldn't hurt.

As the noontime sun crossed the midpoint of the day, Foxtamas cracked open the first of many journals gifted to him. He blew away the dust, picked off the cobwebs, and dove into the unknown tales of the assassin of Evon…

# 9

# "SHARP YOUR AXE, SHAPE YOUR MUG,"

Novels make it clear where you're meant to start. But this?

Should he begin at the first journal and read through them like a book? Take note of the loose pages and scribbles? Or disregard it all and let the secrets lie?

No, the latter was impossible.

Ultimately, the fox settled on what he estimated to be the first of the journals. Opening its yellowed, brittle leaves felt like taking a step back in time. The book's smells of aged paper and long-lingered dust overwhelmed him; his nose traced the scents of the room wherein these notes were born of darkened ink in dimmed firelight. Foxtamas wasn't in the ship's cabin any longer—he sat shoulder-to-shoulder with a much younger Rillem.

The first page lacked any of the paragraphs he expected. Instead, a list of names cluttered the parchment, names that the fox suddenly remembered.

- *Sir Beasle Metaltalon (Beez)*
  - *Harpy Eagle*
  - *Iron and Copper Cast Talons*
  - *Brute Muscle*
  - *Greatest Friend*

- *Lady Juniper Ratagow (June)*
    - *Efete*
    - *Bow and Arrow*
    - *Lead Distance Combatant*
    - *Heart and Soul of the Group*
- *Sir Gericson Violetelle (Geric)*
    - *Red Panda*
    - *Dual Axes*
    - *Lead Close-Combat Warrior*
    - *True, Virtuous, Honorable*
- *Lady Sheridon Isle (Eisley)*
    - *Mossokin*
    - *Sword*
    - *Spy, Camouflage Warrior*
    - *Leader and Mother*
- *Sir Meekial Skitty (Meek)*
    - *Meerkat*
    - *Lance*

- *Speedster*
- *Funniest and Youngest*

*Don't forget them, Cowl*

*Don't forget them*

*Don't forget them*

*Please don't*

*Don't forget them*

*DON'T FORGET THEM*

*DON'T FORGET THEM*

*DONTFORGETTHEMDONTFORGETTHEM-DONTFORGETTHEMDONTFORGETTHEM*

*DON'T FORGET THEM COWL DON'T FORGET THEM!!*

Foxtamas threw down the cover. The sudden change from Velvedier notes to deranged yet sorrowful reminders tore through his heart. These cries…his ears could almost hear them. He figured by the age of the date that this wasn't long after the waning group had departed from Winthrop. If only this Cowl could have heard Rillem's tale. He hadn't forgotten his family—himself, on the other hand, dangled by a string.

But to forget such important people…

Foxtamas looked out the window facing him. Bunns and Acirema paddled away, guiding *The Losmo* down its trail, not towards New Lothlock and beyond, but further, to East Evon and Foxlaris. Would *he* ever forget *them?*

It would be a *blistering* day in Pradifore before he'd allow himself the chance. But…if he did…would he even be upset? A life without them. Or Foxlaris, or the Cammonts, or all those in Winthrop. That being the standard he adhered to without wonder or worry why. No, they were too important, too great to forget. The fox didn't know how to even *live* without them. It seems the only pain caused by memories lost is the fear that plagues you before they're gone.

Rillem must have felt the same. Only the memories remained of his family. Memories worth more than gold. Keeping that alive, even in his mind and writings alone, was enough.

Foxtamas forced himself to move on. He flipped through a few more pages, finding where the actual entries began. Some appeared to have been lost—intentionally. The middle binding housed the shredded edges of pages torn away. A few scraps remained, with titles of *Hucklebee Killing #3* and *Rondlin Killing* #7 scrawled along the top in the jagged owl script. The words beneath, however, had been painted over by the darkest of inks. Not even holding the page to the sun unearthed them.

Foxtamas understood. He needed a way to keep the memories alive, just as he had his friends in the notes prior. But as age and a wicked mind decimated the owl, those truths twisted into evils he *begged* to have cast out lest they send him into further ruination.

The following chapters were, thankfully, still around. Foxtamas' blue eyes skimmed them over, picking up bits of detailed travels and wanderings by the orphaned Cowl.

*...I may set course for the Guardmonts tomorrow. I know Beez is there. To see him, or any of them, alive again...I don't think there's a sweeter dream...*

*...No trail I follow is the right one. I should have known he'd hide better than I could find him. If only he knew who was on his trail...*

*...Leads told me to search Pradifore. Nothing. Just frozen trees...*

*...I stand before the mountains that stand before the ice fields that stand before Roimohr. Is that where he's gone? Beyond the impassible? Is Roimohr even out there? If so, I hope he's there. Warm and away. I hope the rest for all of us.*

Stories of the same kin continued for hundreds of pages. With each, the fox devoured, a prey for the predator. The more he read, the more he heard of places seen only on map or heard in tale. This hermit had *hardly* been such.

*...I've departed the Gilleriso's. They've given me passage along Lake Dolioh. As I told you before, pages faithful, they think me a surveyor named Ikelton. Another lie. How many more must I create in this search?...*

*...Asda Fraye. Waters blue, islands ripe with bright and sandy shores. I wish to stay. My soul...it can feel the tug of rest. Here I'm simply Tolton. No surname, no title, no deadly past. Can I not be Tolton?...*

Foxtamas was in for a *treat.*

"Queenie," asked Bunns, breaking the tranquil silence of the afternoon waters, "yer have any memory of seein' Rillem? As ah kid?"

The princess glanced up from her rowing. She'd let the gilded glimmers transfix her, like paints of dark and light swirling at her fingertips.

"Can't say I do. All my memories before mother died are blurry. I'm betting *you* don't remember either, do you?" she replied, smirking.

"Nae, Ah was listenin', right from mum's belly. Ah had nothin better tae do!"

"Of *course!"* She playfully struck her forehead. "How'd I ever doubt you?"

"Ah dunno, happens tae often."

As the conversation died down, Acirema watched Bunns, carefully. She envisioned him shifting from a proud, jovial rower to the broken boy she'd seen huddled beneath the tree last night. He'd yet to bring the subject to life. It felt like the anger at himself had suddenly vanished, nothing more than a passing dream. Such devastation would take her *weeks* to sort through and get over. How had he bounced back so quickly?

Unless…

"Um…are you feeling alright, Bunns?" She asked with wobbling words. The jackalope looked over at her, confused.

"Never better! Weh're adventurin', ain't weh?" Nothing about him seemed to remember the tears that stained him just one sleep prior.

"Yeah, yes, right. But…you know you don't have to be fun and fine *all* the time. If you need to talk, or open up—"

"Nae lassie, Ah'm not baein' fun," he shot back, winking at her." Ah'm just baein' meh."

"But yesterday, with the map…"

"Ah minor setback, tha's all. Ain't got room tae complain when ol' Rillem got us set with this lassie."

Acirema nodded. She looked away and focused once more on waves. Something had to be up. His rejections felt too strong, too planned. Too…

*"Guys!"*

Foxtamas burst like thunder from the cabin, journal in hand, with the lightning of unbridled excitement electrifying him. "Y'all gotta see all this!"

Bunns and Acirema exchanged confused glances. The fox plopped between them and flashed open the book.

"What in Evon did you find?" Acirema asked.

"*So* much! Rillem went all across the world. Literally from north to south! Just listen to these stories, they're insane!"

"Ah bet!" laughed Bunns. "Yer shoulder better, Scottoh?"

"Yeah, why?"

"Ah'm gonna take ah quick break an' check out tha' crow's nest."

"So you want me to take your shift?"

"Aye, just for ah smidge." Bunns winked at him. The kind of wink that assured 'a smidge' would be anything but.

The paddle nestled back into Foxtamas' paws as Bunns bounded up the ladder. Queenie would have to listen to what the fox found, it seemed. Hopping in the nest, he found it a bit tight, but nothing out of the ordinary. Its apple-basket shape still fit him just as it did when he sailed as Winthrop Pirate.

He plopped down and let his feet dangle out over the sides. Being so high up, his view spanned far, gazing at the glittering river ahead and the bushy treetops equaling him in height. A smile overtook him. Peace lowered his eyes. A warm wind, warning of the incoming afternoon sun, enveloped him as a quiet tune parted his resting lips—or, rather, an ode to his invisible blanket.

Yes, Oh! Yes, Oh!

'Tis the wind at last!

Off we go, off we go,

With it at our backs…

Below, Foxtamas and Acirema listened to the lulling song drift into a lullaby until it petered out into a snore. They just shook their heads. Bunns deserved the rest, of course; yet somehow, he couldn't go without a song to sing or tune to strum.

As they rowed, the landscape of Mechmilne slowly began to shift. At points the tree line cut away, revealing a jolt of rolling fields. Tiny farmhouses guarded the land far from the Runnel's shores. Other times *The Losmo* sailed beside a small hamlet established near the rushing flow. As they passed, the cries of children, jumping and waving their hands with squeals, raced alongside them. They tried to keep up with the dainty ship. Sadly, their growing legs were no match for the stream, and the ship, once a fascination overtaking their afternoon, slipped away as a long, lost memory, never to be recovered until the reminiscing that always comes when old age nears.

Whilst sailing past a winding, stony beach, Foxtamas allowed himself to slip away and gaze into the breaking waters below. He caught glimpse of a river salmon busying along. The fish seemed intrigued by the absurd dark cloud hovering so close to its home. Just that look, the assumption of its humanity and livelihood, was all the fox needed.

Sparks of imagination fluttered around him like the start of a bonfire, asking where this fish had been born, what its family looked like, and now to where it swam and why. The questions rushed to him like the Runnel itself. But he pushed further, deeper, even. He came across trails stretching towards times before that single salmon, signposts to a land predating the boat beneath his feet, Rillem, Foxlaris, his friends, all of it. An urge burned inside him to simply see the world as those now buried had; to experience the potential it would one day provide the traveling trio.

Oh, what families tasted of these waters on their journeys, or hermits sheltered away in the thickets twisting in the shallows. What legends of old could have possibly sailed on the same stream in a ship of their own. Lord Eobin of the Blue? Sir Emri Helmstead? None would ever know. The history of this land lay solely in the faded inks of a few lone tomes.

Yet outside its pages Evon continued unbound. Fields turned to forest without ever making a sound. Somewhere, beyond all sight and mind of the common Evoneer, a flower blossomed in its own quiet nook. Her petals drank daylight and dew until age withered her back down to the ground from which she grew.

Then she was gone.

No one ever knew of her existence except herself, a self no longer with the world. The individual lives and loves of these who called this place home in their lifetime—brief as a memory yet infinite in the moment—were lost. Gone. Dead of the second death.

Their only heirloom remaining? The one sign that, even without a name or face, laugh or smile, proved beyond a doubt they existed? Well, to find it, you simply have to look around.

Legacy is not just in our books. It's in our bones.

Foxtamas waded in that awe. A tree planted in its waters. The fruit of peace growing plump and near his tongue, yet the fear of its rotting driving him away from a bite.

What do lives mean if no one remembers them?

What of love? What of fellowship?

What of this land and the stories within it? Do they not matter? Do we live to be forgotten? What's the point? What's any of it—

He forced his mind off the trails and back onto the logs of the hull, practically spitting away the taste. Traveling those roads led him to a doom Bunns and Acirema would once again have to rescue him from. That...that he *must* avoid. If not for his own sake, then for theirs.

Returning, the fox found the golden afternoon light lagging behind the spacious Mechmilnian trees. Raw beauty. The shade of honey illuminating his fur. Night would not be far behind now.

And by the time it fell, Bunns still slept. Foxtamas and Acirema carefully docked the vessel below a patch of aged willow trees, their branches waving by like silk upon the breeze. It was decided they'd take an evening meal but still prepare something for the jackalope (if he ever woke). It *had* been a tiring few days for him, after all.

The princess brought out plates of sliced apple and dried fish. Foxtamas thanked her, and the pair began to dine on their Rillem-gifted supper.

"Y'know, I asked Bunns earlier, but what do you think we're gonna do after all this is over?" said the fox. It almost felt wrong to talk over the tranquil river waters. A light melody of forest bugs danced in tandem with the cadence of ripples nudging them one way, then the next. The rising moon, steeping the Runnel in a trance of black and rolling, lapping white, set the stage for a nipping wind to usher in a call for night, a call for rest. Had their stomachs not been empty, the pair would have obeyed.

"I didn't expect you to be thinking that far," Acirema replied, voice just above a whisper.

"I guess I get prepared when I'm scared."

"Tell me then, what've you prepared?"

"Well, after we make it to the Fulnoa and have them go into the East and get Foxlaris back—with our help, of course—I might just build a house in Winthrop. Stop leeching off the Cammonts and all that."

"Oh stop, you know that's nonsense!"

"No, really. They've provided for me long enough, and I don't think they'd like me hanging around when I'm any more grown than I am. Just think, Reinden was out around our age and they were *more* than fine with it."

"I guess," she sighed. "It would be a good use for all those woodworking skills."

"Exactly. Who knows, Bunns might join me if he doesn't go off galivanting somewhere. He did say he wanted a family though."

Acirema nearly spat out her fish.

"*Bunns*? You sure you heard him right?"

"Right as rain."

"My word. That's the *last* thing Winthrop needs. A bunch of rogue Bunnses running around—"

"That's what I told him!"

They giggled together. Acirema took pause in her eating and checked above at the crow's nest. Snores still erupted.

"Speaking of Bunns, though," she started, "has he acted...strange...here lately? Just a little off?"

Foxtamas shook his head while taking a bite.

"Not that I've noticed. Why? Was it about the map last night?"

"That's my guess."

"He seemed to have bounced back just fine."

"And that's what worries me…" The princess let her head droop. "Just keep an eye out for him, okay? I don't want him keeping things from us if we can help him."

"Yeah, of course," nodded Foxtamas. He gave her a smile of assurance.

"Thank you. But anyway, this house of yours. What about Foxlaris? Would he live there too?"

"Oh, probably not."

"Why?"

"He's always wanted to go off to Mikyill and such. Once him and Aster get married I doubt—"

"Woah, slow down," once again, Acirema sat shocked at the words of her friend. "I thought *you* liked Asterlyn?"

"I do, or, well, I *did.* But she was always more into him. I mean, she sought him out at Grammo Day, and that was right before this all went down. I don't wanna get in the way of anything. He deserves her, especially after coming back from whatever is happening to him over there." Foxtamas turned to her and tried to show a cheery face. Or at least one of contentment. But neither came out.

"Foxtamas…"

"No, enough about me. What about you, huh? There's gotta be just a few things planned for royalty," the fox asked.

"Just a few." Although she wished to join his joking, Acirema couldn't force a laugh. No, her brown eyes wandered instead. Down the river, across the shore, up to the moon; anywhere and everywhere, except to the future. "Father will have something set for me, that's for certain. Probably more preparation to become Queen, or finally letting suitors flood in."

"That can be exciting…right?"

"Maybe. It might all still be chaos once we get back. Who knows what plans Father has now that the Bridge failed. That was his focus for so long."

"True."

Both sat still, listening to the creak of *The Losmo* as it joined in the soothing summer symphony.

"I just guess that…my future will not be as exciting as yours, or Bunns', or Foxlaris'—"

"Oh, come on now, Acirema! You'll be the *Queen* of *Winthrop*. That's a lot better than being some peasant boy."

"Not by much."

Shaking his head, Foxtamas set aside his meal and turned towards her. His blue eyes sparkled like deep-water diamonds as he tried to smith together some stellar words of advice.

"I know this doesn't mean a whole lot coming from me, but there's not a lotta worth in worrying and making the worst of it now. When the future and all of its challenges come, I know you'll know *exactly* what to do about it." He knew his words were hollow. Had they been given to him, he'd have rolled his eyes in reply. Still, from her graveyard of a face, a grin flowered.

"You're right, and I appreciate it, but you *must* know it's *incredibly* bold for *you* to give that advice," she snickered.

"Hey! Just takes one to know one I guess!"

The friends chuckled together before finishing up their dinner. It became obvious as the stars grew bright and sky above dark that a certain Bunnclar Cammont would *not* be waking. So, for the first time since the start of their journey, Foxtamas and Acirema found themselves asleep at a nice, early time.

# 10

# "Brew the Taste an' Brew It Strong"

"Theeeere yer are, Scottoh. Thought yer'd never join us."

His voice cut through the blackened bliss of sleep like an axe to a sapling. Foxtamas jumped up in shock. He'd been on a boat, no, a *ship,* one with pirates and mercenaries and...poets, strangely, and they were off to this prison island where they'd encountered rocking waves that felt so *real,* and—

He looked overboard.

They were moving.

That's why.

Bunns sailed *The Losmo* down the Runnel without a shred of help. He worked the navigational sail to turn the harsh bends but let the gentle push of the stream carry the vessel along. The early morning hours made him a one-jackalope-band.

"Why are you sailing already?" groaned out Foxtamas.

"Had nothin' better tae do. Ah was oup at dawn while yer tae were still sleepin'. Rillem said weh'd reach tha' old mill at the end o' the day. So, if weh started ah bit early, weh should bae makin' et tae New Lothlock before nightfall."

You couldn't argue with that. Drowsy, Foxtamas nodded and took one long, day-starting stretch before grabbing his paddle. It was right back to boating.

The day carried on much like the previous. Shanties were sung, sails were adjusted, and everyone moved from shift to shift without question. The expanse around them only grew wider, more open. Cuts in the forest led to long valleys hiking up bare ridges. Mechmilne looked to be balding. Through it all, each crewmember accepted one key truth: this land was new, and home lay far, far behind them.

Bunns' eyes kept ready as the colorful dusk faded to the inevitable blanket of night. The mill had to be close. Already the Runnel began to narrow, its waters giving one last flourish before the end. Perhaps, then, it didn't lay at *exactly* where the river stopped. Maybe, Bunns figured, it was hidden amongst the bankside shrubbery.

He peered into the foliage. Nothing. Just darkness.

Or, wait, something.

A little bit of movement.

No, that was nothing.

Nothing *new*, really. He'd spotted traveling merchants breaking along the coast before. None moved as…hastily though…

"FYE!"

*ZWAT!!! ZWING!! ZUNKK!!!*

Arrows, tipped silver upon a maroon shaft, fired from both sides of the Runnel. One narrowly grazed Bunns' shoulder, landing into the mast behind him.

"GET DOWN!" he shouted to the others while hiding behind the central post. Foxtamas stood one step away. An arrow had already pinned his cape to the ground. In his fear, he ripped it away and ducked near Bunns.

Acirema ran out of the cabin.

"What's going—"

*ZIP!!!*

One more step and she'd be pinned to the wall.

"Stay back! Weh're getting' fired at!" Bunns yelled to her. Another volley flew over, again missing the trio. "Get to the cabin, Scottoh!"

"W-W-What about you?"

"Ah got a plan, just go!"

Foxtamas didn't spare a second. He sped off, and once there, looked back to the jackalope for direction.

But he already felt the plan in action.

The entirety of *The Losmo* tilted, just as it had during the rapids, from a sharp turn of the frontal sail. Then, without so much as a warning cry from Bunns, it tilted the other way, upturning the cabin, Foxtamas and Acirema included. The maneuver caught the arrows on the ship's side and threw off the attackers long enough for Bunns to dash to the others.

"Queenie!" he cried, "Yer shoot at 'em from the window. Scottoh, Ah need yer tae row while Ah dodge. Weh can out run 'em an' book et tae Lothlock when weh reach the mill. Got meh?"

"Y-Yes," Foxtamas muttered between staggered breath. Acirema nodded beside him. Her bow, already in hand, was knocked in a heartbeat. "But who are they!?"

"Ah dunno, just hurry!"

With the combined efforts of the boys, *The Losmo* gave one last push forward. The attackers followed close on the shoreline yelling wild, incoherent yaps. Many an arrow flew to the boat but fell short on either the outside log or parting white water. The fox looked on, mortified. His paddle rattled between his paws. Every muscle in his body beat the oar against the water, the whizzing sounds of flying death whistling past his ears. One shot and he'd be gone. Dead in the middle of Evon. Foxlaris wouldn't be saved, his friends left to carry his dead, arrow-riddled body—"

"HOLD ON" the warrior burst out. Foxtamas shot up and saw the low, broken mill rushing towards them. Rotted and falling in upon itself, it blocked the end of the Runnel, squeezing the mighty stream into nothing more than a trickle.

Bunns had no aim to greet it.

Instead, with a sharp shift of the sail, the vessel careened towards the bank.

*CRAAUAUCKCK!!!*

The frontmost hull collided with the rocks waiting on shore. Thee moment they touched land, all three flung themselves off. Such hard footing took them off guard. Standing felt too rigid, running even more so. But they didn't have time to adjust. Two of the quicker troops bounded from the woods in front of them. They charged forward for an attack.

"Get away!" Foxtamas yelled. Clueless. He fumbled for his axe, but felt it caught in the beltloop. He readied his fist in a panic.

It worked.

A bolt from the crossbawn shot out and sank deep in the villain's eye. His partner turned towards him, horrified; however, he too was caught off guard as a paddle, wielded by Bunns, cracked across his skull.

"Atta lad," huffed the jackalope. He patted Foxtamas on the shoulder, but neither acknowledged the other. They only stared at the bodies at their feet.

The bodies of the same Eastern monsters they'd fought days prior.

"Book et! *Now!"* Bunns finally shouted, forcibly pulling Foxtamas away from the carnage.

His blue eyes refused to leave the scene.

Darkness fully consumed Evon. The unkempt branches and briars engulfed the fleeing friends. Grunts trailed them. Yet the flight in the foliage lasted mere minutes as the land beneath their feet shifted.

The trees parted and gave way to a valley long dead. Tall, yellowed grass waved across the moon-kissed land. It led to a ridge looming in the distance. Husks of rotted trees dotted the distance, crackling into the air like the spread of lightning.

For Foxtamas, the grass met him at his elbow. The others struggled to slice through it.

"Are those the ones from Nohsis?" asked Acirema between breaths.

"Ah reckon!

"How'd they find us?"

"Ah don't know! There, bunker down!" Bunns pointed to a fallen tree, now hallowed into a log hidden beneath the grass. The trio barreled behind it.

"W-W-Why aren't we running?" gasped the fox, only for Bunns to nip his lips shut. He lifted up a single finger—a sign to shut up and listen.

"They're tae close tae outrun this time. Weh'll distract them, or fight them, then run," he whispered back. Still, the words meant nothing. Foxtamas' eyes darted every which way, his body on the verge of leaping away towards the ridge. "Scottoh, look at meh. Ah gotcha, laddie. Ah won't ever let ah single one of them Eastern bastards touch yer, got meh?"

Gulping, Foxtamas nodded, his gaze set only to the steadied eyes of Bunns.

"Y-Yeah, I gotcha."

"Good."

Then he froze. The noise behind them, once a jagged mess of running and shouting, calmed. Bunns shushed them again before rising to take a peek.

A monstrous band of Easterners all too familiar from the first night of adventure stalked the field a short way in. The taller commanders lit the scene with lanterns, practically pyres once spread out across the grasses. They barked searching orders in their lost, twisted tongue. By doing so, they made themselves easy to spot; worse, easy targets.

The jackalope plopped back down. A plan scrawled upon his mind quicker than his paw at Flapdragon.

"Ah got et. Yer two start towards the ridge, but keep low. Ah'll draw 'em off and lead 'em left, away from yer. Once Ah have 'em all twisted around Ah'll meet yer oup there. If they spot yer, Queenie, use yer bow."

"I used all my arrows back on the boat." She nodded to the quiver on her back, upright and empty.

Bunns' eyes grew, and his boot rattled in anticipation. The plan may not be fully secure—and that was a risk he couldn't take.

"Use this. Scottoh, yer might have tae shoot."

"Again?" he asked.

"Just in case." Bunns lifted the mallet from his belt (still marked by the face of the minotaur) and tossed it to Acirema. "Now go, an' keep low. The grass is pretty tall, so they shouldn't bae seein' yer. Yer might not bae seein' *them* either."

"Be careful," the princess whispered back, gripping the mallet tight. The last sight she saw of him was a cheeky grin before his fluffy little body, antlers and all, disappeared into the field.

*Finally.*

No more running. No more pain. The hike westward exhausted the very blood within him. Bugbears weren't built for such stress.

Breyhuf scanned the field in front of the party with a snarled yet invigorated grin. Reyhuf, his twin, brought up the rear. Together they'd avenge their fellow soldiers and stomp out this murderous band, just as Vorde Velrick asked. The wolf was right about these Westerners: they craved nothing but Eastern blood on their tongues.

It was time they faced the same suffering. No one could *possibly* hide in the expanse of grass surrounding them, miles on either side of open air. One murmur among the veld and the bugbear would have his prey.

His black, swollen eyes pried deep into the sprigs at his feet. Even with the brightness of his lantern he still found it hard to distinguish between movement and shadow. Wait, there looked to be something at his left.

He turned.

Gah, nothing.

Breyhuf sighed and barked at the scouts behind to pick up their pace. Without more eyes up front they'd be out there until the dawn. Yet, he couldn't quite get the command out. It...it didn't thicken in his throat.

A stinging pain replaced it. Sharper than any cut from his training. And there, his light, had it gone out? Why did it dim? Why did *everything* dim and, and spin, and, why...why was...

Reyhuf watched his brother collapse but feet before him, the star in his neck glimmering in the light of his lantern.

The entire Eastern company halted. Then another of their ranks crumbled to the ground with a croak. The commander twisted around terrified, begging to catch a glimpse of the attacker.

*"There!"* he shouted. The grass parted on their left flank, and a small trail started scurrying away. "Levft! Go, go!" his raspy commands flung out. The platoon obeyed.

In the chaos of the troops zipping one way and then the next, the heavy-armored Reyhuf barked out once again, "Styeborns, go up anz seerch! *Now!"*

"Take tha' yer lil' beastie," Bunns whispered to himself, feet flying through the grass. He kept his antlers tipping out at the top and trail wide enough for the enemies to track. They'd done a fair job following him this far, so it'd be a shame for them to get lost now.

Shouts and volleys of arrows flung towards him. Most would flee in pure horror seeing the shafts fall half an inch from their tails. But not Bunns. Not the Winthrop Warrior. No, every missed shot hit him with a surge of pride. *No one* could beat him. He could stop the running now and fight them, bare fisted, and win without a scratch.

They chased their predator into the night.

Death didn't trail them—it led them on.

*"STOP!! GET BACK!!"*

The cry broke out across the plain. Bunns knew the voice—loved it from the moment it peeped up amidst the cold that old winter night.

He halted in his tracks and peered over the grass. Sure enough, right where Foxtamas and Acirema should have been, two gangly buzzards dove down from the air. Worse, the lantern light had turned course away from him.

"Nonononono!" he scolded through gritted teeth. The sudden stop lasted just long enough for an alp to break through the grass. The poor soul never got off a swing of his dagger as a star fired off towards him, sinking into the depths of the heart. He didn't stand a chance against Bunns usually; he certainly didn't when failure fought the jackalope as well.

*SWISH! SWIPE!*

The first vulture's rapier landed closer to the fox with every hit. Foxtamas had acted in time to retrieve his axe but used it as little more than a shield.

"Stop it, stop!" His words did nothing. The bird's pale, lanky neck, hollow eyes, and snarled beak refused to let up. Beating and beating and beating, wearing him down like a river to a rock. After a near miss against the fox, he pushed closer, and in the same breath, a hammer thudded against his skull, dropping him.

"Hit him, Foxtamas!" Acirema cried from behind the bird, mallet tinged with blood.

He acted.

His hands squeezed through tremors of fear and terror. The fox regripped the weapon and raised it overheard, thrusting it down on the stunned creature. It slid through the neck. No different than the last slash at a tree. A dark, crimson blood splashed back at Foxtamas, flecking his fur. But before he could take notice, the second vulture swooped down and bodied him to the ground.

"Foxtamas!"

"*Gah!! Get it off!!*"

This one didn't care for a weapon. His raw break smacked him across the side of the head—all Evon swirled.

"Get! *Back!*"

*WHAM!*

Acirema slammed the hammer against him once, then twice, then again and again in a fury. The beast turned to her unphased. His talon leapt from atop the fox and kicked her back and stumbling through the grass.

"A-Acirema!" Foxtamas shouted, breath sparse from the weight of the bird.

"Zit ztil!" the vulture snapped back. He raised his beak for another blow. Foxtamas tried to dodge, but even *more* of the hot, sticky blood soaked him. He blinked through it and rolled. The weight paining him grew heavier, practically smothering. Gasping, he slid himself out and kicked desperately at the vulture. Only it didn't flinch.

For a star twinkled from its back.

"Get oup, Scottoh, weh gotta move!"

Foxtamas didn't have the capacity to take it all in. Bunns' voice felt ethereal, everywhere yet nowhere at once. Every sense was overwhelmed. He felt the jackalope's hand pinch around his arm; the wicked taste of blood coated his mouth and smell of metal strangled his brain; his eyes watched Acirema scrabble up in a fit of pain, gripping her side, aching to stand; worst, the roars of the Easterners galloping to overtake them and any yell Bunns mustered, his voice begging him to stand and run and *go, just go,* anything to avoid their death becoming more certain by the second.

He blinked in and out of focus as they sprinted until a bite snatched his tail. The poor, shocked fox gasped for air and tumbled backwards, yanked to the ground.

Pain seared through his lower half that forced from him a whimpered shout. He whipped around and found a dagger, thrown at random, pinning him to the ground, his body helpless in a thickening puddle of his own blood.

That final straw broke him.

Bunns and Acirema looked back right as their friend collapsed. Despite the firelight closing in, they fell back to him.

"What happened?" gasped Acirema, kneeling at Foxtamas' side with Bunns.

"T-T-Tail." The fox, spinning in the pain and chaos, held to consciousness by the strength of a single finger.

"Stay still." With a yank, she pulled the dagger free, prompting a sharp cry from the fox. The white tip—now a paintbrush readied with a stroke of red—held on by a few matted hairs. It would detach by the time they reached the ridge.

The princess glanced the blade over before tossing it aside. Yet…she didn't. Couldn't. Her eyes widened, and mouth hung agape.

"Can yer run?" Bunns asked. He tried to help his friend up, but Foxtamas didn't budge.

"Bunns, I-I can't," he moaned between breaths, hands dirtied by the mud made from his blood. "I'm too scared, I'm hurt, I can't, *I can't.*" The words flooded together into incoherency.

"Yes yer can!"

*"No!* I'm scared! *I'm scared!"*

Bunns just nodded. Any word and the entirety of Evon would know that, deep within, his soul echoed the same feeling.

He turned to the beasts. Any minute and they'd burst through the grass. Without Acirema's arrows, all they had were his stars, and too many had been lost in his rush to kill the vultures. Bunns knew he couldn't carry the fox, or drag him, or move him from his hunkered-down ball. Escape, at least with all three of them alive...was impossible.

Hope vanished. This would be their final stand.

Just over the grass, the lantern, held high by the running Reyhuf, dangled into view. A second more and the rest would arrive.

Bunns stood before his friends. Acirema reached up and pulled him back, but he shrugged her off.

"Stop it!" she cried. "Help me get him up!"

"Nae," he whispered, and turned his head to the approaching beasts.

*"Bunns!"*

He shook his head, reaching instead for his stars. The dead grass rubbed at his sides. The dead, dry grass. No different than the thatch atop the Cammont Household. The kind he and Foxlaris picked to repair Mr. Ochet's roof after the jarring incident that...that burned...

His paws snatched Foxtamas' hand. Not to hold it, but aim it.

"Bunns, stop, I said—"

"Squeeze your hand!"

"Wha—"

"SQUEEZE!"

A bolt fired from the crossbawn. It sailed, not to the head of a troll or weapon of a bugbear. No, its destination lay with the light.

Like an arrow to the sun.

*craaAaAaAAaAAACCKK!!*

It hit true. The lantern's flaming oil exploded from its glass prison. Both shards and flame drenched Reyhuf; the lapping blue flames consumed him. Panicked, he lost control of his body and rubbed against those nearest to him, dousing them and the parched grass below. Within seconds, a fire mightier than the moon erupted in the field.

"Go go go!" Bunns cried, his grip still tight on the fox. Foxtamas forced the last of his strength to his legs. Fear of the fire outweighed any exhaustion or pain.

Together, the trio bolted from the field and to the ridge. Behind lay nothing but hoarse, labored cries and failed retreats. The blaze gorged without cease and discrimination. The deaths had no audience but those waiting to be devoured. Neither friend dared glimpse the carnage.

The moment they reached the ridgetop, tendrils of exhaustion ripped them down to the rugged, leafy floor. From it they had a look out over the field. Massive, infinite plumes of black and maroon started to shield the whipping flames. Dead bodies littered the outskirts of the charred grave. A few had retreated towards the Runnel; others behind them had been caught and swallowed. For what felt like years, their pitiful screams begged for help, for remorse, yet fell on deafened ears. No one alive heard them. No one free to drag them away. The shouts didn't reach beyond the grave.

Foxtamas couldn't look for long. Too many memories arose from the tainted smell of smoke and heat. He focused instead on his tail. Blood oozed from the wound and turned what remained of the tip an ugly brown. The pain drummed against his ears, louder than the rattles of his lungs, the pound of the migraine squeezing the sides of his head.

He scavenged for extra rags in his pack to wrap it with when a murmur escaped Acirema. Her light, graceful voice tried to form something.

"Wha' yer say, Queenie?" asked the jackalope, sweat and sears hot and heavy upon his face.

"Your dagger…from Rillem. You have it?" Her eyes looked up from a bloodied object in her hands. Tears swelled.

"Et's in mah bag, why?"

Trembling, she lifted the knife that had cut Foxtamas' tail. Turning it around, she presented the pommel. The "M" with a boldened sapphire "V".

The realization drowned them. Drowned them just as the river should have days prior. Their trail from Nohsis led to Rillem. Led to his Glum, his hut, and…if the weapon was any indication…his demise.

Bunns shuddered. He breathed a soft "no" and took the dagger in his paw.

This was on them.

All of them.

The smoke finally caught the wind and blew towards the ridge. Everyone lay smothered in its shroud. None could see, none could breathe. Every sense was overtaken by the burnt stench of death.

# II

# "For in our Hearts we're right to feast—"

The Styline creaked more than usual. Its buggy bore the weight of not only Foxlaris and Iota, but the entire Vayneguard, decorated in their coats of white. Each wore a stern gaze. One of anticipation.

One of war.

The deciding battle between the Meki Totadora and the Eastern Army loomed. Both spies and word from the Blue Caps directly confirmed that, at dawn, the two sides would face at the Village's gate. Tactics like these were unusual, especially for the guerilla fighters of the Cult.

It made sense then that rumors spread. Some of ambushes, others of deceit, most prophesying a horrific attack upon Crimsdon Hall. None, however, reached the ear of Foxlaris, oh no. He dismissed the notions at any sign. No, he focused solely on the brandishing of his broken body.

Velrick himself took him for the fitting. A flurry of tailors and metalworkers worked tirelessly to form his armor. The final design blended the Crimsdon color into sheets of flexible, pointed metal, finely detailed with slim furnishings of gold. The plates protected his injuries from worsening. His helmet, fit with a gilded visor, came prepared with a metal ear crafted in; likewise, for both his tail and leg, extra padding formed around them to assure no more damage could be done. As for his weapons, a new axe donned his arm. It melted seamlessly into the armor behind it, creating the illusion of a half-fox, half-metal hybrid. The same went for his sword. Previous captains and generals of Vordemohr had used it, a symbol of their prowess with darkened blade and hilt. Now, for the first time, it was wielded by a Western hand.

His eye darted to the healt beside him. White armor on and silvclaws readied, she too sensed the approaching fight. None knew what to expect.

"There, Foxlaris. Our army gathers." Her pale, metal-laced finger pointed towards the rising Village. No smoke rose from the stone buildings. No lanterns flickered in the early light of the dawn. Instead, a structured mass of black and red stood at the gate, filling in the finality of their formation. It was hardly the full power of Vordemohr, but the fraction showed its might.

"We're the final ones then?" the fox asked back.

"Mostly."

That settled the few nerves still tingling through his body and let his focus shift inward, towards the scar left by the dragon. With the right line of breathing, the lowering world of the Styeline faded, and a void darkened his mind. The boiling scales sizzled his palm. The warrior knowledge flooded into him like an infection through a scar. There his soul stayed. The longer he lingered, the more blood he felt fueling his inner warrior and teaching his body the way it should have always moved. Both he and his blades would soon taste the feast Dearg prepared for them.

"Follow me and my lead. I'll make sure today is full of promise for you. Not death."

Iota's cold words broke the fox's focus. Opening his red eye, he found they had reached the abandoned town and equally empty tarasque. The beasts wished to join the excitement of the morning, not labor in their duties. But such was their burden.

Foxlaris obeyed. The band marched forward, passing through the still streets and stones like a stroll through a graveyard of giants. Even the air, in all its thickness, only whispered.

"Dol has everything planned," Iota began again. "He doesn't speak your tongue, so I will translate if necessary. Just stay sharp and sure of yourself."

"Who's Dol?"

"You'll see. Better to wait on your eyes than fall short with words."

The fox nodded and carried on. All the while, flashes of Dearg continued to consume him.

Roughly a thousand troops stood at the edge of the Village. They formed in rows leading the full way up to the gate. Both Crimsdon doors stood open, gifting a peek in the shadowy, twisted nature of the Darkwood Forguile.

No Cult. No Blue Caps. No Meki Totodora.

The Vaynegaurd and their leaders strolled almost directly to the front, halting and merging into a pre-assembled line. Foxlaris thought himself puny in comparison to the others. Towering bugbears and goblins sapped his upfront fortitude. Luckily, the burning in his chest to serve Velrick and the fallen Easterners replaced the rubble. This *was* his place. None could tell him otherwise.

The cobbled ground below suddenly rumbled a deep, rhythmic hymn.

*Boom.*

Foxlaris felt it through the metal of his arm.

*BOOM.*

The metal within his hand.

*BOOOOMM!!*

Not a single head turned but his. His glance was short but brought with it all he needed to know.

Dol had arrived.

The formation parted at his every step. The middle split no different than Evon as the massive, hulking tarasque, four times as large as his brethren, stomped forward inch by incredible, indomitable inch. His braided mane had been shocked of color and left to a frayed gray that ran through his stony paws and spiked shell. Some of the common tarasque viridian tried to poke through, but the scarring over his body, so thick and wound like threadwork, overpowered it. Relentless slobber soaked his bulging jowl. Beastly were his eyes. Nothing budged the soulless pupils and their simmering mix of crimson and sallow. Every muscle of his gargantuan being hummed with volatility. All except the beast's most foreboding feature.

Nailed into his shell, in between the spikes large enough to impale Foxlaris, sat a crossbow of unimaginable proportions. The Crimsdon-made weapon bore bolts the size of logs, smaller arrows and ammunition tied to the side, and a seat at the back for the alp operator to control. From it wound a conglomeration of ropes and chains fixed within Dol's mouth. One bite and the contraption fired. Alone the crossbow would be fearsome; atop Evon's largest tarasque, it shifted the entire morale of the battlefield.

"General Dol, the Walking Weapon," the frigid breath of Iota whispered to the fox, nudging him to turn back around. "Eyes ahead. He senses respect." Foxlaris didn't know whether or not his commander was serious, but either way, he wasn't about to take a chance.

He faced forward before Dol marched past. It took craning his entire neck up to see the fullness of the general. Once positioned at the head of the battalion, a rigid roar rumbled from hid slobbering mouth.

"*GOOORMIIITIOOON.*"

One word, and the army shuffled. Those relaxed stiffened; shields and weapons flung into the proper position. Foxlaris eyed around at the command and followed suit. He lifted himself to a fighting stance. Had foxes been native to East Evon, he would have blended in perfectly.

Once the brash noise of the readying silenced itself, Dol turned towards the empty forest in a single step. The bottom of his jaw unhinged, and out poured a roar so devouring, so dreadfully blood spilling, that the trees yards away bent back to kneel before the predator. He beget intimidation. He frolicked in the fear. And he beckoned an answer.

Forguile knew the proper response.

As did the lone healt rising from the sickly wood.

He crept forward towards the gate. His armor, a mismatched mess of sapphire-stained metal and leather layered with tufts of blue feathers, stood out in stark contrast to the paleness of his aged, wrinkled skin. Calmness carried him. The companion beside his gait. Every slowed step reminded the Easterner's behind the Village's walls that, had they been in front of such an army, their movements would not be so light.

Foxlaris scuttled back when the healt's eyes came into focus. They weren't matte and soulless like those towering next to him. These were *blue*. Fiery like maddened waves, a raging tempest throttling and thrashing in the midst of a cloudless day. Their power burned like pyres on a hill cloaked by midnight.

He shrugged off the surprise as mere nerves—but nerves never demand an unbreaking attention.

The healt halted just feet away from door and warrior alike. Not an utterance passed among the crowd. His head held high, the Blue Cap gazed across the Vordemohrian front.

"You will kill me today."

Each word bolted forth with a crispness and clarity. The years did not show. "You will kill all of us if you can. Let it be so. May today be the last time our faces meet, both as warriors and fellow Eastern souls. Let our blood stain this forest, stain your Crimsdon doors. Rip the life bit by bit from our bodies and bones. Feed them to your beasts. Burn them for fuel in your waking forges and halls that never tire. Take from us all which you can. "Yet we will not lose this war."

His feathered foot stepped forward.

"Our Author still lives, and forever he shall. You may wipe every Meki off the face of Evon and still he would remain. You despise him when it is yourselves who deserve such wrath. You turn away from your walls when the enemy lives within! Your servitude lies in defending the Plague who rots this very land. How long until you see!? The Vorde keeps us and our land in this sickness, *not* the Author!"

Another step.

“You still have time. Our war is not waged. Roihelm shall indeed aid against the fall of Vordemohr and all who stake to control it. This is your chance, warriors of the East—hear this plea! Hear *him!*

One more.

His final.

*SSHHHLUUNNKKK!!!*

Foxlaris blinked. In a single breath, the mouth of Dol twitched, the string of his crossbow loosened, and the healt, shocked, ruptured through the forest, a puff of fine red mist taking his place and coating the bolt pinning his blue remains to a tree.

“TCHIIIEEELZZZ!” commanded the general. All ranks raised their shields above their foreheads and ducked in unison. The call held true as, spawning from the Darkwood, a vicious onslaught of blue-feathered arrows sprang out. Dol merely shook them off; Foxlaris, however, dropped to his knees.

No shield covered him. Instead, he forced himself close against the Vayneguard who protected their leader with ease. The volley of arrows slipped into the ground left and right. As they did, Dol blared another order.

“FFOOEEEERRRDDD!!!”

The forces ran. They exploded in shouts and hollers tumbling through the gate and towards the Cultists slipping from the ragged boughs and twisted roots. Stray arrows picked off a few rushing alps; the same happened to the Meki.

The fox found himself suddenly strewn in the middle of the chaos. Behind, the ranks pushed and prodded him into scrambling forward. Both Iota and the Vayneguard disappeared, too busy obeying orders to keep up with their Western tag-a-long. Who could blame them? The ferocity of Dol, the ceaseless cries of war, the chance to finally end the blue-capped pests—little did such excitement often culminate.

So, with the world still spinning around him, Foxlaris joined in with the last few rows of soldiers. He *refused* to be left behind and become a burden once again.

Further ahead forces clashed, far deeper into Forguile than he expected. The remaining warriors he sprinted beside finally broke through the gate and into the forest, and as they did, the sun vanished. Only trickles flittered through. Drips of light off a roof. They exposed the thick thorns and brambles reaching down from the shadows. Foxlaris thought night had come upon them. The Cultists, they could hide anywhere in here. How would they battle against them? Where even *was* the battle?

His pace slackened in the darkness. The rest scrambled and rushed down paths of their own. Some kept to the main trail despite its thinning whilst others darted to the right and left, seeking a quicker, brighter way forward. Not the fox. All was foreign, dangerous and exotic in the worst of ways.

After what felt no longer than a few minutes, he looked behind and expected a tunnel of light, only to find an all-consuming black of overgrown trees and leaves. Where had he ended up? Worse, now so far in, the cacophony of fighting blared from every angle. Foxlaris stumbled over root and rock, trying to follow one of the few lagging soldiers deeper into Forguile, yet quickly lost sight as a cough overtook him.

"IOTA! *IOTA!*" screamed his hoarse voice.

No response.

*"PLEASE!"* he beckoned again, trotting somewhere, anywhere away from where he'd gone.

The confusion of the Darkwood soured his mind. He'd no way to the fight nor to those there for his protection. He'd no way forward. He'd no way out. What if no one heard him? Would he die here? Die, a broken boy, in the middle of East Evon? Oh, why was he even there? Why couldn't the River have taken him! He wasn't meant for this. No, he wanted home and family, not war, not fighting.

Any place but this.

Any place but this.

Any place but this…

A place that only worsened the more he wandered. His brown eye eventually adjusted, revealing more of the sickly forest floor. The trees bent low to the ground, forced down by invisible chains. Some leaked a thick, inky sap that pooled into the scene of a murder at their base. Foxlaris swore he felt their wounds while trembling past. Gashes that never healed.

The small peeks of light turned a pale, ghastly violet as rolls of mist flooded in. The fog took away what little vision he had left, leaving the fox blind to nothing but purple and the blackened stalks surrounding him. It hid patches of thorns that blanketed the rocky ground and crawled up into trunks. Had his armor not been forged to precision, the briars would have ensnared him.

He waded through the violet sea until the light of a small clearing parted it just enough to see through. The trees circling the edges stood tall, their claws too short to fully tear out the sun. Relief flooded him. He grasped the hulking roots gnarled into the dirt, the dead grass buried beneath an eternal coat of brittle autumn leaves. The world returned to him. He actually *saw* what he felt and stood taller, calm. For that, he was thankful. Until a back-shattering weight slammed into him.

Foxlaris collapsed to the ground. The attack flattened his lungs and stole the breath from his body. While flailing for air, he flung the mass away from him, catching a glimpse of the assailant.

A young female bat, no older than himself, stared back with a jittering blue glance. She dressed like the Meki healt from before, with a full coat of sapphire feathers and dyed armor. Unlike him, she held no room for peace. Just two thick, readied daggers.

“GHIYAAA!!” she roared, hopping up and charging at the winded fox. He tried to scramble away, kicking leaves and rolling over onto his back, anything to move from the bat’s path.

*“Stop, please! Don’t!”* he shrieked. In his scraping, his paw pushed down on something hard in the brush. He knew that feeling. That grip. The sharp, metal edge sparkling, a thin candle in the darkness of a storm.

It was then he let the dragon move his mind.

"Lead me, Dearg-Fu'Ath."

Foxlaris leapt to his feet, sword in hand, right as the Meki arrived. The bat swung her blades in a flurry. Yet completely missed the fox. He wove backwards like a whipping wind and side stepped her thrust. The dodging gave him the precious seconds to peel back and set his stance, letting his dragon knowledge inform him of where to attack. Once prepared, he launched, meeting her daggers and scraping the edge of her wing.

The mark fueled a kick from the Meki. It landed true and knocked the footing away from Foxlaris. His eye flickered from brown to red—rage thumped through him like a heartbeat. The attacker flew forward with a shout, only to face a flash of crimson and the gleaming edges of both sword and axe. Part of her armor took the blow. The exposed sides of her back caught a slice that streaked down its length. She crashed behind Foxlaris, though scrambled up in the same breath, avoiding the incoming pangs of pain.

The bat's blue eyes shuddered. This wasn't the same beast she'd traced stumbling through the Darkwood. Now, just feet away, he stood tall, broad, arms ready and broken smile bared.

*"AAAHHHHH!!"* Foxlaris unleashed the rage he and Dearg-Fu'Ath shared. His axe shielded his rush, throwing away the futile attacks the Cultist tried to conjure. Blade after blade, hit after hit smashed between them, all in the thorny, brutal outcrop of Forguile. Every blow grew the fox's prowess. The skills burned into his mind flowed forth from him like a breaking dam, overpowering the bat with excellence unseen. Finally, after both sides accepted their fair share of cuts, the axe-hand of Foxlaris slammed into her stomach, lifting her up and cracking her body into the leaves.

The fox pounced, pinning her. He saw the light twinkling in her sapphire eyes, the thundering waves calming as her blood melted into the ashy ground.

*Sword to the neck, slice firm and true. Quickest confirmation of a kill.*

His body read the sentence Dearg wrote within his flesh. One loose of his sword to close the chapter on the poor, poor cultist.

"Y-Y-You…you're…Westerner," puffed the bat, words strained, accented.

They carried such power to erase those of the dragon. His ear pressed closer. Blade fell away.

As if lifted by a second wind, a slight smile grew on her dying face, and a blast of blue illuminated not just her eyes, but the blackened grove. "You see our land. You know the Vorde. He poisons us. H-H-He poisons *you.*"

The red drooped from his single eye. A blink swept it away, back to its natural hue. A rag wiping off blood.

"He's used so many, so long. You're next. D-Don't fall for the trap. Go West…go home. Warn them. S-S-Save Evon from him…Westerner."

He became enveloped by the brightness of her gaze. The words…they mimicked those from the healt, only now more personal. Go West. Go…home. Home. Winthrop.

Friends.

Family…

…Foxtamas…

No. He, he *couldn't,* there was no way. They, no, *he,* his own *brother*, betrayed him. He did this, he sent him over to die and turned him into this monster, put him in this battle, made him the warrior he'd become! No, Foxtamas couldn't save. Couldn't fix *this.* No one there could.

But here…

*Velrick* saved.

*Velrick* made this monster useful. Breathed into him new life. Turned his hands into literal weapons. Weapons for a cause—to uproot the lies of Roihelm and his followers. The follower beneath his blade.

He looked deeper at the bat. Cocked his head.

Had he truly been so…weak? To crave home! *HOME!* Home that wanted him *dead!* Home that stifled all he could *be!*

No. This, yes, *this* was home now. A home that wanted him, *saved* him. The liar in his clutches tried to ruin that with barren, fruitless words all to give control back to the one who so long ago abandoned it.

He was weak before. Failing again now would make him worthless.

Foxlaris wasn't worthless.

He used to be. But never again.

Never.

*Again.*

In the center of the Forguile clearing, the blue of the bat met the returning red of the fox. A purple light simmered between them. The Meki watched in horror as, a blade's width away, the eye of her killer melted into the color of bubbling flesh, searing away the earthen shade. Flames soared from his socket.

Red consumed him.

His sword danced across her neck. Hot, spurting blood painted the fox, but he paid it no mind. He savored the life draining from the bat's body. Nothing saved her. No Roihelm, no fellow cultist. She left Evon staring into the madness her very words provoked.

Once he made his kill certain, Foxlaris rose. Blood soaked his hand, axe, and helmed head. The taste of piping metal flavored his tongue. He glanced back at the ruined body. Fallen feathers, wounded wings. Something about it...changed him. It was his first kill, but it was more than that.

He had...accomplished something.

The thrill of slicing her neck, seeing her fear, and tasting her blood faded, but this time, after such a burst of passion, he wasn't empty. No. Not even close. Something from deep, *deep* within brewed. An unkempt, untamable hell.

Purpose.

*"BAAHAHAHAH!!!"*

His laugh screamed into the abyss surrounding him.

Yes! *PURPOSE!* For once his life felt complete and realized, set straight on a path physically beneath his feet!

His joy connected him to the decrepit trees and rotting ground. Forguile! *The East!* Oh, how they were the same, the very, very same! Tossed aside from a supposed *home*, broken into a form so ugly and repulsive, but given new life, new purpose, *here! YES!* They shared the thorns, the fog, the darkness only those who live within can ever truly appreciate. He was the East, and the East was him. A creature once forced away now blended in seamlessly! Brilliant! *HAH!*

No fear of the forest held him back. He embraced it, just as he did his purpose. A purpose to serve, yes, but one larger than that. One more. A purpose for power. To show how no one could hold him, or withstand him, or make him anything less than he knew himself to be.

He'd serve his Vorde. And he'd rise far and beyond any measure Evon could bring.

The sweetness of freedom, bloodied honey slicking down his chin, made the fox leap away from the grove and dive headfirst into the wood. Nothing stopped his beautiful rage. He flowed as a petal amongst his kin. The dark met dark, the scarred shared their stories in hollow crags, in empty nests, amongst forgotten trails and between the tips of briars. Together Foxlaris sang with the East its haunted hymn. One voice, warbled and wounded, but alive nonetheless.

In his flight, his ear perked at the clash of weapons echoing yards off. The fight! Of course, the fight he'd entered to prove himself. It had worked, alright. Better yet, he'd still time to engage more than a lone, lifeless bat, but the *entirety* of those bird-following fools! Yes!

Yes, to war! To war, *to war!*

Iota, blood-stained and exhausted from the relentless slaughter of the morning, finished off a Meki bugbear with a pointed shove of her Silvclaw to his face. As the beast fell, a ghastly, giggling roar shrieked from behind. She whipped to see the fox, red-coated like herself, charging forth into the hectic fray.

His Dearg-wrought knowledge leapt from his weapons as they wound through a weary alp, cut clean across an unknowing tarmin. Death danced with him. Some of her fellow soldiers stood gawking alongside her; others found the sudden aide a needed boost to finish the battle. Already the fight had drawn longer than expected. One good push and the remaining Blue Caps would either die fighting or run off without their fellow cultists.

The Vayne didn't care about the war, or whether they won here or later. She saw the fox. Saw his brutality. His barbarity.

His…purpose…

Her claws retracted. The beat of her heart stirred as memories stored far away bent the bars of their prison. This wasn't the same Foxlaris who asked if she was an elf; this was exactly what Velrick had always, always wanted…

The fight looked so terribly small from the upper rooms of Crimsdon Hall. Those wishing to watch saw the quick glimpses of blue and the light shakes of trees, but nothing more. Vorde Velrick, though, saw all he needed.

He stood staring out the massive glass window adorning the palace's War Room. Beside stood Getophry, loyal as always, and behind, among the catered breakfast and stuffy books, maps, and charts, a full table of Vordemohr's finest generals.

"It was one thing to send Breyhuf, but Reyhuf too?" spat Mrattle, an old, high-pitched tarmin, too skinny for a real bout of fighting.

"Let the boys play," Ghroat, a hulking, red-tailed vulture replied. He spoke each word with rich deliberation, as if they'd be written into stone. "Better them than us. How would you take to walking that far into the West? Uncharted, no less."

"Worry about the maps one more time—"

"A worry well-planted with such an approaching invasion!" the vulture cut him off.

"But worthless in light of today's battle." A new voice, that of the smooth-talking viper, Yilgelti, slithered into the conversation as she joined the meeting. "Word comes. The victory horn is blown."

"You hear that, my Vorde?" asked the cockatrice. Velrick didn't take note of the tasteless talk. Nothing, it seemed, would break his beady concentration from the glass.

"Oh, I knew already. Just thinking on other things, Getophry. Bigger things." In his paw he stirred a morning concoction. Part spirits, part juice. It added to the calm.

"I see. Are you thinking you've found a new Vayne, then?"

"No." It wasn't a toothy grin that marked him. Or a smile. The look he gave wasn't one of joy or happiness. His face scowled into a twisted look of aged, righteous ferocity.

"I've found our new Champion."

# 12

# "WE DARED TO WALK WHERE MOUNTAINS SLEEP!"

The smoke forced the trio down the ridge. At its end rose an oak taller than the rest of the wood, with foliage large enough to house them for the night. The threat of Easterners had gone; sleep took their tired, weeping souls.

Bunns awoke first. He watched the fat drops of rain plop around him. Dawn had barely begun and already Evon was drenched in the bleakness of a stormy morn, the winds chilled as they battled below a heavy, lonesome sky of gray. He leaned back and rested his head upon the bark. The toll of rowing, running, and fighting kneaded deep into his bones. Worse, the pain of the bruise again began to flare. Sleep beckoned him, even for an hour more.

He couldn't. His mind wouldn't let go of the world, just like his hand wouldn't let go of the knife.

The blue "V" haunted the jackalope. How many times had he shakingly traced it over? How many situations did he devise where Rillem survived, or flew away, or avoided any encounter with the monsters?

It didn't matter. He could still see the owl's ghost. Not the one who struck them in the Glum. He saw the gentleman. The noble warrior who, somewhere far back at the Runnel's end, lay slain. No family. No Velvediers. No…anything.

A single tear trickled down his cheek as he closed his eyes, begging to catch up to sleep's call before she faded away. His mask was back on.

Clenched firm around his head. Would that be enough for an ounce of rest?

It was decided the stormy day wouldn't be one of traveling. Foxtamas' tail needed attention, and drudging on towards who knows where in such conditions would only prove ruinous. Thankfully, Acirema's preparation on the boat meant that, for at least a little while, their packs were fit with provisions, and resting wouldn't be so bad a choice. For their bodies, anyway. Guilt soaked them more than the rain. Few words hovered between the friends, but none were needed. They knew what the others felt. No point in tearing open the wound any further.

The next morning came with the twinkle of sunshine and a rejuvenation to push onward. After a quick breakfast, the company bid farewell to their oaken friend and headed back up the ridge. It was well agreed that New Lothlock wouldn't be far off. Heading north from where they stood would be just as effective as starting back at the Old Mill. A little traveling would find it.

Despite the slice still paining him, Foxtamas led the party through the soft, open trees of the ridgeline. The spaciousness of this part of Evon took him off guard. Where hid the fallen logs, the thickets of ferns and thorns? Mechmilne thinned around them, a fact that, to his surprise, brought reassurance. The adventure was *moving.* Foxlaris grew closer with every lone tree, every sparse clearing.

Through those clearings he watched the remains of the field. It smoldered from end to end, a black stain upon the earth. Burnt bones and flesh still sizzled beneath the decomposing bodies, shriveled beyond recognition. A light misting of smoke drifted from them. Like their final breaths still being stolen away.

Foxtamas forced his gaze away and to the ground. The smells of hellfire and blood were too much for a dawning day. They changed him, certainly, but he rather they work subconsciously, in his mind's shadow. Grammo Day weighed heavy as is; this…this didn't need to accompany it.

"How far might it be?" Acirema's calm, quieted voice sounded unnatural after the deafness of the morn. By now the ridge began to lower, ending in a blank slate of grass that broke into a hilly valley surrounded by a light scattering of trees.

"I'm not too sure," Foxtamas replied. "He just said past the Mill. We've gotta be close, but I was expecting a road, or trail, or something."

"Did we pass it?"

"I don't know how we could've. Did you see anything, Bunns?" The fox peeked back behind him to see Bunns, deep in a world of his own, lollygagging with hops and skips.

"Nae laddie. Ah'm retired from leadin'. Ah'll just bae stickin' tae fightin'," he called back.

"Well at least keep your eyes open."

"Always do."

Noon sneaked up on them. By the time the trio realized it, they'd already fallen deep into another forest, begging for any notice of travelers or wayward road signs pointing, if not to their desired direction, at to least *a* direction.

"There's no way we're lost, right?" Foxtamas asked, his words slightly tinged with terror.

"Weh can try goin' back tae *The Losmo*." A good suggestion by Bunns.

"*If* we can find it again." Yet was crushed by the assertion of Acirema. His ears flopped down.

"I swear I'm going insane or something," the fox said, "*that way* is north. We started close to the Mill, so if we follow *towards it*—"

A growl of thunder rumbled the ground, like the storm from the night previous on a tour of revenge. The trio looked first at each other, then at the shaking, trembling trees surrounding them. It grew louder, backed suddenly by swaying and breaking branches. Why…the noise…it came for *them!* Sped dutiful to their very spot!

Yet no one cowered. Especially Foxtamas. No, his face beamed He knew that cascading roar. He'd listened to it many a night during the long Winthrop summers.

The Ratatoskr, the high-flying delivery squirrels of Evon, burst overhead in a volley of visceral speed. Each nimble member bounded from limb to limb, practically soaring through the foliage. They had no ground, only Mechmilne and the open air. Oh, to be beneath such a scurry. Hundreds of squirrels, all burdened by acorn caps, belts, letters, and parcels, zipping past like autumn leaves on a winter's wind. The action filled the trio below with zeal. It didn't matter how long one knew them—their spectacle transcended friendship.

*"HAHA!* LADDIES! AYE, HERE, HERE!" Bunns shouted into the crowd, jumping and waving. His outburst caught a few rushing glances. Those who recognized the jackalope widened their eyes and chuckled. One, however, couldn't just pass on by.

"My eyes've *finally* gone!" Parcelage Ruel Burrowfoot dropped down from his procession, shaking his head and tut-tutting his tongue. The squirrel leader wasn't the slightest bit winded. His gray-tipped ears and note-littered sashes stood at attention, if not a tad petrified from the surprise. "I know a certain mama-jackey who'll be over the blasted *moon* hearin' this!"

A unanimous "RUEL!" burst from the friends as they enveloped him in a hug. Hearing his jittered voice felt like being welcomed back home.

"There you rascals are! Had the whole village scared to *death* you three did!"

"Oh no, is everything alright?" Acirema pulled away, anxious.

"Mostly so. We were passing through that afternoon after you left and heard the story from ol' Gregabbit. Poor Miss Corlawn. Didn't find the note you boys left 'till right before we arrived, and even after was beggin' us to go searching for you. I told her I would've gladly, but stopping a mission for a lost brother, nope, couldn't do it. I share your pain, Foxtamas, really do."

The fox, a little teary-eyed, nodded his thanks.

"Ah shouldn't have promised weh'd bae back so soon..." Bunns whispered under his breath.

"And of father? Any word?" Acirema cut in again. News of Mrs. Cammont warmed her heart, surely. But the king...she needed to know all she could. They'd last spoke at Grammo Day—practically a lifetime ago now. Perhaps hearing of her absence had led him to form a search party, set the Watchers out on duty, something...

"No, m'lady. We weren't even allowed inside. The Watchers took our parcels at the door."

She let her head fall. Eyes glue to the leaves at her feet. Ruel bit his lip and squinted his face, noting the beaten looks the trio carried. He whipped the conversation around as quickly as he ran. "B-But why are you three *here?* Foxlaris is in the East, isn't he?"

Foxtamas sighed before nodding. In as few words as possible, he summarized their adventure, going through the attack at Nohsis, the minotaur, Teardic, Rillem, and now the quest to find New Lothlock. The Parcelage chuckled at the Hucksubtle chapter, knowing he and the boys just barely missed them at the Tavern. Worse, he confirmed the stories he told Teardic. Havoc spread like a sickness wherever the Easterners traveled. Now, a week into the journey, the statement held truer than ever.

"We'll make sure to avoid the field then. Nasty lil' maggots. But New Lothlock, right. It ain't all that much further up, just head, oh, northwest from here. Few hours maybe on your footspeed."

"Yer sure? Weh was thinkin' the same all morn!"

"You have my word. Oh, and before I forget, we'll be passing Winthrop on the way back south. Anything you wanna send on home?"

Each passed the other a glance. So much had changed since they'd left the impoverished village life. Now, to take that step back...

“Tell mah ol’ mum tae calm et down ah bit. Weh won’t bae tha’ much longer Ah reckon,” Bunns said with a smirk.

“And don’t say anything about the monsters, the fighting, *this—”* Foxtamas pointed down at the bandages around his tail. Ruel snickered. “But also, that when we do come home, it’ll be all four of us. Promise.”

“I’ll make sure me and the boys are there for it, Foxtamas. Anything for you, m’lady?”

Acirema clung to the conversation like a petal from a wilting flower. Only Ruel’s call awoke her, forcing her melancholy into a kind twist of her face.

“Oh, um, the same, really. Poor Winthrop has had enough loss lately. Just…make sure everyone is staying calm, Ruel.”

“You’ve my word. Don’t fret, princess, things’ll return to normal here soon, especially once ol’ Foxlaris is back in town. Now, I best be getting on, but you three stay safe, or else I’ll tell Mrs. Corlawn every secret I’ve kept from her!”

“Come on, not tha’! She’ll whoop meh until next year!”

“Good!” His laugh echoed as he bounded away, a streak of brown rattling up the bark and flinging through the foliage. The byes the trio called back drifted behind him. A moment later, serenity returned to Mechmilne Wood.

The direction held true. Soon, small signs of life approached: broken wagon wheels, overturned posts, rotting apple cores from merchants late to their upcoming stop. The sun traveled with them, arriving at an explosion of color and vibrance dripping across the sky. Although a short day, it held promise that, in only a few short hours, the friends and family of Foxlaris Scottsworth would again be back on the trail towards him.

“Wha’ weh thinkin’? Should weh approach ol’ New Lothlock playin’ ah lil jig?”

"And look like a league of loons?" Acirema slighted to the bouncing jackalope.

"Oh, quit actin' like yer ain't been enjoyin' 'em, Queenie! Just wait, yer put one of them poems of yers tae ah tune an—"

"*HALT!*"

The thundering *BOOM!* of the voice froze the friends. Just a few feet ahead two hulking shadows stomped towards them. Bunns didn't recognize the beasts, instinctively grasping for his stars. Had the Easterners caught up already!?

No. The closer they came, the more they resembled creatures so unique, so unheard that only legends recorded their existence.

Grizlyms.

Identical to the tales. Both bore the likes of bears with their grumbling snouts, tar-black coats, and paws powerful enough to snap bones on a single try. Grizlyms, however, stood taller. *Much* taller. Looking up, Foxtamas rose only to their waist. Quills layered across their backs with barbs as sharp as their teeth. No hero ever made peace with such a beast; their ferocity often matched those of dragons, minotaurs, and whatever other creature mustered a fight of courage.

When a king fought a grizlym, you sat up in your seat.

The approaching pair wore marvelous gold armor. Rays of the setting sun beamed across it, practically blinding the trio. Both carried gilded broad shields and halberds, each with the symbol of an eloquent "R" wrapped by thorns and berries plastered front and center. Any lesser Evoneer would tarnish the presentation's brilliance.

It felt like two sparkling towers had formed before them. Fighting wasn't an option; running would be just as foolish. Instead, petrified by fear, they listened to the bassy, almost unintelligible voices of the soldiers.

"You trespass into the Dukedom of Rokanoe, stewarded by Duke Osiglada III by ruling of King Wittisus IV of the Kingdom of Garon and Surrounding Country. Show your Permissions of Entry or Notes of Passage or forfeit your company to imprisonment and questioning by the High Elder."

"Any attempt to leave will result in treachery of duly noted offerings and thus an offense to His Highness requiring immediate action leading to the direct punishment of death."

Stunned.

No one dared swallow, nor blink, nor breath. Who knew how little they had left with their lives if they did.

Slowly, Bunns eased his paw from the star pouch and raised it up.

"Aye, um, weh ain't wantin' tae enter into nae Dukedom. Just tryin' tae reach New Lothlock, tha's all."

"Yet you take the route through *clearly* marked territory. Present your documentation, NOW," the leftmost grizlym demanded. Bunns turned back to the frightened pair behind him. Documentation? Where in Evon *were* they!?

"Sirs, um…we don't, well, *have* any, but we are more than capable of turning and banishing ourselves from the Dukedom. Our mistake, surely." Acirema gently bowed as she spoke, hoping to communicate her respect.

"You risk the payment of death, girl?"

The threat made her gulp. Both hulking bears faced each other, giving the other a disapproving nod.

"You've admitted your crime. By law of Duke Osiglada III and the Dukedom of Rokanoe, we hereby confirm this party as prisoners until further notice." Both grizlyms pulled from their armor heavy, dyed sacks. Panicked, Foxtamas waved his hands, stepping back in a rush of fear.

"No, please! There's a misunderstanding, please, *please!"*

*WHACK!!*

The golden halberd cracked against his skull. Foxtamas dropped to the ground. Before either Bunns or Acirema could take in the horror, a stuffy, blinding bag smothered them.

# 13

# "FUL-NO-A! FUL-NO-A!"

"Nae, yer right for *NOT* doin' et!"

"But Bunns, *look at us!* Who knows how long we might be down here! And what about the rest of the journey? Could be *months* until we make it!"

"Aye, but weh're still livin', ain't weh?"

The back-and-forth commotion shattered the darkness bounding Foxtamas to his sleep. Head aching, he lifted his lids to find a dank, decrepit crypt surrounding them. The floor on which they'd been thrown was more mud than dirt. Bars of rusted steel formed the leftmost wall, blocking their way of escape. The cell had hardly enough room for the trio to sit comfortably. Worse, darkness loomed over it. Only a short flickering in a hallway past the door shined light on the worried faces of his friends.

*"Unnhhhgg..."* Foxtamas croaked. "What...happened?"

He dragged himself up and leaned his head against the bars. Something about the frigid rust helped soothe the pulse beating through his brain.

"Foxtamas! Are you alright?" Acirema only had to lean forward to touch him in the cramped room.

"Yeah, yeah...uh, kinda. Just a headache. What about y'all?"

"Aye, weh're fine. They put some sacks over our heads an' tossed us here. Weh slept some. Nae clue the time," replied Bunns. He too sounded groggy, like passing on the extra sleep had been an intentional decision.

"Mm. But what…what were y'all saying? What didn't Acirema do?"

"Something smart," she started.

"Something stupid," Bunns finished. Both whipped to face the other, faces scowled with a testy anger.

"She wanted tae tell our captors she's royalty!"

"Yes, so in the chance they are *generous* we might be able to escape, what, the questioning, the trials, the *death*—"

"Death! Lassie, yer askin' for et! Yer saw them grizlyms, they ain't ones tae play fair!"

Foxtamas waved his hands at the pair, eyes closed as the rambling nonsense further pounded his head.

"Guys, please, quiet just a bit," he groaned. "Acirema…I think Bunns is right. Hide it until we need to use it, like a secret weapon or…or something, I dunno."

The princess stared down at the muck. Legs pressed tight to her chest. Had Foxtamas not grown up alongside her, he may not have read the squeeze of her eyes, the fingers rubbing the inside of her palms. She hungered from the need to help.

"You don't have to let your reputation precede you for once," he started, trying to meet her eyes despite the blur of his vision. "We're so far north I doubt they'll recognize you. Let's all just be villagers for a bit, how about it?"

Slowly, Acirema let out a light grin. And an even lighter nod.

"That works." Sweet as the dew at dawn.

"Yer ever heard of this place, Scottoh? What's et, Rokanoe?" asked Bunns. Foxtamas closed his eyes again to try to help him think.

Rokanoe.

Rokanoe…

"Nope. Sounds close to Resolutia, but that was just an allegory. Have y'all?"

"Nae, not even Queenie."

"Father never mentioned it," cut in Acirema, shifting herself over to find some section of comfort in the cell. "Dukedoms this far in are...odd. You usually hear of them further west and beyond in the islands."

"So is it new?" questioned the fox.

"Ah doubt et. Look et this place, lil' nasty, ain't et?"

"True. But...what about Ruel, then? He said New Lothlock was only a little bit away. Why not mention an entire *dukedom* sitting in the way? With grizlyms guards ready to arrest you?"

"These grizlyms," Acirema said, "they come from stories, right?"

"Yeah, or, well, *used to*, I guess. Evon's gotta lot of creatures, but I always took those as myths." Foxtamas shook his aching head in confusion.

"Aye, if weh needed some big ol' beastie an' weh were right tired of dragons, Ah'd make Rizzeh play ah grizlym. Would've chosen ah bigger lad had Ah known they'd bae the size of a tower."

The trio chuckled, like a glimmer of sunlight on their souls. Yet the quiet afterwards left Foxtamas shivering. He thought on the issue, of being knocked out cold, locked in a moldy dungeon in a dukedom they'd never known by creatures never once thought possible. Where had this adventure *gone!* Worse, where would it go, how would it end!?

Before he pondered further into the trappings of fear, thumps echoing off the dim, lantern-lit walls bounded down towards their cell. The icy noise silenced their beating hearts. They timidly turned to the prison's edge, waiting. Waiting for whoever approached. Waiting...waiting...waiting...for him.

In walked a creature familiar yet foreign, unique yet common. He stood tall and slender, posture straight like a sapling finally coming into its own. The barren whiteness of his skin was hidden behind long, silken robes draped over his body, practically doubling his size. His head, the face of which looked like a starved, beardless dwarf, held the brightest of emerald eyes and locks of golden hair. It twisted past his pointed ears, ending just beyond his slim shoulders. Expressionless he walked. Slim, silver walking staff tapping the stones in stride. None dared guess his age or life, only that elegance had been, for the longest, his closest companion.

Trembling, Foxtamas moved away from the bars and against the soggy wall with the others. He leaned over to Bunns, whispering in a raspy, ragged, ruined voice,

"E-E-E-E-E-*Elf*..."

The being must have heard, for he whipped around to face them with a raised brow and mouth spread thin to a line. The look made the friends think themselves lower than the mold growing behind their backs.

"Greetings."

They expected a voice as dream-inducing as his looks. His cadence came more real, more northern, more grounded than the legends foretold. "I am High Elder Ilindil VIII of Roimohr, Steward to His Majesty the Duke and servant of King Wittisus IV."

Roimohr.

The word struck Foxtamas harder than the grizlym. Roimohr, the legendary land beyond the eternal ice fields and trenches of Evon's northern waters where all good souls go to die...and where a certain Blue Phoenix is said to call home.

How had this elf...

"As you've been informed, my duty is inquisition of those we find burdened by probable cause for concern in our borders. You three come yoked with such a weight."

Every breath was bated. Every swallow audible from a league away. Fear choked the hope and dignity from the travelers, forcing them to huddle close and take in the slow, deliberate words of the High Elder.

"But today is a rarity. Rokanoe is prided on its long legacy of truth and honor, but we are still capable of knowing our faults when they come about. You three were detained, but under improper circumstances."

Though they kept staring at the elf, each felt the sudden flip of emotions within the other. Improper...as in...unjust? Or as in...wrongly, meaning instead of a cell, they should have a noose around their necks along with the bags from before?

"See, this fortnight is our Festival of Rising Nights. We celebrate the day when King Wittisus mercilessly defeated the vile enemy of Garon, Lord Bearnabas of House O'LeDial in the Battle of Sleepless Fields. However, among the achievements of that night, he returned to his keep and found that, after a fight of her own, Queen Periosha had delivered the king's first and only son: Duke Osiglada. Every year we celebrate these dual victories in our lands—though, in doing so, we must be weary of any members of House O'LeDial that still lurk and wish to usurp our majesty's throne."

Foxtamas nodded despite his thrashing head, parched mouth. He understood the innerworkings of such kingdom heroics. Together, he and the others gripped every syllable, awaiting a single word of hope.

"Those traveling for the festival often take the main road in. We allow those of royalty and familial ties to enter other ways, but only with the proper documentation. If nothing can be produced, well, you see where they're doomed to end up. This time our guards were too hasty in their assumption of guilt and missed all the key warnings that you travelers were simply that. No gaudy clothes, no weapons of war, and, well, you three don't appear to be *bears* from my eyes."

Ilindil smirked to himself. He adjusted his stiff position and walked to the cell door of the chamber. A careless dangling followed. Not one of Tops. Or sword.

Of keys.

"Our negligence has robbed you of an entire night on your journey, and for that we are rightly ashamed. However, we wish to both repay and honor you in our Rokanoe custom. The three of you are welcomed as honored guests to our Festival of Rising Nights. All, from every vendor and shop, performer and storyteller, is yours, free of charge. As much of a burden it may be to stay one more day, we ask you do. If you choose such, the only payment we require in exchange for the free goods is a breakfast with the duke tomorrow morning. Afterwards you may be on your way with his blessing. Such a badge is more worthwhile than a day of travel, I assure you. While the road may be regained, such kindness is hardly offered twice."

The elf swung open the cage door. He rose above the captives with a smile still etched upon his stone-like skin.

"Well?" he asked.

Foxtamas glanced to the others. They matched his concern.

"What are we gonna do?" whispered the fox.

"I'm not sure," Acirema replied, hushed. "We've already wasted so much time—"

"Aye, but weh could get yer some arrows and better food than just ah few ol' berries. Et'll only bae an extra day." Bunns wasn't wrong. Thinking of the festival foods and offerings made Rillem's supplies stored in their sacks seem like table scraps. Better yet, it was *free*. The poor villager inside of (mostly) all of them knew to never, under any possible circumstance, refuse such an offer.

"He's right. We made up time on the Runnel, we can take a day. I'd rather us make it to the Fulnoa prepared than barely getting by." The words of Foxtamas sealed it. Nodding, the trio turned back to the High Elder who chuckled at the quick conversation.

"Smart decision. Thus, it is my divine pleasure to welcome you all to the Festival of Rising Nights and, officially, the Dukedom of Rokanoe!"

Bags again covered their heads—this time for their own good. Ilindil assured them that, even though simple travelers, they still needed the layout of their dungeons protected. After some twists through the hallways, the warmth of summer sunlight and brisk, peppy wind bathed them. Like waking from a dream. Free, alive. But frivolous once the sacks were pulled from their faces…

A town, larger than any they'd ever seen, filled the fullness of their vision. They stood at the start of a cobbled street, wide and packed by gleeful festivalgoers snaking through the towering buildings of homes, shops, and alleyways branching out like eternal boughs of an aging oak.

It somehow felt both cramped and spacious at the same time. The length of it reached the horizon until it faded to a clouded blue. Mountains from the hands of Evoneers.

Banners spanned across the road, hanging from window to window. They'd been painted brash colors of red, purple, and gold, bursting in a bolded "HAPPY BIRTHDAY!". The same sprinkling of shades melted into flags and posters all down the way. The berry and vine covered "R" reappeared among them. It snuggled on the overcoats of grandfathers, the wheels of merchants' shifting carts, and doorknobs leading into the looming rooms.

All shook with a restlessness, with a joy you tasted through your eyes. For the trio, it felt like Grammo Day all over again, hosted now at Mikyill, not the lowly Bridgeburrow.

Foxtamas spun around to fully grasp the world around him, and, overtaken by such a lavish surprise, practically stumbled into the Rokanoe Keep rising just feet behind them.

Never had a castle reached such heights. From where the friends stood, they could only glimpse the monumental front gates and stonework of the outward walls. It felt like staring into the sun. The gold of the bars blinded them, and the white, crackless limestone walls burned a fiery blaze. What could *possibly* lie beyond them? How many more towers, dungeons, rooms, secrets?

The fox forced himself to turn away. Somehow, they'd stumbled upon Evon's greatest hidden secret.

And they'd become its honored guests.

"Wow..."

His word encapsulated all three of their heart-racing, turbulent emotions.

"Et's...huge," commented Bunns, eyes watering.

"And ours for the taking, right?" Acirema smirked and winked at the boys. "I kid. But still...where do we even start?"

"No clue," the fox replied. "There's so much to see. It's almost too much."

"Aye, *almost.*" It was the jackalope's turn for a silly little wink. He puffed out his chest and started deeper into the town. Despite their hesitancy, Foxtamas and Acirema trailed behind, diving into the Festival of Rising Nights.

The friends waded through the sea of people. The incoherent jumble of shouts mixed into the melody of the minstrel music flowing from windows and shops alike. The crowd paid no mind to the songs nor the outsiders—no, they busied along, giggly, smiling, chatting about. Further in, at a square wider than the central road, vendors blocked off many of the alley entrances. They tightened the streets and kept the overflow of Rokanoe visitors to just the main stretch. It worked wonders to not overrun the city.

As the company passed, one such alley-blocker waved their way.

"Hi-Ho, travelers! Come close, come close!" It felt odd to hear someone acknowledge their presence. Still, they listened and gathered near the gopher calling for them.

Aged, but with a jolly smile and freshly furnished cooking garments, the pleasant little soul rubbed his hands in excitement.

"Welcome to Aydaltown! Word's already spread of your troubles last night, but never fret! How've you enjoyed the festival thus far?"

"Oh, um, it's good, just starting out," Acirema replied. "We're from a smaller village and not used to such um...merriment."

"This is *nothing*, my dear! Wait until the shows they've planned for tonight. Not sure there's any wonder greater in all Evon! But you've done nothing so far, did I hear you right?"

"Yes, though there seems—"

"Well, if you'll have me, I'd be honored to start your day off right! Here, take these, all of you." Out from the cart the peppy merchant produced a tray of muffins. Their golden-brown shells were doused in a happy helping of butter-flared sugar and blueberries, like a broken geode of fruity sweetness. The friends couldn't look away. How *scrumptious* the muffins looked! The price, however, made them better yet. "Go on now, eat all you can stuff and celebrate with the rest of us! Be merry, my friends, be *merry!*"

And merry they were. Bunns snatched as many as he could carry and started scarfing away. Foxtamas and Acirema, though a *tad* more polite, couldn't help but tear into the tiny treats. Each bite of the rich, creamy flavor made the words of the gopher roar to life. The journey could *absolutely* wait. Only celebrating a duke they barely knew concerned them now. And, by his own decree, experiencing all that Aydaltown could offer. No worries. No fears. Just pure, untainted bliss.

The muffins were only the beginning. They ventured forward—a new fire within them—and discovered a massive fountain at the town's center. It spurted leagues into the air, not just from the central nozzle, but from statues circling around its base, outlining the beauty. Former kings, queens, dukes, and duchesses guarded the waters, their stonework keen of any blemish.

The same could *not* go for the road that twisted around it. Long had Evoneers trampled it, and the constant scuttle of the festival did little to lighten the load. As the trio traversed past, they took notice of the…oddities…among the Rokanoe citizens. Foxtamas spotted gowrow, sprites, and harpies, Bunns picked out a unicorn, fouke, yeti, and kempy. Their Grammo Day game spotted all the beings they *knew* existed; now, they encountered creatures those they'd only dreamed about.

One unblocked alley further down from the main square led to an open park of sorts. The bronze signs along its wrought iron walls told how the duke set apart this space to capture the land's original look, before Rokanoe's founding. Bugs buzzed, trees swayed, and the grass hummed to the light tune of town song slipping in. Small wooden seats sat between the trunks that, joined by the stairs beside them, led towards a stage at the back, readied for any daring play or production. The hidden amphitheater made Acirema's heart jump. She'd only experienced traveling shows in Winthrop, the kind with shabby, patched costumes and actors too laden with ale to remember their lines. This…this would be different. The drama didn't look to start until later that night. She'd be back. Until then, they pushed back to the street, finding across from the park an open weapon shop and barrels of arrows and bolts for the taking.

Their journey took them up, down, and all around Aydaltown. Foxtamas forced them to stop and listen to a nymph minstrel sing a ballad about the duke, his homeland of Garon, and how he spent his childhood learning and growing to be the leader they had today. He couldn't believe his senses. An *actual* minstrel played but feet from him. Not a high-strung Bunns or quirky little merchant, but a taleteller, a performer of myth and legend! In the surrounding crowd, the fox faded into just another face. The singer paid him not a smile, but he didn't mind. The words were enough.

Afterwards, they dropped by a poetry reading for youngsters and their families, merchant stands overflowing with crowds, and, a highlight for Bunns, a live demonstration by the local Blacksmith guild. There, one burly black bear (thankfully not an O'LeDial) hammered the finishing touches into a shield, presenting to the audience of eager onlookers a hand-forged Rokanoe crest. He explained the different elements and their importance—the berries represented bounty, the thorns the overcome trials faced in past, present, and future. It made the double W's of Winthrop seem like the scribbling of a child.

The sun crept into a late afternoon by the time the demonstration ended. If the gopher's words held true, some spectacle would soon begin further towards the main square. The trio filled the remaining time with a few final stops (one being the lovely muffin man from before), watched a quick procession of flag twirlers and horn blowers, and just about went in search for a game of Flapdragon in one of the many taverns before, as the crest of the light sank beneath the horizon, a horn bellowed from the fountain and the center of Aydaltown. Something was about to start.

Something, quite literally, magical.

# 14

# "Two Brothers Forged in Stone!"

*FWWWWOOOOOOSSSSHHHH!!!!*

The water, once crystalline and bubbling to a foamy pearl, twisted inside itself and created a roaring flow of leaping flame. The entire fountain burned in a blink. To the shock of those stuffed and huddled around it, no soot nor ash stained the stonework. It was as if the water never left.

Cheer erupted. Almost ear-shattering. The trio, wholly absorbed both mentally and physically, added to it with shouts and hollers of their own. All became one, screaming mass.

The fire wafted down the tiers and filled the fountain in a blaze. As it did, a rich groaning, akin to that of a working grindstone, hummed from the statues at its edge. Foxtamas peeked over the shoulders of those at his front to see what was happening. He laid eyes on a stone elf, bow in hand and hair blown back in an eternal breeze. In one moment, her glazed eyes gazed forward; in another, they looked directly at him.

The forty-or-so others followed suit. Their stone bodies came to life with thick, crunchy cracks. Once free from the bonds, they sloshed towards one another like dangling marionettes, their weapons raised high. Gravens held golden feathers to minotaurs; efetes stood readied against gowrows.

The fire leapt high into the darkened sky once they met, this time to the electrifying pound of drums, fiddles, flutes, and strings. The orchestral sound breathed life into the statues, huffed vigor, action, rage.

Battle consumed the fountain. Swords snapped against shields, backed not by the *clang!* of metal, but the *BOOM!* of a drum, the rhythm of the music matched to the choreographed fight. How *wonderous* a sight! As if the battles of imagination roared before them. No play nor tale had ever brought such raw emotion; the swinging, soaring music captured the soul of every onlooker.

Suddenly, as the fighters danced around the rim of the fountain, the flames silhouetting their figures shifted hue, thundering into hundreds of colors in the same moment as, from high above on the overhanging rooftops, a chorus of a hundred trained, organized voices cascaded downward, flooding the audience.

Blues and violets ruptured across the square.

Blacks and reds rose as the choir and orchestra deepened.

Green and gold painted the night once the flutes took hold.

It was almost too much to keep up with. Every passing minute a new chord, color, or crescendo further enraptured the audience. What had their lives been before such a show? How could they live without hearts bombarded by the bassy blasts, their eyes no longer illuminated by the constant craze of commotion?

At last, after an hour of excitement, the finale began. Water once more gushed from its home, yet it did not extinguish its new neighbor—it embraced it. The two worked in tandem to climb higher than before, in a prism of mixing, bleeding colors, the music rising to meet them. Had any Evoneer before witnessed such a sight? Would they ever again?

As the two elements bonded, the statues tossed out their final blows. Some finally fell whilst others, after taking hit upon hit, soared to the occasion and struck down the foe. Everything built louder and louder, higher and higher, the action peaking before one burst—

The elemental fountain exploded in a piercing of light. The final note rang out. It overclocked every sense, forced the audience to the ground, hands to ears, eyes shuttered closed, the brightness thickened, full and heavy, luminous, the width of the sun and the girth of all the stars flaring, flaring in sparkle, in glitter, in the awe of a night turned day, daylight pedaling backwards, a crown of gold rolling off its head and into the bosom of a new power, raw and dignified.

Then calmness.

No more music. No more color. No more fire. Just the gurgling sounds of simple, puttering water.

Foxtamas crept to his feet, stunned and dizzied. The thump of his heartbeat pounded against his head. He looked over those getting back up and saw both the statues and fountain alike now waxed with a glimmering gold.

It earned one final belting of applause.

"W-W-What did we just *see!?"* the fox called to the others. He turned back to the crowd behind him and had to adjust his eyes to the blackened figures clogging the street. He squinted out a few blinks. The people slowly took form. He blinked again. Even clearer. Yet in the flurry, he spotted no raccoon nor jackalope.

"Guys?" he asked again, spinning around. A faun yes, even a couple clurichaun. But no one he knew.

*"Guys!"*

Foxtamas pushed against the crowd, swiveling his head every which way among the shadowy figures. How had they gotten separated? They were right there, beside him! They couldn't be far if they were that close, right? Right…?

It felt easier to wade against the thrust of Nohsis than the sea of creatures clogging Aydaltown's square. The pushing, shoving, hulking masses practically suffocated him. With every step he took some brute would force him backward. *"Bunns!"* he spat into the shifting crowd. *"Acirema!"*

Nothing.

The constant presses grew futile. Already he'd waded far from where the trio had watched the show, somehow ending near the square's eastern side with buildings and their endless alleys of shadow. He watched the waves crash against each other. Person after person. Their family, their friends with them. He's traversed the winding Main Road of Winthrop just fine at night. But this wasn't Winthrop. No, it was the furthest he'd been from it since he'd arrived, in a foreign land with foreign races and foreign people. What danger lurked around every corner to the unguarded and the unaware? In the darkness at his back? The stalking souls in front of him? What if—

No. This was *not* the time to get scared. Bunns and Acirema were out there, just a little lost, like himself. Soon he might even hear their cries of *"Foxtamas!"* He couldn't get scared. He couldn't get scared.

"Don't get scared," he whispered to himself, voice as faint as he could make it.

"Don't get scared."

The fox formed an outline of a plan. Further along the thick stone wall he was hugging, one of the vendor carts had their extra crates of supplies stacked away for the night. A few hops on top of them and he'd have the clearest view of the sloshing Evoneer mass. The move didn't feel foolproof, but Foxtamas knew the limit of his options. If anything, it gave him a goal to move towards, and with it, precious seconds to keep the army of fear at bay.

Thus, with a deep, slightly shaky breath, he dove back into the sea.

Only to be hit by a wave.

Right as he started for the cart, two figures stumbled into his path: a young efete girl, no older than himself, and a gnarled, shaggy sasquatch with fur twisted and disheveled beneath a stained smock.

"I told you, go away!" she cried out, pushing him back as she plunged deeper into the crowded street.

"And let you slip away with my Tops!?" No mercy coated the coarseness of his voice. The pair squarely blocked Foxtamas' path. He glanced at both sides, even beneath, looking for some opening past the bickering, but the two boxed him in tight.

"You don't deserve them, you ugly brute!"

"I'll take whatever I like!"

"You're a monster!"

"Aye, an' what are you gonna do about it, eh?"

The beast bowed over her, causing her to stumble and quiver down to the ground. Foxtamas tingled with fear. He was right: danger *did* lurk for those alone. But the thought didn't stop him. The sasquatch's move opened a sliver of room behind him as he pressed further upon the girl. Seeing his chance, the fox shot towards the gap, squeezing through as the yelling continued, heightening.

"Hey, *FOX!*"

His blood froze over. He didn't want to look. Oh, he did *NOT* want to *LOOK!*

Quaking, Foxtamas peeked behind his shoulder, only for a second, a glimpse at best. But met the fiery eyes of the knotted hulk staring him down.

"You tryna get involved, huh? Tryna shove me out the way?"

He didn't feel his hands leap into the air.

"N-N-No sir, I'm so, so so-r-r-ry, I'm just passing through, l-l-looking for my friends—"

"I'll find 'em myself and show 'em a mangled lil' corpse if you don't back away!" the sasquatch—quite literally—spat back. Foxtamas replied with broken breaths and a stutter of empty air. The grating words shred open the gates of his keep. Fear, once again, flooded in, and as it did, the fox burst away. His steps stumbled over one another. He had to find the others. He had to. They'd strengthen his mind's defenses. They'd be safe together. They protected him. Without them he was scared, weak, and nothing.

He had to find them.

He had to.

Yet a shaking sigh of relief found *him* once he arrived at the merchant's stand. Foxtamas leaned against it, panting. The crates stood stacked beside him. Three steps maximum to reach his view. It was easy. No fear, no worry. Just step up and—

*"Really? Abandoning her like that?"*

His head jolted back. A breath, icy as a Pradiforian wind, graced his neck. The fox jumped forward and turned around. Nothing stood behind him apart from the empty darkness of the alley.

"Who's there?" he shouted, voice wavering with a fake mustering of courage.

*"You saw her innocence."*

From the other side. He whipped back around and found, sitting on the cart, a figure, slim and hunched over, wrapped in a coat so dark and tight it obscured the features of his face. Its cover did little to stop the stinging of his words. Though, how similar they sounded…like those of an…elf.

"What do you mean?" Foxtamas asked as he stepped back from the man.

*"The efete you ran past, not even batting an eye. Not even a word. Really?"*

"Sir, I'm just trying to find my friends. I'm lost, I-I'm not made for that, I-I-I—" the brutal honesty sputtering from his mouth didn't help his case. The figure raised from the cart, shaking what would have normally been a suitable spot for a face.

*"And yet you still prance around playing hero."*

The fox squinted and tilted his head.

"Hero? No, sir, I'm no hero."

*"Then why do you carry an axe of dwarven steel by your side? For show?"*

"Oh, um," Foxtamas mumbled, reaching down and feeling the weapon bolted to his belt. "It's, uh…a gift. I barely know how to use it."

*"Ah, so you hide away while the innocent die before your very eyes. Do you ever try? Do you ever step up, hmm? Ever be the* hero?"

Foxtamas gulped, loud enough for the shadow to hear. He again resorted to waving his hands and backing away. The figure pursued.

"Sir, I-I-I'm sorry, I'm just here for my friends, I—"

*"I'm not asking this for me, boy, I'm asking this for* you. *Stop him. Save her. Feel the glory. Taste the reward. Do you not see?"* With every step the air

grew thicker, grew colder. The roar of the festival goers ever so slowly hushed. Foxtamas locked onto the cloak's invisible eyes. "Take the blade in your hand. One stroke is all you need with your power. One hit to end it all. Take it, boy."

"I…I, no, I can't—"

*"TAKE IT!"*

Fear won.

Foxtamas pushed down his head and dashed away, diving back into the crowd. The cart, the crate, the view, none of it mattered. He had to get away from that voice, that…*thing!* Oh, how he ran, tossing aside creature after creature, swimming to save his skin. He was alone with no friends and no direction. He needed them. He couldn't do it without him. He couldn't do anything without them. He wasn't anything without them.

With no real thought, the fox fumbled into a cleared alley, hoping to break away from the shadowed man. He booked it down. The cobble clunked beneath his broken boots. Pants hung heavy on his breath. Foxtamas pushed every worry from his mind and turned a sharp corner, skidding over the street and into the figure.

*"You're a horrible listener."*

"GET AWAY!" the fox screamed, his vision staggered by the shock of the shadow. He violently twisted back around towards his exit. The walls, however, had changed. Foxtamas stood before rising rows of impenetrable bricks blocking the way he entered. Sealing him in.

He felt the consciousness start to leave his body.

No.

*NO!*

He had to get away, he had to get out.

Instead of trying to climb, he turned back towards the cloaked man and sprinted past him, down the rest of a darkened lane. Near the end lay a gap to the left, a slim crack between the back of one building and the start of another. The squeeze was tight, but he pushed through, popping back out into the central highway. Where at? No clue. But it didn't matter. His legs buried deeper into the stone and pushed the fox's body as far as it could go. Creatures blew past left and right. Not even one cared to notice.

*"Why do you flee? Do heroes run?"*

The voice…it spoke from the back of his mind, disembodied. The breath from before now blowing across his brain.

"Stop it!" he cried.

*"No,* you do!" it spat back. Foxtamas stopped the sprint to close his eyes, trying to unhear the words pounding within his head. *"Not even a swing! Not even a* shove!?"

"I SAID *STOP!"* he wept. The fox clawed at his head, and for a second, he let his eyes slip open.

He shrieked.

The residents of Aydaltown melted away. No one seemed to even care. Shadow wound up their legs and pulled them down with long, skeletal arms into pools of misty, murky nothingness. One moment they stood laughing in the arms of another; the next foggy dust drained down the desolate street.

*"WHAT'S GOING ON!"* Panic gurgled his words. Foxtamas no longer sounded like himself, now a lunatic on the verge of foaming at the mouth. Although he rose to run, he found nowhere to turn except the fountain a little distance away. The sprint upturned the swirling darkness at his feet, like kicking a black snow, ashen rot.

*"Look around, fox. You can't save because* you. can't. fight.*"* The voice returned to form. It rose high, a giant taller than any building. The cloaked figure loomed over the pathetic Evoneer. He took the shape of an omnipresent mist slowly soaking through the town. The booming cadence ripped the light from the stars twinkling above, stole the lantern flame decorating every door.

Where else could Foxtamas turn? The gloom thickened around his boots. He galloped backwards to avoid the mist, leading him face to face with the fountain.

*FWWWWOOOOOOSSSSHHHH!!!!*

Just as before, fire roared to life from its spouts. This time the heat blasted against him, pushing him away and closer to the looming doom.

Yet the fire was not alone.

At the fountain's edge, the eye of the stone elf glanced again to Foxtamas. Her golden brow furrowed.

*CRUNCH! CRACK! CREAK!*

The full might of the golden army awoke and marched forward past the fox. They drew their weapons, each marred by thin, razored edges. Before Foxtamas fully realized the situation, he was surrounded. The blazing fountain at his back; the golden warriors of the dukedom encircling him; and, above, shrouding the night sky and shredding through it with blasts of thick white lightning, the cloak.

"Please let me go, please! *Please!"* The whimpers barely made a sound. They mixed with the puddle of tears pouring from the fox's stained face.

*"No. You* must *fight. Forfeit your life now or take the stand you cower from. You're too scared to save a life; how about your* own*?"* roared the figure.

The statues readied shields and swords, knocked arrows and gripped taut knuckles around their spears. The soulless gaze of their gilded eyes revealed all Foxtamas needed to know.

Puppets. One move by the shadow and they'd slay him, no questions asked.

He took a single step back. The flames sprang at him, begging for a taste, a lick of their treat. They'd have their turn once fear's army finished ravishing what remained in Castle Foxtamas. The frontmost gates lay buried beneath the feet of invasion. Floods of soldiers, bearing the symbol of unbridled worry, swept through in a rampage, killing all in sight and plundering what little they found to value. It wasn't about control—it was about conquest. Now, as the houses and barracks went up in flames, only one corner remained.

The throne room.

To take the seat, to fully smother the kingdom, oh how *close* fear was! Nothing could stop them.

Nothing, that is, besides the fox himself.

He knew he couldn't fight against the statues or against the shadow. He also knew, however, that this couldn't be his death.

Foxlaris…he still lived, somewhere in the haze of the East. Someone had to find him. Fear might cripple his every movement, but his spirit, his love for his brother…that could never be broken. All it required was a little pinch of passion.

He'd gone to Foxlaris through flames once before.

He could do it again.

Foxtamas cast a look to the sky above. Tears drenched his face. His arms and legs shook without control. He let go of the breath held tight in his lungs and turned to the fountain. It would be a tall, harsh climb, one that would likely scar him for however long he had left. But Foxlaris lay on the other side.

*"NO!"* boomed the shadow. Tendrils of smoke and mist raced down to stop him, but it was too late. Foxtamas leapt into the heat, arms ready to grip the hot, sizzling steps.

But he didn't.

He fell through them.

A haze of sparks, all a bright, bubbling blue, erupted around him. His body plopped onto a stony ground. It felt the same as the streets of Aydaltown. Once his vision came to, Foxtamas saw its true nature.

Tattered. Overgrown. Broken by sprigs of grass and unkempt weeds.

He scrambled up. Sapphire sparks floated in the darkness covering him. They burst out from where he'd jumped like shards of glass suspended in the air. He approached the tear. Through it, like watching from a small window, he saw the cloaked figure running towards him—plastered in the warmth of firelight; the fox speckled by the blue glows. They twisted in the air like stars the size of embers. Where was he? Where had he gone?

*"ADAL!"* a voice screamed in the distance. Foxtamas whipped around. There lay no array of buildings in this darkened dimension. Only a grassy plain with a lantern jostling far off. Something carried it. Something sharp and sleek and fading, as the bottom of a staff whacked against his head.

Foxtamas dropped to the ground.

The broken world around him fizzled. Sleep ebbed away to the tune of distant, dreary, lingering words shouting over his body.

*"FOOL!"*
*"You fool!"*
*"You stupid,*
stupid
*fox!"*

# 15

# "Gateway to the North"

*"S...Sc...Scottoh..."*

Something shoved his body.

After it, a shake.

A slap.

Then a rattling he couldn't avoid.

"Mmmmm...huuuh?"

Foxtamas peeped his eyes open. The rising dawn blinded him—the swirl of gold and pastel pinks glowing across the sky. Thankfully, the outline of Bunns blocked it out.

"Ye...Yer...Wha' are yer doin'...here?"

His heart fluttered. After the nightmare, Bunns...Bunns was here! But his clothes—what happened?

The jackalope slouched over in a dashing suit of Rokanoe Red. Its edges were sharp and gilded, the buttons like acorns both across the breast and cuffs. It *had* to be a joke. The pounding, pounding, *pounding* headache had to be tricking him.

But something else was off about Bunns. He didn't stand as tall, speak with a joke beneath his tone. No, he was...worn, and he was tired. Heavy bags of a lusterless gray sunk below his already sagging eyes. Both ears plopped behind his head. His antlers would too if they could. It took full concentration for his small body to keep itself standing.

Foxtamas, despite the crushing pain, jolted up from the cold, cobbled Aydaltown street.

"Bunns, what happened?" he asked, steadying the drained warrior. The fox led him to the side of a building and helped him take a seat.

"Et's...ah blur, Scottoh," Bunns wheezed.

"Just take it easy, okay? One step at a time. You're not looking yourself." The fox's words were none the more vibrant. A mixture of exhaustion and pain suppressed them.

"Ah know et. Lil' more dashin' than mah usual wear, ain't et?" The jackalope cracked a small smile but couldn't hold it. His head fell back against the stonework. A moan escaped him. "Ah was right behind yer an' Queenie at tha' show last night. Ah was lovin' et, but this ol' tailor lady, ah lil' gnome, told meh Ah couldn't bae out there celebratin' lookin' like tha'. She promised meh some real fancy festival clothes. Ah thought, well, why not, yer know? The elf laddie said et was free."

He slowed, opening his eyes back up and gazing at the sky piddling past rising roofs and street so winding and endless one could mistake it for Nohsis. What did he look now but a castaway slapped carelessly on its shore.

"So, Ah follow her tae her shop down some alley. Weh get in an' the lassie starts tae measure meh all oup, but she makes meh take off mah stars, knives, an' hammer. Ah really wasn't thinkin' all tha' much an' just went with et. Didn't take her tae long tae get meh all suited. Real lovely job. Ah just kept thinkin' how jealous yer two were gonna bae. Had big plans tae surprise ol' mum with et tae. But...before Ah could even thank the lass, she'd gone. And taken all mah weapons with her."

Foxtamas' eyes widened. He glanced down to Bunns' hip. Barren. The missing star pouch looked worse on him than any illness.

"Did you find her, or chase her, or get them back? Where'd she go!?"

"Aye, Ah chased her alright. Ah booked et out the door an' saw her runnin' down the alleyway. Right when Ah started to close in, she yelled out a word Ah couldn't make out, adal or edel or somethin'. Next thing Ah know, poof, mah tailor an' mah stars are gone. Ah big ol' wall appeared in ah blink an' blocked her off. Ah tried going back around tae the shop, but et was all jumbled around. Ah...Ah was in some maze,

Scottoh. Et kept movin' an' twistin' on meh. Every turn would take meh down some new alley tha' led tae another alley then another, then another, then another, then another…"

His words turned to mumbles. Tears started swelling over his eyes as his mind traveled back to the labyrinth, the abyss, begging to escape.

But nothing. Even when free now, he still felt the walls. The doors unmoving. The windows open to nothing more than barren rooms.

"You alright?" Foxtamas slung his arm around him. Small tremors rumbled beneath the noble garb.

"Ah tried tae climb, an' scrape, an' all tha' Scottoh. Ah…"

His breath stuttered.

"Ah thought Ah was stuck. Forever."

"Hey, look at me," said the fox. "You're not, okay, you're out, a-and you're free, and we're safe, alright? It's okay, Bunns. It's okay."

The jackalope let himself be pulled in closer for a side hug. His mind felt the walls widening, the street once more coming into view. He was right. It was okay.

"At dawn Ah finally found mah way out. Et led meh right tae yer. Yer was sleepin' in the middle of the road like some lil' abandoned baby, yer know tha'? While Ah hadn't gotten ah wink since the jail."

Smiling, Bunns nudged away from his friend, playing off his nightmarish night with a grin. Foxtamas let it slide.

"Trust me, I had a night of my own. It's…starting to come back to me now…" Flashes struck him. The cart. The shadow. The statues. Like lightning turning the midnight into morn, he caught glimpses of the horror that befell him. One word, however, latched thick into his mind.

"Adal. That's what your tailor yelled, right?"

"Aye. Had tae bae some spell or somethin'."

"Maybe. I think I heard her yell it too. Or, well, someone did. It was right before I passed out."

Flames. Fields.

"Passed out?"

"Yeah, or, knocked out I guess."

Fighting. Hero.

"By who? Did yer get in ah fight?"

Mist. Axe.

"Almost, I, I—"

He reached for his hip.

Nothing.

Foxtamas scrambled to his feet. He turned around everywhere, grasping for the weapon that, just the night before, had hung faithfully by his side.

"My axe! Bunns, you see it?" he sputtered out, frantic. The warrior rubbed his eyes and searched around their side of the building.

"Nae, nothing. Was et stolen tae?"

The words froze him in place. First Bunns' weapons. Then his axe. What else had gone missing? Or, rather, who…

Breathless, the fox sprinted back into the street. His head spun down one way then down the other, searching for anything in the abandonment and desolation.

"Bunns, where is everybody!?"

Fighting off the constant allurement of sleep, Bunns shook his head, confused.

"Ah…Ah dunno. Ah just thought they were sleepin' in. Must, yer know…bae nice…" A delicate snore bookended his line. Foxtamas, though, couldn't be more awake.

"No, something's not right here. Come on, get up! We gotta find Acirema!"

"Yer…yer just now figurin' tha' out—UH!" Bunns choked as the fox gripped him by his newly refined lapel and dragged him forward. "Aye, watch mah suit!"

"Get up! She can't be far. You can sleep when we find her."

A barren wasteland had more life than the long, lone streets of Aydaltown. Gone were the banners of red and gold, vendors offering their wares, legends finding new homes in the hearts of youngsters. Just gray. Stone. A murky day looming overhead.

"*ACIREMA*! *ACIREMA*!"

The pleas echoed into nothingness. While Foxtamas yelled, Bunns slumped behind him, hardly able to put one foot in front of the other. The fox took notice. Any further and he'd have to go on alone.

"Acirema!" he shouted again. "Where are you! *Acirema!"*

As he readied his hands for another shout, a quiet snore met his ears. Really? Had Bunns fallen asleep already, while *walking?*

Foxtamas glanced behind him. His eyes widened.

"Wha'?" the (hardly) awake Bunns asked.

"That wasn't you snoring?"

"Nae, not yet."

"Then who in Evon…"

Confused, Foxtamas stopped their trek in the middle of the road. He scanned the corners of the bland buildings for any sign of movement, noise, or life. Nothing stirred, apart from an alleyway further to their left.

Both boys rushed over. Hidden beneath the shade, disheveled and asleep, lay their princess. An empty bottle of ale rolled out from her hand. Never had they seen her in such a disheveled state. Had her father, nay, the people of Winthrop seen her dirtied tunic, ruffled fur, and heavy, hungover snores…the already bleak future of the Village would, somehow, turn for the worst.

"Acirema! Hey, wake up, wake up!" begged the fox, bending down to shake her awake. Softly, her eyelids fluttered, revealing brown, bloodshot pupils. They searched around at the faces for a moment. How odd yet familiar…almost like they were…

*"AH!"*

Acirema burst awake in a flurry. Her hand flung away the bottle, choosing instead to hug the necks of her friends.

"Y-Y-You, both of you! I thought you abandoned me, like I did you, oh, no, I'm so sorry, so, *so* sorry—" The words fumbled from her mouth, and a flushing of tears poured down her cheeks. To catch them, she squeezed firm her hug. Never had friends felt so sweet.

"Aye, et's fine, Queenie," Bunns soothed.

"Shhh, calm down, we're here," added the fox. Acirema nodded through the hug. "Just tell us what happened. We...had our own adventures last night. How'd you end up here?" He pulled away and allowed her to lean up against the wall, but kept a grip on her hand. The gesture alone almost brought her back to tears.

"It started after the show. Some director of sorts was calling people down to the park for a play, a reenactment of the festival's battle. I...I thought you two were with me. I never cared to look. I was so dumb, so foolish to just leave and—"

"It's okay," Foxtamas whispered, looking directly into her broken, misty eyes. "We don't blame you." Acirema smiled. For a moment, the trio waited in blissful, bated silence.

"It's all a blur after I arrived. I somehow got a seat amongst the crowd and started waiting for you two, but the show, it began so early, so *quick*. Before long they started calling for volunteers to play certain parts. Not talking or anything, just stand-ins for the actors to work off of. I didn't raise my hand, yet they called me out and had me play the role of Queen Periosha. I was hauled up by the director, some stubby fellow, who helped take off my bow and quiver and dress me in a gown they'd prepared. He finished it with this crown on my head. It was...cold. Not like the wind. Like a blade.

"The next thing I remember is being up before the crowd. The actors did their parts and whatnot, talking to and about me. But then the one playing King Wittisus, he...he bowed. His fellow actors followed. Then, when I looked at the crowd, they all did the same.

"They chanted about their loyalty and servitude and honor to me. I was so confused, but then I blinked. The stage disappeared. Somehow, they had me on a castle balcony overlooking the kingdom. Hundreds, maybe thousands were down below me, chanting my name...honoring the queen. I-I-I thought it was real. I thought I'd woken up then and there and ascended the throne.

"That feeling, it startled me to my *soul.* I couldn't comprehend it. I felt the pressure mount, the failure already choking me out. All those eyes looking up to *me. ME.* I wanted to fling myself off that ledge and never face their looks and gazes and faces ever, *ever* again. So much could go wrong in an instant. Who would they blame? Who would they turn to?

"I-I couldn't take it. I threw the crown from my head and awoke from the illusion. The director began berating me for my behavior, but I didn't care. He snatched off the dress and kicked me aside.

"I cried the entire time."

Breaths staggering, Acirema shook off the memories before she continued.

"I made it back to the street. By then everything had calmed down, but I realized you two never showed. I could have looked but…I didn't. One of the few places open was the tavern. I went in, asked for whatever they could give me to black me out. And…they did. My last memories were of those people. The whole multitude of them. Fake, I know, but how *real* they appeared, how *real* the consequences and pressures of the unknown. They put me in a stupor and now I'm…here. With my head hurting and vision blurring and…world still spinning. Oh, I'm so, so sorry…"

"I oughta ban you from saying that word." Foxtamas winked at the raccoon and passed over his flask of water. Acirema raised it to her lips like a beggar. Its coolness eased the worry on her brow more than any ale or brew. "You're not alone, though. Bunns got tricked by some tailor and ended up in a maze, and I…I swear I fell into some dream, kinda like what happened with your crown."

"Tell me about it," she asked, water dripping from her lips. The headache obviously had full control. Any other time and the poor princess would have beaten herself up for such a look. Still, Foxtamas obeyed, and recounted all he could from the night before, listing off getting lost, the cloaked shadow, and the antics that ensued.

"That's when Bunns found me, axe stolen and the back of my head bruised...again."

"Goodness, I can't imagine," she said beneath her breath. "But it sounds like we each were stolen from, right?"

"Yup, but only our weapons."

"But they let you keep your crossbawns." Shocked, Foxtamas lifted up both wrists. Sure enough, the little contraptions still hugged his arms, leathers straps tied tight as always.

"Hmm...I don't think they meant to. In the dark they'd look like regular bracers." He looked over the empty cityscape, squinting. "I don't know what's going on, but we can't trust a thing here. Look what one night did to us. It's some kinda magic for sure, like at the show. Just..."

"Used to scare us and steal our stuff?"

"Exactly." The fox turned his attention back to the group with a furrowed brow. "When I fell through that fountain, I think it broke a spell of some kind. It's like I'd gone into a different world, one where the whole of Aydaltown disappeared. The shadow didn't want me to see it."

"Mine was the opposite. The director, he *forced* me into that world. He must have known how real it seemed."

"It's all tricks then, right? They wanted us to see something before robbing us. Bunns, that how you felt?"

No response.

Just a snore.

As promised, the second the jackalope found himself a wall, he collapsed, practically dead. Thankfully his noise stayed minimal—waking him would be a mistake.

"I'd assume so. Look what it did to him," Acirema said, despite her own body jealous of such precious rest.

"But the magic and madness started *after* he noticed she'd stolen the stars. The tailor who took them yelled some word, 'Adal', the same one I heard, then the walls changed."

"You saw her though, didn't you? Running in that field or whatever?"

It was then the full picture of the night clicked with the fox: the memory of falling into the sparks of blue and seeing the light painted fresh before his eyes. The shadow…it too heard the call, looking to it like a signal, like…a name. He hadn't gotten the axe before knocking Foxtamas out; perhaps doing so was a last resort. Perhaps more pressing matters were at hand. Perhaps…

"The shadow controlled it all," Foxtamas burst out, brain galloping like a blink of lightning.

"W-What? What do you mean?" asked Acirema.

"It's like, um, in the tales, when there's a huge load of magic, there's always a wizard, or witch, or some council strong enough to summon that much. That tailor, a robber just like your director and my cloaked attacker, needed the help of the head mage to stop Bunns from gaining on her. So, the shadow knocked me out and went to help."

"But what about the crown? He did that too?"

"Maybe, or it just held a certain magic within it. Either way, he must've been leading this…coup, or something."

Acirema nodded, trying to rein in all her friend deduced. The silence of the streets seemed to prove his point.

"By coup…you mean they're trying to attack the dukedom?"

"I mean they have to be…right? Who else would they go after?"

"We seem to be the only ones who saw them. We also seem to be the only ones, well, *here* anymore."

The fox felt his heart beat quicker, his breaths pinch short. Had *they* of all people been targeted?

"No, it can't be, Acirema. Why would they openly attack a small band of travelers with dukedom guards everywhere? That would land them in the dungeons."

"Well then, what if they were *part* of the dukedom? Like a personal wizard or something along those lines?"

Both the brilliance of enlightenment and the hazy fog of disbelief almost brought Foxtamas to his knees. The cloaked voice returned—this time by his own volition. He listened to it over and over, picking over the notes, drawing lines across his mind to noises far too similar. The pitch. The cadence. The choice words. He'd heard it all before, in a stupor of surprise. In the first waking minutes within the Rokanoe dungeons.

"Ilindil," he gulped. "The High Elder. The shadow, when he got angry and broke character, sounded *exactly* like him. It must be him, Acirema, it *has* to be! And if so, then the whole operation is…dukedom made. A royal decree, a special mission, a-a-an *attack*—"

"HALT! STAND DOWN!"

The thundering voices of the grizlym guard pair woke Bunns and alerted the others. Both their towering, spiney bodies blocked any chance of escape from the alley. "The duke expects your presence for breakfast. Follow us or be detained."

The promise. Back to bite them. A deal they'd made in innocence. And a deal they'd made with a certain High Elder…

# 16

# "'NEATH KINGS AND COURTS,"

The bag over his head wafted of rotten hay. Once it led them to a lost, muggy cell; another time to pristine paradise; now, to Foxtamas, it felt like being led to the gallows.

A million scenarios zipped across his mind whilst walking in the patchy darkness. Was Ilindil working for the duke? As an advisor, yes, but were his actions actually bloody orders he could not, and would not, refuse? Or was such a plot thicker? Deeper? Maybe the elf was working *against* his lord! The acts of magic treachery against three innocents, meant to undermine the integrity of Osiglada's festival and paint the duke guilty of such crimes. If true, however, why take the weapons? There existed no shortage of them in Aydaltown and perhaps the wider Rokanoe Dukedom. Obviously it left them defenseless...perhaps defenseless enough for a trap. Was such a plan already in motion? Were the guards bringing them *right now* into the final stages of this plan? Would they be pawns, examples, hostages!? No, *no!* They couldn't be, it was too horrible to think, too hard to escape, too hectic to contain in his worried mind a second longer.

Thankfully, before he could fully succumb to the panic, they arrived.

The grizlyms gracelessly ripped their sacks away after seating the trio in stubby wooden seats. They sat in a room unlike anything else in the dukedom. Massive, it stretched both long and wide, crafted of marble but covered with the ornamentation of tapestries, paintings, and curtains blocking out windows thrice the size of guards. Chandeliers dripped from the vaulted ceiling. Gold seemed to melt from them, revealing the layers of silver and bronze holding up dozens of thin, simmering candles.

And somehow it was still secondary to the table and breakfast waiting before them. The friends sat along its length. It looked to be carved from the center of a massive northern timber, waxed and preserved with the original scarring and rings. Atop an almost endless amount of food sprouted from plates and trays of rose-tinted silver. Apples glistening, grapes sprawling, pastries steaming, fish sizzling; never had the trio dreamed such delicacies, much less been inches away from tasting them. The fox's hands began to tremble with hunger. The shadow's terror had taxed his strength, but also his stomach. To snatch just one scone, one berry…

"Ah, so these are the travelers I've heard so much about!"

Deep.

Bold.

Bearing.

The voice of a ruler.

The trio didn't notice the duke behind the mounds of beckoning breakfast. Foxtamas peeked behind a tray of iced poundcakes.

He gulped.

A griffin sat across from them, bulky in scale yet decorated as fine as any king. He bore the narrow head of an eagle. The crown which adorned it, shaped with the Rokanoe styling of thorns and berries, reflected a golden spark, the very same which colored his squinted eyes. Feathers, white as porcelain, trailed back to his wings. Broad and dark, they extended past both his bulky body and seat, perched to his sides like miniature guards (in case the grizlyms beside him were too slow to act).

Draped over his shoulders was a bright maroon gown. Small bits of gilded armor glittered beneath it. His arms, however, were kept bare. Visible veins pulsed royal blood through his tanned lion body. Each paw ended in five jagged points; the beast needed no need for a weapon at his side when he carried ten every hour. Only his wooden staff stayed by his side, locked in his right hand like a shabby scepter.

The griffin spoke entire commandments with a word, demanded respect by a single stare. So ruled Duke Osiglada III.

"Welcome," he started once more, chuckling at the awe in their faces. His words reverberated so thoroughly through the dining chamber they almost sounded buried beneath the earth. "Your joining here today is a blessing. I cannot fully extend my gratitude for your staying and enjoying our festivities."

"Oh, um, no, Your Highness, the thanks is on our end." Acirema bowed slightly as she spoke, though it did little to hide the slur in her speech. Like Bunns on the table's other end, she was beginning to feel the effects of a long night and miserable choices.

"Y-Y-Yes, thank you so much for our stay. It's been, um, a real pleasure," added the fox, matching his friend's royal customs.

"Splendid! It's too often I'm forced to miss most of the fun, but if our guests enjoy themselves, then I claim it a job well done. Truthfully though, it was High Elder Ilindil who conspired the idea. He felt so disturbed by your treatment and demanded it be made right. He also wishes to extend his apologies for not dining with us this morn. I'm told he had an eventful night; not something a shut-in like himself is used to." Osiglada chuckled before reaching over and grabbing a freshly-filled glass of wine.

Foxtamas, meanwhile, froze.

Did the duke know about Ilindil? From the sound of it, he seemed oblivious. His theories, then, must be right—betrayal loomed, and the ruler had to be warned.

He shot a quick glance to Acirema. Her brown eyes already looked his way. The same thoughts spun around her head. Bunns, well...stayed in his own little world.

The duke's tidings eventually sounded like the nonsense rants of his mother. He couldn't care less about the ornamentation and novelties; no, his focus lay on one thing, and one thing alone: the steaming strawberry and cream pastry plopped before his sagging eyes. How the dollop trickled down the flaky brown sides, glistening over sugar-topped strawberries encircling the open rim. The inside had to be a flowing, flowery, *flavorful* delicacy. Neither dreams nor sleep would ever taste as good as how he imagined that dainty little dish.

Paw twitching, Bunns eased it towards the table, until a shout fired towards him.

"No!" called Osiglada. "I ask we discuss a quick matter before starting our meal. *If* that suits you," he snapped, golden eyes pressed on the weary warrior. Bunns nodded. His hand retracted. The broken little heart inside sank.

"Amusing as it may have been, last night's leg of the festival did not go on without its…rumblings, you may call them. Guards and citizens alike reported acts of theft across Aydaltown, particularly around the time of the show."

The ears of the trio perked up. Small glances again passed amongst them.

"Excuse me, Your Highness," said Acirema, "we too were part of that group. This morning we found our weapons stolen, and—"

"There's more." The griffin raised his free paw forward to silence her, a dark stare joining it. "Among these claims came forward eyewitnesses. Every account stated the same—a trio appeared before the attacks, one made of a jackalope, raccoon, and fox…"

The duke sapped away their breathes. They knew their innocence, but felt a heartbeat thump inside their chests, the room seemingly darkening the longer the Rokanoe ruler gazed into them.

"N-N-No, we, we *didn't*, we—"

*"SILENCE!"* Osiglada cawed, shutting down Acirema's claims. "Do you know the feeling of betrayal? How much I must *grieve* for my people who *I* helped rob? Me, the man sworn only to let them *prosper!?"* The griffin forced away his stare and let his head droop to his chest. He pressed his break tight and forced a warbly, tear-tugging tone. "I welcomed you three in. I gave you all you could ever want for the price of a single meal. And yet…your inhibitions remain the same. Why not take from me? *ME!?* The one who has it all! Why the innocents! Why

*them*? Was it not enough? Was it the thrill you sought, not the goods or gains, but the excitement from ruining entire generations with one swipe of your filthy, *nasty* paws—"

"It was Ilindil!!" Foxtamas suddenly shouted, shrill, like an arrow piercing the air. It cut short the monologue.

Silence held the room still.

Until the golden eyes raised.

"What did you say...?" questioned the duke. Foxtamas shrank in his seat. He felt himself fall back into the night before, fire creeping towards him, swords pointed at his throat. Oh, why had he spoken!

"Ilindil, he...he's the one stealing. Each of us, we got attacked by magic, a-a-and the man who attacked me, he had the same voice. I'm worried it might be a plot against you, sir, and we're just ploys, pawns in some game—"

"You would *DARE* put *BLAME* on my *KIN!?*" roared the beast, bolting from his throne and swiping away piles of food from the table. His snarls dripped drool down his gown, the fullness of his mass dominating over Foxtamas. "You think the man who raised me would for the throne would stoop to drollery reserved for life's lowest? I don't know what's weaker—you or your *lies!*"

Shaking, the fox dodged the volley of spittle foaming from the griffin's beak. He couldn't take it. The danger and pressure became too much, the fear of being killed by one smack of his claws overriding his thoughts. The duke yelled on, but poor Foxtamas did not comprehend a word.

"Be glad I'm more generous than you, *all of you!* Either admit your guilt and return all of which you stole, forfeiting any right to step foot into the Dukedom of Rokanoe, or keep denying with pitiful lies and spend your dreary, miserable days rotting in our dungeon. I cannot believe I let you sorry souls free at the start! Such a mistake will *NEVER* be made again, do you hear me!? That is a *decree!*"

Exhausted as they were, Acirema and Bunns nodded to all Osiglada spat. Foxtamas tried. Oh, how he tried. The room, the dressings, the table, all felt like they were closing in on him while the griffin and his grizlyms grew in stature. In his panic, he avoided beady gilded gaze, landing on the staff wrapped by the duke's claws instead.

It had yet to catch his eye, but this time, it looked...different. A light blue hue permeated through it, highlighting carvings deep in the aged, gray wood. Feathers; wings even, spiraling down from top to bottom. Each etching glowed with the same blue aura, like sunlight hitting a stained-glass window.

Right as the markings became clear, the tiniest of sapphire sparks trickled out from it, no more than specks. A single blink would miss them. Foxtamas watched as they traveled behind him, disappearing into the walls.

The stones shifted shades right as they met, growing into a heavier gray. The curtains darkened from red to maroon. The room... it *was* dimming. This was no trick of the imagination, oh no...it was the staff. It was the magic. It was...Osiglada.

No, it was worse. Far, far worse, worse than all the mounting monstrosity he'd pieced together thus far. The feathers, the color, the hinderance of Foxtamas and his journey...

It was Roihelm.

Foxtamas bit his tongue and stared at the duke's paw. Once more the bird appeared in the journey, and once again for the worse. He cleared Ilindil's name only to impart the crime upon himself. Osiglada ruled the magic, controlled the nightmares of Aydaltown, but not without him—not without Roihelm. The duke's reasons didn't matter. Foxtamas cared solely for the phoenix.

Like his nightmare the evening prior, the thoughts that troubled him at Hucksubtle returned. The Author of Evon, a sigil of life for his late parents, causing catastrophe for thousands, unfathomable pain for himself and his brother. Could it be...true? He'd hid the thought once, but now, staring down fresh evidence irrefutable...what choice did he have? He couldn't lie. Not against something so demanding. So devastating.

Roihelm *had* to be involved, clear as day.

The same blue sparks that guised the fountain now floated before him. What more did they accomplish apart from slowing the trio down? Roihelm had stolen from them, locked them away, used his mystical prowess to pin them back from finally finding the lost fox. The nightmare of last night…his doing. The horrors of the running, the residents, the soldiers, fire, all of it. *His doing.* Perhaps in tandem with the duke, perhaps using him like a puppet, whatever theory sounded best. It mattered little. At its heart, the Creator stood against Foxtamas Scottsworth.

Evil, it appeared, brewed in Evon.

And such revelation resolved into a realization of rage.

He wouldn't take it. He wouldn't bow down, wouldn't succumb to a plan like that. Foxlaris was *HIS*, and no one, not even Roihelm, would stop him.

Passion flooded him. Just as it had at the graveyard when his brother's name was scrawled in runny ink. Fear evaporated; reason ran away. The drive that kept him alive time and time again despite *every* mounting odd rose unbounded. Foxtamas would *not* be stopped.

He raised up his left arm.

He aimed down the sights of his crossbawn.

He squeezed his fist.

Tight.

# 17

# "Two Hearts, One Hearth, Our Home!"

Training. Dearg. Sleep.
Training. Dearg. Sleep.
Training. Dearg. Sleep.
Training…

Foxlaris forced himself to pause. The sweat burned his red eye inside out, the short breaths building towards a coughing fit. If only his body had not been so broken. If only the dragon knowledge was not so alluring, so tempting to exploit and use on those who dared hold a blade against him. At times he wondered if Dearg led the charge.

No.

Never.

The ruined skin he carried was his own. The warrior mind became trained, not tarnished. He'd proven bravery and loyalty alike. Had any other even tried to match him? No, how could they. They didn't know redemption. They didn't know the sweet, sweet relief of purpose.

They also didn't know Foxtamas. Bunns. Acirema. They might be better for it, but not him.

Not him.

They drove him. Seeing their heads on spikes, bodies on burn piles. *That* no one knew but him. That no one *predicted* like him. Him.

Foxlaris. Fighter. Easterner.

"M-M-May I venter?" The warbly, sloppy voice struck him harder than any blow. Foxlaris whipped around, sword in one hand and axe upon the other, to find the mauled messenger, Kyrell, standing at the opening of the training grounds.

"What now?" Foxlaris asked. Blunt. Cold.

"Vorde Velrick, he, um…he requests, uh, az meeting wiz the genrikls." The alp stumbled out, trying with his all to translate his Eastern tongue into the Vorde's language. His nub trembled at the sight of the fox.

"Now?"

"Yez. And, um, your room, ztop by your room."

"Hm."

It was good enough. Kyrell bowed his slimy head and bolted away. A trembling sigh trickled out.

The chamber door creaked open. Foxlaris had hardly the time to notice any furnishing other than the red-graced color of his bed. Every morning he left it strewn about, yet every night he came back to it well-fitted. Even now, barely into the day, some alp had already completed the task—better yet, he'd left something in the process, too.

A chest sat upon the bed, drizzled with layers of silk ribbon. Rather fanciful. He brushed them aside with his free hand and unhitched the crate. Inside lay a fresh new attire meant to replace the armor and robes he usually wore.

He pulled first the tunic. Dyed a rich black, the material felt soft despite its unordinary thickness. He traced thin lines of metal woven into the threads. An intricate pattern sprawled out in tandem. Red lines, hardly visible unless in the right light, spread across like veins. The golden cufflinks and buttons exemplified them.

Beneath it lay the rest of the outfit, composed of leggings matching the striking design, a maroon cape and hood with gilded edges, hard, sturdy boots, silver belt, and, to complete it, a golden gauntlet with its matching hook. The look of a warrior.

He could hardly believe the care and condition of such finery. The longer he stood ogling, the more the attire appeared not like new clothes, but a new skin. His acceptance personified.

Two final items rested in the chest's bottom. He took out the first and rolled it through his hand—a gold spiral, no bigger than his finger. Metal rose petals wound up it, hiding in its core a sapphire glistening in the low lamplight. It clicked when he noticed the bottom formed the shape of the stub of his lost ear. The fox wound it around, clipping it into place. A blue rose grew from his head, like the start of a crown.

At last there sat a small note of Crimsdon-crafted paper, so red the fanciful penmanship upon it had to be white.

*My Blue Rose,*

*I hope you find this parcel well. Inside are not just new garments, but the robes and threads of our Champion. Wear them well. I've little doubt you won't.*

*Meeting is on the third level, General's Room. We'll be awaiting your arrival. You've shown your brawn—now ready your brain.*

*Yours,*
*Vorde Velrick*

Champion.

Could such empowerment fit in only eight letters? Three syllables? One word?

His finger felt the ivory ink. Cold to the touch, hot beneath the skin.

Champion.

Him.

Champion.

*THUNK!!*

Gasps fled them. The generals, Vordemohr's highest commanders, looked at one of their own tossed upon the Crimsdon meeting table.

"Dead. Burned in gruesome, Western fire."

Velrick moved his hand away from the smoldered skull of the bugbear Reyhuf. The wolf gazed over his colleagues, eyes scanning their mortified expressions. "You all knew him and Breyhuf, his twin. You served alongside the pair. Loyal to a fault. Loyal, even, to the end." He crept away from the table and towards the wall of windows behind him, the view overlooking the vastness of Forguile and the Village that struck out from it. Getophry followed close.

No one dared speak. Mrattle and Ghroat forced their eyes away from the severed head; Yilgelti and Iota let their minds wander to the past talks and banter with the bugbear boys. It was one thing to die—it was another to burn.

Before anyone could respond to the horror, the hulking doors behind them broke open.

In walked Foxlaris.

The Dress of the Champion fit him without wrinkle. No longer did any splintered orange show. He bore the mold of black, red, and gold, like a shadow you're meant to see, a knocked arrow lying in wait. He walked with demand, and he got the attention he asked.

"Welcome, Champion of the East! Generals, lend your service to Foxlaris. I know his accomplishments have been passed around as myth here of late. Come, take a seat," said Velrick with a sudden excitement. He received a grateful nod from the fox who settled the chair next to Iota. The one that once belonged to the steaming skull before him.

The red eye glanced around to the others. Their stares cut him. The vulture Ghroat side-eyed him with a yellowed, sickly gaze; Mrattle joined him. Yilgelti's quiet rattle felt like a roar, a call to return home, return West.

But they mattered not. Velrick beamed at his presence.

Once situated in his seat, the wolf began again, more open, more boisterous than before. "You sit next to the betrayer of our sister side, the one who *single-handedly* turned the tide against a foe we've battled for ages. Now, dear generals, he is the key to our present worries. The knowledge he has topples even the most accurate of speculation. But you shall see that momentarily. For now, we turn to you, dear Reyhuf..."

The wolf moved closer to the table and took his seat at the head. All focus turned to his burning red glare. "It is now undeniable—the West is slaughtering us. Scout by scout, soldier by soldier, anyone we send across is returned to us by bones and body lone. Need I repeat the rumors brought back by the survivors? Their blame is on *us*. We are, once again, the other, the *enemy*, the sickness to blame for everything plaguing their perfect society. How much worse is it that we can only learn of such horror by maiming our own?"

Velrick paused. A shudder ran through his body. He cast his eyes away, looking only at the table, only at his own reflection in the polished Crimsdon.

"We may deny it. We may try to run from it. But war...war *is* coming. Hear the marches. Hear the horns. War is coming to Evon."

"You're certain, my Vorde?" spoke the scrawny screech of Ghroat.

"More than I care to admit."

"B-But how can they?"

"Through invasion." Once more, the wolf stood up, forcing his jittering nightmares out step by step. "This time they'll bring an army to our shores instead of a bridge. We're a threat that needs neutralizing."

"And so, what do you propose?" asked the viper.

"Him." His long, clawed finger fired out, aimed straight at the fox. "Our Champion."

"What, for peace talks?" Mrattle scoffed. The fat coating his slimy skin jiggled as he chuckled. A single eye noticed.

"Don't jest with impossibilities. No, Foxlaris came to us for more than the vanquishing our inland foe—he will teach us about the greater one knocking on our doorstep." As he continued, the Vorde's gait waded him around the table, to behind the fox. "He's the only Westerner you've ever met. The only one here in our domain. Can you even *question* the wellspring of knowledge brimming within him? The tactics we could only squabble at? No matter how many troops we send over, none could ever gather as much as he already knows, here, before us in this moment!"

The tarmin shook his jowl.

"Oh, come now!" he spat. "You can't just dress up some stowaway cripple and act as if he's a *mastermind* compared to us! It's folly!"

"*QUIET!*" the Champion roared. He burst out from his chair and stared down the over-sized frog sitting across him. Little did he notice the wolf stalking behind his shoulder.

"Don't get foul with me, boy! You think that old title outranks us?"

"I'll kill you..."

"Oh, shut it already. Don't act tough—this, this *farce* is nothing more than another odd tactic begging to fall to pieces. We've *troops* and *men*, Velrick, and you trust this—"

Mrattle didn't see it coming. The fox leapt across the table, throttling his body into the tarmin, tackling him. He pinned the general's throat beneath his peg before reaching down and skewering his slimly cheek with a golden hook. The frog looked like a fish dangling from a line. Try as he did, no normal sound came through. Just little putters of pain while squirming under the fox's sizzling stare.

"You call *him* Vorde. You call *me* Champion. Doubt either of us again. I *dare you.*"

Foxlaris ripped the hook through the skin. Bubbling blood of black and green smeared across his face, the table, and the stuttering, screaming tarmin. He paid it no mind. The Champion of the East leapt back across and to his seat, hook dripping.

"I hope that answers your question, Mrattle," sighed the wolf. "Return to your seat, please. We have a meeting to conduct." Velrick's smile perked as he floated back to the room's front. The slobbering general, however, slumped back in shame, his webbed hands slipping to hold the black slick from spewing out. Ghroat side-eyed him. Yilgelti's slithers felt like drums against his head.

The red eye gave him no more time of day.

"As I was *saying*, we have a leg up over the West. Foxlaris, if you would, tell us what we are too unfortunate to not know. Armies, cities, weak points, all you can."

The fox nodded. He passed one look around to secure the attention of his peers.

"The West is scattered," he began, voice quiet yet commanding. "There's no central army like there is here. The most unity it's ever seen was Grammo Day, and that ended in failure. It does have strong points. The Fulnoa, the City of Mikyill, the Kingdom of Efeters—each has their own army of fighters, but they're only loyal to their leaders. Small villages and towns lie between them. Some have forces, some don't." The faces around him bobbled with pleasure (apart from Mrattle). Some felt a little tingle of pride settle in.

"What of numbers? Troop makeup?" Ghroat probed.

"Or distance from us?" Iota added.

"That...I can't promise anything. I've seen scrapes here and there. Most fighters are either Fulnoa dwarves or conscriptions. Together they have many, but their might is nothing compared to Vordemohrian soldiers, and most are too spread out to assemble. The Fulnoa and Mikyill are nowhere close, Efeters being even farther southwest."

"So any chance of a union would hardly be timely?" Yilgelti asked.

"Exactly."

"Which is why we must prevent it."

The smooth voice of Velrick entered once more. He gripped in his hands old, strained scrolls, some the red hue of Crimsdon, others made from worn, rugged cloth.

"If they wish for war, they shall unite, no way around it. But if we can stop it, the story changes." Carefully, he unfurled the papers, laying out sheets one by one. "We must hold them apart. Attack each central bastion one by one. If this can be accomplished, we turn the tide and invade *their* land before they're given the same chance. These places, the Fulnoa, Mikyill, all of them will fall weak. They'll be helpless to start a war."

The meeting table lay covered in dozens of maps of old. They spanned from Vordemohr on one side to the complete other shore, passing by names such as *The Setting Valleys* and *Grovistok Grove.* All, however, missed their left-most half. River Nohsis separated the page and left the West a mystery apart from the Mechmilne shore.

"These are the only maps we have of the West, and as you can see, it's nothing more than guesswork past a tree line. Foxlaris, it is your duty to fill them in best you can. Likewise, decide where the first attack should be."

"Is that not a little quick, my Vorde?" asked the viper whilst eyeing the canvases.

"Would you rather fight one congested hoard? Moving now is essential. The longer we wait, the longer we give them to form an army we cannot even begin to visualize."

"I understand," she hissed beneath her breath.

"Good. Confer with whoever you must, but time is of the essence, Champion. Tomorrow evening at the latest. The command will be one given under the guise of nightfall."

Foxlaris hated the nerves he felt. Power now finally fell in his grasp. But where to use it, where to wield it?

It didn't matter. *He* was the Champion. Figuring it out would come to him, moreover after he constructed the map.

"It will be done," he said, voice strong, assured.

"Thank you. I know this all is taking us by storm. I too wish we had a longer period of peace and celebration after the Cult's defeat. But times like these…they are unprecedented. We've waited long, battled hard. Stopping now only guarantees our failure. It is now, in these critical moments, we show our worth. Now, once again, East shall meet West."

# 18

# "Now Bend the Knee and Bow the Wings"

*TTHHUNNKK!!*

*"GGGAAAAHHH!!!"*

The staff dropped to the floor. Blood from the duke's pierced hand dripped upon it. But it didn't land on the royal rug beneath the table, or the ancient, hand-crafted tiling beneath that.

It landed on wood.

Rotting wood.

Littered with the remains of season-old hay.

Everything changed the moment the staff fell. The walls suddenly lost their beauty, becoming slats of plain, dry planks. Too turned the table and breakfast. The marvel vanished into a feeble wooden beam propped up by a pair of metal buckets. The food? A spare few fruits and hardtack loaves. Not a strawberry pastry in sight.

The chamber revealed itself as the upstairs of an abandoned barn. And yet that was not the worst of it.

The grizlyms disappeared. A mole, outfitted with a grimy tunic, glass-heavy goggles, and boots a few sizes too big for his feet, replaced one while a graven (a larger raven with parsed feathers of solid gold), beak and face burdened by thick scarring and body bearing a much nicer violet tunic and cape, took the spot of the other. Both looked dumfounded. Luckily, the duke demanded the brunt of the attention.

At least, what was left of him.

Duke Osiglada III of Rokanoe was no more than a greasy, curly-haired faun dressed in a hand-me-down vest and patched-up slacks. He too had scars and cuts like the graven. They ran up and down his tanned olive skin and across the close-shaven beard and curled horns protruding from his mop. His emerald eyes widened in horror as the blood sprayed from his hand. No booms boasted from his voice—only the whines of a liar.

The bustling paradise of Aydaltown used to sprawl beyond the windows. In a single drop of the staff, the curtain pulled away, it vanished. Replaced by overgrown fields flecked with brown and tainted green. A rotting stone path trekking through it. No keep, no buildings, not even a fountain ready to spurt flavored fire. Just the remains of what once was.

Bunns thought himself in a dream. No dukedom could just up and…disappear. That only happened to small little settlements, and only those cursed or haunted at that.

He became a believer when he saw, piled up along the wall next to him, a stockpile of *obviously* stolen goods. Tops, grain sacks, fruit barrels, clothes, weapons, and, shimmering on the edge, his star pouch.

If it was a dream, he didn't want to leave.

—Until he looked at his clothes.

The suit of red and gold vanished along with the castle, replaced with a coat of sackcloth. No *wonder* it felt so itchy!

*"GAHH!!"* the faun's screams broke through. He dropped to his furry knees and started to wiggle at the bolt, spitting out whatever words—and curses—he could find.

He gained no sympathy from the fox. Already Foxtamas had the other crossbawn poised at the faux guards, forcing their hands up and away from any weapon they may have hidden away. A fiery mix of anger and passion still burned within him. Before turning his attention back to the mumbling mess of a "duke", he motioned for his friends to retrieve their weapons from the pile. They could watch the mole and graven. The faun…the faun was his.

"You better start explaining *everything*, got me!?" Foxtamas yelled. It was his turn to shout, to loom over and see the pain of another. He kicked away the staff with his boot and ensured the blue hue faded from it. Before long, it blended in with the rest of the decaying barn.

"We're thieves, okay, the three of us, we're *thieves!* It's all fake!" cried the faun, clutching his hand. The bolt seemed to have pierced the other side. "The entire town, we made it up to rob you, it's fake! *Fake!* I'll tell you everything, just spare us, please, please spare us, *please!!"*

Pitiful begging—a squeak compared to his voice seconds prior. Even so, it did little to move the fox's heart. He didn't see any room for mercy. Foxlaris was dying in the East because of him, because of all three of them. They'd wasted *precious* time. All for what? An axe? A bow?

The faun didn't deserve anything but a bolt. This time aimed a little higher.

"Foxtamas!"

Acirema's cry woke him. Like smoke billowing from a chimney, the passionate rage blinding him simmered away, and he turned to the princess. Beneath her headache and the shock of the vanishing keep, she shook her head. She felt his same need for justice. Only with sanity on her side. "He's right, spare them. There's a better place they can go."

"I'm Adalgiso, but friends call me Adal. The mole, he's DeWitt, and she's Garrona. We go by the Rokanoe Raiders."

The day had reached noon. Burning overhead, the sun beamed down upon the barren, empty homestead. The tall grass let the wind guide it along; the cracked path baked under the midday heat; somewhere in the barn a wooden plank creaked.

The only action about the farm took place at the cell. All along it had been nothing more than old iron bars melted together and bolted into the ground. Still, it served its purpose—holding down a small band of miscreants.

"Like I said," Adalgiso continued, "we're thieves. Have been for a lil' bit now." Earlier, Acirema had graciously extracted the bolt and tossed in a rough part of a sack to wrap it with. He rattled off the information intently, though now much calmer and with an assured suave that, had he not been locked in his own creation, may have worked on the weak-minded.

Foxtamas was not one of them. He stared down the thieves from the remains of an old tool bench. His friends joined him, though they mostly dug through the confiscated goods brought down from the barn. Seeing Foxtamas take charge still felt odd. But being on the brink of exhaustion…they welcomed the change. He worked well with his anger out.

"We fell into some trouble with the dwarves a few weeks back and got locked up until that earthquake hit. It was so strong the bars holding us in snapped right in two. The place is loaded with a million an' one exits, so we took the first one we could find while the place was losing its mind. We just so happened to jog past some office or closet or whatever and saw that there staff glowing."

"Figured it could be worth a lil' somethin'!" DeWitt, the tubby mole slumped behind the faun, piped up, only to be met with sharp glares from his mates.

"Was I asking you to speak? Huh?" Adalgiso spat at him. He continued without missing a beat. DeWitt, however, rolled his eyes in a tiny act of defiance. "So yeah, we stole it. We were out of there without a trace."

"And got right back to robbing," Foxtamas said.

"Close. I tested the staff once we were far enough out in the Dwarfmoors. It's a weird sorta thing…" he paused, looking around for a way to explain it. "My thoughts, they…come to life, I guess. Anything I think is placed around us, but it's not real. It masks reality in a way."

"Like the barn?" Foxtamas moved in closer, desperate to hear the mastery behind the tricks.

"That exactly. I imagined the dining room, our disguises, that suit your jackey wore. The magic didn't change a thing of how it felt, just how it looked. Thing is though, you let go, it all goes with it. Your connection breaks."

"And yet you still had the gall to drop it." Like a bump in the night, the shady yet sharp voice of Garrona spooked the conversation. She shifted her golden eyes (very much real this time) to her leader, then the fox.

He gulped.

"Oh, I'm sorry Miss Goldwing, did you want to take an arrow to the hand? Fox, go ahead and give her one, I bet she'd love it, wouldn't ya?"

"Do it. Give me something to jab in that neck of yours."

"Still mad you weren't in charge on this one?"

"Of course you'd like being locked in a cage."

"I bet it *reeks* of trauma in here for you."

"More than playing pretend in your little fantasy land?"

"Ooooh, low blow, that one. Go ahead and shank me if you're cutting that deep."

"Don't tempt me."

"H-How about wih just try a-and calm down—"

"SHUT UP DEWITT!" They shouted in unison.

The mole cowered back to his corner as his friends fired at him. They stood face to face in a yelling match. One more word and an actual fight might break out.

Trying to avoid adding tension, Foxtamas turned back to his friends.

"We aren't like this…right?" he whispered.

"Ah'd bae back in Winthrop sleepin' if weh were," replied Bunns.

Once the rage subsided in the cage, the fox started the questions anew. This time, however, he felt pushback from the faun. Like heaving a boulder uphill.

"So…last night. Why'd you do it? You saw what kinda pain it put us through."

"Unintentional." Adalgiso fiddled with the bottom button of his vest. He barely paid the fox any mind.

"What do you mean *unintentional?*"

"You heard me. After we broke out, we didn't have time to go find one of our weapon stashes. So, we needed some arms. You three carried plenty."

"But how's that supposed to be unintentional?"

"Oh, that part's not, but you all gettin' scared is." He finished the fiddling and gazed back up to Foxtamas. Something about his unkempt hair and growing smug attitude made the fox tingle with anger. "See, we're more honest than you're giving us credit for. We bring you in, ruffle you up a bit with the dungeon and all, then make you feel like kings. The stealing comes *riiiight* at your zenith. I sprinkled a lil' extra magic around to make you feel great about yourself and trick you with your pride.

"I was the one tasked to you. Remember that fight? The one you *blatantly* brushed past? I had such a *spectacle* planned! You were 'sposed to rise up like a warrior, feel like a champion to *all* of Aydaltown. But…gah, you just ran away!"

"So you had to *terrorize me?*"

"Of course, what option did I have?" he sniped, smirking with a nasty grin. "I was mad at you for being so stupidly scared. And that axe…it's a beauty, far better than the usual hooks I use. Still can't believe you ran away, and not just away, but into a *burning fountain.* The *foolishness!*"

"Not another word!" From behind, Acirema came storming in, finger pointing straight at the cell. "You put someone through physical madness and wonder why they end up scared?"

"Please, princess, don't act like you're any better."

Her bloodshot eyes widened. How did he…

"Oh, come on! We heard every word you said. I don't care to know where this Winthrop place is, so don't start filling me in. Bunny boy was right, bringin' it up wouldn't have gotten you a single favor. Say, bring him over, he seems more reasonable—"

"Be quiet!" Acirema yelled.

"Gonna lock me up in a different little hole? Goodness me! You're lucky we didn't just poison you when we had the chance, running away like a child when we *tried* to make you feel good. I knew I should've taken that job, but oh no, just *had* to let DeWitt run it, didn't we?"

"I tried meh bist—" the stuffy mole started in his warbly accent but refused to finish. Garrona would sever his head from spine if he said a word more.

"Took the last of our liquor to calm you down. Whew, lemme just say, *some* princess."

Foxtamas yanked her back, a split second before she bolted into the cage. His calming hand held her, felt the heat rising from the blood boiling within. Tears leaked from the edges of her eyes. Born not of rage like the rest of her actions. Just pure, pure brokenness.

"Why not just rob us like normal thieves then?" Each word left her lips cold.

"You mean you'd rather I punch you in the gut, put a knife to your throat and let these buffoons dig through your stuff? I didn't know the show was *that* bad!" Rising, Adalgiso looked down at the racoon, a head taller than her. "Like I said, we're honest. Why not give a little spice to your life and let you pay with, oh, I dunno, a few things of your own? Like bartering, just...one-sided."

"It was torture."

"It was *fun*. You're too high strung to enjoy it. All you are. Just a band of an overbearing loon, witless ruler, and scared little fox trampling around thinking they can navigate this world, acting like you won't stumble into anything wrong time and time again. And you know what I wish you? Good. *Luck*."

His wicked smile just about cost him a bolt to the head. Foxtamas had raised his arm before his words finished, anything to defend both his friends. Some scared little fox he would be.

"Do it," Garrona piped up, causing the faun to step away from the bars, giggling to himself. He slumped down to the dirtied hay and watched the princess huff away.

Foxtamas caught up to her at the pile of recovered goods. Knees to her chest, she plopped down on an old grain sack once belonging to a passing vendor. Bunns lay passed out beside it.

"He's lying you know," said the fox, "just trying to get under our skin—"

"I am *not* freeing them." Never had her soft, floaty voice turn so dim.

"What?" he asked, taking a seat beside her.

"They can rot there for all I care."

"I…I know how you feel. But leaving them to die like that—"

"What, will make me like my father? Better that than running off, right?" She fired back, her words wobbling into a mess of tears. Foxtamas tried to muster some calming thought. Nothing formed. Instead, he slid closer and put her head on his shoulder.

"Shhhhh. No one thinks that. He's just mad we caught him, like…like a child, y'know. It's a small nursery in that cage right now. Just a buncha kids." Slowly, a glimpse of a smile floated to the surface. Despite how desperately she wished to drown it.

"What will we do with them then?" she whispered.

"I'm…not too sure. We might just wait until morning. You two need to sleep. I'll keep watch on them and toss in a couple apples or something to keep them happy—"

*"HEY! FELLAS! COME HERE!"*

*"DEWITT ONE MORE WORD!"*

*"I'LL STRANGLE YOU!"*

Foxtamas bolted up, glaring over to some tussle down at the cage.

"Did he mean us?" asked the princess, standing and wiping her face.

"Gotta be, right?" replied Foxtamas.

"Unnggg…what yer need, Scottoh?" Bunns lifted his dreary head. One of his floppy ears perked at the screams. Just enough to ruin his golden slumber.

"Nothing, Bunns. I think our prisoners are going crazy already."

Despite his forthcomings, the jackalope joined the drama. He followed his friends back to the jail and saw firsthand the animals and their fighting.

The graven pinned poor DeWitt to the ruddy ground, her sharp golden feathers ready to attack at the next sound he made.

"Stop it, *stop it!"* Foxtamas shouted, banging against the bars. "Let him go! What did y'all need!?"

"Nothing, he's acting the fool," Adal muttered with a shake of his head.

"No, let him speak." Once again, the crossbawn raised. This time the bolt would be for Garrona.

"I-I was wantin' tih b-bargain with yih," DeWitt stumbled out. He caught his breath and slipped up past the bird. "Wih can take yih folk up a secret way tih the Fulnoa."

"Nae, nae, nae," protested Bunns, waving his hands. "Weh ain't takin' ah single other 'secret way' naewhere, got meh? Tae many bad things been happenin' when weh do."

"Where yih plannin' tih go then?"

"New Lothlock," the fox replied.

"Yih'll only bih headin' south and wastin' yih time. There isn't much of a clearer way from here. Only a day's walk 'till yih make it to the Last Ring then the Dwarfmoors. Even quicker now with the gorge opened up."

"And *you three* will be leading us there?" chimed in Acirema.

"Aye. I figured wih could offer it tih earn a lil' bit'a freedom." Unsightly as he may seem to the Rokanoe Raiders, the mole was not without his charm. A bit of red poked from under his thick cheeks and thicker glass goggles. How had a poor soul ended with such a rotten band?

Foxtamas signaled to the others. Together, they turned their backs to the cell and formed a huddle, speaking low to hide the conversation.

"Thoughts?" he tossed out.

"Yer really want tae trust *another* route like tha'?"

"I mean, we're lost without it. And if it's only a day…"

"What if they betray us?" asked the princess.

"Ah won't let tha' happen. Ah'll keep tha' staff ol' Adally had close tae mah chest."

"Plus, they don't have weapons—well, apart from the graven, but Bunns, you can watch her."

"Weh each gonna take one then? Like ah guard tae ah guide?"

"Ummm…I suppose so."

"I get DeWitt," Acirema said. "Lucky."

"Wha—Bunns, you *said* you wanted the graven—"

"Ah'm jokin', Queenie!"

"Guys, focus. The faun's mine then."

"We *really* doing this then?"

"Do we have much else of a choice?"

"How 'bout lettin' ah poor ol' merchant stumble on their bones, eh?"

"I wouldn't be opposed."

"Stop it you two. We'll be no better than them at this point." Bunns and Acirema passed each other a knowing—and exhausted—glance

The trio broke form and turned to the cage. Even with the higher ground, Foxtamas felt the anticipation of the deal bubbling within him.

"We'll agree to the bargain, DeWitt, but under a few rules. We leave tomorrow, get the staff, and each one of you will be guarded by one of us. You'll be free once we reach the end of your trail. Got it?"

"Yissir! Oh, thank yih so much, wih appreciate it, don't wih?" He looked back in a flurry of excitement, only to meet rolling eyes and shaking heads. Adalgiso, however, glanced up and added a grin.

"Fine by me. Every duke needs a little holiday here and there!"

# 19

# "To Our Good Kindly Wolver Kings,"

Another early morning welcomed them. Now plenty rested, Bunns was up handling the Raiders while Foxtamas and Acirema double-checked their supplies. Fresh water, fresh fruit, new (although stolen) arrows and bolts—they were set.

Bunns used old rope from the barn and tied the hands of the thieves together in front of them. DeWitt made no complaint, Garrona said no word, and Adalgiso chose to barely keep his mouth shut. Nothing phased the jackalope, though. He could handle anything after that night of torture.

Once rightfully bound, the journey northward began. Acirema held the front of the line with DeWitt, letting him steer the party in the right direction. Bunns took up the middle with the graven (staff in hand), and Foxtamas handled Adalgiso in the back. An odd line of travelers for sure.

The mole's path led them down the abandoned road on which Aydaltown had once sat. It carried on through the overgrown field a way before turning right and fizzling out on the way up a barren ridge. Once topping it, the terrain turned hilly. Only small bits of trees and forest dotted the region. Long, sloping plains of short, chipper grass spread across. Flower patches sprang around. Bits of yellow, blue, purple, and red sprinkled amongst the viridescent sea.

Despite the loss of the trail, DeWitt held true. Acirema barely had to keep watch on him. He steered the company along the dawn-bathed ridge line one step at a time.

"So, DeWitt," the princess piped up, "where exactly are you leading us? I know you mentioned some places yesterday."

"Yip! Lots of windin' through these here hills before yih reach the gorge. Wasn't really a gorge 'till the earthquake hit, used tih be an old rotten ridge wih climbed up. Wih hid stashes up there thit no one ever found. Just pist it is the Last Ring. It's just called thit because, once yih go through it, yih'll be out of Mechmilne and tih the Dwarfmoors. It's a real treasure of a place." The pep in his funny little accent made it seem like he wasn't even a captive. His cheeks glowed a ripe red, and his smile helped push them out.

"Ah, I see. But what do you mean by stashes?"

"Weapons, mainly. Sometimes food, but wih're used tih being good on thit. My idea, actually. These two can't keep up with a blade tih save their lives!" Acirema watched him bobble between chuckles. She held back a curt, quiet smile.

"Good on you!"

"Yip! They may nit give mih a whole lit of credit, but I'm real smart. Always prided mihself on mih brain."

"I agree. Takes a lot to remember a trail like this and offer to lead us. But..." Acirema paused, taking a moment to stare back at her friends and their 'companions.' The beady eyes of Garrona; the careless posture of Adal; she felt the contempt built into them. "Why stay with them? If they don't value you, your smarts, your care..."

"Oh, it's nithing, really. And mih reason, well...it's a long story," sighed the mole.

"We've got plenty of time, right?" she smirked.

"Just a few hours." DeWitt chuckled to himself again and pointed for his raccoon partner to take a turn down the hill. "Well, I'm from a big family—or, um, *was*, I guess. Mih parents were farmers. They had a million an' one responsibilities tih do, and keeping up with eight kids wasn't the easiest. I...wasn't cared for all thit much. I never found I was loved or wanted. So...I ran away. Tih Mikyill.

"I was already seeing how smart I could be, y'know, with tinkering on things and building and all thit. The only ones who really saw mih skills and liked them were the thieves. Mikyill's underground is well nasty. Mih group, the Boundless wih called ourselves, was a smaller one, sure, but had power. I worked with them for some years and grew as a thief and thinker. Made weapons, plans, traps, all sorts of things. It all wint good and will until the conquering."

"Conquering?" Acirema turned to him, bewildered. "I never heard word of Mikyill being conquered."

"Oh no, nit Mikyill, us, the Boundless. See, there's this one big thief group dominatin' the lands. Their long an' proper name is the Brigands of the Long Dark, but most jist call them the Abyssmals for their base kept in Evon's biggest abyss. All the caves around us lead tih it somewhere or 'nither.

"But anyway, wih lost our war tih them, and so wih had to join them as fealty. I didn't mind. It got mih out of Mikyill and with new people. I ended up meeting Garrona there. Wih bonded quick and did our missions for a while until Adal came. He took tih us. We three bonded even quicker, and he decided our lives would be better if wih left the Brigands behind. Thing was, he was tied into the politics of it all, so leaving was a horrible idea. But...wih did. Wih ran right away and up north.

"So, I guess I stay with them because...it's the only family I git. It's like a home for mih. Yeah, wih fight and all thit, but all families do. It's...the only place I've felt included. Winted."

He didn't realize it, but the tears brimming against his goggles had started to fog up the glass. DeWitt shook them away and took off the spectacles. As he did, the calming touch of the princess grazed his shoulder.

"Thank you for sharing, DeWitt. I know it's not easy reliving those kinds of memories. You have a lot of spark, you know that? Better, a wonderful heart and mind alike. I say speak up to them. If they care as much as you say, I'm sure they'll listen to you. And if not, well..."

"I know wit yih mean," he nodded to her, trying to find a grin while wiping his eyes. "Jist been a little hard here late, what with being jailed and this earthquake and all. But I will. Promise. It's…sort of like having tih yell at yir parents."

"I imagine so!" The princess laughed along with him. The cooling air brushing back the heather of the hills rushed through her purple tunic and fur.

Imagine she did. But oh, how she wished she hadn't.

The travelers were low in a shady valley when the refreshing sounds of a waterfall found them. The long boughs overhead blocked all but the small drizzles of sunlight. Crushing in, the waterfall bounded from its landing nest of jagged rocks and into a tranquil pool below, almost as if wrangled from flashing whites to gentle ripples by some strict, unseen mother. The break made way for a mid-morning breakfast. Foxtamas tossed some fruits and flasks to the others; the thieves, however, bent over for a drink and nibbled on their apples like children.

Garrona did *not* agree with the arrangements. The waves lapped too far from her beak. Any further to reach them and she'd disappear into the pool.

"Hey." Her call was almost inaudible to the jackalope beside her. His meal was long scarfed and water long drunk.

*"Hey!"*

"Wha' do yer need?" Bunns asked, ear perked.

"Untie me for a bit. I can't reach the pond."

"Hah!" The warrior shot up and wiped the crumbs from his garment. He edged away from the glittering bird and closer to the tree behind him. "Nice one, lassie. Ah ain't about tae fall for tha'."

"It's just one second," she added with a voice of frozen stone.

"Aye, tha's all et takes."

"You wouldn't last even that in chains, much less rope."

That wiped off his smile. He turned back to her and found the golden glare boring into his head.

"I know you have stars. I try and run you'd pin me in a heartbeat." She inadvertently soothed his pride. Bunns raised his eyebrows in delight. She *did* need water to survive…and no one ever moved *too* fast for him to catch…

The jackalope loosed the knots. He let the haggard string fall, and the glittery wings of Garrona swung wide to her sides for balance as she lowered her beak into the pond. Gushes of water swelled in. Drips and drops covered her like a black flower on an early spring morn. In between the gulps, she paused to speak back to Bunns.

"Be lucky. Those stars would barely have scratched me."

And thus his pride was strangled. Bunns felt physically assaulted in the moment, only replying with a scoff.

"Really? Comin' from the beastie who tried tae steal them?" he attacked, angsty.

"Wasn't my plan," shot Garrona between sips, "Adal wanted more weapons. I'm just fine."

Back to the water.

"Aye, with wha', yer feathers?"

*SHLUNK!!*

Still face down, Garrona shot one of her golden weapons with just the shake of her silky wing. The blade landed inches from Bunns' feet, forcing him back and a star into his paw.

"Why yer—!"

"A demonstration. Not a threat." Finally, after taking her fill, the graven rose and wiped away the watery mess from her beak. Bunns pulled the object out and observed it, testing the razored edge and balance between the shaft and vane.

"Et feels like a throwing knife," he commented. Never had he seen anything so sharp as it was regal. Even without a handle it balanced perfectly upon his paw.

"Exactly. Better than stars."

"Trust meh, Ah've heard tha' before..." Bunns twisted the feather around in one hand and the star in the other as vague, repressed memories of Rillem flashed by. The Velvedier metal burned at his side.

There was no use guarding over the bird. Bunns kept twisting and tossing both weapons beneath his tree opposite the captive. She stared at him. Stared through him, even.

"See, thing is with knives, yer only got one good point an' two good sides. Mah stars, they got plenty o' both."

"True. But they give no good handle. Your hands will be worn and weary before long."

"Meh. Stars are sharper."

"Knives are deeper."

"Not if yer throw et hard enough."

"Hardly."

She paused, tilting her head and securing her golden lock on the jackalope. "If I were to run right now, you'd toss that star. It would hit, I would hurt. But without a perfectly open spot, that's the most I'd feel. You toss that knife and strike me just right, I'd fall. The life would drain from me. You'd have to dig through the messes of hot, pumping blood to even retrieve your weapon from my body. Worse, you throw that feather as fast as I can, you'd feel the dying beat of my organs, see the entrails leak out while I cling on and endure every sting, every last touch of the insides I kept secure for so, so long."

Bunns gulped. He looked away, finding someone, something to focus on other than the merciless pictures the golden raven created.

"Oh, quit tha' talk. Ain't no reason tae bae all dark an' moody. Yer ain't lightened up once since weh found yer. Lookit yer mole friend, he's been chipper all morn."

"That's DeWitt, not me. Don't act like you'd be any better off in this situation."

"Lassie, *yer* tossed meh in one!"

"Hm." Garrona whipped her head away. She ogled another drink but decided against it. Sitting in the quiet of the grove was enough.

Bunns chuckled to himself. She'd come around on stars one day. Her weapon though…few things had impressed him more. He felt it over again. The gold somehow never heated, keeping a sharp, frigid sting. The bristles looked like they would move but instead held their shape, like an artist's imitation carved from stone. Even still, something about them seemed off. He'd seen feathers before, but none so…scarred. Scratched. Some marks from claws, others from blades both thick and thin.

The realization froze him. He glanced back to Garrona. His heart sank.

"Yer said something about chains before…wha' did yer mean by tha'?"

The golden eyes glanced over her shoulder. They did not beam as confident as before. Seconds later they vanished. Retreated back to the pond, to the falls, to the calm. Although she could not see him, Bunns nodded and leaned back against the bark. Perhaps the story was his to figure out. Like a poem, only with signs of anguish instead of the scribbles of an author.

"Gravens are almost extinct in Evon."

The syllables cut worse than any star, knife, or feather.

"Myths have been made about us. That we hoard gold in hidden places. Can sniff it out. It's a lie. Always has been. But some, they still believe, and when they cannot coax it from us, they take what they can.

"Our feathers."

Her paused roared. She waited for the waves to have their say, the wind to drop its two Tops. Though, really, she waited for only one person: her poor, broken self.

"My family was from Pradifore. I was young. I may have had a baby brother. He comes to me in dreams. His crying, anyway. A thief group, Scellar's Sons, killed them for their feathers but kept me. I was caged for years. I'd grow new feathers, they'd pluck them out. It's called livemining. I made them rich. They sold me. I made a new band rich. They sold me. I never left the cage. I'm smaller than my fellow gravens. Weaker, so I'm told, at least. I've never met them. I was alone.

"I was eventually bought again. But freed this time. It was the Brigands of Long Dark. They told me my freedom would be paid in servitude. They gave me a weapon, and I obeyed. After life like that, being nothing but a moveable gold mine, it was enough. All my fear and anger came out. I forgot how to feel anything more. I still don't. No one beats me in fights. Only DeWitt would talk to me, and when Adal came, him too. So that's what made me." Inch by inch, she creaked her head back to Bunns. The gold faded to evening yellow. Tears wobbled like a dying sunset over the ocean. "I can't lighten up. I don't know how."

Anything Bunns could say would only fall short; any emotion he stirred inside could never reach the raw pain the poor girl endured. He stacked his own life against hers. How could any of his worries come close? What did it matter that he feared for his friends, took the weight of the world on his shoulders? It paled in comparison to hers. Everything did.

"Bunns!" The unmistakable call of the princess came from the grove's end. He sprang out of his thoughts and looked over to her. DeWitt, still bound, had already started taking off. "We're heading out, come on!"

"Ah hear ya, Queenie! One sec!"

Pack on his back, he went to call for Garrona, but found her ready by the waterside. Her wings held the rope.

"Tie it back. I can't myself."

Bunns...he...he couldn't. He couldn't put her back like that, not after her life and story and—

"Hurry."

Brown met gold. For the first time, the warrior wavered.

He felt the coarse strands of rope enter his paws. They rubbed his callouses worse than any star ever could.

"Ah...Ah'm sorry," he muttered as he bound her wings in front of her.

"It's fine. Some things are never meant to change."

The path forward took them back up another ridge and set of hills. Slowly, more trees sprang up along the dips and crests. Mixed with the flowers and long patches of grass, the scene felt like paradise. For most of the travelers.

Foxtamas had yet to say a word to his faun, but not so for the latter. Small jabs and jests peppered their walk. Thankfully, the fox spent most of a lifetime in the presence of a little snickering sidekick. Keeping up his "stoic" look drained him, but did give him time to think. Make connections. And, after a good few hours, finally bring something of substance up to Adal.

"Osiglada…"

"He speaks!" The faun jumped in surprise.

"Is just your name backwards…" Foxtamas side-eyed him. He watched the loon bow and chortle.

"Cracked the code then? Surprised you're still on that."

"You left some loose ends."

"As any honest thief would."

"Wittisus…Garon…"

"DeWitt and Garrona, atta boy. They forced me to add those, said I was 'stealing all the credit.' You think I was? Stealing, *me?*" Foxtamas shook his head. Regret drowned him. "I suppose so with Aydaltown. Was originally 'Adaltown' but Garrona hated the sound of it. I agree, much more natural."

"How did you even think of it all?" asked the fox, this time with true sincerity on his voice. Adal's green eyes rolled; the twirly horns shook.

"You think it's fair you get to berate me with questions after not answering even a single one of mine?" joked the faun.

"I'm being serious."

"I know. Truthfully, and I mean fully true, it was an honest mix between the three of us. DeWitt lived in Mikyill for a time, knew all about street layouts, vendors, festivals, all that stuff. Garrona helped with the legends. Some gravens believe creatures we think are just myths actually exist, kinda like themselves. So, they're huge in the little culture gravens have left. Grizlyms, sasquatches, Roimohr, elves, all that made-up stuff was on her."

Foxtamas' heart skipped a beat. Had he really called Roimohr…made up? A legend, yes, but…false entirely? He'd never given such an idea credit. If he doesn't believe in that, then his connection to Roihelm…

"And the rest of it, all the royal nonsense, was yours truly. Buncha stuff from my past, no need worryin' about it."

"Wait…what?" The fox turned to him with suspicion. His thoughts had blocked the faun's words. "You…royal stuff?"

"Heh, yeah, *royal stuff*. Just, y'know, stole a couple crowns and bid them adieu."

"No, you mean more than that," Foxtamas probed. He looked up to the little beats of sweat foaming on his olive forehead. Just like when the staff fell, a tone of panic coated his throat.

*Finally.*

Adalgiso was caught once again.

"Listen, it's nothing, okay? Yeah, I'm royalty. Or, *was*, I guess."

"You're serious?"

"As I said, I'm an honest—"

"Honest thief, yes, I know. But…tell me more. I'm interested. Really."

Adalgiso shook his head, his hands itching to break free from their bindings.

"Gah, fine. My uncle's a king far away from here, at the border of Plentis and Roistlind. When he ascended, he gave my mother a plot of land to the south. She became duchess, and the whole family lived in a small keep with a little village surrounding it. Nothing crazy, but we were rulers. It's all I knew for the longest of time." Gradually, a much more proper, tedious accent graced the lips of Adal. His mind didn't traveling back to his past.

"However, she fell ill with Rooklin's Fever, the kind that takes you a little every day. She became too weak to walk after a while. Her lungs practically shred themselves to ribbons. When my uncle heard word, he cut us off within the week. He took both land and keep and gave them to some new steward who paid his way in through Tops.

"We...had nothing but a hut. Mother died there. Before, though, I made myself ready to war against him and do anything I could to hurt him like he hurt his own sister. I had blades, I had poison, oh I had it *all.* I was ready to assassinate him at a moment's notice, Foxtamas.

"When she finally passed...I couldn't bring myself to do it. I knew I'd lose. He had guards and an army and loyalists, and all I had was a corpse to bury.

"I grew to realize I wanted nothing with that system. It's all corrupt, from the top down. Who wants to work their whole life to please one man? Especially one who cares only for their coin. So, I made a vow. A promise to my mother. I vowed I'd make something better, some new system, new *society* that would one day topple him and all others that ruled in the same stead. I vowed to change Evon."

"I...see. But how'd you end up in thievery, then?" Foxtamas asked.

"It made sense, just not at first. See, there's this abyss hidden deep, deep in Evon. No one's made it to the bottom, but close to it lies the Brigands of the Long Dark, or Abyssmals, some call them. They're thieves, yes, but on a different level, like a cult. Mystics you could argue—I would. They take orders from whatever they think is down there. The leaders do, anyway. The outskirt recruits just go on stealing and robbing but give the Abbots and Abbesses a cut.

"Thing is about the place, it's *growing*. It's a kingdom in and of itself, far larger than whatever my uncle figured he had. So...I joined. Not to be some petty thief, no, no, I wanted *control.* I worked up, pulled strings, you know the deal. And I made it far. But again I saw its corruption. Too many orders and ranks and all the nonsense that put the people on the bottom.

"That's when I met those two nut cases ahead of us. Garrona, wow, she'd been there years. Horrible life she led. DeWitt was new, also newly *alone*, but he'd befriended her. They were a stellar pair, I tell you. The more we connected the more I saw myself and my mother within them. Both came from hardship and neglect…livemining, homelessness, the lot of it. Just more victims this land pumps out.

"It came to me then that *they're* how I truly start. Not from within a place, but with those who are like-minded and personally affected, just like me. Thing is, you may join the Abbysmals, but you sure aren't meant to leave. They won't have it. So, we kind of…didn't tell them. Off into the night with as little fanfare as possible. They still want us back I'm sure, but we've done well to avoid them.

"Once we made it far enough south, we re-branded. The Rokanoe Raiders. A fresh start to a fresh life. Took the name from the ol' word for 'escape,' by the way. It's what the dwarves yelled at us the, um…first time? Maybe second, I'd have to ask DeWitt. But there, that's my glorious tale of treachery and insurrection, sure to shock and awe all who hear it."

Adal, smiling, gifted a bow. One more and his invisible audience may beg for an encore.

"I, uh—thank you for sharing, but…"

"But what?"

"Why do you steal? Like…how do you want a better world, or system, society, whatever, but still do something so wrong?"

"Why not?" The answer had its usual jest, yes, but also a hint of seriousness. Foxtamas just about stopped the march to stare up at him.

*"What?"*

"You heard me. Why. Not." "Yeah, but how does that make any sense—"

"Because what moral high ground is telling me not to? Hm? What rule out there proclaims that no Evoneer should never, *ever* take a little something of what's not theirs? Hmmmm?" Try as he might, Foxtamas kept stumbling on his words. He knew he had something to counter the outrageous claim, but nothing appeared, despite his digging. "Kings steal. Kids steal. It's all the same. No one's better than anyone else, right?"

"And you're trying to build some *paradise* with that kind of mindset?"

"Yes, and it's *easy*. On your tombstone will be two years, maybe two dates if you're lucky. Then there's that tiny little dash. You've seen it, I know you have. That's all we got, Foxtamas. Birth, middle, death. That little middle is the jumble we call life, where nothing makes sense and everyone goes around doing whatever they wish. Some get bogged down in bad situations like us Raiders. Others like yourself lose a brother to the East. Things happen. The only job we have is to survive until that day at the end comes for us. My society would make that middle, that surviving, just a bit better. And I think I'm doing a fine job of it now. We rob, yes, but we don't kill. Everything is fine until you start hurting someone. Losing a bag of flour won't split the world again. It makes our lives better. *Easier.* People can join us if they wish. Spend a little of their middle here as a Raider. If not, well, time's always a-tickin'."

Foxtamas hardly believed his ears. How could someone stake their claim on such a sad, heinous, philosophy? What breaks you down enough to think of life as nothing more than a dash on a stone?

And yet...

Could he refute it?

Could he point to the passage in some universal law book that *proved* stealing was wrong? Could he find the subsection that disavowed Adalgiso's methods? Could he flip the page to where his morality outweighed that of the faun's?

No.

No one could.

Something within told him otherwise, but there, on the hills, through the trees, Foxtamas Scottsworth had absolutely and utterly nothing.

Only the faint, misty feelings inside.

"Yeah, but...it's still not right. Somehow I know it's not."

"Life's not right, pal. That's why we do what we do. Say, you give me one, and I mean just *one* reason to stop stealing, I'll give it up. Throw it right away and never nab anything again."

"Deal." It was his turn for a joke. The fox offered out his hand, but just far enough for the faun's oily fingers to be out of reach.

"Funny. But I accept."

"Good. Might be only thing saving that corrupt soul of yours."

"Many have tried, Foxtamas. Many have tried. Sometimes I think it's *their* souls that need saving. I'm doing just fine."

From the look of him, however, he wasn't. His step had less bounce. His voice less suave. Somehow even his horns looked lower than before. Foxtamas surmised talking of his past had that effect. Thinking back to his uncle, his mother, all the trauma haunting him like a gallant ghost—it exhausted him. His true colors still waved true, though. Even if they were nasty, mucky, and dark.

The Aydaltown scheme started to make more sense. Having the staff let him live that stolen life. He was a duke; he was loved and celebrated, given a life with amazing shows and adoring citizens. It's all he ever wanted, and the staff obeyed. The staff connected to Roihelm.

For believing him a myth, the faun sure did appreciate the bird. Foxtamas further pieced the plot together. The Rokanoe Raiders had no clue of the power they possessed. They tossed it about without a care, abusing it for their personal profit wherever they could. Yet still the Phoenix had his way. He…used them. Used them to slow Foxtamas down, scare him, leave him ready to die in a fiery demise. Roihelm stole any autonomy the thieves thought they had. Really, *he* was the thief. Puppets working for him. Worn, broken puppets. Maybe Adalgiso wasn't so wrong after all—

"Hey, lookit! Thit's it!" DeWitt's cried. He and Acirema, still far ahead in the lead, had broken through a small grove and bounded to the top of a knoll. By the looks of the mole's rosy face and Acirema's giggling smile, just beyond the fox's sight would stand their destination.

The gorge.

# 20

# "THEY THE LORDS FOR WHOM WE CALL—"

The rotten ridge looked like a torn apart loaf of moldy bread. Tall, deep, and wide, the massive mound stretched outward for what looked to be miles. No trees grew atop it. Only short twigs and scrubby brush. The once gentle slope had eroded away to nothing but chalky brown rock, the front side of it completely sheer. Thankfully, a miniscule gap cut its way into the center. It led down some dark and twisted corridor, hardly visible to the crew so far off. Still, it was a path. A path forward. A path to Foxlaris.

"The hike around it could take a day or tih," enlightened DeWitt, leading the march closer to the rockface. "Climbing over was a bit shorter, but nit much. Last time wih tried, that little path cut it down tih minutes!"

"If you don't get lost," Garrona mocked from behind.

"I've got it all mapped out, so we've nothin' tih wirry 'bout, primise!"

As the last slope ended, the six stood face to face with both the dead ridge and the gorge that, had anyone not known better, looked to have been the fatal blow. The gap opened wide. Further in, it appeared to shrink and snake around in the rich, shadowy gloom. All stood ready, though. DeWitt let out a jitter of excitement and stepped forward.

*"ROKANOE RAIDERS!"*

The cry burst from above. While the trio looked around, shaken, Adal and the others thieves inched backwards from the crack. The voice sounded familiar. Worse, it sounded *close.*

A robed figure emerged atop the ridge. She cast aside her hood to reveal a squirrel, fur stained in purposeful black soot. Her gray habit fell long past her feet and stopped short where her left arm used to be. Fabric dangled in its stead. She widened her eyes of black, grimy teeth spitting as she yelled.

"Or, should I address a certain *Duke Osiglada* instead?" Her deep, demanding roar echoed over the ridge. As it faded, a small legion of black robes emerged. Their faces were obscured by black cloth, and each stood armed with bows and swords. The ridgeline seemed to have suddenly grown a large set of midnight spines. Perhaps it wasn't so dead after all.

"Oh no," DeWitt whispered to himself, shuffling back.

"Who's tha' lady?" asked Bunns.

"Abyss-Abbess Ophalin," Garrona sighed. "Of the Abyssmals."

Adal gulped. The attention from both above and below now centered on him. Was he nervous? Perhaps. But nothing except his stammering heartbeat would ever show it.

"Ah, Ophy! Call me whatever you like. How about 'friend,' eh?" The faun shot up. He slide back until he hit the others. Together they formed one petrified clump.

Foxtamas had barely taken a breath. He felt Acirema's calming touch, sure, but as reality set in, his focus lay less on the banter between the old foes and more on the sharpness of the arrowheads dangling above him.

"Aydaltown. Really, that's all you have these days?" the armless Abbess called back.

"I told you to make it different!" spat Garrona, kicking him in the process.

"I did! Sounds completely different with the Y!"

"Oh, trust me, Wittisus and Garon are far worse," continued the squirrel. "We heard their mention from travelers we apprehended. They told stories of a mythical land with free riches and hefty accusations. It sounded too much like a certain faun's fantasy." Casually, she shook her head in disgust, kicking a loose rock down towards the party. "We had to take that bait, thought we could capture you once and for all. Looks like we were beat." Ophalin turned her empty gaze away from the thieves and to the friends. Though far, they made out her poor attempt at a grin. "Leave these traitors to us, children, and we let you continue through, no harm done."

"Lying scum," the graven muttered under her breath. Acirema whipped her head towards her, eyes wide.

"What do you mean?"

"They'll kill you the second they have us. You know they exist. It's a liability."

"So what do we do!?"

"Follow my lead," Adal whispered back, his voice just audible for the whole group to hear. "We book it into the gorge on my signal."

"W-W-What signal?" croaked out Foxtamas.

"You'll see."

The fox didn't have a clue how that was supposed to help. Honestly, neither did Adalgiso. He'd figure it out when the conversation made it there.

The faun pushed his way out the pack's back and lifted his bright green eyes to the sun and squirrel.

"Ah, rookie mistake on the names," he yelled in reply. "But y'know, Ophy, and this might shock you a bit, but I'm actually *glad* you found us! Been carryin' this real heavy weight on my soul for too long."

"Enough games, Adalgiso. Children, like I said—"

"No, really! I never got to explain why I ran away, and, well, call me a fool, but you deserve to know."

That nabbed her attention. She gazed further down, baring her teeth at the thought of his wicked, wicked crime.

"Wasn't actually my idea at all!"

"Of *course* not," she hissed.

"No, on me heart! Someone convinced me."

"Who?"

"Someone you know *way* too well."

"I said, *who!?"*

"Your ol' favorite!" The faun winked. "The Lord of the Deep."

"LIAR!" belted the Abbess, covering one of her ears at the very sound.

"I take it back; that's the one thing you *can't* call me. As an honest thief—"

*"SILENCE! SILENCE!"*

"No, hear me out! He pushed me away, Ophy, *me!* I'm a Brigand at heart and he told me to flee!"

"ONE MORE WORD AND I SHOOT YOU DEAD!" roared the squirrel.

"Fair, I see." Adalgiso held up what he could of his bound hands. "But one last thing, incredibly important. He told me something else you oughta hear. You listening? Good. These hills, this gorge? Well, these fine 'children' sent a little messenger on ahead, and it's about to be *flooded* with Brigand-hungry dwarves!"

The squirrel's eyes widened, and still no white showed. She sprang up frantically, searching over her shoulder, readying herself for the sound of war cries and slaughter. So too panicked the men at her side. They pushed each other around, disarming bows, drooping swords. The small army disbanded into maddened cries.

*"NOW!"* Adal called, half-whisper, half-shout. He pushed the group forward amidst the chaos, forcing the journey into the twisting, winding gorge.

The crack started wide but quickly slimmed and squeezed the band into a line. Bits of rock and silt poured down as they ran. Fallen rubble cluttered at the sides peeked out to trip them. Above, the whirlwind of shouts echoed across the dry walls. The slim tunnels made the sky look to have shattered, as if they sped through one of its twisted cracks.

The rope bindings hardly helped. After being pulled through a wedge between Adal and Bunns, Garrona piped up.

"Cut us loose! We can't make it through like this!"

"What if you run off?" asked Acirema.

Bunns didn't listen to her rebuttal. He whipped out a star and slashed the bonds away. He tossed the weapon over to Acirema to do the same for DeWitt while Foxtamas, hands shaking, snipped the faun's off with his axe. All three freely moved their wrists. Bliss, even for a moment.

After minutes of the single-file fleeing, the gorge finally opened, and their speed picked up.

"W-W-What are we gonna do?" Foxtamas asked, breathing sparse from the nerves sizzling beneath his skin.

"Get out of here quick or turn tail and fight them. Your choice!" Adal fired back, pushing him along the dusty trail ahead. It wasn't long until the expanse widened further. Only for the path to split.

They had reached a crossroads.

"Aye, Witty, choose ah way, hurry!" shouted Bunns.

"I-I'm thinking, just give mih a—"

Shouts. Cries. Rage.

The towering walls around them began to come alive—wrathful Brigands thundered their way.

"Are we going to fight them?" Acirema asked while looking above and spinning.

"Probably," answered the graven.

"We don't have weapons!" spat DeWitt, completely dissolved of his task.

"Here lad, catch!" Bunns popped out the hammer and tossed it into his large, clamorous hands. The mole wiggled it around. A good fit.

"Foxtamas, the axe," said Adal, eyes scanning the upper walls for the first sign of the attackers.

"W-What? My axe?"

"Yes *your* axe!"

"Right now!?" *"Yes!"*

"But what if I—"

"Use your little wrist things, I'll give it back when I'm done, promise!" Grumbling and shaking, the fox slid it from his belt. Oh, what was he *doing!*

The second it left his paws, a sharp *GAH!* exploded from above. He shot up his gaze to watch a Brigand, bow in hand, collapse as a star, followed by a zipping golden feather, sank into him.

Bunns chuckled, sneaking in a quick wink to the bird.

"Forgot tae sae they're ah tad faster tae."

Her golden eyes stared at him expressionless; her beak did an amazing job holding back a smile.

Three more black hoods appeared as the first fighter fell, this time with bows already knocked. Arrows flooded down, snapping against the rock behind the six sitting targets.

"PICK A PATH DEWITT!" Adalgiso cried out, dashing further up to avoid the assault.

"This way!" The mole slipped into the rightmost path and dragged Acirema along behind him. The four followed closely behind as, from the crack's edge, the Abbysmals hurled orders to keep the thieves in sight.

Yet again the ridge's sides packed them tight. Thick plumes of dust grew the quicker they shuffled through. Visibility started to drop. *Fast.*

Suddenly, a thundering cry banged against the walls at the party's rear. A Brigand dropped down to their level on links of thick, jagged chains. He gripped a gleaming scimitar in his hand. The light caught it through the dust.

The cultist peered through the haze to locate his prey. His soulless black eyes locked onto the fox.

He adjusted the blade. He charged forward.

*"YERAAA—"* the Brigand slashed into the air, but did so too late. The sapphire-encrusted axe was already lodged into his stomach. Sticky, oily blood soaked through his habit.

Adalgiso kicked the creature away to free the axe. His body collapsed in a black heap.

"Don't just stand there, Foxtamas, keep going!" he called to the fox, stunned at how close the warrior had been to running him through. Had the faun not been there…

The group's front fared no better in the upturned dirt. DeWitt did all he could to recall his lefts from rights and trail heads from dead ends. The low visibility didn't help.

"Are we almost there!?" Garrona shouted. She slung her wing upward and fired a golden feather into an archer trying to lower a chain.

"Wih're getting there, jist stay close!" replied the mole. Eyes squinted behind his goggles, he barreled further into the dust. Right into a shadow charging his way.

A taller Brigand, armed with dual knives, kicked him back and into the others. DeWitt gasped. Dust filled his throat and crunched beneath his strained bite. He rebounded in a single step, however, and whipped up Bunns' hammer. It swung out right as the attacker pushed closer. A hard, whopping smack.

But not enough.

One of the knives stabbed through his leg. The rugged trousers slowed the strike but didn't stop the pain from searing down his thigh. He crashed backwards again in a yelp, this time unable to reach the hammer. The bloodied blade went up for another strike.

*THUNK!!*

Acirema's arrow struck true. The Brigand stumbled backwards from the blow, gurgling before the life within slipped away.

"DeWitt! Are you alright, can you walk!?" panicked the princess, shouldering her bow and helping him up. Blood had already started soaking the clay ground beneath him.

"Yih, yih, I-I'm fine, jist come on, wih gotta keep moving," he panted. The mole put weight on the leg and let the pangs strike him. Through it, he let out a chuckle of relief. "I've gotten worse!"

The Abyssmals refused to let up. More slid down from both ends, arrows constantly raining overhead. The crossroads only worsened. Three paths became five. Five, seven. Seven an endless spring of wrong turns. DeWitt's focus faded. Despite his memory overpowering the pain, one slip and he'd lead them to their deaths.

Adal saw his fellow Raider giving out from the rear. Someone needed to help that fool along.

"Bunns!" he shouted, pushing him and the fox closer to the jackalope. "Use the staff in this bend, make it look like a dead end!"

"Wha' yer mean?" asked the warrior.

"Dead. End. Hold that thing tight and imagine one, and *don't* let go!"

"Ah, um, got et." He tried to, at least. The second DeWitt led them down another, tighter path, Adal forced the others against the wall. Bunns' paws white knuckled around the staff, his eyelids squeezed as hard as he could get them.

His tensed muscles suddenly felt a cold tingle, like that of snowflakes drifting down at the start of a winter morn, dancing across his hands. The sensation strengthened as he envisioned around them a dead end.

No snaking path. Nothing beyond.

Just a wall of the rock, covered in the rich, rigid scars and rubble as the rest of the gorge.

He opened his eyes. There, right where he pictured it, floated a haze of blue sparks. He could somehow still see through them, watching as a pack of four Brigands ran past the wall. None of them suspected a thing.

"Perfect, now hold it," the faun reminded him. All leaned against the wall and panted, thankful for the break. Foxtamas let his gasps for air turn to regular, calming breaths. He too took a fascination with the magic. Though he tried, he couldn't figure some foul thought about Roihelm. It wasn't the time. Wasn't the place.

"Are we almost out?" quietly asked Garrona.

"Yip, wih're close. Bunns, if yih keep holding thit, wih should be clear tih—"

"THEY HIDE!!" boomed the shrill, unmistakable voice of Ophalin. From the sound of it, she was no more than a few yards above, stalking the array of crags leading out of the gorge. "BOULDER THE EXIT, NOW!"

"That rat!" stammered Adal. He pushed closer to DeWitt, trying to get a good eye on where the squirrel could be.

"We'll be trapped!" squeaked the fox.

"Aye. Wha' next, Adal?"

For the first time perhaps in the full length of his life, the Duke of Rokanoe had no words. His bearded mouth didn't even try to stutter some faux hope. He simply glanced over at Garrona. Then to DeWitt. They looked to him not as a fellow Raider, but a leader, a father, a duke. He led them this far—where would they go now? What would they do?

Maybe....running wasn't the answer. For their trio, anyway. Maybe they needed to take real strides in ridding Evon of the system they hated. Maybe, just maybe, it was time for the Rokanoe Raiders to practice what they preached.

"Run." One soft word, but one boldly spoken. "Keep hold of the staff until you're out and cloak yourselves with it. DeWitt, what's the path?"

"Oh, um, jist tih more lefts then a right. Hard tih miss."

"Perfect. The Last Ring is right there once you exit. Go in, and be careful not to stay long. You never know what to expect."

"You three are staying?" Acirema interrupted.

"What—no, they'll kill you!" seconded the fox.

"They wouldn't know how. Just go! Get out before they seal us all in here, got me? Get to the Fulnoa, save your brother, finish the mission. We'll be fine." The faun fired off a wink before physically pushing Foxtamas closer to his friends.

"Aye, will do, laddie, thank yer!"

"Yes, thank you all," added the princess. The two started running down the skinny path. Foxtamas, however, lingered for a second longer. He gave the faces of the Rokanoe Raiders one last look. The cheery, pained mug of DeWitt; the eloquently annoyed countenance of Garrona; the rowdy yet confident grimace of Adalgiso. Just yesterday he detested them. Now, in some random ridge far away from home, he saw a glimmer of their humanity sparkling through.

"I better get that axe back!" he called out, grinning.

"You will, promise! I'm an honest thief after all!" Foxtamas' keen ears picked up the faun's devious little laugh as he followed after his friends.

He'd made the right choice.

Left.

A slim little trail.

Left.

A wider path, more rocky, dusty.

Right.

Open, similar to the start.

Daylight.

The staff worked wonders. Bunns pushed deep into his thoughts and made them a small shield that, to anyone not within the blue, sparkling bubble, was just another piece of rock. It protected them from the busied Brigands above and those snaking through the corridors.

As the gorge opened back out, and the ground below morphed from fruitless scrub to fresh, breathing grass, a rumble roared behind them. The trio turned back just in time to see boulders crushing down from above, upended by robed cultists. Dust covered the sight. Heinous *BOOMS!* melded with striking *CRACKS!* akin to being blind in a lightning storm.

Shakes, rattles, blows—then silence.

It took a moment for the winds to sweep through and clear away enough of the debris for the exit to peek through. When it did, nothing looked the same. No more darkened entry. No winding road. Just an immobile, unalterable wall of crumbled stone.

Absolute serenity.

Bunns, awe-struck and choked up, let his shielding thoughts lie. The icy touch of the staff left him, and the sky-like blue running through it faded back to an old, weary brown.

It was only them again. No tricks, no magic. Mostly.

Even without turning his back he felt it. Some…call. Some pull. A hand tugging at his shoulder to just turn around, just this once.

And he did.

And he gulped.

The Last Ring of Mechmilne was upon them.

# 21

# "PRAISE THEIR REIGN OH ONE AND ALL!"

Never had trees grown so tall. A meticulous mix of oaks and pines and maples and birches soared skyward. All lined together in a perfectly thick, almost wall-like row. It traveled both ways. The fullness taking up right and left. Looking down far enough, it began to curve, making the slightest form of a ring.

These trees were forebearers. Not the young'uns the friends played games around, grew chummy beneath. These held bark that outlasted kingdoms and families. Trunks twisted up like castle spires. Their inners were that of hollowed age eyed through squinted splinters and cracks. Some looked dead, weary. But no elder stood so tall. Did the Ring not roar with fiery leaves and branches of green? If not, it could easily have been mistaken for a series of statues. Symbols of an age no one, not even the stories and legends, would ever reach.

The first fruits—first roots, first boughs, first falls—of Evon.

Bunns took the first step forward. It felt miniscule. No different than a pace towards the Fulnoa. The closer he inched, the more mountainous the trees became.

"Come on," he uttered, turning back and motioning for the others. "Weh don't wanna bae followed." Foxtamas and Acirema gave one last look at the gorge before joining up with him. It felt almost...wrong...to enter, like they needed an order or decree to pass into this woodland realm. It was just them, though. Just them.

The trio stepped in. The moment his foot passed beneath the shade, Bunns felt the cold tingle return, this time not isolated to his hand. It graced the tip of his antlers, snaked over his shoulders, soaked through his boots, and tapped the tiniest of his toes. The same sensation overtook the others. At first, they thought it a fresh forest breeze. But it couldn't be.

There…wasn't a breeze.

Or any air, for that matter. Everything moved and swayed with its own cool touch, completely adrift from any notion of wind or gale.

The age of the outside crept in stride the further they walked. The stalks felt frozen in time. Their makeup was off, the long wooden strands and bark smooth to the touch, soft like a quilt. So too were the bowing branches, free from rough bruise or breakage, and the leaves upon them, the grass below and springy wanton bushes. Acirema uplifted her hand to the warmth of a passing oak bough. The leaf wasn't slick nor brittle—it felt as gentle as a lapping wave, soft like a newborn's skin.

The concern should have started to build. Worry mounting an attack. Such oddities and wonders hardly go without surprise. And yet those feelings never met the travelers. A mist of relief flowed through their chests instead, clouding their minds.

"This is…different from the Mechmilne around Winthrop," the princess commented, running her fingers along the gray, weathered trunk of a passing birch.

"Yeah, it's…calmer, y'know? Real light, and…"

"Like ah dream," Bunns added to the fox's thought.

"More than that though. Like…like I've always been here…" The majesty of the twinkling daylight falling through the branches, casting their world in a thousand verdant shades; the easy, undisturbed breaths of silence; the endless paths forward, all touching and weaving together as one singular thread; this was home…was it not?

No.

Foxtamas shook away the thought. What had gotten into him? Village Winthrop was his home, and Pradifore before that. Not this place. They were just passing by.

"I see why Adal said to make it through quick," Foxtamas called out. Acirema, in her bliss, caught the fox's words and turned back. She cocked her brow.

"Who?" she asked.

"What do you mean *who?* Adal, the…the, um, the…"

"Tha' ah new story? Never heard tha' name before," Bunns interjected, patting him on the back as he passed in marching order. For half a moment, Foxtamas looked at him, shocked. Then it slipped away.

He shook his head and rubbed his eyes before carrying along with his friends.

"Neither have I. Must've been a dream or something."

"See wha' Ah mean? Dreams are dirty like tha'," Bunns replied.

Nothing but the calm of the forest and the crunch beneath their boots filled their heads as they trudged deeper through, fully absorbed in the dense thicket. Eventually a small conversation sprang between Bunns and Acirema. What about? None could tell, especially Foxtamas. He heard the hum of their voices but not a mumble of their words.

Noises pervaded the Last Ring. High above and hidden below, behind the bark and between the leaves, sounds spread. The bubbling of a river. Laughs of children, four boys, six girls. The bob of a fishing lure. Folk melodies played in the last trickle of firelight. The first kiss of two lovers. An apple's pluck from a tree. A buggy driving down cobbled street. Low murmurs of a lord's council. The light snore of a babe.

All these and more whispered around like the first notes of autumn air. They moved the trees where no wind would, caressed the fox's ears and enveloped him in their past.

Soon smells twisted in with the sounds, entering through the black gates of a ready nose. The first wafts of well-baked bread. Hardy grit of a carpenter's project. The delicacy of roses in their springtime prime.

The timeless age of castle hallways. A cave's murky, metallic mint. The finely fermented aroma buried deep in the back of a book.

His senses overwhelmed him. These sensations, they glimpsed not into the world present but reached within the past. He felt them for what they were: memories of Evoneers old.

Foxtamas let himself infuse with them, taking each one breath at a time. He walked with the daughter of Harlitelle and Hawkirsol Jaspamine as she took her first steps; flipped through journal pages as Sir Emri, now aged, in his final resting cabin; dragged a shovel behind his father, Chaffwin, as they prepared the fields in the southeast of Efeters; worked in the dance of kitchen ladies preparing for Lord Belmonti's coronation; floated down some river called the Lazy Lady Sue, that, had not it been for the always nasty mix of an encroaching storm and even more encroaching mothers, would have been filled with the village children and their antics which, one day, would be no more.

He lived lives a million. His being melted into the past, like dew strung out across a clothesline. None of the souls still lived in his present day. But, for them, their lives *were* present day. Nothing of a Bridge or Foxtamas had been written, nor would it for years, decades, century after century.

This...yes, *this* was life. Life collected and stored, bottled and labeled as its own special type of preserve.

It empowered him. Sight, sound, and smell released his deepest desires for what came before, for lives of endless, boundless adventure, all there to experience, to yearn for, to adore, to treasure until Evon crumbled down to ocean and ash and dust. He felt back with his stories. His books. The beating of his heart when reading of some daring fight, the call to step out and explore the wonders waiting for him, no longer inside faded ink and ripped pages, but in the physical touch of his palm. That nature surrounded him. It was with him.

It *was* him.

Foxtamas forgot fear. He would go wherever. Do whatever. He'd felt his heart fulfilled, seen the world and how it begged for him to meet it in return. Nothing could stop him.

This feeling…it completed him. If only he could give more to it, please it, return all which it had given to the poor fox. Perhaps, however, answering the call was enough. Doing what it said would be payment plenty. Maybe, just maybe, living in its uninterruptable joy and praise was all it required.

Bunns and Acirema paid their friend no mind. Instead, they focused on the world around them, for the deeper they went, the more the Last Ring began to change.

The fallen leaves stirred from their bunches and nests. Together they floated down an invisible stream, no different than *The Losmo* upon the Runnel. Once at the ground, they kept rowing. The clumps brushed past the trio's feet and sailed right on past.

So too did the vines and moss weave with minds of their own. Bunns noticed one link of thorns snaking its way up to the top completely unaided. The mosses followed, only slower, more deliberate, as any fine lichen would do. Just beyond their trail, a few sprigs of grass started along, single file, mimicking a colony of ants. The tree roots beneath slithered by like rugged, brown snakes hidden amongst the brush. Rocks rolled by their lonesome, branches rising and falling to wave. The Last Ring rustled with life unseen in the rest of the land of Evon—but Bunns and Acirema took it as it came. It didn't never bother them. Nothing did, in fact. They simply carried on, letting the forest thrive as it always had.

After some time swimming through the memories, Foxtamas slipped out, and his mind returned to the Last Ring. A sudden drowsiness blanketed both him and the others. Their lids felt heavy and stomachs rang of emptiness. The wear of their adventure collapsed upon them at once.

Wordlessly agreeing to stop, they picked a small, semi-enclosed grove. Towering and profound maples and oaks wrapped around the stout space, just large enough for a fire. Farther down at its edge rested a pond no bigger than a table. A dirt plateau raised it up as the means of an end for a spring which sprinkled upwards through the trees and into the darkness of the wood. Along it grew a few rose bushes. The flowers had been scarce thus far in the Ring; they sweetened the camp with a fragrance like that of a clear morning.

The little bits of sky above began bleeding into the rising shade of midnight. The perfect time to whip up a meal.

"I'll cook something up," said Acirema between a yawn. "You two start the fire while I gather some water."

"Will do, Queenie," Bunns replied, sleepily saluting the princess.

The raccoon glided to the small spring and knelt beside it. She undid the string of her pack and looked inside. What did she even have prepared to cook?

Not much. She pulled out an empty flask, a flattened loaf of bread, and a pair of pears and apples. Where had any of it come from? No one in Winthrop carried glassware like that, not even in the Palace. Perhaps it was a gift to Father, and she'd slipped it in during her rush to escape.

As Acirema tied back the bag, a little sting of metal graced her neck. Her brown eyes flickered down. A pendant, one encrusted with a bright, blue "V". Where had *it* come from?

She let it dangle in her palm. The craftsmanship came with a cooling touch. Despite the darkness, the "V" sparkled in the little light left. The longer she held it, the more a creeping sadness started to overtake her. She couldn't place the feeling. Like a random summer storm, it darkened her mind, casting shadows long and looming across her mood. Had she not already been on her knees it would have dragged her down so. Where had this feeling come from? Where in her past could it have resided? She gave it a thorough dig, searching in the blurry, faded mess. All she found, however, was what the one thing she had hoped to avoid: home.

Acirema physically recoiled and spun away her head, eyes sealed. She didn't dare see their faces or their words of the disappearing princess, Aisar made over.

In her anguish another memory bit back, barbed fangs sinking far. She wouldn't be free from it. Not this time.

She had to face the moment upon the tower, before the minotaur. When she considered…leaving.

Leaving it all behind.

It solved everything. A boiling pot of water melting freedom frozen within her heart. To have no one rely on her, look up to her, expect of her, think of her—oh, a dream, a *dream!*

Acirema Feiht, another face in the crowd.

But…if she did…what *of* those people? Of Mr. and Mrs. Cammont? Of her friends, of Father? Could she truly say goodbye and leave them and live a life isolated and alone from everyone and—

Again the princess shook away her thoughts, freeing the fear clouding her mind. Flask in hand, she scooted closer to the pond but stopped before dipping in the glass. There, drifting along the top, swirled a small troupe of purple lilies. Each was shy, closed off. Their usual vibrant hues of mauve and lavender had faded; the long, layered petals covered the dullness of their center core. One such flower drifted away from the group. It rubbed its graying arms against the spring's edge, no more than inches from the hand of Acirema.

Something about the bobbling little bulb enchanted the princess. The colors seemed…fresh, but depressed—ready, but tempered. She didn't feel right disturbing it. The sight was one of distinguished, natural beauty, the kind that pumps through poems and muses the arts.

That was, until the swaying waters beneath sparkled with a sudden blue blare.

It allured her. Calmed her in her feverish mind. Made the thought of pushing the lily away not just an act of delight, but one the flower needed to survive.

Slowly, Acirema lifted her paw and lowered it into the chilled dew of the spring. The two pushed forth the flower together. Almost instantly the core erupted with color, pushing back the petals and letting the sun-dyed center dazzle the Last Ring. The lily soared over to its sisters. There, by just one passing grace, the others too unfolded, their shimmering middles bursting to life.

Acirema felt the warmth of the glow spray across her face. Her grief and indecision drained away. A heavy cloak of happiness wrapped her as the dance of flowers filled the pool. They whisked and whirled like ballerinas across a silver ballroom floor. Each moved their petals in tune with a woodland melody, one of *drips* and *drops* and the hum of their central light. The flow washed through the princess. She swayed along with them. Stepped in time, twirled in rhythm. Giggling, she danced like a little girl trying on her tiara and oversized dress.

She found purity in that moment, waltzing beside the flowers.

She found peace.

The boys had their fire lit and roaring among the maples. A healthy mix of sticks and kindling abounded only a little ways behind them, and a quick spark from Bunns' stars was enough to start the flames.

They slinked themselves between the rolling roots of the trees. Backs against the bark, a haze of sleep lapping at their shores. Had the kicking pangs of hunger not hurt, the jackalope would be far and away, sailing on the sea of dreams.

To keep him awake, Bunns fiddled with the thick layer of leaves and the acorns he found strewn throughout. Mrs. Cammont always used the nuts for a brief snack here and there. Most times when she prepared them, she doused the hardy shells with honey and sugar. Other times, Bunns found them on the counter, freshly baked, still steaming, even.

These had no such flattery. He popped them into his mouth as is. Dry, a bit dusty. He broke through the ever so annoying outside and crunched down on the rich, earthy center. A fair enough appetizer.

He picked another. Then another. One after the other his hunger decimated. Though, after a little while, the proceeding acorns felt...heavier...in a way. Bunns could no longer toss them up and catch them in his mouth without having one sting his tongue. It felt like throwing in a rock instead of a nut. The next weighed more, and the one after *that* weighed twice as much!

A single acorn eventually strained every muscle in his arm. Once he gathered the strength to hold it, Bunns looked it over, marveling. Nothing made it stand out from the others. It still glistened back the flickering firelight on its smooth, curved shell. The hat atop it, sitting a touch askew, protected the cradled baby maple inside just like the rest.

*Hah!*

That had to be it. He was feeling the weight of an entire tree in the palm of his hand!

Bunns pushed beyond that, though. It made him think of the potential, the miracle of something so grand, massive, and stunning sprouting from one, tiny seed. Had he underestimated it? By popping them away into his mouth did he undermine all it could be? Acorn after acorn, tree after tree populated his stomach, rising, compounding into an unbreathable, unbearable forest inside of him. How small they would start, but how remarkable they would become!

"Y'know, if you keep eating them, there won't be a Last Ring left," Foxtamas called over, smirking.

Bunns squinted.

"Real funny, Scottoh," he shot back. Foxtamas *was* right in way. He glanced back at the acorn, then to the towering trunks surrounding him. Maybe it wouldn't hurt to let one tree get a chance to grow.

Carefully, Bunns scooped out a finger's width of dirt beneath the leafy layer and plopped in the seed. He covered it up and poured out a little splash of water from his flask. As it absorbed into the ground, it reflected a light, sparkling blue.

"Grow big, laddie," whispered the warrior, patting it down for good luck. He smiled to himself.

Foxtamas didn't notice a thing. Not Acirema's return to the camp, her comments on the dinner situation, and the plan she formed with Bunns to snack on their rations. Sleep already beckoned him away.

He bunched together a small covering of maple leaves to settle upon. The dirty, tattered cape covered him like a blanket. All he needed was something *just* soft enough to act like a pillow. The leaves would do for *that,* too.

He outstretched his weary arm and wrangled up the last few at his fingertips. They did the job well. The fox smothered out the little rocks and bumps below his head, and, once done, finally found rest.

Until one part of his pillow escaped. It wiggled free from his arms, just like the process of leaves had beside him earlier. Groaning, Foxtamas raised his head and saw it marching away, pale maroon marking it in the firelight. The leaf stood tall, and its veins ran true. They reached long into three distinct paths as if to pump the separate portions with life and strength, giving away to such a lovely hue. It could not have fallen away but recently. Perhaps, if still attached to the tree, it would have faded into a different shade, different color. On there it waved as a symbol. An outreaching hand. No mere step would have crushed it while still upon the branch.

Now, long and far away…the leaf battled brittleness. The further it pranced the slower it became, walking, then stumbling, then dredging across the thickness of the forest floor. Its edges wound in upon itself; the vibrance of its crimson dulled to decay and blackened with a spotted rot. Foxtamas, even so distant now, felt the *crunch* as it collapsed to the ground. It made the sound of being stomped into the earth. A pitiful death.

If only it had stayed at the branches longer, worked harder, aided in the wonder of the wide, forest colors. What then? Would it still flutter above him? Prepare for the impending autumn?

What a pleasant time to thrive within, like a performer playing their part in a production. The wholeness of the world changing from green to gold, reds and oranges sprouting to guide in the winter winds and seasoned pies, to tell the pumpkin princes and collard kings it's time to rise. Nature's fullness gathering for the harvest.

One such autumn always came to the fox. A harsh one at one point, but now, years on, anything but.

Foxtamas didn't realize he'd entered a dream. He only saw himself looking up at the swaying, vermillion branches on Nohsis' western border. If he could watch them forever, he would. But a small squabble of children beckoned his attention.

*You look out towards the water and find them.*
*Two friends*
*a small jackalope and raccoon*
*giggling and chasing each other through the shallows.*
"N-No! I don't wanna, I'm scared!"
*you shout.*
*Your bare feet aren't anywhere close to the slick,*
*lapping edge of the River.*
*They stand planted in the sand.*
*Firm.*
"Come on, why not!"
*coaxes the older boy.*
*The burn of his orange coat,*
*the darker paws and deepened brown eyes—*
*It's Foxlaris.*
*The younger version, yet still older than you,*
*how you always see him.*
*Shallows wash over his feet.*
*He could go deeper, of course.*

*He usually does.*
*But not*
*without* you.
*His little brother.*
*You scramble to put your thoughts into words.*
*The River, it flows so* fast.
*One wrong move and it will hurt you.*
*Sweep you away.*
*Was that not its quest?*
*Was standing in it,*
*splashing around its waves,*
*not some dumb, reckless act of rebellion?*
*No.*
*You won't dare.*
*It will hurt you.*
*You can't have that.*
*You can't be hurt.*
*But how to put that into words?*
"It's s-s-scary!!"
"It's not here in the shallows!
Come on, I'll hold you,"
*Foxlaris assures you.*
*He stretches out his hand to his baby brother.*
"B-B-But—"
"You'll be okay. We both will, trust me."
*Somewhere in the words speaks an argument*
*not even your army of fear can deny.*
*Slowly, you, the little Scottsworth boy, nod.*
*You uproot one foot.*
*Then another.*
*Step by step you inch,*
*the bristling rumbles of the water still sweeping by.*
*You make out small blue sparkles*
*reflecting the crisp autumn sun.*

*It is…beautiful*
*the closer you get.*
*So much so that easing in would be a waste.*
*No, you have more thrill,*
*more passion than that.*
*You jump.*
*SPLASH!!*

"AAHH!!"

Foxtamas bolted up in a tossing of leaves. He patted down his arms and legs, expecting them to be wet from the waves of Nohsis.

"Easy, laddie," said Bunns. The fox looked over at him, and for the first time since entering the Ring, he remembered where they were.

"How long was I out?" Foxtamas asked, lifting himself and putting his back to the tree.

"Long enough to assume you were gone for the night," Acirema replied. "We were just about finished with dinner." The core of a pear sat beside her and the rippling fire. Bunns busied himself with the last of his loaf. "I can still make something for you if you want."

"No, I'm not that hungry, thanks." He passed her an appreciative smile when the back of his ears perked up. A noise graced them. It didn't feel like a memory or trickle from the past. This…yes, this felt…present. A pull from an invisible hand there with them in the snug little grove.

The melody played soft and sweet, no lighter than the twinkle of a windchime. Foxtamas whipped his head around, looking for the source.

"Do y'all here that?" he blurted.

"Here wha'?"

"Just listen."

The moment the pair focused on the sound, its enchanting hum met them. The longer they listened the more their ears attuned to it being a full song. Its words couldn't quite be made out, but the choral rhythm and airy, swaying notes hugged them like a quilt from Mrs. Cammont.

Suddenly, the orange flows of their fire faded away. The trio watched as a bold, righteous blue consumed the flames, and as it did, the licking and lapping slowed, moving mere inches at a time.

The effect carried past it—the Last Ring froze, paused in time.

None of the friends spoke. The enchantment of the sedated blue fire mesmerized them, forced them to stare within the flames, their waves twins of the sea, the veiled gales of the sky. From the fire flicked blue sparks, pops of heat. They lingered within the air instead of fading to the ground.

Up they floated, forming around the trio a small set of pulsating blue stars like a localized night sky. So too moved the fire's smoke. Now a shade of morning cerulean, it enveloped the encampment, a swirl of mist bleeding through the trees. It smelled not of ash and soot but cotton and mint, a pleasing aroma, a spirit of peace.

The music grew louder as the sparks glowed and smoke expanded. Keen voices of the spectral choir blared their notes sharp and clear as crystal. The trio knew not what the words meant. Only how they made them feel.

*Lo Yenqeeh, Lo Geor, Lo Folsym.*
*Ai ta rytale ro ereek Dun, het ereekest Duna.*
*Fedron in meki clowse elmi Rihm.*
*Ev whistah;*
*Whit ta meki Helm.*

Tranquility absorbed them. No one felt any fear or reservations, confusion or bewilderment. All was calm. All was bright.

Within his peace, Foxtamas looked up and saw a larger, deeper glow of blue illuminate through the mist. He rubbed his eyes, finding it radiating from the chest of the princess.

"Acirema," he muttered, voice too rested to speak any louder. "Your necklace…it's glowing!"

Confused, she looked down at the bursting light. The small encrusted "V" of the pendant burned bright, casting a beam brighter than Nohsis at sunset. In her surprise, she look over at the fox, and gasped.

"So are your eyes!"

They burned with blue flame; a beautiful crashing storm; the shade of snowfall on the midnight of a full moon. Foxtamas felt them as such. His blinks captured the cold of blistering frozen winds. If only he had some mirror to take in the sight!

"Aye, look et!" Bunns exclaimed, pushing back his tunic and showing the pommels of his two throwing knives (neither of which he could remember owning) pulsating as well. All three giggled a silly, almost childlike laugh as their bodies overflowed with the color.

The mist and embers grew to their zenith. All was dyed in the same sapphire shine. Foxtamas sat in awe, stripped of any feeling but wonder. He glanced around and noticed the roses near the entrance starting to shimmer like his eyes. They morphed from their maroon to the same stunning, mystical blue.

Foxtamas chuckled. Somehow, it felt *right.* They were home among the others. A blue rose, lost no longer to its old red ways.

No other world existed beyond the grove. Life consisted of the undisturbed verses, the undulating shadows cast by the stilled fire, and the sweet, sweet air chilling the bottom of their lungs. It was just that. Just the grove. Just the friends.

Again sleep beckoned them as it had before, but, really, was it sleep? No, not any longer. This was the call of comfort.

One by one their lids fell as their bodies gave way. A floating feeling overcame them. A rise away from the world.

Foxtamas held out the longest. That dormant curiosity stirred until the end, a calling for one final look at the mysticism embalming him. So, mustering the last of his might, he peeped open a dazzling, glowing eye and saw a new light, brighter than the others, wisping around the bow of Acirema and the stars of Bunns. A graceful sound, bold but in the style of a whisper, echoed from within it. The last picture before his lids gave out was that same brightness floating towards him. He felt it grace his arms.

Then all fell silent.

He awoke on soggy grass. Dampened beyond dew, with rain, and a heavy wash of it. So cold it jolted the fox's limp body to life.

He lifted open his eyes. Saw the sky above. Its midnight colors fading, pulling from beneath long draws of shifting purple and pearly whites.

Dawn came.

Yet he couldn't focus on it.

Memories played before him. They sprinted out of the gorge and stepped into the Last Ring. After that…blanks.

It didn't seem they had camped there, for no lofty leaves or bowing branches blew overhead. There weren't *any* trees, in fact. Not even a forest. Just…grass…

Foxtamas wiggled himself up from his pulpy pad and took one long look around.

Moors. Far as the eye could see. The greenery lay brushed with hints of brown and gray as it covered the long, shallow hills rolling in every direction. A heavy morning mist already blanketed the land. He turned back to look for anything other than knolls. Maybe something lay through the haze. Maybe there was—

The heart of Foxtamas stopped pumping.

The head of Foxtamas stopped thinking.

The eyes of Foxtamas started swelling.

"G-G-Guys…*GUYS! WAKE UP! WAKE UP!!"*

He shouted, shouted, shouted, and shouted, throat dry and hoarse and cracking. The crossbawn on his wrist shook with such fury it nearly unhooked itself as he pointed forward.

Bunns' ear popped up at the call, forcing him to turn and see what so enthused the fox. Acirema joined him. And felt her lungs empty.

There, in the distance, standing as a king before the enemy, bold and brilliant, expelling the fog and claiming the dawning day as its own, was the journey's end.

The Twin Mountains.
The Brothers in Stone.
The Guardians of the Guardmont.
The Gateway to the North.
The Home of the Dwarven Lords.

The Fulnoa.

# 22

# "FUL-NO-A! FUL-NO-A!"

The makeshift map slammed upon the table. Two flickering candles waved their light over it, doing what they could to highlight the white lines and brighten the dark, barren war room.

Foxlaris had scarcely left it since given his order. The only moments of reprieve he spent with Dearg. Peace came easier there, like he could leave behind the markings and tracings to focus solely on himself, the beast, and nothing else. He tried for it to be that way, at least. The anger always returned. The searing rage burning through his veins. It empowered the fox but brought him back to the maps every time.

He let out a rugged half-cough of a sigh before staring out at the empty room. The glow absorbing him made him feel small among the looming black stone. The wall of windows was no different. It presented a wide, vast overlook of the Eastern night. A rising mist, twisted with tinges of flaky gray and a dark violet, spread thick across the sky to hide the shine of stars. It trickled atop the biting canopy of Forguile, through the raging barracks, taverns, and streets of the Village, and against the hardened stone of Vordemohr like midnight waves crashing on an obsidian shore.

The forest around it grew darker than the sky. Sharp ridges rippled across like hidden blades, shielded fangs. Upon them spread small dots of light. They used to hum and puff little streams of smoke before the war against the Blue Caps. Now the only blips came from lone travelers, pilgrims to the citadel, or those close enough to mix with the orange haze shielding the Village. Though, among the mist and the darkness, Foxlaris swore he spotted the twinkling of lights. New lights. Maybe not stars, but…flakes of gold flying through the air. Rain on a sunny day. Snow against a sunset.

Enough.

The fox steadied the red-tinged paper with his hook and flattened the corners with ancient tomes plumped by bits of disheveled, half-remembered Western maps. He'd given them a fair shot, but nothing lined up to the present day. The work lay on his shoulders alone.

His lines were of a white chalk that glowed in the candlelight. Carefully, he dragged his fingers back over the markings. Bridgeburrow lay at the heart. Somewhere Eastward he'd scribbled Vordemohr, and across the opposite end of Nohsis lay Winthrop. From there the white strokes turned into the leaves, rivers, and ridges of Mechmilne, encircling the glowing city of Mikyill before departing at the Dwarfmoors. Past those stood the Fulnoa. Strong, bold lines made the Twins burst out like an ivory "M" sailing on a maroon sea. The map stretched further northward but devolved into scribbles and dots representing Pradifore.

Foxlaris knew it wasn't perfect, but he *did* make it solely from memory. Any knowledge of the North had grown too fuzzy. Too far to remember.

Other parts hadn't. The ridges running through the shoddy sketch of Mikyill came from a late-night break-in devised by Bunns and executed by the trio of boys. Aisar had been gifted a collection of Mikyillian treasures from Gniw for his faithfulness to the Bridge pact. Acirema unknowingly leaked the possibility of other artifacts being involved, and, due to the friends being in their era of thievery, took it upon themselves to investigate and salvage whatever mysteries lay within.

They laid eyes on the cart unloading the payload. They shimmied closer from the cover of bushes. And they grumbled and scurried back home. It was just paintings. Paintings, however, that showed the bright, busy city and its place amongst the Mechmilne growth.

The rivers came from the stories of Dr. Wardly or Tihrio and their escapades bashing bandits and flailing in the waters after "secure" vines failed as they swung across, the ridges etched from Mr. Cammont's tall tales meant to lure the young children to bed. Then, of course, were the Fulnoa.

The Kingdom of Dwarves—so foundational to the fox's development that he and the others replicated it mountain for mountain among Winthrop's grounds. Their bunks, books, tools, tracks, all of it they marked by the dual triangles connected by a tiny line at the tops. The love of the lore carried long into adulthood, but it was born beneath the summer boughs and between the play fights of stick swords.

Foxlaris would block a blow and sweep at Bunns only for Foxtamas to come up from behind. His stick cracked upon his back. A hit. And then another. Bunns returned with a *whack!* Acirema joined. They all joined…

Hit, hit, hit.

Beat, scar, bruise.

No one stopped. No one stopped. No one stopped. No one stopped. No one stopped. No one stopped. No one stopped—

"STOP!" the fox finally let roar. How the memories burned! Seared him more than any cough or splinter! Why'd they have emerge from the back of his mind, why'd he have to pick them up to put down the map, why'd they still exist, why'd they remain when *nothing else did!?*

His jittering hand clawed against his temple. Red streaks cut past the bare flesh as he begged for relief.

*They did this. They did this.*

*Forever scarred…forever changed…*

*They can never leave.*

*They'll always be there…*

*Always with him…*

*Always…*

What could he do to erase it all?

*SLAM!!*

The Crimsdon door guarding Velrick's study burst open. Light from the outer hall flooded the dim cove. Books were piled high. A haze drifted from the burning wicks of incense littered across his shelves and desk, choking the small room in ripples of purple scented by spiced lavender.

He lifted his red eyes. The wolf, wrapped in his nightly garments of a gilded habit and belt and hunkered over a freshly bound journal with quill in hand, watched as Iota stomped in despite Getophry yanking her back.

"Vorde Velrick!" she yelled.

"Leave her, Getophry." The words dripped from his mouth. Once done crossing a "T", he turned to face the midnight guest.

The cockatrice obeyed and let her free, closing the door behind his exit. Instead of the usual bow, she stood firm, pale body still armored as if on the verge of returning to war.

"Yes, my Vayne?"

"You must be out of your *mind!*" cried Iota, taking a step closer to the desk. "How can you make that—that *child* Champion!?"

"Oh, please," Velrick sighed. "It's far too late for your complaints—"

"This isn't some complaint."

"No, it certainly is." He rose. His frame looked ghastly amongst the low light and smoke, yet the piercing glare of his eyes was undoubtedly real. "You're upset you've outlived your purpose."

The healt scoffed at such an accusation.

"Really? *That* is how you see me?"

"Of course! What, am I wrong?"

"Yes!" she shouted. "Everything we've built and fought for rests on *that fox!* You somehow think he's deserving of the title? No, beyond that, capable!?"

"Mhm." Velrick kept his composure. He felt it fueling the Vayne's rage. His words were neither snarky nor sinister, but forceful. Demanding. "You only think the opposite because your days as Champion have passed. You're more than that now, aren't you? You're the *Vayne*."

"Don't pull that now. It's nothing more than a glorified title for retirement."

Iota lowered her gaze. Speaking the truth without the guise of the game felt wrong on her lips. Then again, none of the talk felt right.

"Thus, you wish to be Champion again and have all that he has on your shoulders."

"Fine! Yes, but not for my own gain," she heaved. "I'd rather it be on me because I know if it rests a *second* longer on him it fails. He's not deserving, he's not capable, he's not strong enough for it!"

"Or…" Slowly, Velrick leaned back into his seat, fingers itching the tip of his chin. "I've been wrong, and this isn't about our goal at all. No…" The corners of his eyes pinched. He closed them for but a heartbeat.

*Stone hall.*
*Left door.*
*There, Iota's portrait in the line of Champions.*
*Second in line now.*
*I'll need to update it.*
*The threads between them all lead to her,*
*but look how hers slacks,*
*thins,*
*as it comes to me.*
*She's headed for betrayal, isn't she…*
*Wait.*
*No.*
*She can't be.*
*Her line thins, but another one from her grows*
*Trace it with the needle*
*Yes, down the hall, far, far, far—*
*There.*
*To the latest wing.*

*The one with Dearg and…*
*the boy.*
*Look at them, how close they've grown*
*since I opened the river between their minds.*
*Practically cobwebs of string, of thread.*
*They feed each other,*
*rage begetting prowess.*
*Soon they'll be one in the same.*
*But Iota's connects to him, too.*
*Not intentionally.*
*No, she's…scared.*
*About him, of course, but about…*
*This.*
*About…*
Me.

"You care for the boy."

After looking at the threads woven between souls, usually the wolf would gasp and gape for air. The magic still did that to him. He couldn't show it here, however. Not with his Vayne. Not when he had her so close.

"Don't reach like that, my Vorde," snapped the Vayne. Her words bit like the frozen metal of her shield. Had she been able to lift it and hide her exposed, wounded soul, she would've.

"I don't reach for what comes to me, Iota."

"You know I care for this!" She stamped her boot down. It inched her closer. "Never has there been any more dedicated to this than I. From all accounts it's *you* who cares for *him."*

"Mm. You would say as such." Velrick lurched forward and slammed his claws upon the loose leaves and ink stains of the desk. "You see him as a pawn," he growled without darting his eyes from her, "and some pawns are hard to lose when trying to win the game. But Foxlaris is not like that." Velrick flicked his burning eyes towards her own. "He's the king."

The chair creaked as he shuffled back up. Around he strode, towards the Vayne, and stringing together words which wrapped around his visitor like chains.

"I *despise* his Western blood. Do you know how my stomach turns when I look upon him? When I see what depravity has been created on our sister side? Don't you know how *close* I've been to taking my chances and running him through? Ending him there? Reinstating *you?*

"It plagues me as that cough does him. I am overwrought with an inward battle you can't see. No one can! But every *single* day I choose the right side. The *good.* The one that gets us a step closer to taking back what's ours and seeing the blue light drain from that bird's eyes."

He stood but inches from her. The harrowing imagery had blinded the woman until his pause. When she woke, her vision filled solely with the wolf.

Her heart thumped. Eyes blinked against the maroon glow.

"Don't worry about the risks," Velrick whispered with a growl. "I won't let him ruin it. But be warned, dear Vayne." A slow, heavy-pressed claw traced across the pale, expressionless face of Iota, dragging long until resting in the middle of her neck. "I won't let you either."

*SLAM!!*

The predator and prey broke away as the Crimsdon door broke open. Heaving a hoarse breathlessness hunched Foxlaris. His hand crunched a wrinkled map while the claw dabbed away the sweat pouring from his fractured, yet giddy, face.

"I know where we start the war."

# 23

# "Midst Moors and Mont Alike!"

"I can't believe it..."

Foxtamas had yet to move. The others took a seat on either side of him. Together they stared off at the rising mountain peaks, the nipping wind rustling through their fur and the pale-green grass beneath them.

"Ah can't either, Scottoh," Bunns replied. His grinning cheeks made blinking away the tears easier. The jackalope patted his friend's back and leaned upon their knoll. Looking out, the Dwarfmoors seemed like they could roll on forever. Only a few scarce bristles of brush sprinkled across. Instead of forests, dark, jutting rocks ripped up from the hills, grazing the scene with a roughness amongst the clear path forward. "But can yer remember how weh got here? Or did Ah fall an' hit mah head or let an Eastern laddie get ah good jab in?"

"I...I'm lost too, Bunns," Acirema mumbled, the realization quieting her words. It was as if a fog finally started to clear both from the moors and her mind. She turned back behind them only to find more of the same. No Mechmilne in sight. "There was the...gorge, right?"

"Yeah," said Foxtamas, focus still planted forward. "I remember getting out, and running, and...I don't know."

"It felt like I slipped into a dream just closing my eyes."

"Could bae this lass." Bunns pulled up Adal's staff. "Who knows wha' all et could bae doin' when weh're not lookin'."

The fox moved his stare to the stick, where it hardened and paused his beating, rattling heart and soured the sweet smell of the breeze.

"Probably," he muttered. Even if it didn't make sense. He'd never fumble through his detesting feeling out loud, but within, he tried to match Roihelm's neglect with their waking so close to their destination. Maybe it was an accident—after all, how could the bird have such care and poise after the unceremonious ripping of Evon and Evoneers alike on Grammo Day? Or perhaps it's a cruel joke. Or an apology. Or, or, or *something*.

It didn't make sense.

But it didn't have to.

The Fulnoa stood in the distance, seen with *his very eyes*. Foxtamas wasn't about to allow a couple aimless questions quiet that thunder rolling through his soul.

"Makes sense tae meh." With a single hop, Bunns jumped back to his feet, mindlessly twirling the feather-carved stick. Acirema watched, cringing.

"You going to carry that the rest of the way?" A trickle of hesitation came with the question.

"Why?" asked Bunns, tossing it up and catching it like an oversized baton. "Yer want et?"

"No, I just don't want to see any, um…accidents…you might cause with it."

"Hah!" he elated. Bunns slammed it into the soft moorland, leaning upon it with a grin. "Wha' do yer mean?"

"She means," began Foxtamas while rising to his feet and offering Acirema a hand up, "that we don't want pirates or dragons suddenly popping up in the middle of the Fulnoa."

The jackalope staggered. Wobbled. One hand gripped the staff while the other dug into his heart.

"Ah don't believe wha' Ah'm hearin'," he jokingly gasped. "Is this wha' yer think of meh? Tha' low?"

"I mean…" Acirema innocently glanced up into the sky.

"Nae, Ah see how et is, Queenie. Here, take et. Yer can use it as scepter trainin'." Bunns tugged it loose and tossed it over. The poor princess barely reacted in time to catch it. "Ah didn't need et anyway."

"Good one," Foxtamas whispered over to her, "he's already set off this early in the day."

"At least I avoided the dragons!" she snickered, nudging the fox with the staff, grin wide and foolish.

"Ah got all Ah could ever need right here." As if summoning them, the stars jumped to Bunns' hand with a flash over his pouch. He whirled one around his finger while the other flew in the air. The showing off loosened his limbs, woke his brain from the heavy sleep still slipping on his lids.

The star plopped perfectly into his hand. Before he could toss it back up again, a little sting of light hit his eye. It wasn't the sun's bouncing off the weapon, though. This glimmer was…blue.

"Wha' the…" Bunns brought the pair closer. His eyes widened.

"What is it?" Foxtamas asked, leaning over his shoulder. There, burned into the stars like a still-glowing brand, were two words written in a flowing, flowery hand.

"Lo…Geor?" the jackalope twisted them every which way to find some other form of pronunciation. "How'd tha' get there?"

"Lemme see," said Foxtamas. He took the pair from Bunns and handed one to Acirema. While they inspected them, their jackalope dug through the rest in his pouch. All glowed.

*Lo Geor* glistened every which way the fox turned it. Touching the words stung like the nip of a Pradifore tree. The sensation didn't hurt at all. It only felt…present, in a way.

As he went to flip it, another blue hue caught his attention, this time from his wrist.

His crossbawn glowed. Both did, in fact.

"Guys, look here!" Foxtamas lifted up his hand. The same glittery writing stretched across the crossbawn's side, spelling out *Lo Folsym.*

"Nae way!" shouted Bunns. "Queenie, get yer bow out, hurry!"

Acirema unshouldered her weapon. She whipped it around and found the final pair of sapphire words: *Lo Yenqeeh.*

"Hah!" The jackalope jumped at the revelation. "Look at tha'!"

"But what does it mean?" she asked, looking deeper at the burnt edges. "It looks...Old Evonian."

"No clue," replied Foxtamas. "Only word I know is that 'Fulnoa' means '*brothers.*' Nothing past that, though."

"Same," Bunns added. He somehow engaged in the talk despite whipping the stars up and down and marveling at their new found shimmer.

"Hmmm...could it be from the staff then? Like the same magic or whatever that got us here?" Despite twisting it over, Acirema couldn't find any matching words or carvings.

"You mean like a...service stamp?" the fox asked.

"A what?"

"A service stamp, or a medallion. It's what you put on your woodworking job once it's done to mark that it's yours. We had to use them all the time in Bridgeburrow."

"That exactly!" beamed Acirema. "I'm not sure who or why or how any of this magic works, but yeah...that feels right."

The icy caerulean markings failed to waver interest from the pale blue mountains beckoning the trio from the horizon. After more back and forth speculation, the friends set off, leaving behind the restful knoll and charting a course further into the misty morning sprinkling the Dwarfmoors with dew.

But it was not about to be a quiet trip. They'd hardly taken a few good steps when Bunns reached back and whipped out the Banjalope. The thumps were steady. Heavy. Thick. Foxtamas rubbed his hands together and readied his voice. Acirema, however, eyed them both with hesitant confusion. That kind of unspoken unity between the boys only ever meant one thing—she was in for, in their words, a "treat."

Cast across the mountains bold,
Like silver poured from cragged mold,
Our home arose in quake of morn,
A shadow bright in Evon born.

Ful-no-a! Ful-no-a!
Two Brothers Forged in Stone!
gateway to the North,
'neath kings and courts,
two Hearts, one hearth, our home!

Trace way the folds of kinsman trail,
From icy peak to inward gale,
In starlit Vern of kith and stove
We're all one line of veins below.

Ful-no-a! Ful-no-a!
Two Brothers Forged in Stone!
The Blue, the Brown,
An' everyone down,
Love this life and live it proud!

Sharp your axe, shape your mug,
Brew the taste an' brew it strong,
For in our Hearts we're right to feast—
We dared to walk where mountains sleep!

Ful-no-a! Ful-no-a!
Two Brothers Forged in Stone!
Gateway to the North,
'Neath kings and courts,
Two Hearts, one hearth, our home!

Now bend the knee and bow the wings

To our good kindly Wolver kings.
They the Lords for whom we call—
Praise their reign oh one and all!

Ful-no-a! Ful-no-a!
Midst Moors and Mont alike!
The Blue, the Brown,
The kings, the queens,
The peaks, the coves,
The feasts, the sleeps,
Sing every soul below this stone:
Here's to this life of home and throne!

Bunns ended the final line with a wallop of his feet into the mushy moor and a sizzling strum on the strings. The Ode to the Twins—dwarves sang it at gatherings and when announcing their presence across Evon. It was marched to, feasted to, held as a symbol of the mountains' pride. Despite rarely ever seeing a dwarf, Foxtamas and Bunns knew it by heart, one of the first songs they learned together. Nothing commanded more power and presence than the Ode, and nothing could better set the stage for their journey ahead.

The trio bounded over the Dwarfmoors. They filled the trip with more dwarvish tunes and wonderings of what would greet them when they arrived. The endless speculation sent shivers down the fox's spine. Thankfully, Bunns quieted them with a promise to tell Lord Enaled all about their childhood games and stories, only for *that* to further agitate and embarrass the princess. Their boisterous back and forth were the only sounds thumping through the land apart from the light whistle of wind twinkling the grass like hanging chimes.

The plains, however, filled each traveler with a sense of unexplainable dread. Every way they turned fell…empty. The rolling green ran off forever past the curved edge of the horizon. Had the Fulnoa and Guardmont Range behind it not been there to point them north, they would have felt no more at home than splashing in the sea. None of them knew a life without trees. The missing branches covering the sky and extending Evon upward left them feeling alone, lost. Even with a goal, even with a destination, what did it matter when it felt so lonely and foreign?

The chill of the realization tickled like an unreachable itch.

All was not just mist and hills, though. As noon neared, the friends found a quiet little pool resting under a rocky outcrop. A tiny school of fish swam amongst the hanging moss and lichen dripping down towards their waters. The stomachs watching them growled.

Bunns fell to his chest and waved a silent paw over the pond. Little glimmers of brown shined amongst the midnight blue waves. They were trout, and they were blind. He knew he could nab one of their speckled backs with hardly a splash.

His hand drooped closer. Tongue edged outside his mouth. A plump one waded directly under the white paw. It would be his final move.

*THRUNK!*

The jackalope jumped back as the water flicked upon him and the fish floated to the surface, a crossbawn bolt skewered into its side. He shot a mean glare to the fox whose arm was still raised at the prey.

Bunns tried to tune out their chuckles by grabbing the first part of their meal out. He wasn't upset that Foxtamas killed it; he was mad that it was a good shot.

It wasn't long before the meal, the walking, and the day waned away. A blistering sunset sank on the Eastern edge. It shredded through the cloudy veil and let free bleed threads of pink and gold, the glow of which outlined the distant Guardmont mountains like gilding on a royal coat. The evening tassels faded at the edge of the looming Twins. They stood closer now. Their blue shadows grew less hazy, more pronounced. The trio were able to make out the stony veins traveling to snow-capped peaks. So too did they find the gray, thorny grove bunched at Fulnoa's base.

The Cranarbor.

Acirema sat gazing at them. They'd made camp in a dry gulch that ran under dual protruding rocks covering them like a roof. The moors were too wet and branchless for a fire. Instead, they ate through the rest of the dry, gathered Aydaltown goods in the hushing, biting wind. It worked.

Foxtamas went to sleep first. After the run-in with the Rokanoe Raiders, Bunns thought it smart to start taking watches throughout the night. The fox volunteered to stay up when they headed to bed. It came from a mix of duty to his friends, of course, but also a valid need for rest. The end of their adventure crept further with every passing second and step—and the beginning of new worries rushed in just as swiftly.

Tucked beside him against the rock, Bunns plucked away at the Banjalope. Not as wickedly as while marching, just a few light strums that started some dwarven song he couldn't quite remember. He'd need more for tomorrow. Another round of the Ode or "The Wolverton Rumble" and they might just snap his instrument in two.

It soothed the princess sitting across and out in the open. Made her wonders about the leafless forest less tragic and more mysterious. She *wanted* to reach them, explore them. Feel what it meant to be let loose beneath the darkness of their dormant canopy.

She sighed and turned back to the boys. The sight caught her in a chuckle.

"You know," she started, "for someone so worrisome he seems so peaceful when he sleeps."

Bunns paused his strumming and looked down. Sure enough, a smile had spread across the fox. He held tight his blanket-cape. Just like he always had.

"Aye. Ah'd bae too if et was mah only way tae escape." He strummed another few notes, these slower, on the verge of a lullaby. "Ah think weh're all gettin' good sleep after the travelin', eh?"

"Very true," nodded Acirema. "It has been good. Nothing compared to after the gorge, though."

"Aye." Bunns smirked thinking back to it.

"What do you usually dream of?"

"Oh, Ah hardly ever dream."

"Come on!" Acirema jested, turning away from the sky and towards him. "I *know* you dream, Bunns."

"Nope." The edges of his smirk faded, but a joking wink replaced them. "Ah'm tae busy livin' mah real life tae bae doin' all tha'."

"Hilarious, Bunns."

"Ah'll bae yer court jester soon enough."

"Mhm."

"Wha' 'bout yer, eh?"

The question made her eyebrows furrow and eyes flutter back to the sinking sky.

"Hmmm. They're all over the place and…and very lively."

"Oh ho ho," snickered Bunns, leaning in closer and speeding up the strings. "Let et spill, Queenie."

"Okay, maybe not *that* lively. It's just small stuff like…flying. Or visiting the sea. Reading with tea…in a field, with flowers, and mountains, and friends…"

"Tha's really nice." The jackalope nodded to her even though she couldn't see him.

"But it's more than just the places, it's like I'm…I'm there, with the smells a-a-and the tastes, and I forget about everything else—" she felt her words slurring and slowed, letting the thoughts drip one by one instead of rush. "I'm almost more content to stay there."

"Ah figure that's why Scottoh's smilin' right now." Both took another look back at him. He'd yet to move. "Easier just tae close yer eyes an' get away. But, after ah bit…"

"You have to wake up and face it." She met him with a graceful nod. The lightest glimmer of tears swelled on the crest of her eyes. Even in the dimness, the same sparkle shined from Bunns.

Acirema didn't know what made her say it. Something, lingering betwixt the sunset and Bunns's strums, summoned the words from her mouth and into the biting breeze.

"I'm not going back."

"Wait, wha?" asked Bunns, eyebrow lifted. "Wha' do yer mean?"

"I mean..." her breath tensed, and her head fell to the ground. She pulled her knees tight to her chest. "I'm running away. I...I just can't do it, Bunns. I can't fulfill my role as queen."

The jackalope set aside his instrument and scooted closer. His wide-eyed face of shock didn't change.

"Yer can't bae serious! This is wha' yer've trained for yer whole life."

"But it's not the life I *want,*" she protested. "Being out here, seeing the world, it's *actually* fulfilling. I can just...be. There's no expectations grinding me down to dust."

"Queenie, Ah'm serious, this doesn't seem right—"

"I don't care!"

Bunns jumped at her sudden flare of temper. He'd never seen her act as such, speak with such fire in her voice. Even in the battles of the past weeks, when death ran towards her.

"I'll ask for immunity at the Fulnoa after we convince the dwarves to help us with Foxlaris. If Father's reputation precedes him this far north, then they'll have no reason to refuse me, especially after Grammo Day."

Acirema shook her head. Each sound from her mouth stung like a knife drawn over her lips. But how could she keep this in? It was either let it out or let the blade dice her insides.

"It's what *needs* to happen. They don't need someone like me," the raccoon whispered, flashes of Winthropians like lightning flaying her sight. "The poor things. Not someone so selfish, so needy. So..."

She wiped away a tear.

"Lost."

The princess turned back around so she wouldn't be seen. In the distance, the Fulnoa seemed closer somehow. Their shadows wider, thicker.

"Yer really serious then?" Bunns asked. He didn't have the strength to go against her, not with her emotions so raw and open.

"Yeah, I am. I kept pushing it down on the way up here, but after we woke up from the gorge, it just felt…right. Like the only way to lift the pressure off. It's either that or drown, Bunns."

"Aye, but…wha' about us, eh?" he asked softly. "Finally gonna leave yer ol' peasant pals behind?"

She smirked, even though he couldn't see it.

"You know I can't. I'm not *that* strong."

"Then stay."

"No.

"Yes."

"No, Bunns."

"*Yes.* If Ah don't fight yer on this, then Scottoh will."

"Let him. It's not an easy choice, but it's mine to make."

Bunns groaned.

"Just…gah, think on et!"

"I *have!*"

"Nae, Ah mean *really* think! Yer'll tear apart the Village! How many folks look oup tae yer, huh? Yer the only hope they have tha' weh'll get ah better tomorrow."

Even with that, Acirema still didn't turn back. The jackalope sighed. With a hop, he jumped in front of her, watching as she dashed away a pair of rolling tears.

"Bunns, just stop, alright? I get it—"

"Nae, listen. *Ah'm* one of those tha' looks oup tae yer. Ah know yer are wha' weh need, and Ah know yer have et in yer. Yer have the power to *change things,* Queenie! An' yer want tae throw tha' away?"

She stared at him with quivering eyes. But the longer he preached, the more they drifted off, beyond his ears and antlers and to the Twins looming behind.

"Yes, et'll bae hard, but with ah lil' grit and—"

"What is that?" she whispered to herself while squinting up.

"Wha's wha? Grit? Yer know, determination, willpower, pushin' through—"

"No, I know what grit is, *look!"*

Bunns twisted around and followed her hand pointing towards the Fulnoa. Four little white dots dashed away from the mountains. One sped faster out of the formation. It twirled up and down as if trying to lose the others.

The second he spotted them, Bunns dropped both the conversation and his jaw.

*"HAHA!"* he roared, bounding up from the gulch, waving his hands, and shouting back to Acirema. "*PERYTON!* ET'S THEM! SCOTTOH, LOOK SCOTTOH!"

"Stop, let him sleep!" shushed the raccoon. She scrambled out and pulled him back down as if he was no better than a runaway child.

"Et's the dwarves, Queenie! Flyin' right oup there on their steeds!"

"Shhh, calm *down!* What're you even saying?"

"They got the peryton, the deer thingies with the big ol' wings, an' they fly, an' scout, ah lass, *just look!"* He broke free from her grasp and sped back out. Acirema followed, sighing.

"There!" Bunns pointed up to the flying specks. They'd grown closer. Visible, flapping wings of green sprouted from pearl-like deer blistering through the air. Thick-geared dwarves mounted each one. The leader lurched hard to the left with a tight pull on the reins strapped over the beast. It led the party closer to the camp.

"Is this…real?" Acirema rubbed her eyes, but the flyers remained.

"Aye lassie! Just like the stories! Look at 'em go!"

*THUNK!!*

Something fired. From atop one of the trailing peryton a net sailed forward. It spun around with weighted ends, collapsing and covering the leading deer and its rider.

The pair sank through the sky like hail. Nauseous, ear-splitting squawks roared from the falling peryton. Its wings fidgeted, unable to flap under the ropes. It writhed into a ball of white, green, and brown, the bucking of which flung off the rider. He too cried as they plummeted, not from fear of the ground, but from his futile efforts to unstrap himself from his steed.

Neither of the friends watched as they hit the moors. Its soggy hills didn't cushion the thud.

Oh, the cracking. The wheezing. The pitiful peryton moans atop the tearful curses of a dwarf.

They only glanced back as the pursuers landed around the site, no more than thirty feet from them.

"G-Guys..." The groggy voice of Foxtamas made them jump. He stumbled over with squinted eyes trying to navigate the scene. "What's going—"

"Shhh!" Bunns hopped up and dragged him back down.

"That...peryton?"

"Aye, but somethin' ain't right."

Nodding, the fox scooted closer up on the moor to get a better look.

The chasing dwarves dismounted by unclasping a series of hooks and chains from the leather saddles strapped to their steeds. Their antlers glistened with a light coat of silver that matched the sparkles scattered throughout their eyes, two ransomed night skies. For such brilliance, they stared off with an air of disagreement with the task at hand.

All four wore the same basic outfit. They had brown, fur-lined boots and greaves, a thick cream parka laced over a tight-pulled tunic, and a leather helmet tied to their hood with a pair of glass-fitted goggles dangling from the side.

The eldest dwarf, denoted by his frayed, gray beard and white curls swirling from under his cap, had fired the shot. It worked like an oversized crossbow, with a wooden cannister and miscellaneous gears plugged where a bolt usually sat. The net that hit the target had been the only one—his age, it seemed, brought experience. He secured the weapon to the side of his ride before hopping down and unfurling a spool of rope tied to the saddle.

The other two were younger. The first to approach the fallen dwarf was a lady with fiery red braids, pale skin, and a limp that rocked her side to side. She steadied herself with ax axe. Following came a smooth-shaven man. Little specks of stubble littered his scarred face. They crawled up over his eye and towards his shaggy head of black hair. Unlike his counterparts, he wore gloves instead of callouses, both hands of which were filled with a muzzle and lead ready for the injured peryton.

The fallen dwarf had wiggled his way out from the net by the time the others surrounded him. Blood pumped from his mouth and a jagged wound running across his bald head. His nose was already broken and twisted before the crash, but now too were his leg and wrist. Every inch away from his captors came with an aching cry. He squeezed his icy blue eyes instead of succumbing to tears.

"It didn't have to be like this!" the woman yelled at him. "You knew—"

"STOP IT!" the captive jeered, biting and baring his teeth as he did. "YOU CAN'T DO THIS!"

"We don't have a choice." She extended her hand for the older dwarf's rope.

*"SLAVES!"* The word physically hit them, but they didn't budge. The elder lifted the net and reattached it to his side while the others secured the braying, huffing deer. "ALL OF US!"

"Did you even think of Wysta?" asked the bearded man, a slight warble in his voice. "That she'll never get to see you again—"

"S-ST-*T-OP!"* He barely got the word out before letting his head sag into the grass. The woman worked to hogtie his hands and feet together. He just sat and stared. Let the pain of his leg and wrist lead him to a state of willing, silent unconsciousness.

The others followed. The smooth-shaven got the injured peryton up, muzzled, and tied to his own. Thankfully the flight back wouldn't be far. Had they let the escapee make it a few more miles, the beast would have ended a white stain on the moorland.

The other two helped lift the man on to the lady's steed. He stared blanks as they wrapped him tight with an extra set of chains. The gaze sunk directly into the fiercely aware and undoubtedly awake eyes of Foxtamas.

He'd yet to blink. None of them had. It was a miracle they weren't found amongst the chaos. If they had been…

"Don't file a report on this," the lady whispered to the younger man. "He can't know we've had another escape. That'll be twelve this month."

"And if he finds us lying?" he asked back.

"We'll make it fifteen. Don't think we won't."

He nodded. Once straddled back with the squeal of leather and clicking of belts, the trio launched back into the air with a sharp whistle from the eldest. The peryton lifted themselves with ease and raced onward with the rush of their legs, almost as if they were treading an invisible, skyward road.

The sight begged to be majestic. Foxtamas tried his hardest to make it so in his mind, but the more he did, the more he focused on the horror. The bloodied skull; the cold crack of chains; the teary-eyed captors. He watched them fly away without a blink as if waiting for them to turn around and explain what had transpired. They disappeared towards the mountains instead, returning to pale dots, only this time showing the leather on their backs and the etchings of a triangle with a little line jutting out from its left side.

# 24

# "The Blue, the Brown,"

Little sleep came the rest of the night. Bunns opted to take the watch, but even then one of the others stayed up alongside to stare off and ponder beside him. The conversation of Acirema's leaving never stirred again. Their first sighting of the dwarves overshadowed it just like the Fulnoa themselves.

The moment morning arrived, they furled their blankets and left the outcrop. Silence strung between the friends until the camp lay out of sight. Part of them wanted to focus on the dew soaking their boots and frayed edges of their capes, or how, despite the bright summer sun, the wind grew bitter, forcing them to unroll and tighten their sleeves. But they knew it was never an option.

"They looked…reluctant." Foxtamas slowed his gait to glance back at his friends and the sloping Dwarfmoors behind them. Without realizing it, the journey had been bringing them to an incline. Their point of awakening looked like it lay in a valley painted against the morning sky.

"They did," replied Acirema. "He must've been a friend."

"Or fellow warrior," Bunns added.

"But why bring him back, then?" asked the fox.

"Might just bae loyal folk, Scottoh."

"I get that. But…dwarves aren't like that…right?"

"Maybe, maybe not. I guess you need to know why he escaped to begin with."

"Why's that?"

"Well," the princess rubbed a finger across her chin. "If you know that, then you might find what made sure he couldn't."

"Like bad orders, or a bad system or something?"

"Probably."

Foxtamas nodded despite not liking the answer. A little tickle scratched at his stomach. A knock at his door. If such darkness lay at the dueling peaks towering above them, then the plan, the entire goal to save Foxlaris...

No.

They were too close to think about that. For it to be true.

Too close...

"I just can't get over how, y'know, brutal it all was."

"Tha' canon though...et was ah smidge cool."

"*Bunns*," prodded Acirema, shooting a hard glare down at her beaming friend.

"Wha'? Ah can't make an observation?"

"No, he's right," chuckled Foxtamas. "Just wish it wasn't used to shoot a peryton down."

"Aye, Ah didn't figure dwarves had anti-peryton weapons at the ready."

"Doesn't sound Dwarvish at all," the fox agreed.

"What *is* Dwarvish then?" Acirema stopped fully in her tracks as she asked the question. A light scoff escaped her, and she turned her head as if in disbelief. "I thought I knew a little something about them, but now they have flying deer and late night escapes and who knows what else."

"Queenie!" Bunns halted as his face squinted into a laugh. "Yer *met* their lord! Yer should bae knowin' more than us!"

"Well did I *study* everything about them like a certain pair of peasants?"

"Pair of *peasants!?"* Foxtamas finally stopped. He gripped his heart and stumbled through the dew while Bunns did the same beside him. "You hearing this, Bunns? That's all we are to her?"

"Apple ain't fallin far from the Aisar tree," the jackalope moaned.

"And to think I was so ready to tell her all we know about the dwarves, to save her from the *years* and *years* of stories, songs, tales, legends—"

"Our poor, humble offering tae her majesty. Will et ever bae enough?"

"It never is, never is."

Acirema bit her lips to stifle her giggles. She couldn't *dare* entertain such disrespectful behavior.

"You both deserve to spend the rest of your days rotting in the dungeon, you know that?" Her words sputtered as the laughter boiled over.

"Ah've been waitin' tae mah whole life, lassie," Bunns replied, winking.

"I'll pass it along to Father." She winked back but added a nod. A curt one, meant to keep her ravings the night before a secret. She'd thought on the words he'd gifted her before the riders arrived. And…they didn't make the decision much easier. But for the moment, she knew the quest didn't need such worries, especially so close to the goal.

Bunns got the message.

"I guess if you *really* want to know about the dwarves we can tell you," said Foxtamas. "*IF* it gets time off my sentence."

"Hmmm, interesting offer." Briskly, Acirema started to strut back forward, leaving the boys to watch her wander off towards the mountains. "Depends on if you really know your stuff!"

The second they caught up, the dumping and defending of the dwarves began. Neither of them could back down from such a challenge. Foxtamas rubbed his hands in excitement.

"Okay, so the basics. The left one there is the Blue Mountain, the right is the Brown. Blue is led by Enaled and the Brown is led by Foehn."

"You've already told me *that* much," said Acirema.

"I figured. But they're both Wolvertons, the reigning clan. They've had power for, what, a long while, right?"

"Thousand years Ah reckon," Bunns threw in.

"So yeah, a *long* while. Enaled and Foehn are cousins, and their children will take over ruling once they pass."

"Are they not allowed to just…retire?" asked Acirema.

"Nope. I mean, some have, but that's rare and often involves some sorta family drama."

"I see. Are they in another round of that? I remember Foehn not being there at Grammo Day."

"Ah'm not sure. Ruel hinted at et ah bit but there's nothin' tae concrete."

"Interesting." Acirema lifted her finger and shut one eye. She dragged it to the Blue Mountain. "So do they both do the same thing? Or does one specialize in something different than the other?" A perfectly political question.

Foxtamas scrunched his face to push deeper into his knowledge.

"They're sworn to guard the North together and keep order there, both in Pradifore and the Seasondoms."

"Tha's why they're some of Evon's finest warriors," added Bunns, smirking.

"Exactly. They do a lotta other things, but I'm not sure how directly they divide it."

"Other things being…?" she asked.

"Cutting and shipping Northern timber," said Foxtamas.

"Minin' for jewels an' coal," said Bunns.

"Crafting new Tops," said Foxtamas.

"Sortin' and organizin' old Tops," said Bunns.

"Keeping records, stories, scholarship," said Foxtamas.

"Runnin' ah army of pertyon," said Bunns.

"Housing whole families of dwarves and others," said Foxtamas.

"Makin' infamous feasts famous 'cross all Evon," said Bunns.

"That's right, almost forgot that one," said Foxtamas.

"Oh, and determinin' borders an' reconstruction after northern wars," said Bunns.

"Gosh, yeah, that one too," said Foxtamas.

Acirema stood wide-eyed. It never occurred that the dwarves controlled *so much.* They always seemed to be the fun, adventurous axe-wielders that bumbled and drank like in the boys' stories. Even Father downplayed them, like just another ally Mikyill constantly bickered with. That wasn't the case at all—Evon *relied* on them. They'd been instrumental in the Bridge Pact after all, being the designers and suppliers.

And yet one of their own tried to escape.

What were the trio getting themselves into?

"I—I can't even imagine how just two dwarves oversee all of that…" she finally replied, a tad hoarse and breathless.

"I mean, they both have councils," the fox assured. "They manage and appoint the right people to oversee these smaller things. Still, they have to keep up the image of their mountain. I don't even know what kinda job that's gotta be. I don't envy them, that's for sure."

"I don't either…" The princess started back up her pace, but her stare remained stuck in place.

"Oh, don't bae gettin' stuck in the weeds of all tha'!" reminded Bunns, hopping out ahead of the others. "Yer missin' the art! The music! Et's all brimmin' with beauty, an' Ah bet they won't disappoint one bit when weh strut on in there."

"You're right," nodded Foxtamas. "It's gonna be so strange actually *seeing* it all, y'know? We're gonna get to walk the same halls as the legends, touch the same rock they did…"

"It sounds incredible." Acirema tilted her head with a polite smile to the pair. "All of it. I just hope they actually let us in."

"Without ah doubt!" laughed Bunns. "They'll get one look at yer and start bowin' on the spot!

The conversation continued throughout the morning. Acirema kept the questions rolling one after another. Most the boys could answer. Some, like why the mountains were named "Blue" and "Brown," stumped them. *They just kinda are* wasn't the most satisfying answer.

Above, the Fulnoa finally lost their shade of blue and loomed with a sharpness that made them feel as if they could tumble down upon the trio at any moment. The giants shielded the entire sky. Cuts of decade-old snow tucked beneath jagged edges replaced the clouds; only the colors of rough, faded blacks and striking grays remained. None dared comprehend the scale. They towered to heights that felt fictional. The monstrous power made their hearts race with every step closer. How did something so daunting even exist? Worse, when would the pure excellence and majesty begin to wear off?

All questions ceased when, near the early edges of evening, the friends stood against the Cranarbor. The moors beneath them stopped, replaced only with dense, bare soil and rock.

They appeared fairly large from further back, but now, standing before them, they felt on par with the Twins. Not a single bough or branch in all of Mechmilne reached such peaks, fading off into view from the ground. They had trunks both barkless and cracked, so immense in width that it would have taken triple the trio to hold hands and wrap around them. The branches were equally thick and bare. All wore coats of a patchy grayness that seemed to sap away the usual umber hue. The color wound down from the brittle tops to the massive roots rolling across one another and the craggy path forward like tails of dark, dormant dragons. What little light dripped into the forest became buried beneath shadow, twisted until barely enough to illuminate the uneven way forward.

"Maybe we should find a road in," squeaked Foxtamas. Vertigo absorbed his vision. This couldn't be real. This couldn't be the Cranarbor, the legends, the last step before their destination. And if it was, it was too much. Impossible to take in and process and be around and experience and—

"Come on, Foxtamas, look how close we are!" Acirema patted him on the back and brought him forward. "What road would there be anyway?"

"Th-th-the main one, y'know, where they have the big doors a-and bring stuff down to Miky-y-yill and other places."

"Oh yeah, tha' one," said Bunns. He shot a blink-quick wink to Acirema. "Bit far though, eh?"

"Not if we l-l-look. Or maybe the, um, the Wolveroad. That's gotta be somewhere, right?"

Bunns too patted his back, but his paw never left. Instead, he eased the fox forward as he replied.

"Weh could bae out here tae nightfall if weh do tha'!"

"That's fine."

"Really? Bein' in the Cranarborium at night?"

"I-I mean, well, if we found it, we could go the other way, not towards the center—"

Acirema joined Bunns and pushed him forward. Together, they entered the forest despite the Scottsworth's stuttering. It didn't take long to cease.

At once the already cool air chilled. It shuddered through the unwavering stalks one way before pausing, lying still, and sweeping back out the opposite direction. It crept like a breath.

Acirema spun around with her head craned upwards towards the endless canopy. The sneaking glimmers dotted her stripes.

"You said these trees were alive, right, Foxtamas?" She bent back down only to find him just as lost as her. A smile had fully and fiercely taken him over. He grazed his hand over the smoothed trunks, careful not to linger, almost as if he had been trying to pet fire.

"Oh, uh, yeah," replied the fox. "They're an army."

"How in Evon..." Acirema whispered as she pushed forward, starting the march deeper into the wood.

"They were asked to serve by Roihelm during the War that Split the World. The dwarves and other people on the West's side needed help, and there weren't a whole lotta fighters left. So, the trees obeyed. They shed their bark and their leaves and took off out of Pradifore. I grew up knowing about them before I learned a thing about the dwarves."

"These lads as big as yer house then, eh?" asked Bunns, bounding off the jutting rocks and roots and clambering over their path.

"Some," replied the fox, his smile quieter but just as warm. "Just without the bark. Or ice."

The princess carefully nodded. She took a closer look at the trees they passed. Was that…a hand? Or an askew branch? Did the slice in the wood mean an eye hid beneath it? Or were the roots she stepped over the outcropping of knees?

"What happened next?" she shot back with a slight pound in her chest.

"They were given tae the dwarves as ah gift," answered the jackalope. "Laddies have ah whole massive army at their disposal. They were meant tae bae guardin' Evon an' all, so et checks out."

"And now they just…sleep?"

"Aye. Well, most of 'em. One lad, Waynoor the Waking, he stays oup an' listens for the Dwarf Lords tae call."

"Only their combined call can wake them," Foxtamas added from behind. "Makes sure that if they're gonna be used, they're gonna be used with both Mountains on the same page."

"Ah don't reckon they were ever used, though," sighed Bunns. He could only imagine the roots ripping out from under him and twisting into the legs of the wooden giants.

"That should be good…right?" the raccoon chuckled.

"Ah suppose…"

They pushed further in, cautious to weave around the warriors and squeeze through the cracks of ever steepening rock and wood. Foxtamas' lungs sagged as he lunged up after the others. The pace, however, let him take in the multitude of details blowing past in the dim woodland.

One Cranarbor's top drooped down. It shaped its spine like a petrified lighting strike. Looking underneath, it seemed more like a child nodding off during a school lesson. Another, not too far behind it, leaned against its neighbor who boughed close, as if to hold him. Had its mouth not been yards above and melded into its sleeping timber, the fox figured it may be open, drooling, and snoring. No better than Bunns against his shoulder after their long days at Bridgeburrow. Or Foxlaris in the bitter cold of an ash-tainted Pradifore night.

He'd slowed too much. Any further and the already fuzzy dots of Bunns and Acirema would disappear into the darkness forever.

The fox hiked up his pack and dashed. His boots hobbled over the maze of roots. Little lineages of lichen ripped away from the crags standing in his way. He went up for one final jump. His hand grabbed a random trunk and held tight to balance him as he careened over a wooden jumble. But when he landed back, he paused. Turned to his hand. Snug it deeper upon the giant.

"Hey guys," he shouted over. "Y'all should come see this."

"What's et?" asked Bunns while hopping back down, Acirema tailing behind.

"Feel this."

"The tree?"

"Yeah."

Side-eying him, the jackalope obeyed. He pressed his paw against the gritty skin of the Cranarbor. Instantly, his gaze shot towards it.

"Nah, Scottoh," said Bunns as he ripped away. "Tha' ain't right."

"Let me see." Acirema touched the same spot as the boys. Nothing came. At first.

Gently, a ripple flowed through her hand. Like the lapping waves of Nohsis within the wood, beating, humming, thumping right beneath the surface. The longer she felt the flow the crisper it came to the touch.

"What is it?" she whispered, turning back with giddy grin.

"I'm not too sure," replied Foxtamas. He squatted down to the tree's edge and followed the root bending out from the ground. It too carried the same rush. Beside it ran yet another root, only thinner, curled, and twisted at the end. The fox felt it as well.

The rumble again washed through his hand.

"But I think they might be…communicating."

"But aren't they asleep?" asked Acirema, wide-eyed.

"Dreaming, then."

"Wha' about?" Bunns raised a brow at the raccoon. It only added to her enthusiasm.

"No clue. But it's in all of them, and if I had to guess, the roots underground have them connected.

"So one big dream then?" the princess asked.

"Maybe. It'd be pretty neat if it was."

The ground suddenly felt holy to the trio. Wonder already worked in the shady grove above Evon. What more mystery and spectacle lay below, in the resting dream of trees? Nature spoke to itself beneath their feet. But hadn't it always, with every step, no matter the direction, no matter the distance, no matter the destination?

They kept climbing. This time with silence and the ripple of rest still gracing their palms.

A cobbled road broke through the forest a few hours into the trek. Evening was on the crest of waning, but the streaks of light preceded it, leaving the wood on the precipice of pure darkness.

The roots had long ripped through the path, cracking it and angling the once linear stones into jagged lanes. Dirt too tried to bury it. Had the travelers arrived any later, both it and the night would have been successful.

"This has to lead up to the door, right?" Acirema asked.

"Aye, but which one?" Bunns prodded further.

One end broke from their own path and trailed upwards. The other barreled down on a steep decline, breaking the layered bricks even further.

"Going up turns more left," the fox said. "That might lead…to the Blue? I can't tell with it being so dark."

"Are we wanting to go to the Blue?" questioned Acirema.

"Looks like the quicker way. Yer also know tha' lord."

"Mmm, true."

"And the attackers yesterday were from the Brown. I dunno if they represent *all* the dwarves there right now, but…I think we'd do better avoiding them," Foxtamas added. Together, they peered along the route leading up. They hadn't been lost in their wandering, but this would, without a doubt, put them at the Fulnoa. No more guessing and heading north. No more faulty maps and loose directions.

The path led up.

The path led on.

The path led…there.

"Tae the Blue et is!"

The further up they hiked, the more the terrain around began to shift. Fewer Cranarbor crowded the edges and upturned the stones. In their place came hulking slabs of rock, jutting edges unearthed from slow, sliding silt and others fallen chunks from the sheer stone face above. A few of the trees still clung on by the tips of their roots. One wrong move and they might tumble down towards their fellow wooden warriors. Acirema couldn't help but wonder if that might wake them before any Dwarf Lord's call.

The path beneath them too changed, with stones tightening together and forming the start of speckled granite stairs. Their centers dipped down from centuries of use. Alongside them rose a little barrier wall. It journeyed with the path, marked by smoothed edges imprinted by a single triangle bearing a small line jutting from its right side.

"What are we even gonna say?" Foxtamas murmured under his breath as he mounted the stairs behind the others.

"Wha' do yer mean?" asked Bunns.

"Like, like how do we even get in, or if we do, how do I explain Foxlaris, or why we're here, or what we even need?"

"Me and Bunns can take on the formalities. You just be ready to explain what happened," the raccoon called back.

"Sure y'all can't do both?"

"You know the details the best." She turned around and flashed him a joking little grin. Bunns didn't hide his snicker.

"I'll spill everything right here so y'all can know just as much—"

"Come on, Scottoh! We're tae close tae bae havin' these worries now. Just look!" Bunns pointed at the steps aside. Torches, flickering with a low, steady hum that brought a desperate light to a darkening hour, perched on sidewalls up ahead. The Blue Mountain couldn't be far beyond them. "Weh made et this far. Ah doubt weh'll bae failin' now."

An entire tempest of rebuttals almost burst from the fox's mouth then and there. Thankfully, he found restraint. Bunns might not be right, but he had to believe he was. The doubts and worries and shaky hands and dry mouth and army pounding at his door would have to wait. His friends were there—how could he have anything to fear?

"You're right…let's keep going."

The torches led up only a short way before ending at an outpost. It was stout, dug into the side of the mountain a short way to create a natural roof and smoothed columns to hold it up. The walls guarding the path wrapped around it in the form of battlements. A pair of axes leaned against them, matched by empty barrels and a stack of crinkled cheese cloth coated with crumbs. Loose silt and rubble cluttered the corners. Nothing about it screamed glamour. Or tidiness.

But it didn't need to.

The trio stood together on the last stair. No one dared take the final step forward. Their eyes opened wide, mouths sagged in breathless shock. There, glistening with golden waves like the careening glows of a setting sun, a melting blade, a scathing flame, sat the door. Forged of bronze and stamped with the triangular Blue Mountain Crest at its center. No rivets nor nails nor hinges could be seen. A forgettable detail etched with the finest of care.

Foxtamas took the first step. His mind focused on the beating heart thrashing away within his chest. Those…those were the walls of the Fulnoa. The rock of *myth*. The stone of *legends*. And beyond that door lay…oh so much. More than he could comprehend without passing out amongst the dust and trash.

That didn't matter, though. They made it.

*They.*

*Made.*

*It.*

"We made it…" His whisper sounded like a scream in the silence of the evening. Behind, Bunns and Acirema walked up with him, all easing towards the door. "We…we made it!"

*"Haha!"* The jackalope joined with a shout of his own. "Weh did! Weh're here!"

"I can't believe this," shuddered Acirema, hugging on to the fox's shoulder while Bunns rattled off the other. "This is it!"

"Yes Queenie! Oh yes, yes, yes, *yes!"* he continued to cry.

They melted back into children. Foxtamas sizzled together his hands as his grin grew wider than it ever had. Bunns took Acirema by the hand and pranced around, throwing his antlers back in glee. The fox burst out laughing at the sight but couldn't help but toss himself along, spinning with his friends on the darkening Fulnoa outpost.

They broke into a fit of laughter. It winded them more than the entire journey up. Once settled, Acirema, a chuckle still on her lips, looked back at the door.

"How do we get in, though? Do we just…knock?"

Bunns too turned towards the bronze. He cocked his head.

"Ah mean…Ah don't see any other way."

"But we just can't, y'know, *knock* on the Fulnoa…" Foxtamas looked back for agreement, only to be met with shrugging shoulders, "…right?"

"Only one way tae find out." Bunns shuffled forward and extended a hand towards the door. However, instead of landing it, he let it hang down, turning to the fox and welcoming him forward. "Knock yerself out, Scottoh."

"Wait, me?" he asked, confused.

"Not sure there's a better option," replied Acirema who joined Bunns in beckoning him forward, standing on the opposite side. They looked like a mismatched pair of guards yearning for him to follow them into the mountain.

Foxtamas breathed. He took the step forward, but not before turning back around. The peaks of the Cranarbor blocked the view out. He didn't mind. He could still see the poor, broken home of Village Winthrop far at their start, the slow yet rising lively night at Hucksubtle housing broken, thirsty souls, Rillem's empty hut haunted by the secret regrets of his heart, the lonely thieves battling away at their slim chance of freedom. He saw the entirety of the adventure and how, at every move, lives tore at the seems.

But he also saw the door in front of him and what lay beyond—the chance to start mending at least one of those poor, broken souls.

Foxtamas raised his fist.

He closed his eyes.

Breathed.

Opened them.

And saw the smirking form of Foxlaris right there beside him.

How could Eobin reach home without Bwayine?

*KNOCK! KNOCK! KNOCK!*

# 25

# "THE KINGS, THE QUEENS,"

Nothing.

The group stood silent. Foxtamas glanced back at the others, a flicker of worry flashing across his face.

"Do I…knock again?" he asked.

"Um…" Bunns exchanged glanced with Acirema. She just shrugged her shoulders. "Wouldn't hurt."

The fox nodded and raised his hand yet again. The moment he let it fly, the door changed.

An invisible panel, completely flush with the glimmering bronze, moved away to reveal a pair of tight, gray eyes. Dark crow's feet clawed at their corners and pinched as a voice spoke in a bleak, monotone repetition.

"By Royal Decree of Lord Enaled Wolverton, first of his name, High Commander of the Blue Mountain, Dual Ruler of the Fulnoa Kingdom, and Prince Protectorate of Evon, no visitors of any rank or ruling are allowed entry into his domain in light of recent natural disasters pertaining to the unveiling and subsequent destruction of the Bridge of Evon. If needed entry persists, we recommend seeking asylum at the Brown Mountain under the ruling discretion of Lord Foehn Wolverton. We can provide no guarantee of admittance at this time as we have not heard their standing on recent events. I bid you a good evening and happy trails."

*SLAM!*

The eyes disappeared with a ringing from the sliding metal. It faded perfectly from view, leaving the shocked reflection of the friends painted on the door.

"Wha' was tha'!?" shouted Bunns, pushing his way to the front and knocking yet again. "Wha' do yer mean yer *closed?"*

"Watch out." The princess slid past him and gave a knock of her own. "Sir, please! I am Princess Acirema Feiht of Village Winthrop and request a special council with Lord Enaled. We have traveled a treacherous journey here and—"

Behind the door echoed a cranky chuckle that sounded closer to a squeaky hinge than living being. The peep hole slid back open, this time only far enough for one eye to appear.

"I don't care if you were Gniw himself knocking on this door, princess. Orders are orders. Now good evening and happy. Trails."

"No, listen, please—"

*Slam!*

Gone again.

Slowly, Acirema shuffled back in disbelief, blinking away the tears of frustration.

"This can't be right," she muttered. "Why would they be locked down to the point of denying royal entry?"

Foxtamas shook his head, not to rally behind her question, but because a door of his own was being knocked upon.

A battering ram splintered through with a single tap. Invaders clamored in one hoard after another and carried with them torches to burn the walls of security so laboriously built.

His breathing staggered.

A tremble stuttered across his frame.

The corners of his vision started fading into blackness.

"Gah, yer load of spineless peepers!" Bunns banged again at the door with a whole heaping of fury. The resounding thuds brought the fox back to the present, but he could tell by the wobble growing in his legs it wouldn't last long. "Yer claim tae bae warriors, eh?"

*Bang!*

"Leaders?"

*Ding!*

"*Dwarves!?*"

*THRANG!*

He let his paw sit hard against the nipping bronze. Instead of raising it again, he paused. His head turned. And he pressed his ear up right next to his fist.

"What are you—"

"Shhhh," he hissed to the raccoon. "Someone's talkin'."

At first the muffles were just that. Distant to the point of shuffles and commotion. Yet little trickles bled through. One, the bored voice of Gray Eyes, and the other more jolly, almost...emphatic. Both bickered back and forth, easing their way towards the door. "Tae lads now. Somethin' 'bout...orders, an'...scouts."

"You mean the ones we saw?" asked Foxtamas.

"Nah, ones in Mechmilne."

Their shouts crept closer and closer to Bunns' ear. With every word tossed, out the jackalope pressed hard, face twisting into elation and confusion. "They're on about taverns, nah, drinks, aye. Louder lad's accusin' the one who talked tae us. Hah! Ah like this one."

Footsteps broke against the bronze like waves to the coast. Gray Eyes yelled behind them only to be drowned out by his companion.

"Wait..." whispered Bunns.

The stomper slung something back.

"He wants tae see for himself..."

Step after step rattled the door.

"Wants tae see…"

A lock turned. Hinges creaked.

"The jackalope."

The door burst open, narrowly missing the confused Bunns hopping back.

A lone dwarf strode out.

He stood tall, barely glaring over Foxtamas. A heavy, fur-lined coat dyed a royal blue wrapped his broad, heavy-set body, cutting off at his thick belt and buckle. It held up his tanned trousers (tucked tightly into his leather boots) and onto a metal-frame compass, single-handed side axe, and, at his back, a tankard, wooden and carved into the shape of an oak studded with sapphires for leaves. Both wrinkles and tattoos were sewn deep in the hands planted on his hips, the designs disappearing beneath his half gloves. He wore hair of midnight black. Half lay flat against his neck with the rest braided and resting upon it. The same went for his beard which pointed down to a long, lone point. Above, his rosy cheeks pinched into a grin that pushed a squint and covered his honey-colored eyes.

"Oh ho ho! Well I'll *be!*" the dwarf boomed with a throaty chuckle. "I just *knew* it was you!"

Bunns tilted his head. His eyebrow cocked up.

"Wait…are yer—"

"From Hucksubtle, yes!" He extended out his hand to the jackalope. "Never introduced m'self! Name's Dubyr Tywyll." "Dubyr, laddie! Ah didn't think weh'd bae seein' yer here!"

"I didn't think it either!" He shuffled back to shake the hands of the others, all with an exciting laugh hot on his lips. It felt like a dream to the fox. He barely remembered the dwarf beyond his stature as a looming shadow over the fires of Flapdragon. "I haven't stopped singing your praises, Champ! Whole Blue be knowin' your name now."

Bunns' eyes grew, and his smile sagged open.

Foxtamas and Acirema nudged each other with rolling eyes.

"But hurry, come on in! Gettin' too dark and cold out here." Dubyr stepped aside and welcomed them into the bronze door with a bow. "Right this way. My, it's good seein' you folks again. What are the odds, eh?"

Shuffling in brought chills down their spines, not from the wind, but from the eminence of walking amongst the stone. The outpost continued inward as a quiet set of rooms carved out on either side of a hallway that twisted off into the distance. All the rock was an agreeable gray, smoothed down to a glassy touch. Through it ran streaks of gold, sapphire, and opal. They swirled and jumped like spirals, shaping into patterns that made the soulless stone burn with a sizzling touch of life. Torches burned near the top of the tall ceilings. Their light flickered through the veins. It was as if they too were one fire. Nothing lay dim.

The rightmost room housed two bunks built into the wall, an overstuffed chest bursting with odd cloaks and boots, and a dusty stack of books that had recently tumbled over. Across sat the other room, and in it, Gray Eyes. He was noticeably older than Dubyr. Their outfits matched, but in place of a full head of hair grew brittle, wispy curls of a faded blonde. The same matted itself into a beard that hung low on his lips. It wasn't the kind that showed a smile—it always drooped into a frown. He sat in the office, glaring at the entering party from a desk overrun with scraps of paper, stains of ink both wet and dry, pinned notices nailed into the hutch, and wobbling columns of leather-bound tomes. They were just the start. An entire wall of journals and log books towered behind the disinterested dwarf. The dates etched into the side went back decades.

"See, Chester," started Dubyr as he shut back the bronze door, "I told you it was him."

"Mm." The older man sighed and focused back on the scribbled page before him. His counterpart winked and whispered down to the trio.

"Don't let ol' Chesty bother you. He's always a grump like that."

"At least sign them in, Dubyr," croaked Chester, not even looking up. "Remember that you have a *job*."

"I was *getting* there." He rolled his eyes with a grin. "You can take a seat over in the suite while I grab my things." The friends nodded and found a surprisingly comfortable seat on the edge of the stone bunk. The dwarf returned with one of the ledgers and a quill, scratching some notes on a fresh page. "Alright, this'll be quick. We've got Bunns the Champ, of course, and Princess…"

"Acirema Feiht," responded the raccoon.

"Ah, that's right. I thought that's what you told the ol' hoot. Sorry 'bout his arrogance, folks. Real strict on the orders. He's right though, I can't argue there. Just figured I couldn't leave people I knew stranded for nothing. Especially after comin' all the way to this tiny gate. What took you all this way?"

The friends all side-eyed each other, waiting for someone to step up and answer.

"Just the way the road led Ah guess," answered Bunns. "Weh had ah right wild time gettin' here."

"I hear you, Champ. What a *coincidence*. But I'm not complaining! This is just where the scouts stay and work when we're not off flyin' and checkin' out things that need checkin' out."

"Is that why you were in Mechmilne?" Acirema asked.

"That exactly, m'Lady! I was down with Chester a week or so beforehand making sure Lord Enaled's travelin' party could make it down safe. Furthest us dwarves have traveled in ages, so we needed it perfect. After the whole mess there the Decree locked us down up here, so I had to head on back. Not before a few drinks though, hah! And you, the knocker. Your name?"

"Oh, uh, F-Foxtamas Scottsworth." The realization of the situation was just now settling in. Despite the stutter, he found his breath. Gave a hard squint. Grounded himself and stared at the dwarf writing in front of him.

"Scotts…worth, got it. Now, the big one—'Official Statement for Passage and Further Occasion, Entry Withholding'—or, in a friendlier way, what brings you here?"

This time, the stares directed to one shuddering fox. It was time to fulfill his part of the bargain.

"It's, um…for my brother. Foxlaris Scottsworth." Dubyr nodded and started to scratch again, flashing up his mellow eyes. They, along with his words, calmed Foxtamas. The resoluteness of his mission returned, emboldened his tongue to say what mattered. It was his plan, and it was his family. It stoked the embers of passion in his soul.

"He was the one picked to cross the Bridge at Grammo Day. I know it sounds crazy and wrong and all that, but he survived what happened there. I know it. I saw him on the Eastern bank. And now he's trapped somewhere over there. We…we tried to go over and rescue him, but all kinds of creatures attacked us at the River. I don't know what they were or where they came from. They've chased us ever since, most the way up here. Because of that, there's no way we can make it over and save him. So…we came here. Hoping for help. Not much, not an army, but something, anything…"

He paused and stared at the stone floor. He didn't know whether to keep up with his demands or admit defeat right there. Looking at Dubyr would reveal an answer he knew he wouldn't like.

"We…we also heard about the scholars here from Teardic. How they're looking into what happened at Grammo Day. I thought, and I know it's so stupid, that we could help, or trade knowledge, or something." He sighed out his hope and looked up at the dwarf. "I just want to save him. I don't know what all that will take, but…I'll do anything."

The honey mixed with water. Dubyr marked down one final note and eased the ledger closed, still nodding at the fox.

"I hear you, Foxtamas. I do. It's a…brave quest you three've made. I remember your brother. I saw him cross." Sniffling, he patted Foxtamas on the shoulder. "My heart's broken for you, both of you. He's blessed to have you and a great pair of friends."

"Thank you," Foxtamas replied as a lump grew in his throat. "That means a lot."

"Course, course. Now," he paused to wipe his eyes and toss aside the book, "I can't be makin' any big promises here. But…I might can get you an audience with Enaled. It's a maybe, and a mighty one, but—"

"Tha's perfect, laddie!" shouted Bunns, hopping to his feet. "Just wha' weh were wantin'!"

"But wait, Champ. I also can't promise that he'll be agreeable to anything. The lockdown and all's caused a big stir with who can come and who can go. Then there's Lady Henstray and the scholarship and what all we have here…" Dubyr began to pace, pulling and picking at the braid in his beard. "It's all a tossup. Princess, you're from…Winthrop, right?"

"Yes sir."

"And the one on the stage, at Grammo Day, he was your father?"

"Yes…"

"He must have met Enaled. Did you too, by chance?"

"Briefly, just an introduction."

"Hah! That's an in. Better than my other choice." The ideas in his mind visually jumbled on his jumping brows and twisting tongue. "Yes, yes, okay, that'll work. A royal request, prior meeting, gripping story, and, on top of it all, a Flapdragon Champion. It's too good! He's a massive fan of the game, Bunns. You'll be a *hit*."

"How great!" clapped the princess, smile wide.

"Aye!" added Bunns.

"And we can get it done tonight," said Dubyr.

"W-W-Wait, tonight!?" The fox almost toppled over, pale.

"Oh sure! There's a feast tonight starting—" Suddenly, his pace stopped. The dwarf hobbled out of the suite, tankard flailing on his belt, and to the door, sliding out the peephole and eyeing the rising night sky. "Soon. Sooner than I thought."

"Wha's the occasion?" asked Bunns.

"None right now. They've been goin' ever since the lockdown." The peephole slammed back into place. "But no one's complaining. If we leave now and hurry, we can make it. Might can even sneak in a quick tour." He shot a quick, honey-coated wink to the group before digging through the chest and scooping out a few ruby and gold rings. It didn't take long to trade them out for the gloves. "What do you all say? Sound like a plan?"

"Of course!" Bunns dragged the still-dazed Foxtamas up from the bed. He couldn't even mouth a word.

"It sounds lovely," replied Acirema, bubbly.

"That's what I like to hear! Hey, Chesty!" Dubyr called while showing the trio out of the room. "We're heading out."

"I heard," he spat.

"You coming?"

"Later."

"Sure?"

"Mhm."

"I'll take your word for it. And pass it on to Tarietta."

"You're a child, Tywyll," grimaced Chester.

"As long as I'm younger than you!" He tossed the ledger back on top of the pile, moving back to the front of the group without even watching it struggle to avoid toppling. "Righty, folks! Right this way, right this way!"

Bunns pushed the fox forward, his jittering paw tapping his back in excitement.

"Ease up, Scottoh! Yer hear where weh're goin'?"

"I-I know," he stammered.

Enaled. In front of him. Listening to *his* words. *His* plea. What if he said no? Kicked them out? Refused to help? How would they ever find Foxlaris? How would he be saved—

"Ah *real dwarven feast!* Ah bet et'll bae better than bread scraps an' ol' soup."

That woke him. Foxtamas laughed. His tongue tasted and nose smelled the possibilities before his mind could. It was enough to let in the excitement of his friends, open his eyes to the beauty of the situation. The tingles of glee fortified the gates and built higher the walls. A war still raged, but now the passion, fever, and joy of life held the upper hand. Afterall, they were going to a feast.

A *feast!*

# 26

# "THE PEAKS, THE COVES,"

The hallway snaked up a gentle slope before ending at a locked iron gate rising tall with sharp, Blue Mountain-shaped points adorning the ends.

Dubyr tapped the bars and whistled out.

"It's me, Maverson. Chesty'll be out soon too, so you can keep it open." From the outside corner suddenly popped a gnome. Freckled, clean-shaven, and short, closer to the height of Bunns, he too stood dressed in the same scout coat. A clear weariness had overtaken his young body. Still, he nodded and undid the padlock with his key, swinging open the door with an unnerving *CrEaK!*

Dubyr thanked him and pressed on into the expanding world of the mountain. The gate led out into a street bustling with the back and forth of Fulnoa folk. It weaved through what felt like an enclosed ravine. On either side rose smoothed walls of rock with doors, windows, and alleys carved within. Stone stairs led up to second, third, and fourth stories. From them jutted little balconies. Some lay adorned with hanging gardens of moss and primrose, others rocking chairs (thankfully made from wood and topped by cotton-sewn cushions) and candles dangling from above. Quaint alleys dug deeper past the walls and expanded to even further housing, their glow humming from the end of the darkness. Above, thin gilded arches connected the two sides. Miniature chandeliers in the form of lamps swung beneath, illuminating the busy street below.

But busy didn't really sell it. Hustle and bustle consumed every inch of the way forward with a monstrous hunger. Mother dwarves pulled a line of child dwarves, each giggling and cooing to the sibling behind them. They swerved past a sprinting herd of teenagers bulling down the road. Short-bearded and lanky, they shoved at the traffic in their hurry to the feast, not stopping despite the gray-headed couples shouting down a barrage of unheard commands from their balconies. Between it all leprechaun lovers traveled along with hands held for the first time, gnome families bickered about whether or not they locked the front door, and clurichaun wavered from alley to alley before passing out drunk at the entrances. Yet, despite the commotion, the mass continued forward like the staggered flow of a river dammed thick and tight.

"Say!" Dubyr called to his followers over the noise, "you all know how the Blue's put together, right?"

"Ah bit! Only heard about et in stories an' such," Bunns shouted back.

"You're in for a treat then! This here's Cranny Way, one of the Verns. Name's a carryover from before the Fulnoa, when dwarves made their homes in caverns and caves and the like. Think of them like…neighborhoods, or tiny villages."

Foxtamas nodded from behind. He'd heard mention of the Verns but never could picture them as anything other than little tunnels or a version of Winthrop crafted from stone. Cranny Way felt anything but.

"This one's, eh, busier than others, you could say. Doesn't make our gate the most fun to work at, but oh well. Wait, here, come this way!" With a sudden heel turn, the party skirted away from the flow and wiggled their way into a side alley. Instead of another row of homes, it turned into a winding set of stairs. The slumped steps had been reinforced with blue and white tiling that created a triangular pattern upwards. "I'll show you a *real* Vern."

The constant chatter of the road drifted off as they climbed. Around them the walls expanded, growing around the spiral of the staircase.

"How many of these places are there?" asked Acirema.

"Three, four dozen? Something like that? I've never been good at keeping count," chuckled Dubyr as they reached the top of the steps. "They cover the entire Living Realm."

The princess cocked her head.

"Living...Realm?"

Before he could explain further, the group broke the edge of another ravine, this time standing on the jagged edge of a stone platform. Roped fences guarded them from tumbling down into a thin yet raging river miles below. Across the gap lay the other wall with a short, sagging wooden bridge connecting the two sides and leading to a small entrance flickering with torchlight. The ceiling ran on just as tall as the fall downward. It felt like being trapped in a cut-off segment of Nohsis.

"Ah, can finally hear myself think! But yes, m'Lady, Living Realm. The first level where most all Fulnoa Folk live. Above that's the Endeavor Realm with the Mint, Academy, jobs, all that, then you've the Fellowship Realm on top of that where the feast is, and *then*, topping it all off, is the Royal Realm which, as you're probably guessin', seats Lord Enaled and all the Blue Council. But, below it all..." the dwarf strode forward to the bridge and learned over the side. "The mines, and with it, the forge. Too deep to take you all there."

"That's...certainly more than what we have in Winthrop," she joked back.

"I'm imaginin'! Always something new to find here, though. Real magic to it." With that, he motioned for the pace to pick back up. His steps bounded across the clearly gray and wearing wood like it was secure as stone. For the others—Foxtamas especially—the crossing took longer. Shorter steps with even shorter breaths.

Once across, they passed through the short-cut cave and into what looked to the trio as a dream come to life.

This was no ravine. A thriving underground *world* lay before them. Ceilings hundreds of feet high that traveled beyond the horizon line, space as open as the Dwarfmoors. The road out of the entrance turned left and toward a fully functioning village. Quieter and calmer than Cranny Way, it was a short yet steady maze of stone houses furnished with second stories and smokestacks bustling a little fluttering of mist. Those closer to the cavern's wall had been carved out of the rock. Others were built of bricks both tan and gray and, those newer to the Vern, granite. All had pointed roofs of wood that grew patches of moss and lichen atop.

Coziness radiated like warmth from a hearth, so much so that it imbued the easy gaits of the villagers strolling through the cobbled streets. Feast-goers talked with quiet laughs, the elderly snoozed on their porches. Gone was the rumble and, in its place, soared serenity.

But that was not the standout of the Vern. Neither was the monumental waterfall dancing down to the right. It burst from high on the wall and fell with an almost unreal gracefulness, like it lay suspended in the air before crumbling into the crystalline pool below. Its sound was that of a calm summer storm. The lake beneath almost matched the village in size. Its edge snaked to the back wall and drained out a sloping cave where, alongside it, rugged minecarts and steel track exited. The water soaring from above would only delve further into the buried river of the mines.

Beside the waterfall was yet another village. Not one on the ground, but one suspended around the falls. Interlaced ropes bolted to the ceiling held up wood-framed cottages. They connected to each other by bridges wobbling back and forth over the lake, yet somehow seemed to hold the buildings steady. It did not phase the miners who settled there. They strode across their streets with ease, pickaxes hugging sooty shoulders. A shift change was in order. A pack drenched with sweat climbed up one set of threadbare lattices while another, fresh from their nocturnal slumber, descended. It would not be a night of feasting for them.

No, the true spectacle, what took the breath away from the trio and locked their eyes upward, was the art painted across the miles of ceiling. The entire night sky blistered over them. Crystals, hot with a breathing brightness, had been placed as stars on a backdrop of waving, rich blues and purples. The sky swelled like the sea, churned as wind raking through a winter's night. All felt the motion of the beautiful abyss spiral into the infinite right above their heads. Thin lines began to spread out between the crystals. Each passing moment made them thicker. When connected, old constellations formed, those stitched by tales far before Nohsis of vanished creatures and lands long forgotten. Dragons flew; elves danced; cockatrices fought; mossokin slept; the last remnant of these legends in Evon.

"I…I never, never thought…" Foxtamas tried to match together some set of words, but all failed to mimic his mind.

"Oh ho, I get it! I know the feelin'," assured Dubyr. "This here's Constylane. One of my favorite Verns, personally. Real open, lovely view. The stars only come out at night too, so you feel like you're outside half the time."

"How in Evon does et do tha'?" Bunns asks, neck still stuck on the art.

"Something with light tricks or magic. Never really learned. But the stars, they're a special stone called Velihrihm that glows on and off. We mostly just call 'em light rocks, but that's neither here nor there."

"It's a marvel…" Acirema awed in response. "Are the other Verns like this?"

"A fair few. Some have valleys, others more falls, and some just a big couple houses."

After another round of gawking, the party creeped onwards, trekking through the village and around to a small crevice shaped like yet another cave opening. However, it ended only a few feet in with the floor below hollowed out.

"Weh supposed tae jump on down?" Bunns chuckled. A slight ring of hesitation came with it.

"No, we're more advanced than that! Just a minute and, oh, yup, here it comes." A slab of wood descended from the cave's top. It planted into the ground with an echoing *thud!* A pair of beams extended from the edges and met at a point, similar in style to the framing of a house. From the point grew a set of gears, metal pins, and chains rolling back up into the stone. All produced the same rhythmic grind of clanking, clashing metal. "Hurry, hop on!"

The wooden floor below them creaked as they obeyed.

"Will this bring us up?" the fox asked while glaring at the void above.

"Yes sir! They're called lifts, and we've probably a good hundred of 'em all over the place. Great for getting up, but they never stop movin'. You miss it, you're stuck for a bit."

"I kinda just assumed y'all used…stairs."

"Oh ho! We did for the longest. After a while folks got crafty and, well, here we are—"

*SKREEEEAAKK!!*

The lift roared. Its jolt shook the party to the brink of falling as it sailed up into the darkened crag. Little cuts of Velihrihm glowed just enough to not fully cage the riders in black. Still, it didn't cease the pulling of their stomachs or jittering of their brains. The villagers gave each other the same worried look of fear, then excitement, and then nausea.

The lift slowed in the same moment a sudden brightness blinded them. As their eyes adjusted, they gazed out at the Endeavor Realm.

It stood in complete contrast to the Verns below. Nothing formed naturally, no caverns, no ravines. Instead a grand marble hall outstretched before them, carved by years of mining. The ceilings were painted in a richness of scenes. Detailed imagery of past Dwarf Lords, the creation of the Fulnoa rising from the ground, and the many foundational myths practically glowed. Rows of pillars, each Cranarbor-thick and patterned with Blue Crest banners and Old Evonian ruins, traveled down for miles in directions both back and forth, left and right. Among them scurried the crowds. A sweating dwarf in a fine, puffy-necked tunic unsteadily wheeled an overflowing wheelbarrow of Tops. His charge took him to the Mint, a crystalline building rising among the columns. It was shaped like an oversized sliver of diamond and jutted out and over the hurried minters shuffling jewels, gold, Tops, and documents in and out. Through the glass, passersby watched the stories of currency be shaped and reshaped and studded and weighed, and, once complete, packaged for shipment all across Evon. The calloused hands of the Minters worked without break. They could always be picked out from a line by their squinting eyes and bronze headgear sprouting dozens of magnified lenses frayed off to the side.

Beyond the Mint, the Endeavor's hall met the other large buildings and rooms further dug into the stone. A barrage of shops, shaped in a similar styling to a ravine-set Vern, squeezed beside trading posts. The only ones still operable were those with goods already within the Blue. No grain-carrying Efetes had been welcomed in for weeks; neither had Mikyillites or far journeymen from Plentis Plains. Still, a buzzing crowd of dwarves, gnomes, leprechauns, and clurichaun filled the gaps. They closed their shops, clocked out for the night, and headed forward. Yet another river to float down.

"How's there this much!" Foxtamas choked on a laugh while taking in the shimmering alabaster of the marble. Every corner had the same glisten of care. No trim left rough, no wall or entryway bare of detail. Passion outweighed all the Tops in worth. It made his breath shudder. "It was always just battles and feasts and adventure in the books."

"Aye!" Bunns agreed. "How far down does et go?"

"A good ways. You've the Academies, baileys, training grounds, cellars, silos, more shops and businesses—plenty!"

The boys elbowed each other at the mention of training grounds. Never had their smiles or devious, childish thoughts grown so fierce.

Dubyr's path down the realm led them past a row of market stalls all long closed for the night. Beside one lay an open trunk with a faint glimmering of blue.

"Ah, look at what ol' Ganthew's still got lying around!" He snatched up the contents and presented them to the guests—miniature sapphire cones shaved down to the image of the Blue Mountain. The cut made their sparkle triangular. No other stone could boast such. "Ol' Minter who took on trinketing. Crafted a batch of these for his shop at Grammo Day. Had big plans on sellin' out too. But, well..." Dubyr fished around his coat pocket and left a pair of Silver Tops in the chest. "You all have one. Nice little memento, and I know he'd appreciate the business."

"Oh, why thank you," said Acirema, bowing as she took the tiny mountain in her hands. The boys thanked him as well before continuing through the thicket of dwarves. They rolled it over between their fingers, admiring the way it refracted the intense glow of the light rocks above. It felt like holding on to a little piece of hope.

The crowds flooding the hall began to stagger the further in the party pushed. After a sharp turn right, the Endeavor Realm opened to a staircase fit for a ballroom. It led to a second story filled with a line of lifts easily capable of holding hundreds of Fulnoa Folk. However, ugly, sporadic cracks ran across the walls and over the vacant lift spots. Ropes blocked off the entrances. Only one had been spared, and from it came shuffles and shouts.

"Ah, nook it! Still!?" spat Dubyr. "The earthquake from Grammo Day ruined a good portion of the lifts, but I figured they'd have more than *one* working."

"It leads to the feast then?" asked the princess.

"Yes ma'am, but at this rate we'll never make it." He rolled back his shoulders and let out a pent-up breath. His honey eyes scanned above the bobbling heads quickly filing up the stairs around them. One twitched. Another squinted.

Then both grew wide.

"Hah! Hurry this way, folk! I've got an idea!

Another set of stairs, another hall, another turn, another up, another down—all the Blue melted into a maze. Dubyr's route pulled them far from the crowds and into a quiet corner deeper into the Endeavor Realm. The marble faded in favor of the usual dark gray stone. All seemed to mellow until the party turned into yet another spectacle: the peryton stables.

It expanded deep with rows of wood-crafted stalls on either side. Above them pegs held harnesses and saddles, dangling beside signs burned with the names of the creatures. Peryton peeked out over the gates to get a glimpse of the visitors. Their eyes glowed more vividly than the Brown ones had, as did the viridescence of their wings and marbling of their coats. Some even wore the start of a smile.

Story after story of the flying deer rose in the room with stairs zigzagging across to reach the different stalls. At the back, the entire wall was cut out in the shape of the Blue Crest. A sloping ramp ran up beneath the straw littering the floor, leading to the top of the vaulted ceiling and creating a massive expanse for the riders to take off and land. Each level had its own path merging with the main ramp. At any moment an entire fleet of peryton could assemble and fly out within the minute. beyond the rocky crest of the ramp

A few scant torches remained burning in the stables with the last pair of riders, outfitted in heavy green parkas and goggles, checking over the final few peryton and their tack. A couple low yawns and brays kept it awake.

"Oh, he better not've left yet. Ethwill!" Dubyr cupped his hands to shout the name.

"Easy!" called back a voice from one of the stalls above. "I'm still here!" It carried the same rugged yet jolly tone as Dubyr, only a tinge peppier. The responder soared down on a loose rope tied to the upper platform. He bore the same green vestments as the other workers, only with extra leather straps running over his arms, back, and to a utility belt fastened both to his hips and across his chest. Hammers, chisels, nails, and carrots filled the pockets. His hair was a fair blonde, cut short on the sides but long on top, with a beard closely shaved to his tanned cheeks. His eyes sparkled with a sharp emerald that grew when he saw who'd called for him. "What's it—wait, who's this? No oh *ho*, is that who I think—"

"It's the Champ alright!" Dubyr replied. The two dwarves met with a snappy forearm shake before Ethwill passed around to Bunns.

"By the Blue! It's an honor to meet you, truly is," he said whilst grabbing his hand and shaking it. The jackalope gripped harder, his smile beaming at the recognition. "You brought him all the way here, Pod?"

"No, they came all on their own."

"And you let them *in?"*

"What, was I supposed to just send them back to Mechmilne?"

"What if Enaled hears about this?"

"I hope he does."

"Why?" "We're going to him."

Ethwill tossed up his hands in disbelief.

"Dubyr!"

"Easy, Pea. It's a royal request for urgent business. She's a princess who knows Enaled, met him at Grammo Day."

The blonde dwarf wiped away the sweat bubbling at his temples. He nodded with relief and shuffled a stiff bow towards Acirema.

"I see. It's an honor as well, m'lady. Ethwill Tywyll, the Blue's Peryflo and brother of this blunthead."

Chuckling, the raccoon bowed back.

"Acirema Feiht of Village Winthrop. It's an honor—"

"*Yer* the Peryflo!?" Bunns practically shouted, cutting her short. "Yer should've mentioned he was yer brother, lad!"

"Oh, what's this now? Champ's favoring *me*, eh?" Ethwill shot a fiery wink back at Dubyr, the poor scout already shaking his head.

"Don't mind him, he's just antsy. It's been a dream of theirs to come here," replied Acirema.

"Don't drag me into this…" whispered the fox from behind.

"I get it, Champ, no other place in Evon quite like it. But what's this about a request, now?" asked the Peryflo.

"I'll explain later," said Dubyr, walking further into the stables and dragging his brother along. "But right now we need to get to the feast. You still going?"

"Unfortunately. Enaled still wants us there every night," he moaned.

"*Enaled*?"

"Thistaline."

"Figured." Dubyr mouthed back to the group the words "lord's wife."

"You aren't planning to speak to him *tonight*, are you, Pod?"

"I don't see why not."

"He won't be in the mood."

"Sure he will."

"He *won't.*"

"Why not?"

"He hasn't been in the greatest headspace these last few weeks—no, let me rephrase that, these last *ten years*."

"What do you mean?" Foxtamas asked. He nudged his way forward from the back.

"I'll explain at the feast, if we can *get to it*," Dubyr replied, further dragging Ethwill to the stalls.

"Oooohhh, I see what this is now."

"Good, wind hasn't blinded you yet."

"Funny, Pod."

"Just get them saddled, please."

"Don't get me anymore involved in this than I have to be."

"Promise."

"No using my position to get an audience, no word of using my peryton to bypass the other citizens—"

The trio froze. Both brothers kept bickering, yet through it Ethwill unlatched two sets of saddles and began leading out a pair of peryton.

"D-D-Dubyr," stuttered the fox. He was suddenly *more* than alright with sinking back behind the others.

"Yes?"

"W-What's going on here?"

"Just a shortcut. Gonna fly up to Fellowship on these girls and land on a pad close to the feast." He slung one of the saddles over the beast. It ruffled back its silky green wings and lowered down its head for better access.

"*Weh* get tae ride one!?" Bunns bounded, yelped with glee, jumped up and down and up and down again on the quaking shoulders of Foxtamas.

"N-N-N-N-No, no, no, nonono." The fox stuttered without cease. Acirema pushed the jovial jackalope off to rub his back. He didn't even hear her soothing words.

"Come on, you've *dreamed* of this, Foxtamas," she said, trying to tap and rub as much as possible. "It's done all the time!"

"Not by *me!*" he protested. The tightening of the straps sounded like the grinding of an axe. Were the peryton honking or jeering? Bucking to adjust their saddles or practicing how to throw him to his demise? "I'm gonna fall and die and we'll never get F-F-Foxlaris back—"

"You won't if you *don't* get on," pitched in Dubyr. He shared a wink with his brother.

With one final click of a buckle, the peryton pair were primed. Both fanned their wide spread of wings and shook a few loose sparkles from their antlers.

"Champ and the princess, hop on with Dubyr. Fox, you're with me." Ethwill looped a chain from his ride's saddle through the straps of his belt. His black-haired counterpart did the same.

"What's that?" asked Acirema as she and Bunns strode over.

"Just a lil' extra protection in case the girls get a bit wild," Dubyr replied. The dwarf locked one boot into the stirrup and slung himself over.

"Do weh get one?" Bunns didn't really care for the answer as he was already hopping up in front.

"Nope. But I doubt you'll need it."

"Lovely…" muttered the princess. She too snuggled her way to the top, behind Bunns. He gripped the leather reins running down the creature's neck. Moving his head any further down would tangle their antlers.

As they adjusted, Ethwill reached out and dragged the mumbling fox into the saddle.

"It's half a minute up, if that."

"Seriously, I-I-I can't." His protest didn't stop the dwarf from hauling his shivering body up.

"You sure we can't leave him here, Pod?" shouted Ethwill, heavy disdain greasing his voice.

"He's the one talking to Enaled!" Dubyr chuckled.

The blonde brother sighed.

"Stop embarrassin' yerself in front of the Peryflo, Scottoh! Weh're so close tae the feast!"

"Yeah, Scotto," Ethwill grunted as he hopped on behind the fox. "I'm a harsh judger."

"You're *not* helping!" the fox squeaked.

"How's this? Grab the reigns, those leather straps there. Yeah, good, good. I'm right behind and won't let you fall. All *you* have to do is breathe, got me? No, deep breaths, no shudders or stutters. There, just like that. In, out, in—"

The rush of the flying deer knocked the last breath out of Foxtamas.

# 27

# "THE FEASTS, THE SLEEPS,"

It was all black.

The shouts of his friends, frozen tempest of the wind, falling wings of the peryton—an entire world rallied around him.

Foxtamas only squeezed his eyes tighter.

He felt the ground below him disappear. His entire body, gripped tight by a hooting and hollering Ethwill, sank with the falling through the air and then flurried by the sudden boosting upwards. It was like sailing on an invisible ocean, only with waves made from the searing scorch of bitter winds. The cold cut straight to his thumping heart. He struggled to find a breath between the sprays.

Yet, through it all, a little part of the fox stirred. A biting feeling, a hint of…regret. It took the form of a twitch in his eyelid that brought him into the world for only a second.

The Guardmont Range glowed in the moonlight. Their icy peaks shimmered, the sparkles evident from miles away. Behind, their shadows fell like contrasting jagged teeth. It made the mountains appear almost painted with lavender and azure lying beneath layers of rocky white.

The Cranarborium below looked no more than sticks from the sky. They stretched to the base of the mountains and reached up. A fruitless grasp. Their power shrank from above, turning them into nothing more than a spindly forest.

So many other sights and sounds consumed the fox, pulling his attention in every possible direction. Bunns stood and shouted. Acirema yanked him down. Dubyr laughed. Their peryton honked. Ethwill whistled. Deer rose. Leather creaked. Clouds rolled. Feathers rustled. Stars twinkled. Saddle wobbled.

Foxtamas' eyes stayed open for it all.

He couldn't close them. Not even to blink. The old taste for adventure flowed through him once again. Fear retreated so far back it felt like a distant memory, a story the rambunctious elders, always too loud for the dinner table, whisper to the children to keep them awake in the late of night. *He* was *flying* on a *peryton* to a *feast* at the *FULNOA*. If only he could tell that to his younger self. The poor boy wouldn't believe him—he'd be so dismayed to know he'd grow up to be a liar.

In that moment, the rest of his upcoming journey remolded itself in his mind. Joining the feast, speaking to Enaled, spending time within the Twin Mountains with his friends, their love propelling him forward…he'd nothing to fear. Not in the slightest. Of all the times in his life to feel confident, this was it.

Oh, how he loved it.

So too would Foxlaris.

The water against his eyes almost formed to ice.

So Foxlaris would.

He straightened his back and let his grip on the reigns loosen. With the rush of the frozen mountain air flowing through him, Foxtamas howled.

The beasts landed in a dim cavern on the mountainside. It was untouched apart from a few dusty hoofprints in front of a gate similar to the one in Cranny Lane. Beyond, it twisted into a tunnel that led to a quiet, crowded roar.

"See, wasn't so bad," said Ethwill sliding off and offering the fox a hand.

"Yeah," Foxtamas nodded. He tried to hide the smile from the others. "Not bad…"

"Weh *have* tae go again!" The jackalope didn't need the help down. He flipped off the saddle, bounced around, and slid his hand across the braying peryton over and over again. "What ah rush! Better than Ah ever hoped!"

"Maybe after the feast, Champ," chuckled Dubyr. He undid his chain and secured it back to the reigns. Once set, Ethwill clicked his tongue three times. The deer perked up and bolted back into the air. Bunns sighed, watching them dwindle back down to the stables.

"Glad you all had a good time, but I've gotta run and get ready for my entrance. Always gotta look sharp for royal business." He flicked a wink at the princess. She nodded to hide her blush.

"Why of course. Thank you for the ride up," she added with a hasty bow. The others followed with their thanks.

"No problem, m'lady. Pod, the gate?"

"Oh, right." Dubyr fiddled in his pocket for a set of keys and began cranking open the lock. Once freed, it waved open with a creak cutting through the rust. The Peryflo saluted the party and headed off down the hall.

"Say, laddie," asked Bunns as they began trickling down towards the noise. "Wha's all tha' Pea and Pod business?"

"Hah! Seems a bit strange, eh? We were so tight as kids Mum would always call us two peas in a pod. Easy things for twins to be. But the name just kept stickin'. Sometimes even I forget why we do it!" The trio snickered at the story, Foxtamas especially. Neither of his mothers had ever called him or Foxlaris anything less than "baby," "love," or "dear." Thankfully, Bunns had corrected such a glaring error. The same youth that had named him Scotto bounded out in front of him and towards the feast. He'd an unbearable excitement. And it was contagious.

It didn't take long for the tunnel to end and the feast to begin. The stony entrance brought them to a back corner that stared out at the massive, incomprehensibly gargantuan room shaped like an overgrown piece of pie. At its base ran hundreds of long, wooden tables lined with seats thick as thrones. Lanterns, plates, and utensils traveled up and down the lengths. They lay arranged in rows that formed a semicircle around a fanciful stage wedged into the corner, raised from a rocky outcrop studded with jewels and veins of sapphire, opal, and gold.

A single table sat atop it. Crafted purely of marble, a trim of gold smothered the edges with ancient markings worked deep into the sides. Eight granite seats sat behind. The first on the left was studded with amethyst, the second emerald, and the third sapphire. The two in the middle, however, sitting higher with both girth and weight added to their sides, were blitzed entirely with diamonds. The sparkle hurt to look at. Only the finest smith could have refined such a pattern. On their other side came a bleak, cracking obsidian. It stood in desperate contrast to the blazing ruby beside it and the gold encrusted seat rounding off the table. Each chair marked importance. Begged attention. Asserted authority.

Yet they paled in the sight of the sapphire monster engraved just above their heads.

The namesake.

The Blue Heart.

It was plugged in the direct center of the massive wall behind the royal

table, flanked on either side by banners bearing the Blue Crest. Gilded edges took sharp turns along its primitive shaping. Instead of curves, the bends made right angles, strict and precise. The gem stood roughly fifty dwarves tall and glimmered with a marquis cut. Legends say those who stare long enough can see the shimmers beat as if blood truly coursed through. Many didn't find the task difficult. The thrones beneath demanded attention; the Heart simply accepted it.

Barrels, all dripping with dozens of ales, beers, pints, and drinks were stacked against both sides of the stage and the Heart. They wound high enough to hide the frescos starting on the wall and trailing up the sloped ceiling above. Only half an axe and the back leg of a warrior dwarf peeked through.

The Heart of the Mountain stretched well past the bottom level. Two granite staircases trailed up to six other layers rising to the top. Each was plenty spacious and ornamented with its own line of tables, kegs, Fulnoa Folk sitting, standing, walking, drinking, and everything in between. Little gold railings bordered the sides so no one could fall to the story below. That didn't stop some from bumbling awfully close.

Crystalline chandeliers swung above and bathed the chamber in a bright yet quiet light. Every level was dimmer and thus cozier than the one before it. Across from the stories, little balconies were etched into the walls. Musicians of every type filled them, strumming along fiddles and cellos, pounding drums and bells, and working their bony hands across flutes, piccolos, harps, and horns. It brought coherency to the crowd's endless drollery.

Thousands upon thousands of dwarves, most mugs in hand, poured and crammed into every inch of the Heart. Little tunnels opened into it like an actual set of veins. No one seemed to mind, though. They clanked tankards, shook hands, belly laughed, teased and seethed; a feast wasn't a gathering of neighbors and cohorts, but of family.

The trio lost sense of themselves. They'd never seen such a scale of people, even at Grammo Day. It was akin to shrinking down and sneaking into a beehive—the Heart had the same buzz and bustle.

"He better have gotten our spot—oh, yup! Look at ol' Chesty, perfect as always!" Dubyr pointed up to the second level. A barely visible Chester sat sipping down the last of his drink while an older dwarf woman, gray hairs mingling into her coal-black curls, talked mercilessly into his ear. His wrinkles had twisted into a smile. Until he caught sight of Dubyr waving up.

He returned to his stone-faced scowl.

The scout led the way through the chaos, splitting a path up the stairs and through the crowd scurrying around the seats. Foxtamas and Acirema ruthlessly apologized for stepping over, across, and behind the littering of lost gnomes and cranky clurichaun. Bunns, however, just kept on hopping by, eyes wide and mouth open.

"Beat us here, Chesty!" Dubyr patted the older dwarf on the back with a hearty laugh.

"Oh, Dubyr dear! Lovely to see you," shouted the lady at Chester's slouching side.

"You too, Miss Tari. Looking wonderful tonight, as always."

"Oh, you're too much!"

"Chester says the same!" The pair howled. The man between them did not. "You three take a seat, I'll run and get the drinks."

They beat him to it. The trio wiggled their way into the chairs with Bunns sitting between his friends. The table rose slightly too high for all but Foxtamas who, looking closer, noticed hundreds of circled indentions spanning deep and wide into the wood. His interest didn't linger. He connected his sizzling fire of excitement with Bunns' instead.

"We're here, man…We're actually—"

"*HERE!* Hah! Look at et all, laddie!" the jackalope shouted. He spanned his paw across the room and pointed out every detail he could. "Enaled will bae right there! An' the heart, Ah can see et beatin'. Ah *knew* the tales were true! Oh, and tha' lad's blade, look et! W-Wait, nae, his! Aye, an' there, Heartmaidens! An' listen, they're playin' 'Marawyn's Day'!" He almost fell over in a fit of giddy gasps, but Foxtamas kept up his pace.

"Did you forget that's the *crowning stage* down there! Every Blue Ruler started their reign *right there!* And look, next to it, at the art behind the barrels! That's Polroth III's March to the Allmarsh. The gold boots give it away—"

"Is there anything you two *don't* know?" Acirema tried to cut in with a slice of seriousness, but her cracking grin proved too strong.

"Not much, Queenie," replied Bunns, now propped on his elbows to see further into the Heart.

"The mugs," the fox added. "It's like everyone's got one, all special and engraved too. Never heard of them doing that in my life."

"Aye, hadn't figured they'd bae tha' into drinkin'. Ah feast is a feast though!"

"No, it *is* a lot, isn't it?" Acirema took a quick look around. Entire families were slugging back grog. Many a dwarf already crawled to the verge of passing out, foam thick on their lips and beards.

*SLAM!*

Their own drinks arrived. Dubyr slid down the overflowing wooden mugs before taking his own and kissing it with a hefty sip. Crackles of fizz popped from the sparkling blue ale. The smell wafted heavy to the trio—somewhere between a strawberry patch and lavender tree with a hint of cinnamon tying it all together.

"Drink it down, folks! That there's Blue Brother, a Blue Mountain Feast exclusive." He wiped his soaking braided beard with his coat sleeve. "Nothin' in there to get you too riled up. I bet it would be a hit down in Hucksubtle if we tweak it a bit. And if anyone dared go that far south."

Foxtamas raised it to his lips. The sparkles of fizz leaped out to burn his cheeks. Despite it, he took a sip and let the ale sizzle down his throat. Definitely strawberry. Definitely lavender. *Definitely* cinnamon.

He launched an eye-watering cough into his elbow. When he looked back up, both Bunns and Acirema were chugging along, their mugs raising higher and higher.

"Good stuff, eh?" asked Dubyr with a pat on the fox's back.

"Oh, uh, y-yeah, real good," he lied between coughs. "But the mugs, Dubyr." Another cough. "Why's everyone got one? Didn't think that was something common here."

The dwarf downed another swig while nodding.

"It's a newer thing for sure. See, we—"

*Boom! Boom!! BOOM!!!*

The rest of the instruments silenced. Thick, full force beats burst from the balconies. At once the tempo changed to only the rich bleat of the drums. All the crowd ceased their talk simultaneously, sat down in their seats, and turned their attention down to the stage with heart-racing anticipation.

"You'll just have to wait and see!" whispered Dubyr, winking. Foxtamas nodded and turned towards the thrones. The wait made his tapping foot rumble and cheeks spread in a smile.

It was time for the Blue Council to arrive.

The sudden sweep of a fiddle joined the cold *tap!* of the female dwarf's gait as she strutted onto the stage. Applause echoed throughout the chamber. Every step came stiff. Her hair, long, straight, and plain gray falling to her waist, refused to move. It contrasted with her purple and black two-tailed dress, the glittery pattern of which looked like swirls of sand blowing against the dark sky of a dust storm. She wore a plain circlet around her forehead with a drop of amethyst inlaid into the front. Her body was no thicker than the skeleton beneath it, the pale cheeks of which sunk deep into a thin, cruel scowl. In her sleeves she carried her bony, skin-tight fingers, clamped together and hidden from view.

"Lookin' good, Lady Henstray!" shouted a drunk from the lower level. Ripples of laughter followed, met in tandem by a roar of hushes. The lady responded with a single icy glare from her even icier blue eyes. They matched the color of the thickest frost grown in a Pradifore winter. Foxtamas remembered the color. He shuddered.

"That's your lady," the scout whispered again.

"What?" asked Foxtamas, ending his clapping and turning with cocked brow.

"That's the scholar you'll be talkin' to. Mean ol' lady—I think she's nothing but an overimportant librarian myself."

Lady Henstray took her seat in the first chair without even scooting it back. Once settled, the strings ended, and in their place rose a pan flute.

The applause shifted from claps to a roar as Ethwill Tywyll strode out towards the stage. Up went his hands to meet the cheers, now glimmering with emerald rings on every finger. He'd rapidly replaced his tunic with a finer garment—still a rich, velvet green tufted with fur—that clung loose beneath a tightened belt. Added to it was a black cape and a collar shaped in the silver, glistening style of the peryton antlers, rising behind his head. No one would expect a stablemaster to have such enriched style; still, they all clamored his praise.

Dubyr especially.

"*ATTA BOY!*" he shouted through cupped hands. He motioned for the trio to stand and cry out as well. "*PERYTON KING!*"

They found it hard not to chuckle at the dwarf. His cheeks puffed with redness, voice on the verge of cracking every time he called out. Both above and below flyers and other stable workers matched his energy, all denoted by their green, furry tunics.

Ethwill and Dubyr sat down at the same time, one much more exhausted than the other. Between his breaths he winked over to his guests.

"Always gotta hype the boy up," Dubyr panted. "Or embarrass him, depending on the day!"

Tambourines rattled from the line of balconies. Their sizzle of shakes mimicked the clinging of a bag of Tops, quite literally setting the stage for the laughing, bumbling dwarf fumbling up next.

He wore a sophisticated, double-breasted blue suit tailored in the same style as the Minters. Gold buttons flashed from his middle and cuffs. His hair was thin, balding, but still a striking and curly black. It rolled along the back of his head and formed a fearsome beard at his front, the edges of which bounced on his rotund belly that jiggled as he jaunted. The flailing bronze of the Minters' speckles did what they could to cover the receding widow's peak. It didn't fool anyone. Instead, they acted like crystalline glasses, bulging his brown eyes to the point of becoming two bricks of coal slotted into his face.

It only added to his flare. The moment the music shifted, a chant broke out among the screams of children rushing towards the front of the stage: *"TIRSOL! TIRSOL! TIRSOL!"*

Tirsol, the head Minter, replied with a shrieking laugh and the tossing of Tops from his pockets. Not just any, but ones of value, Silver Tops, Garnet Tops, even Opal. They landed in mugs, under tables, in the faces of old, crouching leprechaun women, but mostly in the hands of the children jumping at the front. Once his pockets were emptied, the cheering lowered. The kids scurried away. Tirsol plopped into his seat with a hearty laugh, winking at the pair to his right. Ethwill nodded. Henstray did not.

The metal shakes sped to the fast, sharp hits of a fiddle. Before the Heart had only echoed—now it rumbled. As if one singular wave, the entire crowd stood with the collective roar of a storm. Dwarves below shook each other to release their uncontainable joy. The clapping numbed into a singular, listless noise.

But no one showed.

It didn't stop the feast goers. The shouts kept thundering, the storm stuck in the clouds.

Finally, after the fiddles restarted their opening song twice, the Council member stumbled out from the right-side tunnel.

A gnome. Dressed in an oversized brown robe with gilded edges, floppy sandals, and slouching nightcap dripped over his face. A prickly chinstrap beard wrapped around his sharp face. His nose fell long and curled at its point. It sagged like the blue eyebags sinking beneath his once fiery hazel eyes. He lacked the ornamentation found on peers. His shoulders barely stood straight enough to keep up his robe.

The gnome fluttered a single wave to the crowd while dragging himself to the table. His feet didn't leave the ground. It didn't quiet the ear-bleeding shouts—if anything, they only multiplied.

"*LADDIE!"* Bunns had to lean across Foxtamas to blurt over to Dubyr. *"WHO'S THA'?" "DREWNOH!"* he launched back.

"*Why's he so important!?"* the raccoon yelled.

"*ALE MASTER!*" That settled the remaining questions. "*USED TO BE OVER LUMBER, BUT...WE HAD MORE PRESSING NEEDS.*"

Drewnoh plopped down in the far-right throne marked with gold. Burped. Curled up. Reached down for a swig of drink before "resting his eyes."

That quieted the Heart. It gave enough of a reprieve for the fiddles to (finally) quiet and change to another round of drumming, this time with quicker, deeper hits. The rhythm built in rigid staccato until, yet again from the right, a red-headed dwarf rolled out. Dirt and soot marked his face and burly arms. Only a mere black set of overalls covered him. Around it looped a tool belt stuffed with picks, hammers, tongs, and every available forge accessory. A matching cloak connected to his left strap and draped over a lame arm. The scar burned into it traveled up to his face. Melted the skin. Made his cheeks and mouth sag. None of his wiry beard or hair grew on that side. It instead flourished like an erupting volcano on his right.

The disfigurement did not slow the blazing energy of the forger. He responded to shouts of "*DRAGYEN!*" and *"FORGE MASTER!"* with snappy points of his hammer. Once beside his seat, he raised a hand and motioned for the crowd to follow. They obeyed.

Dragyen threw down his hammer.

*"DING!"* shouted the Heart.

He threw it down again.

*"DING!"* the Heart echoed.

Finally, he tossed it down again with all his might.

*"AYE!"* both the Fulnoa Folk and their forger acted as if they'd been blasted back by flames. It threw Dragyen into his chair with a guttural laugh. The shock stirred Drewnoh awake. For a second, at least.

The drums suddenly stopped. No more music took its place. Just as quickly as the Heart roared, it ceased. Not even a swallow sounded. The trio glared at Dubyr, but the dwarf refused to acknowledge them. He planted his attention forward.

Everyone did.

*Clop.*

*Clop.*

*Clop.*

*Clop.*

Metal steps. Sure in stride.

The final dwarf entered in resolute silence. He was by far the tallest. Widest. Strongest. His beard and hair were midnight black. They grew untamed. Over his sun-spotted forehead. Unwavering expressionlessness. Burnt metal plates soldered like eyepatches over both his eyes. He walked completely blind. An old scar ripped over where his eyes once lay. The patches interrupted it.

The same cold and matte material formed his black armor. Each angle ended in a point severe enough to slice. In the center was etched a thin Blue Crest—the only glimmer upon the dwarf. The metal too formed his four-bladed axe. It hit the ground before his steps did. Guided him towards the stage's middle.

He stopped precisely in the center. Turned to the Heart.

A metal *STOMP!*

All rose.

None of the friends dared to speak or, in Foxtamas' case, breathe. The congregation stood forward with eyes on the blind, boding dwarf.

A metal *STOMP!*

*"GEN'RAL KRIG!"*

One singular voice. He rewarded it with a nod.

The moment Krig sat was the moment the music returned, not with one instrument, but all. An entire crescendo of drums, strings, fiddles, flutes—every balcony blared a rising royal tune that shook the very sapphire of the Heart. Gasps and bouncing legs joined. Breaths staggered, held.

Then came the Wolvertons.

Enaled walked from the left, Thistaline from the right, and endless applause from the crowd before them.

The Dwarf Lord of the Blue Mountain marched in the fullness of his regalia. He wore a blue tunic covered by a silver robe, the threading of which retold the history of his position as Ruler. Over it lay a hefty fur coat doubling as a cape. Multiple blue and gold rings studded each of his fingers. They shimmered as bright as his golden locks. His hair was a flowing, glowing blond, falling just above his shoulders. The same coloring bled down his full yet trimmed beard. The Crest Crown sitting upon his head locked the mane tight. A gilded sterling silver, it took the shape of the Blue Crest, set in by the prestige finery of dwarven craftsmanship. Sapphires wrapped around it. Runes glowed across the band. Beneath it, however, within both beard and hair, ran streaks of gray. Not light and easily overlooked, but thick, clumped together, like highlights of darkness, dark clouds on a sunny day.

The pattern dressed his entire body despite it barely being over forty. Rugged wrinkles cracked over his forehead; bags begged to drag under his sea-blue eyes. His face, once round, now looked in the early stages of atrophy, with cheek bones sunken and neck thinning below them. Still, he smiled wide. Beamed his bright teeth and waved to those he commanded.

To further their excitement, he raised up the axe held in his hand. Foxtamas and Bunns recognized it right away, their eyes on the verge of popping from their skulls—the Blue Brother's Keeper. One half of the legendary Fulnaxe, a weapon crafted before Evon split, the united power of which could raise the Cranarbor. It was shaped in the style of the Blue Crest, only angled and with the jutting bridge replaced with a smaller, sharper blade. It sparkled just like the sapphire Heart behind him.

His approaching wife held the same royal eloquence. Her hair sparkled a fine white, not from age, but from the uncommon dwarvish gene. She'd braided it with flakes of sapphire and primrose both in the back and on the bangs at the front. On top sat the Guardmont Garland, the partner crown to her husband's. Silver threads weaved an outline of the mountain range. Paired behind Enaled's, it made the full picture of the Blue's dominance. Her face was plump and round, speckled with freckles and gold eyes that squished as she smiled to the Heart.

Round too was her stomach. Full not with food or ale, but child. The bump protruded from her sequined blue dress, the glow of which shifted to silver as she crossed the flickering light of the room. Such a dazzle became the envy of mothers and daughters, but in the same breath, an inspiration.

Her strut and wave moved quicker than the Dwarf Lord's. She arrived at the table's center before he did, but the second he stepped close the two joined hands, Enaled even planting a kiss on her chuckling cheek.

It wasn't a collective shout. Nor roar, nor rumble. Only pure noise rang out in that hall. Enough to shake the chandeliers and form a haze of ceaseless applause. All standing. All cheering. All praising their fearless, fighting family of the Fulnoa.

The couple walked around to their seats, greeting the Blue Council as they went. Once in place, they picked up their mugs. A shared smile passed between them.

The Heart followed by grabbing their own. Enaled began tapping the stone table one beat after another. The hits were steady. Heavy. Thick.

"SCOTTOH!" languished Bunns amidst banging his own mug, "ET'S ET!"

"I-I-I KNOW!" The fox threw back his head in disbelief. His banging hastened. Blue Brother soaked him.

Acirema sighed. And smirked.

Cast across the Guardmont bold,  
like silver poured from craggen mold,  
our home arose in quake of morn,

brightest light in Evon born.

Blue Moun-tain! Blue Moun-tain!
Our rocky paradise!
Gateway to the North,
'neath king and court,
one Heart, one hearth, our pride!

Foxtamas looked at Bunns, but the jackalope had already turned his way. This song…it wasn't the same. They knew by the first line. Their mugs kept stomping to the beat, but as the Ode furthered, they lost any notion of following the words.

In light of Living Vern below
we En-dea-vor to help the whole.
Our Fell-ow-ship of ripe and aged
with Royal hand will bright the day.

Blue Moun-tain! Blue Moun-tain!
Our rocky paradise!
Raise high your pint
and down your fright,
Hug on a brother and love your life!

Sing your song, shape your mug,
brew the taste an' brew it strong
for comes a feast from dusk 'till dawn
within our Heart, one bleating throng!

Ful-no-a! Ful-no-a!
Two Brothers Forged in Stone!
Gateway to the North,
'neath king and court,
one Heart, one hearth, our pride!

Now bend the knee and bow the wings
to our good kindly Wolver king,
he the Lord for who we call—
Praise his reign oh one and all!

Blue Moun-tain! Blue Moun-tain!
Our rocky paradise!
Raise high your pint
and down your fright,
Shoulder your kid
and kiss on your wife,
Stomp on the ground
and stand with pride…
Hug on a brother and love your life!

*HEY!*

*SLAM!*

The song concluded with a final yelp. In the same breath, mugs across the Heart crashed down on the tops of the tables. The jolt kicked them back up to the mouths of Fulnoa Folk, and everyone downed the last swigs of their drinks, thousands of new circles cut fresh into the wood.

Good talk and cheer resumed. The crowd took their seats, careful to wipe away the far-flung ale from the tables and themselves. Enaled remained standing. He shot Thistaline a quivering wink before regaining his smile.

*"Folks! Friends! Family of the Blue Mountain!"*

His boast was that fit for a Dwarf Lord. He naturally filled the chamber with a deep, smooth call, marred by the Northern dialect and worn high with pride.

"I thank you all, on behalf of myself, my wife, and this Council, for joining us here tonight. Feasts are the special moments that unite us all as one. Minters and flyers become brothers, scholars and forgers become sisters—when we're here together in this Heart, it beats as one."

Applause rang out once again. Enaled raised a hand to quiet them, turning to avoid embarrassment.

"It is another night of blessing that we can hold such a gathering. I ask you pour your thanks to those who've made it possible both now and in these past trying weeks. It's been a…a difficult time, as w-we all know, and…and—"

The Lord's focus fell to the table as his legs began to tremble. The words ready on his lips ebbed away. His ring-encrusted hand grabbed the golden edge until his knuckles threatened to shred through his skin.

"And we hope these feasts continue to be a beacon of light in such dark times!" Thistaline rose to her husband's side, holding him up and gleefully finishing his opening speech. "It is our joy to have you here. Let the feast commence!"

She patted his arm and helped him down to his throne. This time, instead of a wink, the Blue Lord offered only a nod, and a shaken, curt one at that.

Heartmaidens, white-clad serving girls with braided, heart-shaped hair, poured from the tunnels across the Heart. They carried in trays of steaming bread with butter leaking from the sides, grilled trout piled high next to chopped, seasoned, and fried potatoes, rolling cauldrons of cheddar and collard green soup, cinnamon porridges, sweet rolls slathered in melting, dripping icing, and, most enticing of all, sugar-crusted muffins filled with blueberry syrup.

Every mouth watered.

As the servers began to make rounds between the tables, Bunns leaned back across to Dubyr.

"So, wha' was with the song changin', eh?"

The dwarf pulled his eyes away from the rolls just long enough to answer Bunns. "What changed about it?" he half-heartedly replied, no jest in his voice.

The jackalope exchanged confused glances with the fox.

"Oh, Ah dunno, the whole *thing*."

"That wasn't the Ode to the Twins then?" asked Foxtamas.

Dubyr fully turned himself around, honey eyes pointed up as if deep in thought.

"No, not that one…nope, this one's just Ode to the *Twin*."

"What happened to the old one?"

"Stopped using it years ago, right around a decade, I think. Can barely remember now."

"But *why*?" Bunns protested further.

"Because of the Rupture."

"The *wha'?*"

The scout's face fell. His rosy cheeks turned a cloudy pale. He didn't even notice the Heartmaiden passing by and laying out his plate.

"Oh no…you three don't know, do ya?" The trio shook their heads as worry built within their chests. Dubyr's expression told it all. "That…makes sense. It's between Enaled and Foehn. They, well…they don't talk to each other. Haven't in years."

"You're joking!" cut in Acirema, eyes wide with disbelief. "I know Lord Foehn wasn't at Grammo Day, but the two lords not even speaking…"

"I wish I was, m'Lady. But it's worse than that. No one's allowed to cross into the other mountain. Blue's stay Blue, Brown's stay Brown. Last I heard most Brown's can't even *leave*. Not because of Grammo Day either. Just the law there."

"How did we not know…" Foxtamas asked the question not to the dwarf, but to himself, mellow voice wistful at the revelation. He physically felt the crumbling of the Fulnoa he'd built in his mind. The falling rock didn't hit him with fear, just…pain.

"They don't like makin' a big deal out of it. Think they'll look weak, like the whole kingdom is tumbling apart."

"Wha' in Evon happened tae cause et then?"

Dubyr scoffed down a quick bite of trout before continuing, nodding as he recalled the story.

"You all won't like this but...the Bridge." Another bite to steady himself, this time of bread with a sip of ale. "See, Enaled and Foehn were more brothers than cousins. They spent their younger days pretty close to bein' inseparable since Lady Rolestelle of the Blue, Enaled's mum, married the best friend of Foehn's pop, Lord Vyleno II. Anyway, both their parents were older and poorer in health than they should've been for their ages. Tough sickness swept through both mountains, and, well...the lords took their thrones at a younger age than most.

"It was, oh, five or so years into their reigns that Gniw approached with the Bridge Pact. I assume you're all too familiar with it. Mikyill and the others would provide the funds, and the Fulnoa would offer the resources and actually *build* the nookin' thing. Enaled jumped at the opportunity. But Foehn stayed put.

"Rumor has it the debate between them lasted months. One reason the Bridge took so long gettin' done. Enaled saw it as a way to further the kingdom's industry, y'know, make it a larger player in an ever-expanding Evon, *especially* one about to double in size. But Foehn hated any *notion* of industry. His focus lay on strengthening the rule the Fulnoa had asserted for centuries. They'd slackened on keepin' track of their dominion up north. Bandits, gangs, and thieves ran wild in Pradifore; the Seasondoms were bickering and infighting to the point of riling up a war. They'd already lost too much control, and he wasn't about to let the rest of it slip away.

"So...he didn't. The Pact never said both lords needed to agree. It was a first in Fulnoa history, the two not agreein' on something so big. Enaled signed the Blue Mountain on while Foehn refused. Lad didn't even show for the meeting." The scout shook his head, stuffed down a muffin, and tossed back another swallow. He needed the reprieve.

"Things only spiraled from there. New decrees came out *daily* on the changes, like who was allowed where and in what mountain and the such. Next thing we knew the Mint and Lumber facilities moved to the Blue, and horror stories started leakin' out 'bout the Brown's Verns dissolving to nothing but a buncha barracks.

"Worst was when Foehn barred any entry to the Brown. He got his loyalists together in one camp then slammed shut the doors. In a single sweep he tore families right apart, all because he couldn't make a deal.

"Now, word is he's his own self-servin' tyrant. They say pride comes before a fall an' all that. Guess it comes before makin' yourself into a monster too."

Dubyr paused for another swig, this one longer and steadier than before. "Peace *is* kept up north, though. If you can call it that. I refuse to take any scouting routes past the Guardmont—I don't want to see what Foehn's axe has done to the place. It's already hurting us bad here. Just look down there at Enaled. Lad can hardly keep up anymore. The work of one Dwarf Lord is plenty, but doublin' it breaks you down. He should be younger, and happy, and…not burdened or stressed like he is.

"It's a miracle he found Thista, though, even more so he's having a kid. You all should've *seen* the place during the wedding. Didn't think we'd ever calm down! Everyone, all the way up to the Council, was worried sick he'd never have an heir. Same with Foehn. Wolvertons *always* have children. Never been one who didn't. If something happens to Foehn, then the entire Brown Mountain will…I don't like to think about it."

Dubyr had been staring straight at the sapphire Heart. He shook away his blank stare and turned back to the solemn guests beside him, eyes low and heads nodding. "Oh, but 'nough of all that!" He clapped Foxtamas on the back with a laugh. "I didn't bring you folk here to depress ya'. Go on, enjoy the feast! We don't have the best cooks in Evon workin' for nothin'!"

"We'll try," said Acirema, trying to chuckle back. It was hard to break through the mire of such a story.

"That's a good leading attitude right there, m'lady. Take all the time you need. We won't be going to Enaled until the end." A smart move. Down below, a line stretched out from the Council's table. Important messages, hearings, reports, and updates were fed to the Dwarf Lord faster than his own meal.

The party cut through their fish, potatoes, soups, and sweet rolls. They didn't realize just how little they'd been surviving on and, worse, how bland it had become. Every bite of bread made Bunns slow his chewing to a crawl. He needed to savor his precious seconds with it.

Gradually, little dots of flame sparked up throughout the Heart. Flapdragon, along with quieter games like Fool's Gold and Half-Stone Breaks, kept the feast flourishing with cheer and hollers.

A devilish glance passed between Dubyr and the Champ.

Bunns stuffed his final half of muffin in his mouth and dashed off to a round starting at their table's end. Acirema joined him. The scout couldn't stifle his laughter from seeing them dart so happy and readily to the flames.

"What a pair, eh?" he scoffed to the fox. Poor soul had yet to move or make comment on the night.

"Oh yeah, they're...somethin' else a lotta the time," Foxtamas squeaked out.

"The best ones are!"

He nodded back, trying hard to make his smile obvious. In his hand he twiddled his spoon through the bottom of the soup bowl. It made the letter "M" and connected its points with a line. The Fulnoa Crest. Branded deep in his mind ever since seeing it sketched in one of Momma's storybooks.

He slashed a new line down the middle.

"I'm…really sorry to hear about the Rupture, Dubyr," he finally replied. "I know it can't've made life easy here. The dwarves, y'all are like our heroes back in Winthrop. It hurts me to know the truth of it. I can't imagine what it's been like here…" Before he could finish, a hardy pat landed square on his shoulders.

"Oh ho, thank you for that, Foxtamas. I know the sorta impact we have here. Every realm's carved and painted with legends from our past, the kind we can't ever live up to. As for livin' here, well…you do your best to ignore it. Not that you ever can, but helps to try. Big reason I took up scoutin'."

"Really?" The fox perked. He set aside his last scraps of food and fully faced the dwarf.

"Yes sir! Was the best way I had to escape. Can't be bothered with a buncha infighting when you're not even there to see it. I chose it over being co-Peryflo with Ethwill when he got the job."

His blue eyes bulged.

"No way! How could you turn that down!?"

"Come on, you met ol' Pea! I can't *imagine* having to saddle and train those beasts all day with that chunk of stone!" Dubyr howled a hoarse laugh and shot down another swig. "But really, I'd only be gettin' in his way. He's better suited for it, and it just kept me too close to home. Scoutin' let's you see places, keeps you involved with the world at large." *Another* swig, this one finally emptying his hand-carved mug. "I won't lie, it hurts seeing this mountain how it is. Just look around! Where else in Evon can you find this much artistry, or care, or—or *passion?* The potential to do something great is right here in our hands and yet…we just keep squanderin' it. Time and time and time again. I'd do anything to heal this place. Bring us back to the legends you think—or thought—we are. Not that I'm doing much these days with sitting down there with ol' Chesty, but still.

"I figure it's all on the brink of gettin' worse. If what you say is true, about the monsters you all saw and fought on the way up here, then it only means Foehn was more right about the Bridge and its dangers than he already is. You give that...*maniac* a flake he'll take the whole vein. Any chance of compromise'll be out the door."

"I just don't get it," the fox said with furrowed brow and boot jittering on the stone below. "Why won't anyone stand up to him? *Both* of them? This is the Fulnoa, Dubyr. So much rests on y'all and yet it's hurting because of a single, stupid argument—"

"They've tried." His words weren't loud, or rude, or cold. Just words. But they spoke many more for him. "Especially early on. Now they're too scared or too complacent, and neither Foehn nor Enaled will lend an ear. Enough peace is kept, so why bother it?"

*SPLASH!!*

The pair bolted their attention to the table's end. There, an opened keg sprouted flames, and from the flames sprouted two fluffy white legs.

Bunns flung himself back out with a messy but passable flip. Drenched, he shook off what he could of the Blue Brother, but not before tossing a hefty bag of Tops to Acirema. She caught the bag with a laugh and started a screaming round of shouts and cheers.

The table had drawn a crowd. Folks on the stories above and below peeped over at the commotion. Even the likes of Tirsol and the newly awoken Drewnoh hobbling up to see the Champ in action.

The cackling jackalope bowed again and again as the chants covered him like a silken robe.

"*Bunns! Bunns! Bunns! Champ! Champ! Champ!*"

Neither victory nor ale ever tasted so good.

"At least we can have fun." Dubyr winked to the eye-rolling fox. Both snickered at the sight. It eased the pain of the conversation. Brought them back to the light of the moment long enough to carry through the night.

# 28

# "SING EVERY SOUL BELOW THIS STONE:"

It was time.

The Heart was slowing and the feast dissipating, dirty mugs and dishes piling just as high as the food had hours prior. Flapdragon fires burnt out. The last trails of conversation meandered back to the wild lands of coming and going. All felt the final exhale of the night. Except for the trio and their dwarven guide leading them towards the Wolvertons.

Foxtamas' fear had come against a stalemate with passion. Both sides agreed to a ceasefire to let the fox dwell over his confusion and heartache with the Fulnoa. He didn't feel scared to walk up to the Dwarf Lord. More so…sad.

The friends followed Dubyr right up to the table's steps and before the lord and lady. They felt the stares of the Council's importance weighing heavy, be it with dried mouths or twitching ears. Up close, Dragyen's scars made a sliver of heat roll down their arms, and shivers wrapped a fist around their spines from the seemingly watchful metal eyes of Krig. The Gen'ral didn't move at their arrival. Hardly breathed. He stared forward, scraggly black hair motionless across his face. Thankfully, to their left, Ethwill winked and flashed a mischievous grin. The Lady Henstray beside him did not seem impressed.

"Your Lordship, if I may—"

"Apologies." Thistaline leaned against the marble to cut Dubyr off. "Lord Enaled is exhausted from meetings this evening. If you'd please—"

"No, Thista. Let him speak." Enaled Wolverton eased up into his seat. The gray hairs weren't just darker up close, but thinner. Beads of sweat rolled across his temples like rain blessing a cracked, wrinkled desert. Foxtamas met his inquisitive peering from behind the scout. The lord's eyes were a darker blue than his own. Sagging, yes, with lids ready to fall at any second, but deeper in, running like ocean ravines, spread cracks in his color. Hard, hollow fractures of brown. "Dubyr is a friend and serves us well as one of the lead scouts. Still stationed with Chester, yes?"

"Yes, My Lord."

"Still groggy?"

"As always."

The two shared a laugh that chipped a grin into the stone of Enaled's face.

"Oh, how good to hear. Now, you're business? I see we have...*guests*...with us tonight..." His words faded as he looked over the visitors. Gen'ral Krig grunted at their mention. Current protocol was *not* to be broken, especially by one as vigilant as a scout.

"Yes, right. My Lord, this is Princess Acirema Feiht of Village Winthrop and her two loyal companions, Bunns Cammont and Foxtamas Scottsworth. They come on Royal Pardon for an urgent request requiring your immediate attention and decision." The proper talk never fit Dubyr quite right, but it got the point across. Following the introduction, Acirema bowed and led both boys to follow. Enaled leaned further forward and squinted at the raccoon.

"Ah, Lady Feiht! Yes, we met at Bridgeburrow, didn't we?" asked the Lord, voice low but still sharp.

"Yes, Your Lordship. My father, King Airsar, was one of the first founders of the Bridge Pact," Acirema replied with a curtsey. The proper talk fit her like a glove, even if it tasted bitter on her tongue. She'd wash it out with ale later. It was an act she'd only have to put on for a little while longer. That thought made it tolerable.

"You're very right. I must apologize both to you and your father. I was regretfully a little less talkative than I should have been for such an occasion. But I am more than happy to remedy that now." He offered up a nodding, tired smile. Acirema responded with her own.

"You've no need to apologize, My Lord. It is more than understandable for such a day. I wish our talk could be more delightful and less strenuous, but, as announced, I come with pressing matters." She motioned behind for Foxtamas to stand beside her. He obeyed with unwavering attention to the Dwarf Lord. "We seek aid for a quest of rescue that only the forces of the Fulnoa can properly wage. This is Foxtamas, one of my fiercest friends and the brightest of Village Winthrop. You may not remember him from Grammo Day, but you will his brother, Foxlaris—the first to walk on the Bridge of Evon."

That perked the table's attention. Enaled nodded and scooted even closer, Thista now warming his side.

"I see then. This rescue, it is for your brother then, Mr. Scottsworth?"

A Dwarf Lord said his name. A Dwarf Lord *knew* his name.

"Yes, My Lord." It felt odd not saying such a phrase to a playing, childhood Bunns or Foxlaris.

From there, he began the same tale told to Dubyr and the other passing members of their journey. He ensured each word was spoken carefully, pronounced with confidence. It worked, taking Enaled, Thistaline, and the other eavesdropping Council members through the harrows of Grammo Day, first attack at Nohsis, reprieve at Hucksubtle, and the ups and downs of the adventure leading to that very speech in that very hall.

"So, we, or really, *I*, come asking for help to cross into the East and search for Foxlaris. We know he's still alive, but with the threat of the monsters we encountered, we can't be certain that we'll make it to him in good shape. Or any shape at all.

"We also want to do what we can to figure out why they've come now. Why the Bridge tore apart at all. Word's spread of the studies here, and we have what I think is critical firsthand experience. It's all we can offer in return. And, well...I want to know why this had to happen, too. And why it had to be Foxlaris."

He said his brother's name staring into the watery eyes of the lord.

"I know we're just small villagers from Mechmilne, and our quest here shouldn't be some reason for reward, but you're our last hope. We came here because of the legends we grew up on. As kids we'd play pretend, and Foxlaris, he…he ruled the Brown, and I ruled the Blue, like Bwayine and Eobin, and—gah, I-I'm sorry, that's stupid to say. There's just…just…"

His stutter returned alongside his final words. The fox glared up at the ceiling. He tried to control his tongue and the tears drowning his eyes.

"There's no one else we know to call upon."

Enaled nodded. Steadily. A careful back and forth, tired and long, to the point of the Crest Crown slipping from his mane.

Every second lasted years and aged him tenfold. He became in the fox's eyes a wizard, bending time and pondering each possible scenario and outcome of his decision. The growth of his wrinkles and ridges in his lips only further painted the picture.

Thistaline took the brunt of the worry. She hugged her husband's side and rested a calming hand over her stomach. If her white hair could pale any further, it would.

"You're certain they were monsters? Not bandits in disguise?" she asked.

"Nae, Mah Lady," said Bunns. "Ah slayed many an' saw more. They ain't anything close tae wha' weh have here." The woman looked down without a response. She knew the words to be true.

Enaled sighed.

"I cannot guarantee anything, Mr. Scottsworth. These times are, as you know, unprecedented." He set his clasped hands upon the table. His many rings had been taken off apart from his simple silver wedding band. "But…I will be in talks with Gen'ral Krig over the following days. Our fighting parties are not what they used to be in years past. Most are hardly still assembled."

At the mention of his name, Krig again perked up, this time raising a lone brow.

"In the meantime, you can discuss your findings with Lady Henstray. I know this has been an important task for her and her husband, Sir Lordell. I suppose you can meet sometime in the morning." The trio turned to the purple-clad woman, only to find her already staring back. She passed a similar grimace over to Enaled, but the icy throws bounced right off. "I can also treat you three to our royal rooms, or the Verandos, as we call them. It's the least we can do one for royalty—and those loyal to it—after such an arduous journey."

Foxtamas didn't know his next choice of action. It was bad taste to hug or shake the hand of a Dwarf Lord. His Winthropian ways hadn't prepared him for this.

Instead, he bowed low to Enaled. The others behind followed.

"My Lord, thank you. Th-th-this is very, *very* appreciated, more than you could ever know." He stumbled through his words, but he didn't care. Neither did Enaled. The dwarf smiled hard enough to push up his sagging cheeks.

"You're very, *very* welcome yourself, Mr. Scottsworth. I thank you for your dedication to your brother. And to us. I assure you we will do all we can."

The others poured out their thanks before departing with a final set of bows. Elation filled Foxtamas. Every step through trails, trees, rivers, towns, moors, all had led him to that very moment.

To a *yes*.

Now it was Foxlaris' turn. He too was one step closer to coming home.

In his joy, Foxtamas turned and glanced at Enaled a final time. He intended to wave or bow or thank him yet again, but he stopped shy. The dwarf's smile had shrunk away. The sag returned. Shoulders slumped, golden hair melting into the hopeless gray of his seat.

It appeared he'd given to the fox what he so desperately wished to grant himself.

Hope.

The Bridge of Evon had taken more than Foxtamas ever could have anticipated.

# 29

# "HERE'S TO THIS LIFE OF HOME AND THRONE!"

"Look, don't touch, and when you do look, don't linger."

Lady Henstray commanded the three bumbling visitors trailing behind her. One stayed close, almost to an uncomfortable degree, his boots clopping inches from the hem of her dark purple dress. The other two, well…at least they were walking.

The night had still been young after the meeting with Enaled. Dubyr helped the trio celebrate with another round of Blue Brother and a subsequent go at Flapdragon. Only for it to turn into another round. And then another. Foxtamas declined the drink to focus on preparing himself for sleep; Bunns and Acirema did rather the opposite.

Long after midnight, Ethwill, aided by a pair of chamber servants, led the group up to the Royal Realm and into the Verandos. The poor torchlight didn't show much apart from the castle-like labyrinth of rooms, halls, staircases and courts built from a mix of tan and granite stone. An entire fortress had been carved into the top of the Blue Mountain.

The Peryflo gifted Acirema her own personal room while the boys shared a cozier one, furnished with two beds, shag rugs, and a rumbling fireplace. None cared for the fineries. They stumbled into the quilts and pillows without question. The full day of Fulnoa lulled them into the darkness of sleep, no help needed. Peace cradled them.

Until the snoring started.

Foxtamas buried himself beneath the blankets. Then the pillows. Then in the thought that throwing his friend's limp body into the smoldering coals would do good to end both of their sufferings.

Thankfully for Bunns, that trail of thinking led him down into the den of dreams. Did he wake to Acirema's banging on the door with a thumping headache that felt like a heartbeat had replaced his brain? Of course. But it didn't slow him down. He'd recover. He'd already done better than the other two who complained of aching stomachs all the way up to meeting Lady Henstray in the empty Heart. Neither sleep nor snoring would stop him now. Passion pushed his steps forward like a mother letting her babe walk on its own.

For the first time in a while, things were going right for Foxtamas Scottsworth.

"These are *sacred* archives you're about to enter. Treat them as such." Her words were just as sharp as her features. It was as if she knew the *exact* thoughts readying on their tongues and the *exact* way to counteract them in such a way to where their entire existence would feel foolish. They were quick. They were nasally. Worse, they were always *correct.*

Their path led them from the Heart and down a narrow corridor that opened into the library. It felt distinct from the crowded Verns and campus-like Endeavor Realm. Wood covered the room instead of stone. Thick, hickory grain ran through the shelves crafted from Northern Timber. They rose high like the Cranarbor, lining the five stories above. Rails of gold wrapped around the balconies of the floors' edges and along the staircases twisting to them like gnarled roots.

And, of course, there were the books. Some thick, some thin, some too tall to store without turning sideways and others so short they lay buried between tomes spanning well past the thousand-page mark. They burned like a rainbow squeezed to fit amongst the wood in picturesque order—and it was a sight Foxtamas could gawk at for eternity.

He spun around as he walked. It nearly knocked him into the tables filled with students creeping through their texts and the other scholars, also clad in a rich purple, pressed against the spines looking for a single specific ledger. Despite it, he breathed in the details. The way the gold lettering sparkled in the bright candlelight waving from above; the frayed edges of the cloth titles; the honeyed, nutty smell of paper young and old, ink damp; the fingerprint grease on the leatherbacks; it enticed him to stay. His heart pounded with belonging. Had Henstray not sped forward with unrelenting *taps!* deafened by the maroon carpet he would have melted into the shelves and never returned. The calling didn't feel selfish, though. It was more like the start of something, a sign that pointed him in the right direction. Where that direction led, the fox was clueless. But the pull remained. And it would linger just like the dust coating the top-shelf tomes.

Henstray wove them through the alleys of books until reaching a wooden set of stairs. They spun downward, and as the group descended, the walls changed. Lanterns emitting a pale yet blinding glow clung to the sides. Their light reflected into shadowy cracks and jags of what used to be rock. With every step down, the stone dissolved into a violet geode, one that grew and encompassed the cave they entered.

At first it didn't seem possible. Had they shrunk down? Were the purple crystals and crevices truly that *massive?* It seemed as such as they pushed deeper, heading down more stairs and into larger rooms. Within the crags sat books just like the ones above, only aged and secured by chains. More scholars worked here than above. Little stone tables and desks filled the corners. Inks of all colors stained them.

"This is the Archithyst," suddenly spat the lady, nodding to a bowing set of researchers passing by. "It is where we store our most valuable archived material. I assume you know of the Rupture?"

Her head cocked back with a raised, gray eyebrow. Only the fox nodded.

"Y-Yes ma'am. Dubyr told us last night," replied Foxtamas.

"His mouth would. Well, it was only afterwards that the Archithyst became the bustle it is now. I say that as an explanation for its busy state. *Not* an apology."

She was understood.

The archives kept crawling down until stopping at a heavy-set metal door. Henstray leaned against it and heaved it open with a turn of a key she produced from her oversized sleeve. Inside, the room was designed like a chapel, with a tall ceiling ending at a point and finely sculpted crystalline pillars and shelves hugging the circular walls. The purple of the geode suffocated buried beneath the incessant clutter of papers, notes, quills, inks, books, tomes, and leaves covering the corners and floors. Plenty were nailed into the rock. They formed little microcosms of research, pods of connecting trails of knowledge that bled from one runny, tanned sheet to the next.

The most formidable was the map of Evon spread across most of the right wall. Neither of the friends had seen the West so detailed. Just about every village scattered across Mechmilne was named, with the far-reaching rivers, bluffs, and patches of trees spreading to the sea given equal recognition. Yet not so for the East. No Westerner had ever seen a full map of Evon. Henstray looked to have tried her hardest.

Scraps of thin, crumbling paper were mismatched across the Eastern side. Faint strokes of ink marked out the jags of mountains running past the Guardmont with bushy trails indicating the long stretch of forest just south. Not a single name appeared. Only the random drollery of bored cartographers.

The dwarf ended their trek at the central table taking up most of the study's room. It was carved of a shimmering purple quartz and housed a pile of recently collected tomes and scraps.

"This place is a true work of art, My Lady," said Acirema, unable to stop looking around.

"That is the hope, princess. Now, come close and listen." The scholar started to flip through the loose pages and sort out new, seemingly unrelated piles. "Lord Enaled mentioned it last night, but my husband, Brown Scholar Sir Lordell, believes based on his prior research that something more went on at Grammo Day than just the destruction of that Bridge. He claims it goes back to the War that Split the World. How he got there, you can ask him yourselves. But, my goal in aiding him is to see what information we have of that time." She flopped down a dusty book pulled from beneath the table. It sent leaves flying. "We've mere scraps of history that predate the Split. Mikyill used to house Evon's scholarship, especially of this era. But they began to trade libraries for castles and slowly stuffed what they could over to the Brown. Scattered it and lost as much as they could. What *rats*." Her tone indicated that the rage against the city wasn't new. "Regardless, the more we piece together a picture of what Evon looked like back then, the better we set the stage for understanding what is going on now. And if what you say is true, Scottsworth..." Lady Henstray paused and let a crisp stare settle on the fox. She swallowed. Hard. "We may be wading beneath a wave already swallowing us up."

With that, she slid over notes and books marked to open at a few select pages. "We'll start by identifying just what 'monsters' chased you three here. There is not much on the lost races of the East. We only know what we do through scraps and legends. Look here." She tossed down a set of ripped, brittle parchment with burned edges. "The remains of songs made after the War. They contain some mention of the Eastern army and who comprised them. We've also crude sketches, half-finished poems penned centuries after the fact, a few tertiary journals, and half a ledger. Like I said—it's a mess."

The trio nodded and began to carefully spread out the papers, covering the table until not an inch of purple remained. All were written in Old Evonian and completely unreadable to the friends.

"Now, for the first creature," said Henstray, leaning over to them with both hands firmly planted among the piles. "What was it like?"

"It was, um..." Foxtamas glanced to the others. They were equally lost as to where to start or even how to *describe* what had chased them.

"Short, and...slimy. They had long ears and these nasty-looking webbed hands—"

"Easy tae sink ah star into," Bunns added with a nodding wink.

"So something like this?" Henstray pulled up a sheet. Drawn in a shoddy mix of dripping ink and charcoal stains stood their beast. He didn't look as twisted as he had while chasing them through the dark lanes of Mechmilne. This one looked…kinder. Polite and positioned at a desk with a quill marking an obscured piece of writing.

"Yes!" shouted Bunns. He reached across to snatch it, but, miraculously, Henstray was quicker and pulled it back close to her chest. She compounded the defeat with a glare. It reverberated her opening warning.

"This is an alp. Specifically, Helios Drawdush of Village Grendis. The artist, if you can call them that, was kind enough to label it. I believe it predates the Split. There's no war or battle attire, just a man in his work."

Acirema squinted at the portrait.

"An…alp, you said?"

"Yes. They're mentioned more than any other Easterner in the more-or-less complete ledgers we have from the Eastern generals. They seem to us how we see squirrels, or even dwarves if you were from here—common and rowdy."

The lady scribbled a few lines of notes on a new page in her already overstuffed journal. Once done, she picked up the remaining portraits.

"And these three? Any look familiar?"

All three shook their heads. None of the sketches chased after them the night of their crossing. They showed slithering, scaly creatures; shaggy, moss-covered, mopey-eyed dopes; and a hybrid with a lion head protruding from a turtle's shell. While not familiar, they still elicited fear. "Hm. I was hoping those leads would be concrete enough. Never mind. Tell me of another."

"There were some that flew," Acirema said.

"Good." Henstray shuffled around the books and notes. The princess paused, but as she did, the icy stare flicked up. "Well don't just stop!"

"Oh, right, apologies. They were large, with black feathers that blended into the night. Their necks, though, they were bare with this rough, red wrinkled skin." Her words slowed again as the scholar whipped out a half-bound book.

"Here," she said, tossing it over to Foxtamas and Bunns. "It's a ledger from an old avian village in the Eastern mountains. Flip through it."

"An' look for wha'?" asked Bunns. He politely slid it over to the fox, ever eager to open it.

"Species names you don't know."

"But it's all in Old Evonian," Foxtamas rebutted. From what he could gather, the place was named something…Loromere. Could be a village, could be a city. He hadn't the slightest.

"Species stay the same no matter the language." Henstray grunted as she spoke. Her focus lay on peeling back notes of her own. The lady had marked the pages in strokes of red and blue. The charts linked to some long unorganized document lying somewhere within the Archithyst. As she flipped, she kept muttering *red skin, red skin.* It signaled a focus Foxtamas wasn't keen on interrupting.

He cracked open the pages and began to scan. Names, dates, hometowns and, of course, species were listed on the left page with the right full of their presumed business in the town. For a split second he felt himself ready to fall into the mystery of the forgotten words. What had the day been like when, Yeligow, a magpie on the third row, entered the city of Loromere. Why had she gone? Was she visiting a sickly parent? Secret lover? What had the journey been to arrive, and who had she gone with? How did the wind taste, stone crumble, and heat of the sunrise feel? And was there ever a sliver of a chance that Yeligow knew just how ancient of a world she lived in and how quickly it would change and cease to be?

"Scottsworth!" shouted the dwarf from across the table. The magpie flew away from his mind.

"Oh, uh, right. Lemme see…I know these, wait…okay, there's a hawk, condor, griffin, vulture, cockatrice—"

"Stop! It was one of those two."

"Which two?" the fox asked.

"Vulture or condor. I couldn't remember the names, but one is mentioned with red skin—" She tossed down a pile of lyrics, ballads, and poems. "In one of these. Hurry, let's get searching!"

The friends suddenly eyed each other. Was that a tone of...excitement? From *her!?*

Now she was *certainly* understood.

The search spanned the four corners of the table. Everyone mulled over their stack of papers, creating a whirlwind of flapping leaves and humming tunes (mostly by Bunns). Most were still coded in Old Evonian, but the occasional lyric had an updated translation written on the back. They found a story of a runaway gnome forming a family in Efeters, an eloquent aubade of two parting elf lovers, a series of stanzas from a lone sailor, chronicles of a Western soldier during the War, and a recipe disguised as a song that taught the listener how to perfectly glaze a maple pie.

Yet no vultures or condors. By a stroke of a luck, Acirema stumbled across a line describing "an ugly gloat / of lard and loaf / with rugged polyps / that jiggle with hops." It continued to describe the beast as a tarmin, the very same oversized toad that hunted them.

"Look here!" Henstray finally called out. She pulled the crinkled sheet closer and read off the slanted, Old Evonian line. "'Wives wrapped our wounds / but couldn't clean the rest, / our slain brothers and their blood / red as the dead vultures' neck.' Vulture it is!" She grinned despite the grimness, humming to herself as she rattled her quill through her notebook. This time her marks were clear on where to find the poem.

The hunt continued for hours, but no one had any complaints. They sorted through more records, created charts along the walls that connected traces of information across centuries to map out the species of "weasel." They found goblins in love letters, trolls in cartography notes, and korrigan hiding plainly in the margins. As the search became exhausted, only one monster remained.

"Aye, he was a big ol' laddie. Tall, chunky underbite, heavy brow," described Bunns. "Et was dark tha' night. Hard tae see, but he was commandin' the troops weh burned."

Henstray nodded between scratches to her notes.

"Commanding who again? His *troops* you said?"

"Aye. Same lot chasin' us all the way oup."

Her quill stopped half-way through the word *chunky*. Wobbled in her wrinkled hand.

"And were these…troops…his same kind?" She asked, hesitant.

"Nah, just ah few were. Laddie was 'bout as bright as them alps Ah reckon. Wha' yer say, Queenie—"

"No no no, *no* more talking!" shouted the scholar. The trio shrank from the table with hunched backs and worried eyes.

She threaded her fingers through her hair as she left the table and paced, loosening frayed gray tresses with every seethed word.

"I need this straight at *once*. You're telling me this wasn't some wild band of beasts crawling over and hunting down easy prey? Stirred by some, some, some *disturbance* that caused them to investigate?"

"No, My Lady," peeped up Acirema. "They came over collected just like any other army I've seen. They had boats and weapons and armor—"

"*ARMOR!?"* The shriek echoed in the violet chamber. "When were you going to inform me of *that!"*

"Weh never thought tae mention et Ah guess." Bunns was done backing up. The yells drew him closer to the distraught woman. One more outburst and she'd be dealing with a lot more than a lack of details.

"Oh, you *children*…don't you see what this means?" She sank down upon a stack of books. Dust plumed around her. "I've thought them savages. Nothing more than remnants of a lost civilization still scrounging around in a wasteland. My predecessors theorized they didn't even *exist*. But now…they're not just out there, and they're not just organized, but they're an *army*. After all this *time! WE* disbanded, but they may never have! Do you three understand the danger this poses to *everyone* in the West!?"

That did it.

Foxtamas' fear broke the truce.

"W-W-W-Wait," he stammered, choking on the rising flurry boiling in his stomach. Instead of letting the intrusive thoughts battle, he opened his mouth to pour them out. "How do we know the whole East is an army? W-W-What if it's just that small group, a-a-and who would lead them? No one's around to hold that grudge or want us d-dead."

He rambled around the true issue stabbing at his heart: Foxlaris. The alp had spoken of the other fox, an alp apart of this larger coalition. No matter the army's size or leader, *they* had his brother.

"You're right, Scottsworth, I can't say anything for certain. But I'd be remiss if I didn't assume that a fully formed army, stocked with boats and armor, ready to invade, must have some strength backing it," replied the dwarf.

"But it can't be the *entire* East, can it?" Acirema asked.

"Ah bet they'd have come over first if et was."

"No, but even small reactionaries can create chaos when the enemy is unsuspecting. I can't fully say what may motivate that. The one who can, however…" She slid a sly wink to Foxtamas before rising from her books, grabbing the top ledger, and cracking it open. "Their leader."

"And weh find tha' how?" Bunns asked with unhelpful sarcasm.

"Follow the trends, Cammont," she answered, her eyes not lifting. "Connect the dots, draw a conclusion, use the past to guide the present, same tactic we've used all morning. My suspicion is that if we find out who led the Easterners before the Split, we may learn something about them now."

Foxtamas cracked his knuckles in anticipation.

"What will that something be, though?" he asked.

"Something," started the lady, finally gazing up and turning the ledger around, "to guarantee we aren't utterly helpless."

Her bony finger traveled up the page. It was part of the incomplete waterlogged ledger that first mentioned the alps. Her nail passed over the undecipherable names of generals and soldiers until pressing to the top. All other words were coded. Expect for one.

Wolf.

"What's a...wolf?" the princess asked.

"Not a clue." Henstray whipped the book back around and closed it. "But he's marked as their lord, or, eh, usurper I guess would be the better translation. The word 'Vorde' isn't used horribly often. Anyhow, I've yet to see that name, be it of a person or species, anywhere else in the archives."

"Then it's a dead end then...?" Foxtamas tried to control his shaking while he spoke. To his surprise, the question brought a smile to Henstray's wrinkles and lifted them in ways very, *very* few things ever could.

"Not at all. Remember, this is only one *half* of what the Fulnoa has." She rubbed her hands together to the point of creating a spark. The eyes of the jackalope grew wide.

"Yer sayin' yer can get tae the Brown!?"

"No, I can't," she replied. "But you three can."

Lady Henstray explained the plan on the way back to the Verandos. Her and Lordell were the only two dwarves allowed to cross into the other mountain, as neither Dwarf Lord wanted the other's scholarship fully inaccessible. However, they could only meet for short bursts to trade necessities, be it information, books, or secrets only the couple shared. It wasn't much, but it worked.

This law, though, only applied to *Fulnoa Folk*. Visitors were allowed to cross so as to maintain a proper image between the mountains. They may be warring, but not at the expense of millennia of goodwill.

Henstray would clear a time with Lordell for the trio to cross. Once there, they'd deliver the day's research and dig through any and all records for a sign of wolf. That would guide them to deciphering the

East's past and, hopefully, a way to gain a step ahead of the encroaching forces. All that stood in their way was an icy wooden bridge and, of course, Foehn.

"Lordell will need to clear it with him," concluded the scholar as they marched up a lengthy stone staircase. "Sneaking in will be certain imprisonment. Lord Enaled's jurisdiction runs out the moment you step on that bridge."

"There's no guaranteed 'yes' then, is there?" asked the fox.

"There never is, Scottsworth. It'll be a tough call for him. On one hand scholarship *is* important, but it's the first to go if a Blue branch needs pruning. Likewise, visitors *are* allowed and good for publicity, but the lockdown decree may override that process. It's a gamble."

"Ah, just perfect tae hear, Mah Lady." Bunns nudged the pair walking up next to him. They hid their smiles.

The party wrapped around the corner and made it down to the rooms. Once there, Lady Henstray bowed, her words of thanks and encouragement ready on her tongue. She still carried a nip in her attitude, but it *had* softened since the morning. Like an early spring day in the last few weeks of winter.

Yet the trio looked away as she spoke; their attention was pulled into Acirema's room.

Enaled, Ethwill, and Dubyr crowded around her bed. When she entered, they suddenly rose to attention. Their faces were drained to a ghastly white.

Before them, to the friends' shock, stood Ruel.

"My Queen," spoke the squirrel with failing strength. He dropped to a single knee and bowed his head. "Village Winthrop has been attacked."

Cast across the mountains bold,
Like silver poured from cragged mold,
Our home arose in quake of morn,
A shadow bright in Evon born.

Trace way the folds of kinsman trail,
From icy peak to inward gale,
In starlit Vern of kith and stove
We're all one line of veins below.

Sharp your axe, shape your mug,
Brew the taste an' brew it strong,
For in our Hearts we're right to feast—
We dared to walk where mountains sleep!

Ful-no-a! Ful-no-a!
Two Brothers Forged in Stone!
Gateway to the North,
'Neath kings and courts,
Two Hearts, one hearth, our home!

Now bend the knee and bow the wings
To our good kindly Wolver kings.
They the Lords for whom we call—
Praise their reign oh one and all!

Ful-no-a! Ful-no-a!
Midst Moors and Mont alike!
The Blue, the Brown,
The kings, the queens,
The peaks, the coves,
The feasts, the sleeps,
Sing every soul below this stone:
Here's to this life of home and throne!

*"Ode to the Twins"*
*— Written by the bard Sir Connoway Krag*
*on the eve of the coronation*
*of Dwarf Lords*
*Eobin and Bwayine Wolverton*

The story of the Foxtamas, Foxlaris, Acirema, and Bunns continues in Book III: *The War that Split the World.*

Available July 2026.

# ABOUT THE AUTHOR

Marshall Cunningham grew up in the woods of Arkansas but lived in the castles of Narnia and mountains of Middle-Earth. He began *The Bridge of Evon* in fourth grade, writing and re-writing it multiple times before its four-part publication across 2025 and 2026. He holds a BA in English and Creative Writing from the University of Central Arkansas and owns Bean's Books in Pickles Gap Village. He resides in Conway with the store's titular schnauzer, his reading and writing buddy, Bean.

You can keep up with him, Bean, his books, and his store at the following:

beans-books.com
@beansbooksconway
@thebridgeofevon

www.ingramcontent.com/pod-product-compliance
Lightning Source LLC
LaVergne TN
LVHW100504110826
845146LV00002B/508

* 9 7 9 8 9 9 3 8 0 1 5 2 0 *